Raven sighed. "I could talk for ten days straight about the incredible *power* of the subconscious mind, about its control over every cell in the body, about its infallible memory, about things I learned about it from Nanosh and Jack Shanglo and the Rom in Europe involving spells and magic, but we haven't got time. And I believe all we still *do* know about the subconscious is only the tiniest tip of a vast iceberg. But believe this: it is a miraculous facility, a veritable nuclear power-plant, waiting to serve us. And all we have to do in order to achieve miracles is learn to harness the power of the subconscious."

Kat laughed. "I know, I know—mind over matter. I do believe in that."

Raven shrugged. "So—believe in psychic phenomena. Tell yourself over and over: I am psychic. I can communicate telepathically with John Raven's mind, with all minds. Practice. And *believe*. And right now I believe we've reached our destination."

Up ahead she saw a sign for Live Oak Springs.

Kat sensed a change come over Raven. Gone suddenly the gentle instructor, the hypnotist who, for the duration of the journey, had been working on her mind, distracting it from the horror of yesterday. Raven's thoughts now belonged totally to him. Sitting there, he looked almost as though he had turned to stone, grave with concentration. Kat disliked the eerie sensation of being completely shut out, and found no comfort in her awareness of what the forthcoming meeting with the Indian, Joe Santee, meant to Raven.

Once again, at that moment, she found herself afraid of this complex, different, mystical man.

RAVEN

Stanley Morgan

LYNX BOOKS
New York

RAVEN

ISBN: 1-55802-180-9

First Printing/April 1989

This is a work of fiction. Names, characters, places, and incidents are either the product of the author's imagination or are used fictitiously. Any resemblance to actual events, locales, or persons, living or dead, is entirely coincidental.

This book is published by Lynx Books, a division of Lynx Communications, Inc., 41 Madison Avenue, New York, New York, 10010. The name ''Lynx'' and the logo consisting of a stylized head of a lynx are trademarks of Lynx Communications, Inc.

Printed in the United States of America

0 9 8 7 6 5 4 3 2 1

For Linda
with love.
Nais tuke,
thank you

ACKNOWLEDGMENT

With special thanks to Ken Rains, a very gifted Romany psychic, for his help and encouragement during the writing of this book.

RAVEN

Chapter One

It should never have happened.

Raven blamed himself for Kat's rape. It was a heavy burden. Heavier now than it had been yesterday, because he'd slept on it, and sleep, giving free rein to the subconscious, clarifies perspective. He owed her something for not being able to prevent the attack.

No man can fully appreciate what the brutal violation of her body does to a woman. And probably no two victims react alike. Though the study of rape was not his field, Raven had read enough to know that some women externalize their trauma through hysteria while others secrete it, riven with shame, planting psychosis deep within themselves that, like a time bomb, might explode later. Yesterday, after the horrible event, he had managed to hold Kat back from the brink of hysterical breakdown with hypnosis, and by one this morning, when she finally retired to bed, he felt sure that that particular danger was over. The time bomb was defused.

But still he owed her.

Standing there on Kat's terrace above the canyon, awaiting the sun's first rays above the San Gabriel Mountains (an anticipation that evoked so many poignant childhood memories), he reviewed the events of the previous day. Despite the availability of mitigating circumstances he was afflicted by a sense of failure. Oh, yes, he had a hatful of

1

those excuses: his angered preoccupation with the incredible things he'd learned at the deathbed of his grandfather, Nanosh; the shock of Nanosh's death later that same day; the traumatic experience of the Romany funeral that followed. All had, he could now claim, diminished his psychic powers.

But it wouldn't be the truth.

What had happened when he was boarding the bus in Phoenix proved that.

A stranger standing in front of him in the aisle had tried to stow a heavy canvas carryall into the overhead rack and missed. He'd caught it as it fell. His hand had brushed hers, a static charge had crackled between them, and in that instant he had read Kat's mind with startling clarity.

So his psychic battery was not dead.

No, what he'd been guilty of was an uncharacteristic and unforgivable lapse of vigilance. He had momentarily forgotten the lesson drummed into him by his grandfather for twenty-five years, since he, himself, was five years old. *The Rom owe their existence to constant vigilance, John. You must learn the habit until it becomes as instinctive as breathing. Danger is all around us, can come at us when we least expect it, like boulders down a mountainside. Be always on your guard.*

Well, he hadn't been. He'd been grieving over his grandfather's death, immersed in anger and bewilderment. And maybe working at the Institute had taken his edge off (you don't get too much murder, rape, and mayhem in the Psychical Research Department of the Alcott Institute in Kansas City).

But, no, that wouldn't wash either. When the horror started he had proved his gifts were as well honed as they ever were. So it was pure preoccupation.

He should have picked those two punks up as soon as he set foot on board the bus, or even before that, waiting in the depot. After the attack, there was so much stuff coming off those two guys—so much hard-core evil—that he was astounded he hadn't immediately flashed on it in the close confines of the vehicle. The small dark-haired one, Luke, had been the tricky one. He was intelligent, hid his aura well, didn't look the part. But Max was as blatant as an ax in the face—six-four, two hundred and fifty pounds, bovine, a killer through and through. He, Raven, should have sniffed that bastard out like a hound sniffs out a fox.

But he didn't.

And Kat got raped.

And Max got away.

That animal was on the loose, armed with a straight razor and Kat's address. And Raven knew he would come looking for her.

His glance went down into the canyon. Max would have to approach this way, if he came to the house at all. Maybe he'd wait awhile, lull both Kat and the police into believing he was in Mexico, then catch her out shopping or coming out of a movie. The only thing Raven knew for sure was that Max had a job to finish.

The one he'd started yesterday.

Max *would* come.

Chapter Two

Yesterday.

Max couldn't get his mind off killing the girl, off how it would be, and what he and Luke would do to her before they finally snuffed her. There were plenty of other things he ought to have been thinking about because the time for the main action was getting mighty close now and his thoughts ought to be covering the whole thing, the way Luke had instructed him, over and over—Jesus, how many times had they been through it? a million?—but the image, the projected fantasy of this sweet bonus crowded the confines of his drug-muddled mind like a great black killer shark trapped in the fetid waters of an undersized marina tank; there just wasn't much room for anything else.

He'd thought about it for the past five hours, since they'd boarded the bus in Phoenix, and that much sado-sexual imagery had brought him to such a pitch of excited expectancy that the beat of his heart was literally rocking his body, and he reckoned any second now he'd either throw up in the aisle or come in his pants, or maybe both, and he didn't want to do either because the first would probably alert and alarm the driver and passengers and maybe screw up the whole scam, and the second would be a crying, wasteful shame because the sizzling white-hot cream-dream he had stored up in his blue jeans was all for *her*—for little Miss Katherine Anne Tyson of Cleves Cot-

4

tage, Canyon Road, Brentwood Park, in the city of Los
Angeles in the state of California (it was all there on the
identification tag dangling from her canvas carryall on the
overhead rack)—and for no one else in this whole wide
sicko world. Oh, Katherine (Kate, Kit, whatever) baby,
have I got a big surprise for you!

Ker-pow ker-pow his heart thudded as his gaze riveted
for the billionth time on the top of her head, just visible
above the back of the window seat, left side, three rows
in front. Nice hair. Blond, sun-streaked California hair,
shining like pale-green silk in the strong sunlight refract-
ing through the tinted window. One hell of a looker all
over, not just the hair. Everything. Slim build but good
jugs. Long slender legs that were showing because she
was wearing a denim skirt with a thin white cotton tank
top. He'd first noticed her in the Phoenix depot, struggling
with a couple of heavy-looking cases and the carryall slung
over her shoulder. Then she'd been wearing a tan corduroy
car coat, so he didn't immediately get to see the spectacular tits; they were an added bonus after she got on board
and removed the coat in the warmth of the bus.

Back in the depot he'd nudged Luke as she entered, and
Luke's scary-looking pale blue eyes lit up as Max knew
they would, but then Luke shook his head and said, "We
could never get that lucky, baby. It's long odds she's heading for San Diego. More like L.A. She looks L.A. to
me."

"Let's switch to L.A.," Max had joked.

Luke's eyes changed, kind of glazed over in that spooky
way they did when something came along he didn't like.
"Keep your mind on the plan, Max. If she takes our bus,
fine, maybe we can use her, but don't go—"

"Hey, man," Max protested, "I was kidding."

Luke smiled, reinstating him.

She bought her ticket and sat there with her bags, mind-ing her own business, staring mostly at the floor, looking kind of sad and lost and forlorn and very, excitingly, vulnerable. And as Max watched her, his desire began to mount. He began to want her something fierce. And when the Los Angeles bus was called and she didn't make a move, sixth sense told him she was heading for San Diego, and then his imagination really took off.

He didn't mention her to Luke again. By this time, Luke—the Master Planner—was in high gear, eyes sweeping the crowd, mind locked maybe into some personal computation of each one's potential worth, even though he didn't yet know who was going to board the San Diego bus and who wasn't. Most of the time Max never knew what Luke was thinking until Luke chose to express the thought. Nor did he care. He readily admitted that Luke was the brains of the partnership; he, himself, was what? The brawn, the violence, the terror factor. Luke's mind was a vast territory that he didn't much care to set foot in unless invited. Max was no planner. And so, relieved of any executive burden, he wallowed in sexual fantasy concerning this great-looking chick who looked like she had a big problem.

His joy welled unbounded when the San Diego bus was called and she headed for the door.

They did get that lucky. She was his.

Screw the women and old-timers. As Luke had meticulously planned, he and Max were first in line for the boarding. Luke swung up the steps and took the first seat by the door, near the driver, on the aisle so he could look back any time and visually communicate with Max, who strode down the vehicle and occupied the aisle seat at the extreme rear of the bus, adjacent to the toilet cubicle, on his right.

So far, perfect. They were positioned. The rest was academic. Max was able to relax a little.

Until the tenth person climbed on board.

Then his heart began its long, unremitting, painful pounding.

She was on board.

An old grandpa came trundling down the aisle in front of her, obscuring Max's view, throwing a rheumy eye at the window seat beside Max.

"Mind?" the old man muttered.

Yes, I mind, you stupid old fuck, Max wanted to yell. It's saved for her. But he didn't. Luke had warned him: Play it cool, be nice, quiet, reserved. Attract no attention. Don't give them any warning what they're in for. Shock is the tactic; terror the prize.

So he played it cool, let the old fart slide into the window seat to his left.

Jesus, he watched her, though. Watched the way her long slim thighs moved beneath the denim skirt, pictured them naked, visualized the color and thickness of the muff of pubic hair where they met. He grew rock hard at the image, and at the certainty that in five hours it would be all his to do with as he wished.

With difficulty he dragged his eyes away from her snatch up to her face. Closer to him now than she'd been in the depot, she was even better looking: good bones, sleepy green eyes, soft wide sexy mouth. But also more miserable. This kid really had a problem. Maybe she'd just found out she was pregnant? He liked that. What he had in mind for her, he'd be doing her a good turn, fix her problem fast.

She looked weak with weariness. Hefting her carryall, she tried to push it into the overhead rack, missed, and almost dropped it on the head of an old crow sitting a row in front.

Almost. But the bag didn't reach its target.

There was a guy coming up behind her, inching along,

eyeing an empty aisle seat on the right side of the bus. Big guy, quarterback type, muscled beneath a black leather jacket, worth watching. Luke had stressed the point: "For Crissake, check everybody gets on board. I'll be up front, won't be able to keep an eye on things. Watch out for potential heroes—hell, yeah, and heroines. The frigging women these days can kick the shit out of you, given the chance. Any guy in uniform or is bigger than Woody Allen, watch him."

Well, this guy was quite a bit bigger than Woody Allen. Good-looking stiff, black hair, dark unsmiling eyes, strong face, maybe a touch of Indian there. Maybe Eye-talian.

Muscles flexed, the guy moved with the speed of a striking rattler. There was this chick's bag, falling out of the rack, heading for an unstoppable collision with the old crow's bean, and this guy, though he was facing away from the action looking for his seat, saw it or sensed it or whatever. He shot out an arm and stopped the thing dead, an inch from disaster.

The chick gasped, looked back at him and up at him, and he gave her a kind of half-smile. Max didn't expect that at all. Hell, it should've been an ear-to-ear ain't-I-hot-shit bobby-dazzler, her looking like she did and traveling alone. It's what most guys would've done. But this cat was cool. Without a second glance at her he lifted the bag into the rack as though it was no weight at all, then swung down into his aisle seat with a smooth muscular grace while the girl moved into the window seat behind the old biddy, obviously nervous about the near-miss.

Oh, yeah, this guy will need watching, thought Max cautiously.

So he watched him, but soon got tired of it because there wasn't anything to watch. Shortly after they pulled out of Phoenix, the guy stretched out the best he could

8

with his long legs and didn't so much as twitch in the next two hours, seemed to be dead. So Max relaxed his gaze on him and concentrated on the girl, and, when he could drag his besotted mind off her, on the other people on the bus.

Excluding Luke and himself, there were forty-six passengers on board, forty-seven counting the driver: full house. The vehicle was a brand-new air-conditioned vinyl-smelling Americruiser, traveling westbound on Interstate 8. It was nine hours from Phoenix, Arizona, to San Diego, California, with a couple of comfort stops along the way.

Luke had been right about it being full. Thanksgiving, he'd said—no, had *stated,* with that incisive authority with which he made all planning pronouncements—is when people travel by bus. Believe me, Max, the pickings will be rich.

So, in the first hour, Max did his part of the thing and gave the passengers the once-over, even to getting up one time and walking down the aisle to ask the driver some dumb-ass question about their ETA in San Diego so he could eyeball the suckers good and close on the way back to his seat, which was when he discovered the name and address of the sweet young fuck who had about four more hours to live, according to Max's plans.

Returning, he paid special attention to Mister Potential Badass, the only guy on board who looked like hero material, but saw no real problem there. Not with what Max had tucked away in the canvas Puma bag under his seat. The guy looked hard and rangy and capable of throwing a football three miles, but faced with that big bad staring eye at the end of a sawed-off Weatherby pump gun, it was truly amazing how quick the hardest muscle turned to quivering Jell-O. Max grinned to himself at the thought of the coming transformation.

Satisfied that everything was under control, that Luke's

9

masterly game plan was moving along smoothly toward its righteous conclusion, Max slipped into the tiny toilet for a sustaining toot of coke, then returned to his seat to while away the time thinking about this and that until Luke signaled the snap and the fun began.

Later on, he could think only about the girl. But early in the run, now and then, lulled by the thrumming, drumming rhythm of the bus, his coked-up, drug-muddled, whirligig mind would lose focus on the killing to come and drift to past pleasures, gliding over the past three incredible months like a ravening thing, swooping down on this or that particularly succulent morsel of flesh. There had been a lot of carrion.

Fourteen.

He'd kept count. That was part of it, the fun, how much they could get away with, what they could do to people and still get away clean. It had been unbelievably easy.

Luke *was* a genius at making things easy.

He'd never met anyone like Luke, never thought he would.

Amazing, how they met.

It was an army brig in west Texas. Max going in for breaking the face of a pig physical instructor with a twenty-kilo barbell; Luke coming out on a dishonorable discharge for knife-wounding a fellow sergeant in a barrack-room brawl. They shared a cell for only one night, but that was long enough. Their affinity was immediate. They sensed it in each other's aura, saw it in each other's eyes, later heard it expressed in words and innuendo. Their common bond: their belief that for most people life was so intrinsically shitty that release from it would be a blessing, the tenet that the ecstasy derived from killing transcended and made redundant all other human experience.

"I'm going out tomorrow," Luke had told him, passing

him a butt like they'd been close buddies for a lifetime, this incredible guy with the smooth, deep, educated voice and cool, creepy manner, so fucking confident that you'd think he was some visiting defense lawyer come to reassure. "Pity. We might have had some fun."

Luke's indolent tone had offered such rich, dirty promise that Max had experienced a surge of regret bordering on panic. Here was a guy he really wanted to be with. Luke was magic. Max had never had a partner, a real friend. Things he'd done, he'd done alone, and it was no fun that way. You needed someone to show, someone to laugh with, build on. He was pervaded by the feeling—hell, no, the certainty—that if he let this chance go he'd regret it and be friendless the rest of his life.

Luke Shand and Max Koenig.

The Odd Couple.

Friends—unbelievable.

In appearance they couldn't have been more different. Luke: short and lightweight, an Al Pacino type, with thick dark hair, sharp, intellectual features, and that easy, charming smile that so effectively—until you read his eyes—concealed the killer mind. Max, in utter contrast, a side of beef, six-four, a blunt, blue-eyed, blond-haired German country boy whose appearance clearly signaled his propensity for violence.

They were opposites attracting like crazy, sharing the common root of conscienceless evil.

It was now or never.

"I'm coming with you," Max had told him.

Luke's pale washed-out eyes twinkled with amusement. "And how do you propose accomplishing that, kiddo?"

Max shrugged. "Through the gate, over the wall. I'll get out."

Luke nodded, acknowledging the desperation. "I'll wait for you in El Paso three days—back row of the Cameo movie theater, last showing. If you're not there by the third night, I'm gone.''

"I'll be there.''

Escape had been child's play. He took a day to study the layout of the stockade, and on the second night faked an appendix pain that sent him to the medical center with a lax escort (who expects you to make a run for it with a bursting appendix?). The guard never knew what hit him—it was a fire extinguisher—then, prison uniform off, stripped down to running shorts and undershirt, he went through a window into an alley behind Dyer Street and made a fast run into the refuge of El Paso's bustling night streets.

Sitting there in the last row in the dark, Luke had been impressed as hell. "Maxwell, you are something else. Together we can purge this shitty world of joyless humanity. Let's go and free some unhappy folks of their mortal burden.''

Swaying to the rhythm of the bus, thoughts of the girl momentarily on hold, his gaze fixed fondly on Luke's dark distant head, Max recalled with piquant clarity their first act of liberation.

First things first.

They needed clothes, wheels, money.

Macho Modes was a hole-in-the-wall outfitters off Trowbridge Street. The harried-looking little guy was shutting up shop when they appeared out of the night. His eyes told them he'd flashed their demon.

"Sorry, gentlemen, gotta close.'' He foolishly tried to close the door against Luke's omnipotent hand.

Luke's response was disarming: the boyish grin, dimpled, apologetic. "Hey, *we're* sorry—but as you can see my friend needs some help. While he was jogging someone stole his car. Look, pants and a shirt, we'll come back tomorrow for the rest, okay?''

12

Greed and suspicion jostled for a place in the guy's mind. Greed won by a short head. "Well . . ."

"Thank you, you're a prince."

The door closed. Luke did a crazy kind of twirl, his arms above his head like a ballet dancer, then going straight out from his shoulders, his right hand passing close to the little guy's neck as it came around. Then blood was spurting out of the guy's neck like a fucking faucet. Straight out. A jet from a lawn sprinkler . . . pow, pow, pow. Max had never seen a severed jugular before. It was unbelievable how far the blood shot. All over a rack of good-looking shirts.

Luke hit him again where he stood bug-eyed, unable to believe what was happening to him. Slash, slash, slash—across the eyes, diagonally down through the nose, back across the mouth. Ten . . . no, five seconds later the prince was dead.

"Ta-dahh! The Mark of Zorro!" proclaimed Luke as the little guy, realizing he was dead, crumpled. "Lucas Patrick Shand—Deliverer of the Oppressed and Misbegotten! I mean, this poor asshole was *unhappy,* Max, who the fuck wouldn't be working in this dump. Draw the shades and grab some duds, I'll empty the cash drawer." He wiped the bloody blade of the cutthroat razor on a hanging shirt sleeve and folded it into his jacket pocket.

"Jesus," gasped Max.

He was no stranger to blood, to literally buckets of it. And he dug it. As a kid, the youngest of five boys, raised on a Pennsylvania pig farm, he'd seen a lot of it and spilled much of it, but never this kind and never like this. They'd hung the pigs up, slit their throats, and let them drip. Early on he'd tuned in to the thrill of power over porcine life or death, the visceral excitement of slashing through tough skin and fatty flesh and watching the blood and life flow out and down into a plastic pail. His brothers and father tuned in, too. If there was only one porker to go, they'd fought for the privilege of murder. Max'd been raised on an ethos of blood and violence. But this—

Was something else.

"Je-*sus*!" he whooped.

Scooping up the cash, Luke grinned. "Never used the old cutthroat, baby? Beats all, lemme tell you. Nothing like a dose of cold steel to put the shits up 'em. You want, I'll show you how."

From there and then Max was in complete awe of Luke, enthralled by his hypnotic coolness, slick inventiveness, total amorality. Educationally, as in every other way, Luke was light-years his superior. Many times Max didn't even know what Luke was talking about or even recognize the words. But in essentials their communication was absolute. Terror was their mutual pleasure; death their common joy.

In the heady weeks that followed they talked little of their past lives; neither had need for such information. Each realized he had embarked upon an incredible fantasy adventure, a unique and unrepeatable roller-coaster ride of indeterminate but possibly short duration which, by virtue of that fact, permitted extreme license. They were to be laws unto themselves, lords of the earth, powers in the land; impervious; indestructible. Gods.

Later that first night, waiting at the foot of the south-bound entry ramp of Interstate 10 in El Paso, wearing new blue denim and good Nikes, courtesy Macho Modes, Luke, one eye peeled for cruising cops, projected the collegiate clean-cutness that was to prove the sucker-bait for all future beneficiaries, Luke—with uncanny instinct— letting stuff go by, then liking the look of a white Plymouth and hanging out a thumb.

Their next beneficiary provided the wheels.

Max recalled him clearly, though thereafter some of the too-many faces disappeared from memory.

Brakes screeched. "Where you headin', boys?"

In reflected street lighting the guy's pink live-right complexion and clerical collar glowed like a welcome-home altar candle.

How did Luke do it?

"Kind of you to stop, sir." Luke at his deadliest. "We're heading for Odessa, but we'd be happy to make Van Horn tonight."

"Can't oblige you that far, Acala's my stop. Hop in if it'll help."

As planned, Max slipped into the rear seat, Luke beside the driver, ready to take the wheel when the snap came.

The Reverend Wesley Parker died a bitch, Max remembered nostalgically, strung up in the woods in the Finlay Mountains like one of daddy's porkers, a-squealin' an' a-twitchin' an' a-bleedin' something beautiful. But it was Max's first try and the old Mark of Zorro took a bit of practice. He got much better at it later on.

"God go with you," Luke said solemnly, dumping the Rev down a crevasse, and then they were heading out on their Goodwill Trail, deep into the heart of Texas.

The Rev was the last guy to be liberated. Women had more to offer. There was so much more you could do with a chick. And the reaction was different. Their terror was pure. Luke explained it: Show a guy a cutthroat and what does he think? He's going to die. So he'll either numb out on you and take it or fight. Not so a chick. Her first nightmare is: Christ, my face! Then she starts thinking about other parts of her body. Then about rape. Bang, bang, bang—you've got three major pressure points right there. Then you've got the noises. Men generally don't scream, plead, cry, beg. Women externalize their terror. Believe me, they're so much more worthwhile.

15

Luke proved his point with a hooker in Abilene. Man, did she externalize. Though not entirely to Luke's satisfaction. She was, after all, a hooker, a tough-ass, incapable of demonstrating the pure terror of innocence.

So they tried again with a hitchhiker out of Shreveport heading for New Orleans (new wheels by now; they boosted a new car every new state; when the car wasn't provided by a beneficiary, another of Luke's specialties was hot-wiring). The hitchhiker was better, yet again not quite. She'd been around and around and up and down and was too facile with the sex, too many truckers maybe, liked it rough. She screamed up a storm when it came to it, but, as Luke judged, hardly representative of the average woman.

The two bored housewives in the Mobile bar came closer. Max shivered now as he reminisced on that sweet night. He came out of that encounter with a headful of new experience in human behavior under dire stress, plus three thousand dollars cash, a week's supply of good coke, and the pleasure of riding a Porsche Targa through Alabama.

Things were picking up.

Who next? Christ, he couldn't remember. After Alabama, where?

Florida. Hell, how could he forget?

Two there. Tampa—then across to Daytona Beach.

The black chick in Daytona. His groin surged at the memory. Artist, living alone in the isolated house outside town. They were there in the basement three days, Luke making a joke production out of it, coming on like a schoolteacher instructing a pupil, telling him after that he'd passed with straight A's.

Max was really into it by then, something surging deep inside him whenever he saw a good-looking girl, feeling how it would be with her, aching to do it, the whole thing so much more than sex had ever been, though that too, so fucking unbelievable when you had the power, when you could feel and see and hear the stone terror.

It's how God feels, Luke had said, every minute of His frigging life.

Pittsburgh, Detroit, Chicago through September; Kansas City and Denver as Indian summer and its clutch of beneficiaries slipped into memory. Finally, in November, Phoenix.

The idea to hijack a bus hit Luke as they sat drinking coffee in the bus station.

Max saw the inspiration arrive. His pulse kicked, knowing something good was coming. "What?"

"We need bread."

"Right."

"Who has bread?"

"Who?"

"People."

"Right."

"There," Luke directed his desolate gaze to a point behind Max's head, "are people."

Max turned to look at the crowd, a motley aggregation sharing the common burden of twentieth-century travel: parents weary of their charges, old folk weary of the hustle, students weary of excess. All stunned as refugees.

"Do they look happy to you?" Luke asked with real concern.

"Hell, no."

"Seems to me we could relieve a goodly few of these poor souls of their purgatory and solve our problem in the process."

Max looked blankly at him. "In here? Now? How?"

Luke smiled patiently. "No, not in here, good buddy. Out there. On the blacktop. Think about it. Thanksgiving coming up. People go places Thanksgiving, visit family, take money with them, you dig?''

It took some time coming. "You mean—hit a bus?''

Luke's flat look said: What the fuck else?

Max's heartbeat kicked again. "Shit.''

"You have a problem with this, kiddo?''

"Hell, no! It's just . . .''

"What?''

"Different.''

Luke nodded solemnly. "Time for a change. The sameness is getting boring, the progress too slow. Fourteen—is it?—beneficiaries in three months. Population—two hundred twenty million. Have you any idea how long it will take at this rate to create Utopia?''

Math had never been Max's strong point. He shook his head.

"By the bus load it'll be forty-five times faster.'' Luke's grin was chilly. "And much more fun.''

"Jesus,'' croaked Max. And then: "How?''

"I'm planning, right now.''

"But . . .''

But Luke was off and running.

The plan was pure genius.

They did a dry bus run, Phoenix to San Diego.

Why San Diego?

Because, Luke revealed with a smirk, it's very close to Mexico.

After Interstate 8 crosses into California at Yuma (which is roughly halfway between Phoenix and San Diego), it runs almost parallel with and so close to the Mexican border you could, with a little wind assistance, piss out of the bus window into Baja California Norte.

Also—

Once you get past Yuma, Winterhaven, and Andrade, there is a stretch of some forty miles of highway—before you hit El Centro—flanked by absolutely miles and miles of total fuckin' nothing except desert scrub, the occasional farm, big rocky outcrops, towering cactus, rattlers, and a zillion escape routes.

Luke knew this because he had once spent a week at the Army Proving Ground at Yuma and had on several occasions driven to El Centro—or more accurately to Mexicali, just south of it—hoping to find a better class of whore in that larger town. Though he didn't succeed, he said, he got to know the road like the back of his prick and knew whereof he spoke.

Now he took pleasure in demonstrating his knowledge to Max as they dry-ran the course.

I-8 being a limited-access highway, they would have to take the bus off at an intersection. Between Andrade and El Centro there were three. The first seemed the most suitable. From it ran a piss-poor state road, 98, the back way to Mexicali.

Once off I-8 onto 98 they could get the bus quickly into desert and out of sight behind any number of rocky upthrusts and cactus groves, even drive the mother into the All-American Canal if it took their fancy.

"Here," Luke had said, nudging Max, pinpointing the spot. "Off here, through there, behind that." And Max went: "Yeah, yeah, yeah," seeing it.

The decision made, they stayed on the bus all the way into San Diego—another four hours with stops—slept overnight in a sleaze motel, smoking grass, planning, then stole wheels after dark the second night and drove back to the takeoff intersection for a closer look at the area in the first light of dawn.

The place they'd first seen from the bus was A-1 perfect—half a mile south of I-8 and just off 98, a small jungle of towering rocks, twenty to thirty feet high, giant saguaro cactus, and the maguey cactus, Spanish bayonet with its stiletto points, all forming a rough circle around a clearing of low scrub big enough to accommodate a bus, and giving total cover from both the Interstate and the state road once the bus was inside. And all around this dry oasis—desert, farmland—nothing. Perfect.

Inside the clearing, Luke did a crazy victory jig like a wide receiver after scoring a touchdown. "Dis *is* de place, baby! Let's get back to Phoenix and put it together."

On the return run Max had asked, just to get it straight, "So, okay, we take it off there and . . ."

"What?"

"Well, like, how do we . . ."

"Get away?"

Max shrugged. "Yeah." Max grinned. "Do we, you and me, drive the bus to San Diego?"

Luke's look clearly said: Asshole.

But his voice said, "Motorbike. You do ride a bike?"

"Sure."

"We boost two in Phoenix, ride them out to the intersection on state roads, stash one bike behind the rocks, ride the other one back to Phoenix."

"Great." Max nodded. "And how do we, you know, *take* the bus—the people. A full bus, maybe. How do we control them, get the driver to . . ."

"Shotguns."

Max beamed. "I like shotguns. Sawed-off. You could really kill a bus with a couple of those babies."

"That's the idea."

Later on, Max asked, "How much d'you reckon, Luke?"

"Takings?"

"Yeah. The bus we came out on was half full, with four Chicanos. Lotta Indians, Spics, Chicanos this neck of the woods. They gotta be piss poor."

"Not necessarily, kiddo." Luke the erudite schoolmaster now. "These people are like tortoises, carry everything around on their backs. Maybe it's only a hundred bucks, but it's there, under the old serape along with the tacos and tortillas and other Mex shit they chew on to kill time. Thanksgiving, the buses will be full, take my word."

"And the old farts," said Max, pressing the point. "There were four, five oldsters on that bus."

"Same thing. These days, they're scared of their houses being robbed while they're away, so what they don't stash in a bank they bring with them—cash, checkbooks, credit cards, jewelry." He grinned. "Reminds me of a joke. Rich father and daughter riding in a coach. Gang of bandits stop the coach, tell dad and daughter to get out, hand over the box of jewels. Daughter takes a couple of rings off her fingers and says, 'This is all we've got.' Bandits search the coach, then drive off with it. Dad says, 'Where did you hide the box of jewels, darlin'?' Daughter reaches up her skirts and pulls the box out of her box. Dad says, 'Pity we didn't bring your mother, we could've'—"

"Saved the coach and horses," said Max. "Yeah, I heard it."

So—

That is what they did.

Bikes were plentiful in Phoenix, all kinds of all-terrain bikes for desert and hill work. But they didn't steal those. Too noticeable, Luke said, on the open road with their weird tires and guards. So they settled for a couple of domestic Japs, one a powerful mother, a Kawasaki 750, which they took out and left behind the rocks, and one a Yamaha 350, which they rode back to Phoenix.

All together the finding and the boosting and the riding took three days.

On the fourth day, just before closing, they pushed into a sporting goods–cum–hardware store on the quiet edge of town, coldcocked the old-guy owner and stuffed him in

21

a closet, took two Weatherby pump guns, a couple of boxes of double-ought buckshot, a hacksaw for cutting down the guns, and what was in the cash register—enough for bed, board, and two single bus tickets to San Diego.

And here they were.

Max slid out of his reverie and straight into panic because Luke was coming at him up the aisle, those starey, ice-water eyes telling him Luke had been trying to reach him and there he'd been strolling down memory lane and being generally unprofessional and Luke didn't like it one bit.

Reaching the toilet door, Luke slammed inside for a quick one and reappeared with the same "get your ass together" look leveled at him, together with a show of perpendicular fingers that told him "three minutes to go."

Now Max was up, up, up, heart boinging in his ears, mouth dry as sand, eyes blurring, every nerve in his body twitching, that bitter, sicky feeling rising from his gut into his throat.

Three minutes.

The enormity of what they were about to do hit him.

Forty-six people . . . forty-seven with the driver. All theirs. And the chick—

All his.

Katherine Anne Tyson. This—

Is Your Death.

Kat was in a state. She lifted her head off the scientifically designed headrest of the body-contoured bus seat (why *couldn't* they get it right? what did they use for a profile model? a six-foot-three orangutan or a pygmy hunchback?) and laid it to rest against the air-conditioned surface of the tinted window, for a mere moment relishing its coolness before removing it because she was sitting over the rear wheels of the bus and the thrumming vibration through the glass did absolutely nothing for the headache she'd been nurturing since Phoenix.

The bus had been a mistake. She should have flown straight to L.A. The voice had whispered to her in the Phoenix depot that enough was enough, three weeks on and off buses was more punishment than the human frame and psyche were designed to take—why, for Crissake, San Diego?

Because she'd never seen it.

Was that the only reason?

Because in three solid weeks of travel she hadn't picked up one single idea she could use, wanted to use. Maybe in San Diego . . .

Was that the main reason?

No.

Because she was afraid to go home.

A terrible sense of desolation swept through her. She felt so—lost. In that instant she knew what it was like to be a lone iceberg floating in a vast freezing sea, could empathize with a Saturn probe sailing silently through the endless black void of space.

How could things have changed so quickly? Where had all the happiness gone?

And on top of everything, it was her birthday.

That didn't help. Too many birthday memories, joyous occasions when they were all together—Mom, Dad, Rick . . .

Stop it. Get your act together, dummy. You're not a kid, you're twenty-two years old and Scott Tyson's daughter . . .

Tears just gushed up then. Oh, Daddy, Daddy.

From her shoulder bag she fumbled for a tissue and dabbed her eyes, thrusting away the pernicious image of England, that beautiful, ghastly bedroom, her father lying there, gray, wasted . . .

Chin up, Kitty Kat, the old Bastard hasn't gotten me yet.

But He had. Only a matter of time. And so little of it. Perhaps three months, no more.

"You all right, chicken?" Mrs. Clavitt, seated beside her, lived in Sun City to escape the urban violence that had killed her husband when they owned a liquor store in Tucson. Kind Mrs. Clavitt knew all about heartbreak and loneliness.

Kat nodded. "Just tired," she said. She hadn't told Mrs. Clavitt about her father, or Rick, or her mother, or anything. It was not her way.

Mrs. Clavitt reached out to touch Kat's arm, a comforting gesture, then leaned closer as though to impart a confidence, indicating with a tilt of her head the man reclined in his seat to her right, across the aisle.

"I don't suppose that could possibly be Harrison Ford, could it?" Sotto voce, a little devilment in her maternal gray eyes to cheer Kat up.

It worked. Kat had to smile at the idea of it, and dipped her head to glance past Mrs. Clavitt at the man who had saved her from embarrassment when they'd boarded the bus, catching her book-laden carryall before it brained the woman in front.

"Don't . . . think so." She frowned, pretending uncertainty. "I wouldn't think Harrison Ford does too much bus traveling these days."

Mrs. Clavitt sneaked another look at the apparently sleeping man and came back to Kat. "Could be his double."

Kat didn't agree but smiled in agreement.

She took another look at the guy, only now appreciating the symmetry of his profile: good jaw, strong mouth, and one helluva nose. Black hair combed back from a broad brow, shaggy around his neck and ears. She remembered now—that momentary feeling of heavy presence behind her at the time the carryall started falling, a radiation of—what?—heat, energy. His leather-jacketed arm had come from nowhere, his hand, strong and tan, grabbing the bag and stopping its fall dead. Also, she now remembered, the shock, the tiny crackling discharge of static electricity that pricked her hand as their flesh brushed. And she remembered his eyes—dark, penetrating, flaring for an instant with a smile of amused collusion, but then as quickly returning to—

She frowned in thought, recalling, trying to. She hadn't much cared at the time, been too unnerved by the incident and too full of her own problems, but her retina had taken the picture and her mind had stored the negative, and now that she consciously developed it, his eyes had returned to an expression of—

Good God, was the entire fucking world heartbroken?

—grief.

Again she glanced across the aisle, seeing him in repose, leather jacket stirring slightly with his even, rhythmic breathing, his face devoid of woe.

"Handsome devil, isn't he?" whispered Mrs. Clavitt, quite mistaking Kat's interest.

Kat smiled yes, while thinking, and hurting like a son of a bitch.

Across the aisle the man in the black leather jacket who really looked nothing like Harrison Ford but whose dark, strong looks had prompted others to speculate that if screen acting wasn't his game it should be, floated in a limbo of self-imposed hypnotic trance. His own grief at Nanosh's death notwithstanding, the experience of the funeral, the intensity of the Romany mourning, had been well-nigh unbearable. This, compounded by the mind-blowing revelation made to him by his grandfather on his deathbed,

25

had reduced John Raven to a state of such mental anguish—encompassing the extremities of grief, bewilderment, and volcanic anger—that his physical containment within the bus for eight long hours would have been impossible to endure without the anodyne of hypnosis.

He was not asleep. Rather he dwelt out beyond the reaches of the world. In blissful nothingness. Healing. Self-programmed to awaken when he reached his destination: Live Oak Springs, the junction stop for the Manzanita Indian Reservation, one hour east of San Diego; or before that moment in the event of any emergency.

Now, three hours before his intended resurrection, John Raven was about to be awakened.

Andrade, the penultimate junction, had long come and gone. Seated to the driver's right, on the aisle in the front right-side double seat, Lucas Patrick Shand stared through the huge windshield at the rushing blacktop, his unblinking gaze both encompassing the highway and identifying landscape features on either side, knowing also from his watch how little time was left. Now—

One minute.

An excited pulse beat in his throat.

Turning in his seat, he looked back down the aisle, knowing that since his angry three-minute warning Max just had to be sitting there waiting for his signal.

Jesus Christ, he couldn't believe it. The dumb fuck was off again, staring bug-eyed at the broad. Zapped out. What had he been doing in the can—snorting C, shooting up? He'd warned him to go easy . . .

Well, hell, nothing mattered now. He'd sure as shit get Max's attention thirty seconds from now. And everyone else's, too.

Reaching down beneath his seat, he slid a hand into the opening of his Puma sports bag, gripped the stock of his

26

sawn-down Weatherby, and in one smooth movement crossed the aisle to poke the gun's murderous hole into the ribs of the middle-aged, overweight driver.

Max saw the move and panicked again. Christ, it was here! In a kaleidoscopic blur he snatched his Puma bag off the floor, fumbled the zipper, but couldn't get it open, his hands shaking like wings. Calm down! You're the Man. They ain't going noplace.

But now the bus was turning off the highway, swinging down the exit ramp, and the people were staring and stirring. What the fuck's goin' on?

Murmurings and mutterings. "Hey, driver . . ."

Luke's eyes flashing at him, lethal lasers. "Max, you AAAASHOLE . . . !"

The zipper—

The old guy next to him asked, "Need any help, son?"

—open. The Weatherby out, pumped, primed, ready.

"Sonny, n-now you be careful with that thing," the old voice quavered.

Max was up on his feet, into it now, blood soaring, everything a blur, feeling the power, gun in one hand, bag in the other, beginning to shout: "ALL RIGHT, YOU MOTHERS, THIS IS A HOLDUP!" shocking them, stunning them, terrorizing them.

Heads turning, mouths gaping, eyes popping, a cry, a groan, a scream.

"FACE THE FRONT! ANYONE GETS BRAVE GETS THIS . . ."

He pulled the trigger, blasting the roof. The noise was horrendous, the effect devastating.

Everyone turned to stone.

"I WANT EVERYTHING YOU'VE GOT—CASH, WALLETS, WATCHES, JEWELRY. EV-ER-Y-THING. IN THE BAG. I CATCH ANYONE HOLDIN' OUT . . ."

He pumped a shell into the chamber, the slick, metallic sound of it as threatening as the explosion.

"Okay, old-timer, you first—dig it out, drop it in."

The bus lurched, swinging onto 98. Max shot a glance behind him, saw Luke in command, covering his rear, directing the driver, watching the people, watching for cops, eyes manic, sending him the nod, everything cool.

Max—keeping up the terror. "You, lady—get your purse in there—take those fucking rings off!" Moving backward, enjoying the power, the fear, the trembling, the tears, feeling the chick behind him, coming up, gut-sick with excitement, knowing this was the best moment of his life; this—and what was to come.

Another step back, coming into line with her, but delaying it, teasing it out, turning to his left, thrusting the bag across the hero in the leather jacket to the woman at the window: "Dig deep, Momma—everything or I shoot off your ass!" Feeling Hero's eyes on him, but not much else. Expecting heat waves of male anger from this guy, the frustration of impotence, the bunching of muscle. But nothing. The dark eyes under the heavy brows just watching, too damn cool.

Max decided then Hero had to die. But first—

A little fun.

"Hey, hey, what do we have *here*. Hey, nice jacket, man." He thrust the Weatherby muzzle into Raven's chest, parted the jacket lapels, revealing an open-neck blue-check shirt, three buttons undone. Nestling in the spriggy black chest hairs was a gold cross topped by an oval, hanging on a gold chain.

"Would ya look at *this*!" Max goading the guy, slipping the muzzle under the cross into the loop of the chain and jerking it and the guy forward. "Why, it's a Come-to-Jesus cross. You religious, Hero? You all for turning the other cheek, like the Good Lord says?"

That was better. Hero wasn't so cool anymore. Beads

of perspiration popping out on his handsome mug and he was swallowing some.

"Speak up, I can't hear you."

Raven's lips moved tremulously. "Not particularly."

"LOUDER—I CAN'T HEAR YOU."

"Not," Raven cleared his throat, "particularly."

"So why you wearing a cross?"

"It's—" Raven's voice was a subjugated whisper. "It's personal. Let me keep it. It isn't worth much."

"*Per*-sonal," gloated Max. "A present, was it? From your boyfriend? You a little fruity, Hero? A big dumb-jock faggot? Well, you're also a fucking liar, because this is solid *gold,* prickhead. Get it off!"

As Raven reached behind his head for the clasp, Max rammed the Weatherby hard under his chin, sneered into his face. "I don't like you, Hero. Something weird about you . . ."

The bus bounced hard, throwing Max backward against Mrs. Clavitt, who cried out.

Max threw a look through the window, saw they'd left 98 and were onto the farm road that led to the clearing.

Luke called from up front, "Max, get on with it, we're nearly there!"

Oh, yeah, he'd get on with it.

Turning, he peered with exaggerated surprise at Kat, like meeting up with an old friend. "Well, *hi,* Kathy, fancy seeing you here!"

Kat gaped at him. How could this animal possibly know her?

Then to Mrs. Clavitt: "Put your bag and rings in here, lady, then let my fiancée through."

"Come on out, sweetheart," he purred at Kat.

Kat gasped, hearing it, disbelieving what was happening, but knowing exactly what this creep intended. Jesus, no. A horrified glance at Mrs. Clavitt, who shut her eyes

29

in pity, shock, and dread. Another across the aisle to the man who had helped save her before, but this time he offered only a hurried shifting of the eyes: Not this time, kid. This is no falling bag; this is death.

Max again, all banter ended. "Kathy, get out here right now or I shoot this old cunt."

Mrs. Clavitt, ashen, crying out as the Weatherby rammed into her stomach.

"Leave her alone, you bastard!" Kat scrambled up. "Leave her alone!"

A grin. "Spunky. I like spunky broads. Grab the bag, Kate, start collecting."

Backing up, speeding up now, wanting to get out of the bus and into this incredible, neat, tight little ass in front of him. It was happening, just as he'd imagined it. This was no longer fantasy, it was *real*.

He heard Luke behind him, giving directions. The bus swung sharply, grated against something, came to a stop with a hiss of brakes. Max glanced out. They were in the clearing, rocks all around them towering over the bus.

Luke took over. " 'Kay, folks, this is how it is. Max and I—and Kathy, his fiancée . . ."

Max turned, grinned, liking that.

Kat shut her eyes, shook her head, trying to let anyone in doubt know the truth of the matter.

". . . will be leaving you now. Naturally, we'll need some time to get away. You will remain in your seats for one hour. We'll be out of your sight immediately, so you won't know whether we've gone or not. If anyone leaves the bus before the hour is up, we will open fire and kill you all." He indicated the hole Max had shot in the roof. "Does anyone doubt what these guns can do?"

For emphasis, he turned and fired across the driver's legs into the dashboard, obliterating dials and ignition connections, unconcerned that stray buckshot going in and glass and metal splinters coming out pierced the driver's knees and thighs. Liking it, in fact, liking the effect the guy's shocked yell and the sight of welling blood and the second devastating explosion in that confined space had on the people, enjoying the gasps of terror and cries of outrage, knowing that *nobody* was going to follow them out of the door, looking to be a hero.

Reaching across the mortified driver, Luke hit the control and the door opened with a flatulent hiss.

"Okay, let's go."

Max grabbed Kat's arm and swung her down the steps.

Luke gave them all one last manic glare. "One hour!" He swung his attention to the driver. "You—close the door after me." To them all: "This door opens, we'll hear it and start shooting. One hour—synchronize your watches." He grinned. "Hey, that's right, you ain't got any watches. So count—three thousand six hundred. Come on, start counting—one, two, three—all together now—four, five, six . . . I DON'T HEAR YOU! COUNT, YOU BASTARDS! LOUDER AT THE BACK!"

He cocked an ear, listened to the spiritless murmur.

"Terrific."

He ran down the steps, waited for the door to close, and then was gone, following Max and the girl through a narrow defile in the rocks.

Kat knew she was going to die. The only uncertainty in her mind was how. She also knew she was going to be raped. The message radiated from this blond freak loud as a drumbeat, even before he started talking it.

Once they were through the encircling rocks, he shoved her into a small clearing surrounded by cactus, the giant ones throwing black shade in the afternoon sun. In a patch of shadow beneath a towering saguaro he pushed her sprawling to the ground, then stood over her, legs spread, and slowly brought the shotgun down to touch her cheek.

"I know what you're thinking." His voice was quiet and slow, either drugged or histrionic, playing out a fantasy. Whichever, it said he had total power over her, whether she lived or died, died hard or died easy. Here, in this desert place, it said, there is no law, no protection. You are mine.

Disbelief battered her. This could not be happening. Yet here was the reality—the sand and stones of the desert beneath her fingers, his dusty Nikes within her view, the cold steel of that terrifying gun against her cheek. Every nerve in her body vibrated, twitched. She was going to die. Ludicrously, she remembered it was her birthday. What a helluva day to die.

"You're thinking, 'This can't be happening to me.' " The voice was singsong, menacing. "You're thinking, I, Katherine Anne Tyson of Cleves Cottage, Canyon Road, Brentwood Park, Los Angeles, California—see, I remembered your address—can't be lying here in the desert, kidnapped from a bus by a coupla sex-maniac psychos who're going to fuck me and make me give head and do all kinds of dirty things to me before they kill me—hell, *while* they're killing me. But it's true, honey. Swear to God, that's exactly what's going to happen. Look at me—"

She was slow and a Nike thudded into her ribs.

"I said look at me!"

Crying out, shaking uncontrollably, she raised her face. His crotch, the long thick outline of his erection, filled her swimming vision. And then, she saw something else, something far more terrifying. He took it from his shirt pocket, brought it down to her eyeline, opened it. The blade of the cutthroat razor glinted sunlight.

She gasped, dying inside, crazed with terror.

He stroked a Z, lightning fast, just inches from her face.

And laughed. "The Mark of Zorro. That's our trademark, Luke and me. We like to spoil things, watch them die. Like a snuff porno movie. You ever see one? This is better. You're making one, Kate. You're the fucking star!"

Now he hurled the Weatherby aside, all action, grabbed a handful of her hair and hauled her to her knees, the razor's blade flat alongside her cheek.

"The zipper—open it."

A sob exploded from her. He thrust her face against his erection to stifle the sound, swiped the back of the blade across her forehead, pressing her mouth against his cock to kill the scream.

"Next time I'll cut you. Open the zipper!"

From the other clearing came the roar of two gunshot explosions.

"Luke just having a little fun, maybe teaching someone a lesson. He's only teasing them, though. We're going to kill them all when we're done with you. Open the zipper, Kate."

Numb now, her face buried in his hard belly, she reached for the metal tag and drew it down. He wore nothing underneath. The odor of his sex filled her face. His hard thick penis sprang free, the hot flesh against her lips.

He jerked her head away, so she could see. "Look at him, ain't he somethin'? Talk to him. Tell him you think he's beautiful. Tell him the thing you want most in all the world is his big comey head down your throat and hard, hard up your wet little pussy. Get hold of him, Kate, put him in your mouth. Lick him. Suck him. And if he don't like what you do, I'll cut your fucking lips off."

Luke came into the clearing. "You starting without me, kiddo?"

"Who'd you shoot?"

"The front tires, just in case. How's she doing?"

"Not good."

"Cut her some, they get better."

Kat's heart exploded in her breast.

Max laid the flat of the blade against her cheek. "You heard the man. Suck or bleed, bitch."

Luke came up behind where she knelt, threw his Weatherby alongside Max's and the Puma bag, opened her legs and knelt between them. What they liked, Max and he, was doing it together, all of it, which on this occasion posed some logistical problems. It was easier naked on a nice soft bed or carpet, with all the time in the world, like with the black chick in Daytona. Here it was stony and they couldn't hang around for three days. So it had to be this way.

He lifted her denim skirt, exposing little white panties, moved his right hand around and over the flat firm warmth of her stomach, dipped into the waistband and ran a finger down into the crevice of her cunt.

"Sweet Jesus." He rose like iron against her buttocks.

Now he jerked the panties down, balling them in a left-handed grip midthigh. "Razor!" With a slash he severed the briefs, exposing her ass, handed the razor back, now thrust his hand between her legs and drove a finger up inside her.

Kat cried out in rage and terror, in helplessness, in extreme protest.

Then they got to her: Max in the mouth, clasping her face, the razor closed in his hand, drawing her onto him, easing in and out of her, using her quivering, distorted mouth like a lubricated vagina; Luke covered in spit, hard up inside her now, gripping her hips, almost lifting her off her knees with the power of his thrusts, both of them grunting, gasping, muttering obscenities, wild with the joy of rape, mad with power.

Max groaning, breathless, swelling in her mouth. "Oh . . . Christ . . . oh . . . Jesus . . ."

Luke panting: "You . . . there, baby?"

Max grabbing her hair, right hand flicking open the razor. "Mark of Zorro . . . now . . . now!"

"Wait! Wait—I'm there . . ."

Suddenly Max was gone from her mouth, backing off, Kat falling forward without support, onto her face, pitching away from Luke, Luke falling sideways, shocked, glaring up at Max, seeing Max transfixed, staring, at the rocks, Luke turning, seeing—

The big guy, black leather jacket, off the bus—

Braced there, set like stone, unreal.

Luke was on his feet, erection wilting, darting a glance at the Weatherbys, ten feet away, starting his move.

Now Max saw Hero—what the *hell*?—somehow gathering himself, face contorting, a fury, hands like claws, outstretched toward Luke, mouth opening—

Max would never understand or believe what happened next. Luke, taking two strides toward the guns, suddenly stopped as though he'd run into a wall, clapped his hands over his ears, took a quarter turn to the right, and flew . . . hurtled face first into the three-inch spikes of a bayonet cactus, impaled a hundred places into immobility.

Max, head ringing as though he'd been clubbed with an ax handle, saw it begin again, the guy's face, turned on him, inhuman. The eyes, coal black, burning with incredible anger. A withering malevolence streamed across the clearing, attacking him, driving him back. The guy's hands stretched out toward him, fingers clawed, body braced, gathering . . .

Max fled.

Lying there, cheek to the ground, Kat saw it and passed out.

Chapter Three

Kat drifted back, felt hands on her body, and went berserk!

"Ssh, ssh, it's okay, it's okay."

Looking up, she saw a familiar face swimming into focus. It was the guy off the bus, no longer wearing the jacket. Kat realized her head rested on something soft and leathery and knew what it was. The kindness, the relief, broke her up.

"It's really okay, the danger's over."

She curled up into him, into strong arms, and let go in racking sobs. "Have . . . they . . . gone?"

"One has. I heard a motorbike. He's probably in Mexico by now."

Now she remembered—the other one. She jerked a look, saw him lying beside the cactus, no longer impaled, on his back, blood oozing from a dozen places, eyes gone. A nightmare vision.

A gentle hand blinded her to the horror, turned her face to his, to the kind, sad eyes she'd known on the bus, not the—that terrifying mask . . .

"What happened?" she whispered, trembling, afraid of him despite his gentleness. "What did you *do*?"

"Let's talk about you. Can you stand, make it back to the bus?"

She shook her head. She couldn't face them, the speculative stares. She felt degraded, filthy, unfit for human company. The taste of him was in her mouth—not sperm, thank God, he hadn't climaxed; neither, she knew, had the other one—but it made no difference. They had been inside her. Remembering how her panties had been disposed of, she felt suddenly naked, vulnerable, and ridiculous beneath her denim skirt. Reflexively she pulled at it, tugged to make it longer, and squeezed her thighs together defensively.

This man saw and understood.

"Come on," he said, "you need a few minutes alone. We'll find another place."

Supporting her, he led her through rocks and cactus and found where the motorcycle had been hidden, the sand torn up in frantic takeoff, tracks running west-southwest toward Mexicali, hell-an'-gone into Mexico.

"I won't be long," he said, releasing her. "I'll tell the people on the bus it's okay, get some help." He moved off, asking from behind her as a parting thought, "Sure you're all right?"

She gave a nod, croaked, "Yes, thank you." For the first time she became aware of the quality of his voice. It was deeply masculine, easy, reassuring, almost hypnotic, a beautiful voice. Yet his presence, knowing what he'd done, frightened her. There was something very strange about this . . .

She turned to reassure him, feeling he was waiting for it.

She was alone. She hadn't heard a sound.

Something very strange.

It took an hour to contact the police. Three of the younger, most physically able, passengers set out from the bus, one heading for a distant farmhouse and a hoped-for telephone, two for 98 and a lift—or even, with luck, an encounter with a patrolling police car. Luck was initially against them all. The farm phone was out of order; nobody was picking up hitchhikers on 98 that day; and the county cops had been called to a six-car pileup and the resulting traffic jam near El Centro.

But then one of the hitchhikers did get lucky, and when the law finally did arrive it was both in style and number: patrol cars, unmarked cars, motorcycles, a helicopter. Highway Patrol, Sheriff's Office, the FBI. And the media. A lot of media. The hijacking of a bus, the shooting of the driver was big news. Mayhem reigned. It was carnival time.

The police questioned; the passengers, still shocked and mystified, answered. Opinions conflicted.

The girl was in on it! That blond bastard knew her, called her by name, said she was his fiancée!

Bullshit—she was terrified.

Don't you bullshit me. That was an act. She collected our stuff for him, didn't she?

Jesus.

"Where is this girl?" a plainclothes cop asked.

Nobody knew. Or cared. Self-interest ruled.

On his return to the bus to let the passengers know they were out of danger, Raven hadn't told them Kat had been raped, merely that she was alive and very shaken. Everyone, even Mrs. Clavitt, was too preoccupied with their own deliverance and the problem of getting on to San Diego to wonder why Kat hadn't returned to the bus with Raven.

Now another plainclothes cop, one of several who had converged on the small clearing in response to the helicopter sighting of two people and an apparent body, was questioning Raven. Kat sat close by on a sunlit rock, withdrawn, hugging herself, avoiding the sight of Luke's body being picked over by a team of detectives.

The cop, a graceless, crumpled, near-retirement bear of a man, tan suit, wide-brimmed hat, complexion like cooled lava, identified himself as Lieutenant Plaidy, Highway Patrol. His gray, thousand-year-old eyes, red-rimmed by sleepless nights and desert glare, witness to every known human frailty, folly, and foible, invited Raven and Kat to tell lies. See what they'd get.

"We'll start with your names."

"John Raven."

"Miss?"

"Katherine Tyson," Kat answered without looking at him.

"This is just to get my bearings, find out what the hell happened, broadly." Plaidy unwrapped a stick of Juicy Fruit, fed it into his mouth, chomped on it, getting it started, the sweet aroma drifting to Raven's nostrils. "Later on we'll be taking statements, hope you folks aren't in too much of a hurry to get where you're going. You all right, miss, you look a little peaked."

Raven said, "Miss Tyson's in a bad way. Those bastards took her off the bus, brought her here . . . violated her. She needs special attention."

Plaidy looked at her. "You see it?" he asked Raven.

"Yes."

Plaidy glanced across the clearing to Luke's body, came back for a reappraisal of Raven, his weight and build. "You do that?"

"Yes."

"How?"

"I pushed him."

Plaidy frowned. "He allowed you to get that close?"

"They weren't expecting me. They'd warned everyone to stay on the bus."

Plaidy eyed him narrowly, getting the picture but finding it hard to swallow. "You took one hell of a chance—

two punks with shotguns. You a Green Beret or something?''

"No.''

"What are you—what you do?''

"I'm a research biophysicist.''

Plaidy's eyes said: What the fuck's that?

"Yeah?'' he drawled while he was snapping the send button on his walkie-talkie. "You there, Buckley?''

The receiver crackled. "Yo.''

"Get Madge in here, through the rocks, take a woman to Medical.''

"Yo.''

"Think's he's in the cavalry,'' he said in Kat's direction, trying to lighten her load. His eyes fell on Raven, deadly serious. "We'll talk. Stay put.''

Plaidy walked off across the clearing to mingle with the detectives around the body. Raven saw him crouch, give it a more thorough inspection this time, look up at the cactus, at the blood now dried black on the stiletto spines, then talk to a couple of men, one with a bag who might be a doctor.

"I don't know how to thank you,'' Kat said softly. "He's right, you did take one hell of a chance.''

"Just remember—keep it simple, as we agreed. I pushed him. The other guy ran off. That's all you saw.''

She nodded acquiescently, his voice soothing, sure.

Raven was still working for control. In the hour before the police arrived he had returned to the bus several times, checking on the driver, reassuring him, urging the impatient to stay put, not wander off into the desert. But he had spent most of the time with Kat, talking to her, calming her, battling the hysteria that surged just beneath her fragile surface, evidenced by the trembling of her body that threatened to erupt at any moment and precipitate her into either a cataclysmic crying jag or, going the other way, into something like catalepsy. There was more here, Raven knew, than reaction to rape. He'd taken the measure of her emotional condition in Phoenix, on the bus, touching her for that instant, sparks crackling between them. He'd read her like a computer printout—father, brother, mother. Altogether too much. The rape, that hideous, totally unexpected endgame, had brought her to the brink of breakdown. In that hour he had worked hard to bring her back from the edge.

She was calmer now, a little tranced, not too much because she had to function, but enough to keep her inside her skin.

"Were you telling the truth?" she asked. "Are you really a research biophysicist?"

"Yes."

"What do you research?"

"People."

"What—their behavior?"

"We'll talk about that later."

She focused on his eyes, frowning. "Will I be seeing you later?"

"Oh, yes. I'll be taking you home."

The frown deepened. "Home?"

"To Brentwood. You're in no condition to be alone."

She stared blankly at him. Her lips moved silently before voicing the questions. "How—do you know I live in Brentwood? How d'you know I live alone?"

Raven smiled, soothing her bewilderment. "The first one's easy. Your address is on your bag in the bus rack."

Something dawned horrifyingly. "That's how *he* knew my name and address!"

"Yes. That's why I'm taking you home."

She gave that a moment, then returned to the second question. "How did you know I live alone?"

Raven was spared from answering by the arrival of a

young woman through the crevice in the rocks. She wore gray cotton slacks and a jacket, carried a shoulder bag, her blond hair tied back.

Lieutenant Plaidy, waiting for her, came right over, bringing the Puma bag containing the passengers' treasures.

"Madge—" He took her by the elbow, drew her aside, murmured the information, came back to Kat. "Miss Tyson, this is Policewoman Tiefort, will you go along with her, please. Here—anything of yours in here?" He proffered the Puma bag.

"My purse." Kat rummaged inside and retrieved her bag. Her eyes met Raven's in farewell.

"I'll be seeing you," he said.

Raven followed her visually until she disappeared, then turned to find Plaidy watching him narrowly.

"Anything of yours in here?" Plaidy asked.

"Yes, a billfold." He dipped in, located it. "And this." He drew out the gold cross and chain.

Plaidy eyed it. "That's a—what'sit."

"An ankh." Raven slipped it around his neck under his shirt.

"Yeah, right. Sex symbol. Greek."

"Life symbol. Egyptian."

Plaidy shrugged. "Close. Your billfold—got any I.D. in there?"

Raven could see the suspicion coming at him like a telegraphed right hook, Plaidy enjoying himself, playing cop. Questions had been posed over there by the body and Plaidy was here for the answers, but in his own way, taking his time, one of the few perks of a fucking awful job.

"All kinds, Lieutenant. What would you like—driver's license, Social Security, credit cards." Raven handed over the wallet.

"Kansas City," mused Plaidy. "You're a long way from

home. How come you were on a bus from Phoenix to San Diego?''

He raised a sardonic gaze from the billfold, caught the direct challenge of Raven's eyes, then backed off, offering an appeasing hand. ''You're right, none of my business, it's personal. Except we have a problem. On the one hand here, we have a respectable citizen—you—going about his lawful business, traveling on a bus for personal reasons . . . and on the other hand, we have one very dead psycho rapist shithead freak who looks like my old lady's colander. Mister, what you did—apparently did—to no doubt save Miss Tyson's life was brave, no denying that, I take my hat off to you. Trouble is, those guys over there, the detectives, don't believe you could've done what you say you did. Or, let's put it a kinder way—they don't see *how* you could've done it. So what they'd like is for you and me to walk the thing through, nice 'n' slow, you telling me where she was being raped, how she was being raped, where the shotguns were—stuff like that.''

Raven accompanied the lieutenant across the clearing.

''Here,'' said Raven, pointing.

''Draw pictures for me,'' said Plaidy. ''See, I have this terrible imagination, or lack of it. I like lots of fine detail.''

The guy's playing Columbo, thought Raven. All he needs to complete the picture is a celebrity-struck wife and a raincoat that ten trucks have run over.

''She was kneeling here, facing that way. The blond ape was in front of her, holding a razor on her, against her face—''

''A razor?''

''A cutthroat.''

''Jesus. No wonder she looked . . . okay, go on, what was he doing to her?''

''He had his cock in her mouth.''

Plaidy grimaced. His glance went behind Raven. Raven turned, seeing the cop coming up, young, dark, clean-shaven, pristine in a light-gray suit, polished black Oxfords. Before he spoke Raven knew he was FBI.

"Lieutenant." A nod to Plaidy but earnest blue eyes trained on Raven. "Mind if I listen in?"

Plaidy nodded, glancing from the agent to Raven. "This is Agent Hendrick—FBI. John Raven."

Hendrick said, "Been hearing about you. Hero of the hour. Remarkable, what you did."

Raven disliked the man's tone, his eyes, everything about him, and sensed that Plaidy disliked him, too.

"Go ahead," Plaidy said to Raven. "What was the other creep doing?"

"He was down behind her, lifting her skirt."

"Was he into her when you got here?"

Raven nodded grimly. "They were going to kill her, soon as they'd finished."

"How would you know that?" Hendrick cut in.

Raven answered, as though Plaidy had asked the question. "The blond guy, Max, was flourishing the razor, near to orgasm. He grabbed Miss Tyson's hair and shouted something like 'Mark of Zorro . . . now . . . now' but the other one told him 'Wait—' "

"Hey," Hendrick interrupted, "you said 'The blond guy, *Max*.' How d'you know his name?"

"His partner used it on the bus."

Hendrick arched his brows. "Yeah? No one else came up with that—that I know of. You're very observant, Mister Raven. One very cool guy. So—go on, the other one—whose name, incidentally, is Shand. Luke Shand." He looked at Plaidy, checking, although it was too late anyway, if it was okay to impart the information. Plaidy nodded his approval.

Raven said, "Shand, then, saved Miss Tyson's life—by

delaying her death. He wasn't quite ready, told Max to wait."

Silence.

"Then?" prompted Hendrick.

"Then Max saw me. He backed away, surprised. Miss Tyson fell forward, away from Shand. Shand got up, made a move toward the shotguns, but I got to him first and threw him into the cactus. Max obviously didn't like the way things were going, so he ran off through there and . . ."

"Whoa, whoa, *whoa*." Hendrick laughed dryly, walking in a circle, kicking sand with a polished toe. "Hey, Raven—" He squinted, like he was aiming a rifle, sizing up the man. "You're—what?—six-two, two hundred pounds?"

"One-ninety-six."

"Nice build. You look strong. But if you'll pardon my saying so, the Refrigerator you ain't. Now from what I hear, this Max character went six-four and maybe two-fifty. Added to which he was armed with a cutthroat razor. Now, you're telling me—us—that while you were busy throwing his buddy face first into the cactus spikes, he was just standing there watching and letting it happen?"

Raven shrugged. Max stood rooted with shock for a moment and then ran off. I told you I'd surprised them. They didn't expect anyone to get off the bus, said if anyone did they'd hear the door opening and start shooting."

"How did you overcome that?" asked Plaidy.

"I climbed out of an emergency window."

"Smart thinking."

"Well, hell, I don't buy it," said Hendrick, squinting again. "Something here doesn't sit right."

"There is one other possibility to consider," said Raven.

"Yeah, what's that?" said Hendrick.

"I might have embarrassed him."

"Huh?"

"Well, I did catch him with his dick out."

Hendrick's compressed expression said: Fuck with the FBI at your own peril. Then he turned and walked away.

"The man gets up people's noses," said Plaidy. "But maybe he has a point. I don't much buy it, either. Max should've come for you with the razor. What did he see, Mister Raven, that I don't see right now?"

Raven deflected the question. "About Miss Tyson."

"What about her?"

"If the doctor says she's okay, when you're finished with her, I'll hire a Hertz and drive her home."

Plaidy's eyes, just for a moment, asked: You fancy some of what you saw? But then he nodded, withdrawing the question with apology. "If the doctor says okay. You'll be with her? We'll need an address."

"I don't know." Raven frowned, thinking about it. Then he nodded. "Yes, I'll be with her. Brentwood Park."

Plaidy peered at him, unsettled. "What changed your mind?"

"Rather me than Max."

"Max? The bike tracks say he's in Mexico."

Raven shook his head. "Max is in San Diego."

"That right?" mused Plaidy.

Later, Raven eased away from the activity and sat alone on a high rock, facing the flat scrub desert to the west, the sun warm on his face, eyes closed, reaching out for Nanosh, sensing his grandfather's presence, despairing of their separation.

I see you, Gramps, and love you.

I see you, John, and love you.

The voice—in his ear, his heart, his mind? But there, not just desperate, wishful imagining.

I miss you, Gramps. God, I miss you.

I'm with you, Heart, always.

I killed a man. Did you see it?

You saved the girl.

I used the gift to destroy.

You will use it as you must.

There will be others.

You will use it as you must.

"Mister Raven!"

It was Plaidy, down there.

"They're going in to the police station. You get special treatment, you ride with me. See—even the worst days are not entirely lousy."

Chapter Four

There they were, seven that evening, heading north on the San Diego Freeway in a rented Ford, a crimson sun on their left hissing into a misty ocean, quiet with one another, closing in on L.A. Kat was outwardly calm enough, listening to soothing Earl Klugh guitar on the radio, but inwardly undone by the bus experience, drifting now and then back into the nightmare despite the Valium and the comforting presence of the strange, strong, quiet man who had saved her life. It was all too preposterous, unreal, the whole thing. Mrs. Clavitt was the last real thing that had happened to her. The explosion, the gunshot through the bus roof, had triggered some kind of real-time freeze, and everything that had happened since, and was happening now, was fantasy.

"You're having trouble with it."

Raven's voice startled her; it had been some minutes since either had spoken. The jump, the way the nerve ends throughout her entire body squeezed shut like an angry fist, told her she was in trouble.

He took his eyes off the road to look at her, into her face, then down at the hands twitching in her lap.

"You'll feel better when you get home, get to bed. Familiar surroundings will restore the reality."

Her neck prickled. "You know everything I'm thinking."

He grinned. It was a comforting, normal-guy grin that dispelled, a little, his aura of mystery, almost of mysticism, that troubled her. "I can't read your mind precisely, but I'd have to be pretty insensitive not to appreciate what you're feeling."

She shook her head. "No, it's more than that. You—know things, do things. You're a big part of the unreality. It's like I'm working on a Spielberg movie and I can't remember signing the contract."

This time he laughed, a charming Redford-type chuckle that dislodged a little more of her anxiety. "That's how you see me, huh, as E.T.?" He offered the back of his right hand for inspection. "See, quite normal. Go ahead, touch it, pull a hair out. Cut it, I'll bleed. I promise there's no slimy green scales underneath."

At least that got her smiling.

"No," she said, the smile fading. "I believe you're from Planet Earth. But don't tell me what you did back there was—the norm."

He was quietly thoughtful for a while, then said, "Time was, Kat, when people thought the earth was flat. It was the norm. Then along came some weird guy who saw a sailing ship disappear over the horizon and thought, Hey, it's either dropped off into space or the earth is round. That notion bought him a lot of trouble. I think they burned his buns."

"Please—I'm not saying you're weird."

"I know. But you're thinking I'm different. Different from anyone you've ever met. That may be so. But you've led a sheltered life." He stopped her protest with a gesture. "No, I'm not saying you're spoiled, haven't known heartache. I know you have. What I'm saying is your experience is limited. Most people's is. A lot of what I 'know' and 'do,' as you put it, most people could achieve with concentration and effort. It's completely natural.

There must have been a time, way back, when all people had these—abilities. But civilization has numbed them out. See that up ahead—''

Up ahead was Los Angeles, drowning in a loom of purply-gray carbon smog.

''Behold—a prime numb-er. One of many. Noise, concrete, greed, fear are all great little numb-ers. In a way, I was lucky. I had an unusual,'' he grinned, ''some may say exotic, upbringing. Maybe I'll tell you about it sometime.''

''I'd like to hear about it.''

''What I'm saying is—''

He was talking, talking her down, talking bad thoughts out of her head with that deep, rich, soothing voice.

''—I want you to relax around me, don't be frightened by anything you see or hear me do. You're in no danger, not from me. I like you and I want to help you. If you want me to.''

''Yes, I do. But what about your life? You were heading for San Diego, you have things to do.''

''Yes, I have. But they can wait a couple of days.''

A conflicting reaction of relief and uncertainty pervaded her. Despite his assurance, this was no ''ordinary'' man. She'd seen him gentle, helpful, all-too-humanly sad, then suddenly capable of extraordinary power and violence.

She began to think consciously about John Raven.

Gradually, there in the car, thoughts of him began to displace her persistent preoccupation with her own ongoing predicament and the flashing recollections of the recent terror. She thought and wondered about this ''exotic upbringing,'' about the extent of his power. She reflected on the possible direction their acquaintance might take, and couldn't shake the premonition that in the past few hours, despite the horror, the course of her life had taken a tangential change for the—better? Well, certainly for something different. And at the moment almost any kind of change was welcome.

"May I ask you a question?"

His smile said this was what he wanted, what he'd been working for—an indication that her mind was capable of moving away from the rape. "Sure."

"Are you psychic?"

He took a moment to answer, then did so with a question. "Do you believe in such things?"

"Then you are. You didn't say no."

He didn't respond.

Kat went on, more positive now. "You see into the future. You know something terrible is going to happen, it's why you're coming home with me—"

He reached to touch her hand. "Hey, take it easy. It's not like that at all." He returned his hand to the wheel, deciding how much to tell her, decided enough to keep her alert, self-protective, but not enough to frighten her, maybe tip her over into crisis. She was real close.

He asked her again, what he would eventually tell her dependent on her answer. "*Do* you believe in psychic ability . . . psychic phenomena?"

"I don't know. I'm not sure. I believe what you say about us being numbed out. Living in cities has done it to us. We've separated ourselves from nature. I've just spent three weeks traveling by bus through New Mexico and Arizona, visiting pueblos, trying to get close to the Indians, but finding it impossible. They're intrinsically so different from us . . . from me," she corrected herself, with a look that said: I'm not sure about you, "that they might as well be Martians."

A smile illuminated his face, a glow of—what?—pleasure, approbation?

"Different how?" he asked.

"Deep down, spiritually different. They're people of the

Earth. They belong. In their presence I felt like something manufactured in Silicon Valley. They were cactus; I was Coca-Cola. This, despite every dreadful thing we've done to them. The tour depressed me terribly. I saw so much drunkenness, unemployment, neglect. And yet they still possess something, a heart, a spiritual core that I've either never had or have lost somewhere along the past twenty-two years."

"Why did you go, do the tour?"

She thought about it. "Research."

"You're a writer."

She expressed a small, sardonic laugh. "Oh, yes, I'm a writer. An unusual one. I'm a writer who never writes. What I am is a great reader. I've been reading since I was three—everything from Dick and Jane to Dostoyevski, Anderson to Zola. I have a master's in English lit. You want I should quote you Chaucer? I am also an etymologist, an expert in word derivation—witness: etymologist from *etymon* from the neuter of the Greek *etymos,* meaning *true*. I adore words, revere language, but I can't put the damn things down on paper. Because I don't know what to write. I don't *know* anything, haven't lived anything. You were right, I have had a sheltered life. I went to the pueblos to learn something, see the country, maybe use New Mexico as the background for a story, find my voice in the mighty waters of the Rio Grande." Again the small, wry laugh. "The Rio Grande. What a misnomer—from the French *mes,* and Latin *nominare*—an unsuitable name. The goddamn thing was a trickle, and if my voice was in it, it was buried under ten feet of mud."

"Your *voice*?"

"It was an expression my . . . father use to use—a writer's voice, his style, the way he expresses himself."

"Your father was a writer?" he asked, picking up on

her hesitation, her sudden slide into morbid preoccupation.

"My father *is* Scott Tyson," she said with touching defiance, willing it still to be so, tears glistening in her eyes.

Again Raven reached out a comforting hand, touching hers, and there it was—the knowledge, received in a single frame of enlightenment, like a scene perceived in one single pulsing beat of stroboscopic light. Decay. Corruption. Pain. Death. The impression was so fierce it forced a gasp from him.

She jerked a look at him, eyes huge. "What?" Her own pain forgotten.

"I'm—so sorry, Kat."

"You *know*!"

He nodded. "Cancer."

"Jesus," she whispered. Blood fled from her face. "How . . ."

"I don't know. Touching you."

She trembled.

He released her hand. "Don't be frightened of it."

She shook her head. "I'm not. I'm just—awed. Really, I'm interested. Ever since . . ." She drew a deep breath, fumbled in her purse for a cigarette, lit it with a trembling lighter. It was a quarter smoked before she could get the words out. "Two years ago I lost my brother. Rick. He was beautiful. Just . . . beautiful." Her voice broke on the word. She pulled angrily on the cigarette and hurled furious smoke at the windshield.

"Do you know what true real-life horror is?" she ran on, sniffing, wiping at tears with her wrist. "It's not ghoulies and ghosties and things that go bump in the night. It's when good, ordinary lives become unraveled. Stephen King wrote it. And it's the goddamned truth. It's when a beautiful kid of twenty-two who that day graduated from college with honors and has a brilliant medical future ahead of him meets up with a fucking drunk truck driver on the coast highway and goes over the cliff at Big Sur. Boy, that is horror. Horror is the family waiting there in the garden at Brentwood . . . with a surprise party, his friends . . . waiting to welcome . . . and the police drive in instead. And horror is what happens to the family afterwards. Horror is unspeakable grief . . . and insane accusations. And guilt. And separation. And divorce. And . . . oh, *shit*." She smashed the cigarette into the ashtray, dug for a Kleenex, and wiped her face. "I'm sorry."

"So am I," Raven said earnestly.

"It's just—well, all things considered, it's been one asshole of a day."

At that moment, as Max Koenig turned off Fairfax Avenue onto Sunset Boulevard and began cruising and perusing this unfamiliar environment, he was thinking much the same thing. He'd never been to Los Angeles. Its size overwhelmed him. A fucking ocean of concrete. For Crissake, it had taken him an hour to get from where the sign said Los Angeles International Airport on the San Diego Freeway to where he was now, and he could see from the map he was still only a third of the way across the city. Not that he had any intention of driving any farther east. Right here, by the looks of things, Hollywood suited him fine for the time being. It looked scabby, and by reputation was the place where he'd find a couple of things he needed. Later on, couple of days maybe, give her time to get home, he'd be heading west, along Sunset, through Beverly Hills, past UCLA—it was there on the map—into Brentwood Park. A right off Sunset onto Reseda Boulevard, near the Will Rogers State Park, and there you had it: Canyon Road.

Where she lived.

Where she was going to die.

Did she really think it was all over? That she wasn't going to pay for what that freak creep did to Luke?

For the hundredth time since it happened recollection of it brought scalding anger up from deep inside Max to fill his heart, his head, with pounding blood. He throbbed with it, fit to explode, wanting to scream. He still couldn't believe it had happened, what he'd seen. The guy—standing there, ten feet away, body braced like fucking Charles Atlas in the ads, hands clawed, outstretched, face twisting, mouth wide open like he was yelling . . . but nothing. No sound. Then something smacking him, Max, in the head, stunning him, vision blurring, and then there was Luke, slammed against the cactus . . .

A blast of a horn behind him shocked him from the vision. He jerked the white Chevette he'd boosted in San Diego to the right. A truck pounded past, the driver's mate giving him the finger.

He'd fled in panic, seeing what the guy had done to Luke, knowing he was next, knowing Hero wouldn't follow, too concerned about the girl. Pushing the Kawasaki hard across the desert, he headed south for Mexico, then suddenly getting smart he decided to do the one thing they wouldn't expect him to do—stay in the States. Turning west, he picked up 98, dropped his speed to fifty, cruised into El Centro, lost the bike in an alley, thumbed an easy ride into San Diego, and hot-wired the Chevette in the parking lot of the Sports Arena. The Chek-Chart map of L.A. had been in the dash compartment.

God, he missed Luke.

Cruising Sunset, the empty passenger seat beside him brought home his loss with terrible impact. Luke dead. He couldn't believe it. Where was the fun now? No more brilliant Luke plans, wild adventures, exciting schemes. For sure, he'd never find another friend like Luke. Wouldn't even try, it would be an insult to Luke's memory. From now on he'd go it alone. The Lone Avenger. He liked it. It gave him direction for his anger, a cause. From now on everything he did would be in honor of Luke: The Master of Zorro. To his memory and his name. Every death a monument to his friend. Oh, yes, there will be many, old buddy. A fucking graveyard full of stones.

Max loved the Strip on first sight. Garish, pulsing with neon, lewd. Strip clubs, porn movies, filth. Whores parading, pimps cruising, faggots questing. Hell. Its ambience bathed his dark blood-hunger like balm.

He chose the first sacrifice to Luke with care, seeing the rightness of it. She was young, leggy, black, reminding him of Daytona, the best time they ever had. She was wearing a thin pink tank top, big sucky nipples showing through, skimpy black leather skirt that barely covered her snatch.

Streetwise eyes shaded by preposterous Daisy cow false lashes ran the car and him through her computer and came up with a go.

He slowed, smiled. She came over, blinding him with teeth. "Hi, sugar, what's your pleasure?"

"I'm lost. Could you please direct me to heaven?"

She laughed, big mouth showing him she liked to use it. "Long way to heaven, sweets, sure you can afford the fare?"

"How much?"

"Fifty."

"Sounds right." Sh-it. "Get in."

She slid in, legs spread, offering Day-Glo pink panties and a flash of the Pearly Gates, reeking of perfume, batting the Daisy lashes, grinning the teeth. "You're a real nice-lookin' fella. Big. I dig big guys. You this big all over?"

"Bigger. Where to?"

"Whoa, boy. Daddy says I gotta have the entrance fee first."

"Yeah? Well, my daddy says to tell you he didn't raise

no assholes for sons. Now, let's get goin' or get your sweet ass out.''

"Okay, okay." She hung a pretend pout. "Take a right, I'll tell you when."

The dump was back of the Strip, a loft above a garage behind a storage yard. Max followed her tight, twitching black-leather buttocks up a flight of external stairs and into a narrow hallway with three closed doors. Opening one, she led him into a room of bare wood walls decorated with centerfolds, a sagging double bed covered in black mock fur, and a scrap of bedside rug. She had her hand out before he'd closed the door.

"What?"

"The mon-ey, man, come *on*."

"What do I get for fifty?"

"For fifty you get it straight, what else. Somethin' fancy cost you more."

"How much for a snuff fuck?"

It took a beat, then hell broke loose in her mind and she yelled "ZAAAACK!" in stone terror.

Max hit her, right on the point. She flew backward across the bed. Footsteps pounded in the hall. Max moved fast behind the door, razor snicking from his pocket. The door burst inward, a black hand holding an automatic leading the charge. *Swish*. The gun and damn-near the hand fell to the floor. The guy fell in, gaping, at his killed hand, then rounded at Max, seeing his own imminent death.

Swish again.

Blood gushed from the skinny guy's neck. In five seconds the room was a butcher's shop.

Max stood there, breathing hard, listening. No more sounds. Quickly, he darted into the hall to check the other rooms: another bedroom and a kitchen, *Playboy* open on the table, scotch in a glass, cigarette burning in an ashtray. Pimp's Paradise. Sh-it.

Back into the first room. Daisy was coming around, sitting up, seeing Max, seeing her daddy floating in blood, mouth opening to—

"Scream," Max said, showing her the razor, "and you get it, too. Do as you're told and you live to fuck another day. Take your clothes off."

Daisy, wanting to throw up: "Let's for Crissake go in the other room!"

"No, I like it here."

"*Je*sus."

Naked, she climbed on the bed, curling away from the gore, terrorized, fetal. Max liked that. Luke would have loved it. Naked himself now, enormously engorged, he climbed up after her. "Look at me."

Blinded by tears, she turned her head but could not see. "Please . . . don't kill me."

"What's your name?"

"Sh-Shelley."

"No, it isn't. It's Kate. It's Katherine Anne Tyson. Say it. Say: My name is Katherine Anne Tyson."

"M-my name is . . . Katherine Anne Tyson."

"Say: I'm sorry, Luke, for being the cause of your death."

She said it, sobbed it.

"Good. Now, Kate, you have to finish what you started. Sit up. Put this good old boy where he belongs. That's it. Quit slobbering, for Crissake, get your lips together. Hey, that's terrific . . . Jesus. Luke, this is for you, man . . . Luke . . . LUKE!"

She gagged, choked.

"Just—one more thing, Kate. Look at me, I have something for you."

She looked up, her last look at anything.

"The Mark of Zorro."

Chapter Five

West of Griffith Park, Sunset Boulevard is the bench-
mark between topographical order and disorder. South of
this long serpentine road a vast sprawl of plain permits
the reticulated symmetry of grid design beloved of America's Teutonic town planners. North of Sunset, as the land
rises into the Santa Monica Mountains, such order goes
out the window. Brentwood Park, like its pinch-nosed
neighbor, Bel Air, is structurally a cow's guts of roads
that twist and meander and dip and rise, now soaring, now
plummeting, enforcing a helter-skelter construction policy
of build-wherever-the-hell-you-can.

The original builders of Cleves Cottage had chosen a
spectacular, if somewhat vertiginous, site for their mock-
Tudor dwelling: a two-acre plot perched on a ridge which
offered panoramic views of the mountains, city, and state
park, and even, smog permitting, from certain windows,
a glimpse of ocean.

It was raining when Raven and Kat reached the house.
The night was black, the street lighting poor, and all that
Raven could see of the property was a pair of black
wrought-iron gates supported by stout fieldstone pillars,
juxtaposed on either side by a run of high, dense hedge of
impenetrable holly.

A slate nameplate inset in both pillars identified the
house in gold lettering.

"Cleves Cottage," said Raven, in a tone querying the origin of the name.

Kat picked it up. "Are you ready for this? It was built by a guy named Henry King, who made a fortune in early television. His wife's name was Anne. The house was a homage to her. Henry King. King Henry. Anne of Cleves. The house is . . ."

"Mock Tudor."

"Who said California glitz is dead."

Raven grinned. "How do we get in?"

Kat rummaged in her copious shoulder bag and found the electronic control. "I hope the batteries are working." They were. The gates opened. Raven drove through, stopping while Kat used the control to close the gates, then the car climbed steeply between dense rhododendrons, emerging into a more gradually sloping lawned area and finally arriving at a paved turnaround in front of the house.

Raven cut the engine, stared up at the house. It was huge. There was a light on in the porch, other lights showing in some downstairs rooms behind curtained windows. He frowned. "I felt sure you lived alone."

"I do. Help comes in several times a week to clean up and tend the garden. The lights are on automatic switches, random display."

Raven got out of the car, stood for a moment in the rainy silence, looking at and listening to the house. It loomed above him, solid, empty, bereft. What he felt induced a shiver of empathetic desolation, a muted moan: "Oh, boy." Then he moved.

While he got their suitcases out of the car, Kat opened the studded oak front door and disappeared inside to cancel the alarm.

Raven entered a splendid hall, the polished wood floor softened by an acre of Persian carpet, the theme reiterated on the curving carved staircase that swept up on the right to a galleried landing. Gilt sconces illuminated the paneled walls; a matching gilt-and-crystal chandelier was centrally suspended.

Raven sensed what was there and shivered.

Kat emerged from a closet under the stairs, hugging herself, looking, in the crystal lighting, drawn and drained. "It's cold. I've turned the heat on. Drop the bags there, we need a drink."

She opened double doors on the right, near the foot of the stairs, and Raven followed her into a spacious sitting room–cum–library, its walls lined with books in carved oak shelving. Tall windows, curtained with green flowered fabric, overlooked the front and side gardens. A thick cream carpet covered most of the floor. The furnishings were rich and eclectic, antique and modern upholstered, the major piece a glorious Chinese-fabric sofa arranged before a wide carved-stone fireplace.

"Some cottage," Raven remarked wryly, opening himself fully to the house, feeling its trauma come at him, press down upon him, its sadness pulsing in the walls.

Kat smiled. "The supreme affectation. Our Henry King had Vanderbilt aspirations, a Newport 'cottage.' " She opened a liquor cabinet. "What would you like to . . . to . . ." She fell forward, scattering glasses.

Raven ran to her, caught her by the shoulders. "Come on, lie down, you're done in." He led her to the sofa, arranged a cushion for her head. She looked like death, lying there.

Raven crossed to the cabinet, poured a stiff brandy, came back to her. "Sip this."

The glass rattled against her teeth. Tears rolled down her cheeks. "I'm s-sorry. I despise f-fainty females."

"What you've been through today—not to mention the past three weeks, the past two years—you're entitled. I've got news for you, you're no Cybernaut. You're flesh and blood and nerves. And yours are about as raw as they get. Drink some more. I'm going to find the kitchen and make us a hot drink. Now—listen to me . . . *listen to me.*"

Something happened to his voice. It deepened, took on a quiet, vibrant authority that probed deep into her, into her mind and body, making them buzz pleasantly, sensually. Gently he caught her chin and turned her eyes to his. They were kind, concerned, but determined, and she felt her will slipping away under the directness of their dark depths.

"I want you to relax. Take a deep breath . . . hold it. Let it go. And relax." He touched her cheek, a caress so gentle it made her shiver. "Close your eyes." The brandy glass was removed from her hand. "Relax—every muscle . . . every nerve. Let go. That's beautiful. Sleep."

She floated, drifted, suddenly an amorphous thing, bereft of bone and muscle, encompassed by peace and lightness, all spirit, yet knowing he was there, trusting.

"I'll be back in a moment," she heard him say.

Raven entered the hall, chose the most likely of four doors. Flicking on overhead fluorescents, he walked into a cavernous oak-cupboard kitchen, so pristine it looked unused, a display piece in a department store window, the floor and every surface polished like glass. Soul-less. Devoid of human aura. Disturbing.

He opened cupboards and drawers, most of them empty, a few utensils, minimal supply of dry and canned goods, including, thank God, coffee. In the mammoth fridge— one lonesome quart of milk. Sitting there, it reminded him of Kat all alone in this mausoleum. Why in God's name did she insist . . . yeah, well, he could now guess the answer to that, but he wanted to hear it from her.

He found the percolator, took it to the sink, half expecting the water supply to have been cut off, the house

eeling so unlived-in. But it wasn't. He ran the water a
while until it was clear, filled the container, plugged in
the percolator.

Over the sink was a big picture window. He stood looking at it, rather than through it, at first seeing only his own
reflection and the kitchen behind him. Outside was unre-
lieved blackness. Fingers of rain tapped against the glass.
The window overlooked the rear gardens and, he calculated, faced west, the rain coming in off the ocean.

Then a spear of lightning lit up the sky, distantly, but
bright enough and prolonged enough to show him the terrace outside the window, its stone retaining wall, maybe
three feet high and thirty feet away. Beyond that—nothing.
No garden. No trees. Black space. The canyon.

He was still staring at the window, hearing the rumble
of thunder, waiting for the next lightning flash, when
something—

—entered the edge of his vision . . . behind him.

His mind blurred. He froze, his blood icing. He wanted
not to look, not to see it, but there was no escape. All he
could do was wait and see how bad it would get.

It hovered near the door, an amorphous essence, drifting, swirly, now collecting, vaguely human, taking more
shape, a face . . . distorted, rearranging, firming . . . now
a shoulder, arm, chest, blue-suited, shirt and tie, one di-
agonal half of a young, once handsome man.

Raven shuddered. The kitchen was ice cold. His heart
thundered in his ears. With his mind he said *Hello, Rick.
I'm John Raven.*

In his mind he heard *Hello, John.*

Why are you here, Rick? You've been over a long time.

I miss her . . . miss them all.

*I know. You went over too quickly. You'll have to be
patient. They'll join you. Your father will be with you quite
soon.*

I know. I've been with him. Thank you for helping Kat
I'll do what I can.
I wish she could see me, talk with me.
I'll help there, too, but I have to be careful.
I know . . . mustn't frighten her . . . mustn't . . .

The apparition drifted, like smoke caught by a fan, and disappeared.

Raven sagged, turned, and gripped the sink, breathing deeply, sucking air. Would he ever get used to it? For every gift there is a price to pay, Nanosh had told him so long ago, warning him, preparing him. You have been blessed, but the price is duty.

Fine.

But he was only human. He got tired and scared at times like everyone else, and couldn't help wishing he could now and then go *off* duty like everyone else—switch off punch out, forget it.

The price was also shock. It could happen any time and there was never any warning, no pinging bell like the one that lets you know an elevator is arriving, no approaching footsteps or discreet cough. They were suddenly there. And never—what made it worse—all of them. Bits. A floating face in a dark hallway. A torso. Sometimes only a hand. It was a matter of energy. Also technique They had to learn how to do it, and most of them weren' very good. Mostly, they were harmless, though not all. They didn't mean to frighten. But their options were limited. There were so few human receivers. What he'd told Kat in the car: too many people had been numbed out.

Since childhood, since first discovering his gifts, he'd questioned: why him? No one knew the answer, not Nanosh, nor Jack Shanglo's mother (whose own gifts had been considerable). None of them. It simply was, they'd told him, and had to be accepted, used, shared.

The gurgling percolator brought him back. In the china

cupboard he found four glazed pottery mugs, each embossed with a personal initial: *K, R, S, M. K* for Kat; *R* for Rick; *S* for Scott; *M* for . . .

He rejected them in favor of two plain ones. It was not fitting that he should use Rick's, Scott's, or her mother's, and no time to remind Kat of happier occasions . . .

Flashing, he saw them seated around the breakfast table there in the center of the room, heard their morning laughter. Her loss had been enormous.

Marion.

Her mother's name was . . . is Marion.

What happened to Marion? Kat hadn't mentioned her.

He filled the mugs, set them on a wooden tray with milk and sugar, returned to the library. In her sleep Kat had turned toward the fireplace, curled in a fetal position, hugging herself, though the room was no longer cold. The movement had dragged her denim skirt high upon her thighs, exposing white panties that must have been provided by the policewoman. No woman could have looked more vulnerable than Kat right then. Raven felt a rush of pity and embarrassment for her. Setting the tray on a low table, he gently took hold of the skirt's hem and began to draw it down, difficult because she was lying on it.

She awoke with a start, panic stark in her face, finding him there, his hands there. She shot upright, pushing away from him, fear and distrust and confusion and terrible disappointment expressing in a stifled cry.

Raven stepped back, palms held up appeasingly. "Kat, no . . . please. I wasn't—it's not what you think." He tried a smile. "I was just trying to make you decent."

She heard the heart behind the words, blinked, sighed, then relaxed. "I'm sorry."

"I made coffee."

She swung her feet to the floor, sat hunched, elbows on knees, face in her hands. "I had a dream. I dreamt Rick was alive. I have it often. Subconscious desperation, I guess.''

Raven sat beside her, handed her her coffee. ''You shouldn't live here alone. Why do you?''

She sipped the drink, gazing without focus at the hearth. In a voice ragged with sleep and emotion she said, ''This house is my lifeline, my hold, I swear to God, on sanity. I leave it, I feel I'm slipping over the edge of some hellish abyss into frightening unreality. Look what happened today. But there's more. I tried living in New York—my mother's there, playing a game called 'being a stage actress.' I *think* she's my mother. I mean, I think she's the same woman who used to be my mother here in this house. But she's almost unrecognizable as the same person. Something happened to her when Rick died. I think she went crazy. I tried living in England. My father's there, dying of cancer. I told you, I came back from there three weeks ago. That experience was literally unbelievable. The bitch he's married to wouldn't let me see him. Now I phone every day to see if he's still alive.''

She was shaking again from the telling, wanting to talk, but paying the price. She took out a tissue, blew her nose determinedly, willing back the tears, trying to steady the quake in her voice.

''This house—is where all the good things that ever happened to our family happened. It's a treasure house of incredibly happy memories. There were golden times here—for a short while. Such joy.'' She drew a tremulous sigh. ''Who made the law, John—the better the times, the bigger the reversal? And don't tell me there isn't one. It happens. And not just to the Tysons. So many of my friends . . .''

She shook her head, disbelievingly, golden hair falling about her face.

''There's a guy somewhere,'' she said, ''with a Moviola, watching your family's life go by, a kind of Chief Editor in the Sky. And as long as you don't exceed a certain degree of happiness—listen to this, this is really maudlin—he lets the film run through. Comes the bit when things are beginning to look up, the really tough times are starting to mellow, the money's coming in, life is taking on a rosy hue, this pervert says: 'I'll give this bunch another forty-eight frames, then cut and splice in a couple of reels of absolute shit, that'll teach 'em.' ''

She swung to face him, throwing back her hair. "You know it's true. It happened to you. I saw your eyes on the bus. What happened to give you that look, John?"

He gave her an appreciative smile but shook his head. "This is not the time, Kat." His glance went behind them, across the room to a carved oak desk and a display of framed photographs. "Those your folks? I'd like to see them."

She got up, a willowy girl with an angel's grace. Raven followed her with his eyes. Something was coming through, a fondness for her that warmed him deeply. And something else. He'd told himself he'd give this a couple of days, see her settled, watch out for Mad Max, then leave her and be about his own difficult business. But now, in one of those fleeting intimations of the future that now and then swept through him, he saw a different picture. Vague, but there. A future that extended beyond two days. Dangerous. And she was with him.

She returned to the sofa with several frames and an album, pleased yet sad to show them.

"This is my dad, taken about five years ago, at the desk over there."

Raven saw a beefy, good-looking man in his mid-forties, California tanned, abundant dark hair, glasses perched comically on the end of his nose, looking up over his typewriter—a relaxed, successful writer, captured during the creation of his next best-seller or Oscar-winning screenplay.

"You ever read any of his work?" Kat asked. "His books?"

"All of them."

Her eyes widened gleefully. "Really?"

"Truly."

Scott Tyson had exploded onto the commercial literary scene ten years earlier with a tough, one-man-against-the-world thriller, *Manhattan Mandate,* that sold a zillion copies; the film, Tyson's own screenplay, followed as a major box-office grosser. It wasn't so much story as style that produced the cornucopia. The "Tyson style" was as distinctive as a cattle brand. The liberties he took with the English language were breathtaking. Tyson had taken all the traditional mores and observances of language construction, thrown them in the trash can, wound a blank sheet of paper in his typewriter, and given the literary world something so refreshingly different it was still reeling. There had, of course, quickly emerged a multitude of impersonators. But nobody worked like Tyson. Nobody thought like Tyson. He was unique.

And there, Raven knew, was the source of Kat's writing problem—her father's success. Fearing comparison, she dared not start.

Perhaps he, Raven, could help her. She needed something equally unique, something to call her own. Maybe not a style, but a subject. He could tell her things. Oh, the things he could tell her.

"This room," she was saying, wan with nostalgia. "So many of the greats have stood here, glass in hand, paying homage. Writers like to see where other successful writers work. I've seen people of no mean stature slyly touch Dad's typewriter, as if it were a talisman, trying to rub off some of his magic. It's crazy. Before *Mandate,* he was earning less than a bus driver. Here . . ." She opened the album, turned pages. "This was the house we lived in before 'the miracle,' as Dad called it."

The snap showed a shabby, single-storied tract dwelling, its verandah sagging, pink paint peeling, the front yard a grassless hen-scratch, neighboring houses almost touching.

"Lennox," she explained. "In the shadow of the San Diego Freeway and in the direct flight path of every plane that landed at L.A. International. It's a wonder we're not all deaf mutes. How Dad wrote there God only knows."

Raven nodded. "I read about his humble beginnings."

"Brooklyn Irish. Which no doubt accounts for his quaint speech rhythms. His literary toughness came from the docks. He was a longshoreman before he came out here."

"Why did he come out, Kat?"

"To be closer to movies, to write them. Ain't that something—an eighth-grade dropout Brooklyn docker aspiring to compete with the Goldman brothers et al.—and doing it."

Her pride was touching; the extent of her loss further revealed.

"And your mom?"

Kat's glow waned. She handed him a framed photo, taken in this sun-filled garden, in front of the house. Father and Mother. He—relaxed, rumpled, jovially unkempt, as though he'd been pulled away from a long session at the typewriter for the photograph; she—print-frocked, pristine, blond hair perfectly coiffed, an unremarkable-looking woman using money to enhance her grading. Raven guessed a five-year age difference, she the younger.

"You and Rick favor your father."

"Yes," she said. Then looked at him, frowning. "How do you know—about Rick?"

69

Big mistake.

"I—guessed. The way you described him: beautiful. I imagined you and Rick looking alike."

Her eyes disbelieved him. "Yes, we do . . . did."

Ice settled on Raven's neck. He felt Rick might be with them, but dared not turn around. He diverted Kat's scrutiny to the photograph. "Your mother's younger by—what?—five years?"

"Exactly five. You have a good eye."

"How did they meet?" He wanted her to talk, to tell the whole story, get it out. He sensed she was a girl who did not readily impart confidences, and that much of her depleted condition was attributable to too much stuff being bottled up inside for too damned long. Besides, he wanted to know all about Kat Tyson.

"She was working part time in a coffee shop, trying to break into movies, getting nowhere. We're going back twenty-six years now, early sixties. Dad was twenty-five, just arrived, working at odd jobs during the day, learning to write at night. Mom served Dad breakfast and, she told us, fell for the big handsome Irish hunk on sight. They married the same year. Give her her due, she helped him a lot early on, gave up the idea of acting and worked full time at the coffee shop, insisting that Dad cut down his day work and write more. After Rick was born she hired a sitter and went back to work. Then I came along and screwed things up again. They must have been very tough years."

"Yes," said Raven, who knew all about very tough years. "How was your father's writing coming along at this time?"

Her laugh was richly sardonic. "Ha! Like mine. No, not quite, he did sell a couple of potboilers. Trouble was, he was copying everyone else, subconsciously trying to. Spillane, Fleming, Robbins. It wasn't entirely his fault.

He had a very bad agent who didn't know books from bucks who kept telling him, every time a new best-seller hit the stands, 'Scott gimme one like this *now*.' Of course, by the time Scott had written half of 'this' it was already 'that,' gone, passé, kaput, and Dad was left dangling, six months research and work in the hole, bills coming in and two kids to feed. It must have been a bloody mess.''

''And then?''

She laughed again, this time tenderly, with great affection. ''Boy, then he got his Irish up. He sat down and wrote what he knew. He wrote New York, the docks, the crime, the brutality of the Mob, the terrifying danger for any man who goes against them—well, you've read *Mandate*, so you know. But he also poured out his own frustration, his fear for the future of his family. He wrote with rage at being jerked around, and he threw the rule book away, took English construction by the scruff of the neck and shook the hell out of it. He wrote *Mandate* from the heart, then fired his agent and sent the manuscript direct to a New York publishing house. And then . . . he took his family to Yellowstone on the first vacation we'd had in four years.''

Raven smiled. ''And when you returned, there was the letter from the publisher saying . . .''

''When we returned, there was the letter from the landlord saying if he didn't get a month's rent that day . . .'' She swelled with a sigh. ''I was—what?—eleven. I remember that day so clearly. It was terrible. I'd never seen Dad so—desolate. He'd overspent on the vacation, didn't have enough for the rent. He was always bad with money. The landlord's muscle was there, ready to throw our broken-down furniture into the yard. Mom was in tears, I was in tears, Rick—thirteen—wanted to fight them. We were all frightened. But what frightened us most was hearing Dad tell Mom he was giving up writing there and then, that he

71

refused to expose his family to this sordid pressure any longer, was going to Long Beach the next day, get a job on the docks. He told the landlord the same thing and got a week's extension.''

''Some vacation.''

''Yeah, some vacation. Ever since, I go cold when I hear the name Yellowstone.''

''And did he—your dad?''

''Yes, he did, a laboring job in the naval dockyard. Mom wept when he went to work, wept when he came home. But by the end of the week he had the rent money, which proved his point.''

''And New York?''

''Screw New York. Those bums took six months to reject his manuscript.''

Raven frowned. ''They rejected it?''

''Ho, yes, didn't you know? *Mandate* is a classic case of eventual best-seller rejection. Five publishers turned it down.''

''No, I never read that. What I read was a stiffish piece in a psychology journal about suddenly successful people.''

''Suddenly successful,'' she mused. ''Oh, yeah.''

''So, what happened eventually?''

She smiled. ''Phil Goodman happened eventually. Dad had been doing it the hard way, sending *Mandate* to publishers himself, probably to the wrong kind of publishers for his book. One of them, the last one, advised him to get an agent, so he stuck a pin in the New York Yellow Pages and landed on Phil Goodman. That was the day our fortune changed.''

She shook her head slowly, staring at the hearth. ''I'll never forget that phone call if I live to be a thousand. Either it was pure chance or Phil calculated the exact moment Dad was due home from work. It was January, cold and raining. He came through the door, wet through and through and miserable, lunch pail in his hand, calling out his usual 'Hi, gang,' and as he came into the kitchen the phone rang. He took it off the wall, said 'Yep?' and didn't utter another word for three long minutes. I watched his face change, run through a string of emotions from utterly pissed-off to bland interest to frowning concentration, gasping awareness, bug-eyed disbelief, and finally it crumpled and he started to cry. Tears rolled down his cheeks. Mom and we kids were stunned. We thought at least his entire Brooklyn family had been wiped out in a terrible disaster. Finally, he said, 'Okay, thanks, Phil . . . Jesus Christ, thank you!' And hung up.'' She smiled at him, tears in her own eyes. ''His exact words. I have never seen such *joy* in any human being before or since. He couldn't speak. He slumped at the table, face in his hands, and said very slowly, 'Two . . . hundred . . . thousand . . . dollars.' ''

Raven pursed his lips in a soundless whistle.

Kat nodded. ''Two hundred thousand dollars.'' Laying the photographs on the coffee table, she got up, crossed to her father's desk for a Kleenex, saying from over there as she wiped her eyes, ''All families should experience such a moment. It's the time when you *know,* without a doubt, that there is a God. I'm not talking about money as money. I'm talking about the incredible sense of—of *release*—from pressure. The joy we experienced was unbelievable.'' Smiling, she returned to him. ''We went crazy. Dad went crazy.'' She laughed, the first genuine expression of unrestrained pleasure Raven had witnessed. ''On the dresser . . . was a stack of bills—electric, telephone, loan company, a snitty reminder about an overdue car payment. Dad grabbed them, roared gusto defiance they must have heard in Fresno, took a ballpoint and scribbled 'PISS OFF!' across every one of them so hard it made grooves in the table.''

Raven laughed with her, caught up in her bubbling remembrance of the moment.

She shook her head. "Oh, boy, what a time we had. First to New York to sign contracts, then back here to look for a house—our first own real home. Of course, first time out, this place was far too ostentatious, but Phil and the publishers told Dad he was going to be rich, with a multiple-book contract and a film deal under way, and Dad thought—what the hell, why walk slowly up the hill when you can zoom straight to the top. So—here we came and here we are.''

Her mood changed. "A few good years. Excellent. Too much, I guess, of everything, including expectations. The California disease. It has to go on forever, getting better and better.''

For every gift there is a price to pay.

Raven asked, "What changed it, Kat? Was it only Rick?''

"Mostly. But there were cracks before that. Dad didn't change, he was too busy. Fame didn't touch him, he hated the fuss. But Mom . . . Well, people *have* to change in such circumstances, don't they? That's the point of working your butt off, so you *can* change a life-style you don't like. What did it for Mom . . . well, several things. Through Dad she became a celebrity. People wanted to get close to her to get close to Dad, you know what this town is like. So here you had a woman, a failed actress in her twenties, being courted and flattered, in her thirties, by the cream of Hollywood.

"Not immediately, of course, because it took a year to publish *Mandate* and for all the razz to begin. And that first year here was the best of all. Mom *reveled* in doing over this house—it was pretty shabby—having the money to spend and Dad's blessing. Rick and I had transferred to Pali High and loved it, so she could relax about us. She blossomed, bloomed, shed ten pounds and five years and never looked so good. God, it was great to come home from school and find her *here,* talking wallpaper and fabric and furniture, Dad in here with his chattering typewriter, the lovely garden, the pool. It was fabulous, too beautiful to be real. Rick used to say to me . . .''

Pinch me, Kat, we're dreaming.

Raven's mind blurred. His nerve ends fizzed with re-action to the voice behind him. He stared at Kat, expecting her gaze to switch direction and the screaming to start, but she hadn't even noticed his tension, still going on . . .

''Pinch me, Kat, we're dreaming.''

We'll wake up tomorrow morning back in Lennox . . .

''We'll wake up tomorrow morning back in Lennox . . .''

Seven-forty-sevens shaking the house.

''Seven-forty-sevens shaking the house.''

Now the voices were almost in unison, a beat apart, Rick leading, reading her mind. Raven was overwhelmed by a searing compulsion to swing around, to stop this, or clamp hands over his ears to shut out the sepulchral tone.

His rigidity finally penetrated Kat's preoccupation. She glanced at him, did a double take, frowning. ''Hey, you okay?''

''Fine.''

''You're not. There's something.''

He affected a sheepish grin. ''Tell the truth, I need the john.''

''God, why didn't you stop me, rattling on. Across the hall, under the gallery.'' She collected the mugs. ''I'll make some more coffee.''

Raven stood, reluctant to turn, but did so. There was nothing there. They crossed the hall, their footsteps echoing on the oak, silent on the carpet. He entered a small cloakroom, pink lighting and flowered wallpaper, a big pink mirror above a vanity unit, then spotted the toilet through a second door. Finished in there, he returned to the washbasin and soaped his hands, avoiding the mirror. He hated goddamn mirrors.

Hands washed, he reached for a fluffy white towel, eyes fixed down there on it while he wiped. Then there it was, creeping into his vision, into the mirror, a hand, reaching, fingers spread, reaching to touch him, his shoulder . . .

He whirled. "Rick, no!"

Now the face, emerging as though surfacing through water, shimmering, swimmy, distorted, one side of the face dragging down like melted wax, the left eye too low, down on the cheek, now suddenly too high in overcompensation.

Panic raged through Raven's mind, the room was too small, the thing too close. Hurling the towel aside, he grabbed for the door, fingers stiff as sticks, fumbling the dead bolt. Ice behind him, pressing up against him, the voice in his mind, booming inside his head . . .

Raven.

"No!"

Lock back, door jerked open, Kat standing there, gaping. "John, what—?"

Out into the hall, into blessed space, a split second to think. "I, uh, I locked myself in! Anything mechanical, I'm a klutz."

She didn't buy it. Her gaze went back into the little room, then at him before she moved to pass him. "You left the light on."

"Oh . . ." He moved faster, got there first, ducked inside to pick up the towel and hang it on the rail. She was standing by the door, watching him too intently.

"It's cold in here," she said, frowning.

"It's cold everywhere, the wind's right off the ocean. And you've just come out of the desert."

She didn't buy that one either. The central heating was on, a small rad under the towel rail. "Coffee's in the library, I made instant."

They went in. As they sat, Kat asked, with a determined edge to her voice he hadn't heard before that told him more about her, "John, what really happened in there? I heard you shout, cry out."

He couldn't tell her, not tonight. "Truth is, I suffer from claustrophobia. Rooms that small, I get panicky." He shrugged self-deprecatingly. "Sorry if I frightened you. You, er, were telling me about your Mom when I interrupted."

Sipping her coffee, she picked up the thread, but her heart wasn't in it, not like before when she'd drifted into it naturally, relieved to talk. Now, dispiritedly, she was just finishing the story.

"She became, gradually, a Hollywood wife, too much money, time on her hands, servants to do things, Rick and I getting older, not needing her so much. Maybe that was all of it—nobody needed her as much. She'd kept Dad afloat in the bad days and now he was earning millions. Oh, he didn't desert her, mess around. But he was committed to a pressure schedule, burned a lot of midnight oil, and writers are solitary creatures."

For every gift . . .

"Gradually she submerged herself into Hollywood silliness, played Narcissus with her A-Team buddies, talked gossip and diets and face-lifts instead of wallpaper, fabric, and furniture, and clothes-shopped the hell out of Rodeo Drive. Things like that. But don't get me wrong, life here was still golden. I believe if Rick hadn't died . . ."

Raven tensed, his conditioned reaction now to her use

of Rick's name, fearing an appearance. But nothing happened. Maybe that was worse, the not knowing.

". . . it still would be. When we got the news Mom went berserk. Dad and me, too, but in a different way. The doc sedated Mom, but that had to end, and when she came out of it she was different. She was like a star that had collapsed in on itself, heavy inside, dark and too compact. One night, at the dinner table, out of the blue, she suddenly pitched into Dad with a searing indictment, blaming him for Rick's death, for best-selling his books, for earning the money, for buying Rick his car. She yelled that we'd been happy in Lennox, and if he'd stayed in the shipyard none of it would've happened. Then she took another tack, screamed that marrying him had deprived her of a glorious career in the theater. It was just—awful. Poor Dad, he sat there stunned. Talk about life unraveling. I saw him begin to die right there . . . saw us all die, as a family. The golden days were over. The Chief Editor in the Sky had spliced in two whole reels of shit—and they're still playing to a packed house."

"Why England?" Raven asked, wishing he could alter time for her, take her back, rewrite the script and make it come out right.

"He went over to promote a book, liked London and its civility, found peace over there away from Hollywood and Mom. While he was away Mom went back to acting, used her name, and when Dad came home she was in Maine, doing summer stock. He told me, here in this room, that he'd met someone in London, a titled woman, big estate in Buckinghamshire. I died a little more. He flew to Maine to talk to Mom about divorce and found her in bed with her director. Seems she'd arranged the scene for Dad's benefit."

Raven grimaced.

"Mom got this house and a freight-car load of money.

Dad returned to London, then invited me over to meet Lady Elizabeth Allenby—this was about a year ago, six months before he became ill. Christ, what a nightmare visit that was. Lady Elizabeth is a cow, a young divorcée with two kids of her own. She hated me on sight. She . . .''

Kat roused herself, shook her head dismissively. "Raven—enough. How can you *stand* this litany of self-pity? How come you've let me talk so much?''

"Because I'm interested. How else can I get to know you? And it's not self-pity, it's your life.''

"Well—enough.''

He held out his hand. "May I see the one of Rick?''

"Of course.''

She passed him a silver-framed eight-by-ten color photograph of a radiant college senior, uniformed for football but without his helmet, ball in his right hand drawn back, the quintessential hero quarterback going for the long pass. Posed, of course: a fun photograph for the family. Rick, grinning his face off, brilliant smile showing perfect Tyson teeth. Handsome as hell, traces of Kat and Dad around the mischievous Irish eyes. Raven's height, six-two, but fifteen pounds heavier. He could see this, despite the padding.

He could see something else, too. Rick was wearing a quarterback number, ten, but, holding the photograph, Raven knew it was wrong. Angling the frame, light from a wall sconce behind him struck the glass, momentarily obliterating Rick's face. The spasm of concentrated light drew Raven in, into the picture, into the campus, into that day. For ten beats of a heart time stopped. He was running. Running hard. Now turning, leaping high, stretching. The brown howitzer shell of a ball smacked gorgeously into his hands. And he was off, cleats biting, knees pumping, almost hitting his chest. A hip jiggle and the cornerback was empty-handed, facedown in the mud.

A tricky last-second swerve and the first safety was grappling winter air. Fifteen yards and one safety to go. Brute of a guy, six-five, hands like baseball mitts, coming at him, grabbing him, the neck of his jersey . . . rip-and-zip . . . him going on, shoulder pad flapping, but over the line, pounding the ball into the turf, crowd going crazy . . .

He came back.

Kat was staring at him with her now familiar look, half scared, half fascinated. "What's the matter?"

"He's wearing the wrong number."

She gasped in a sibilant hiss. "My God, you're uncanny."

"He was a wide receiver, a flankerback."

She nodded, drifted back to that time. "It was the last game I saw him play. He won it for Stanford in the last seconds . . . an unbelievable catch. He had his shirt ripped off going over the line." Tears glistened in her eyes. "He borrowed the quarterback's so I could take his picture."

She blinked and a tear rolled down her cheek. "How did you know, John? How do you do it?"

He shook his head. "I don't know. It isn't conscious effort, it just happens."

"It's . . ."

"Creepy." He smiled.

"I think it's wonderful. It's like being with someone of a future time."

"You're still frightened of it."

"No, I—I'm getting more used to it. I want to know more about you, all about you, what you can do. Will you tell me?"

"Well, not tonight. You should get to bed. I think we're going to have company pretty early tomorrow, you should get some sleep."

She frowned. "Company?"

"The police."

Her eyes widened. "You can see that?"

He laughed. "No, that's a rational assumption." His smile faded. "Kat, bad things happened at El Centro today." He glanced at his watch; it was one in the morning. "Yesterday. The cops down there will want to keep tabs on us both, especially me, and they'll probably do it through the LAPD. My guess is they'll come calling first thing, make sure we're here."

She nodded, suddenly drained. "Yep. Come on, I'll show you your room."

"Look—if you'd rather, I'll sleep down here."

She looked squarely at him, eyes brimming with emotion. "John Raven—a few hours ago you risked your own life to save mine. You've brought me home to protect me and keep me company. Don't you think the very least I owe you is a comfortable bed?"

He smiled acquiescently. "Okay."

They climbed the stairs, Raven with the bags, their footfalls muted on the thick carpeting, the house sepulchral and silent around them. Nine bedrooms, all with bath or shower, she told him, leading along the landing to a guest bedroom overlooking the rear of the house, the room done in earth tones, smelling pleasantly of pine furniture polish, but, like the rest of the house, possessing an aura of abandonment.

"Will this do?" she asked in the doorway.

"Absolutely."

"I'm next door," she said, pointing back toward the staircase, meaning: So you'll know where to find me.

"Fine."

There was a moment of awkwardness between them, Kat hesitant, he sensed, to quit human company, to be alone in this memory-haunted house.

He thought quickly to fill the gap. "You said there were

several reasons for living here alone. You gave me only one.''

''Oh. Well, another reason is that Mom refuses to sell it. With property values in hyperdrive it's a fabulous investment.'' The stark altruism of the explanation pained her. He saw her soul close down on it, her eyes apologetic. ''She never comes here and never will,'' she continued softly. ''And I couldn't bear the thought of it languishing untended—you know, by family.''

''No.'' He waited. There was another reason coming.

''Also—'' A small, fluttery smile. ''At times I feel incredibly close to Rick here . . .''

That thing happened to his neck hairs again. He was suddenly, intensely aware of the door-sized closet mirror immediately to his left. No, he begged, his gaze fixed rigidly on her, fighting the compulsion to turn his head in that direction.

''He didn't die here,'' she was saying. ''So I know he can't be here.'' Getting it all wrong. ''But now and then . . .'' She frowned.

''What?'' Raven pressed gently, his calm tone concealing the pounding of his heart.

She shook it away with a silly-me smile. ''He had a favorite after-shave—*Habit Rouge De Guerlain*. I used to buy it for him, birthdays and Christmas. It was a running joke between us, you know—'I wonder what this can be' when he opened the package.'' A frown pinched her brow. ''Now and then I swear I can smell it in the house. I did tonight when we got home, just the faintest . . .'' She shrugged. ''Maybe the gardener uses it, he comes inside to do the plants.''

''That's probably it.''

A borderline sensitive. Raven had tested many of them at the Institute. The almost-not-quites. He hoped for her sake, considering what he'd seen in the house, she never made it all the way. It would drive her crazy.

"Well—I'll say good-night."

"Good-night, Kat. Listen—if you need me, don't hesitate. Any time. Wake me, I mean it."

She smiled her thanks. "I'll be all right, I'll take a pill."

"Okay."

She closed the door.

The room enfolded Raven, the mirror pressing in. He drew a deep, slow breath, summoning ch'i, filling his hard body with power, his mind with defensive strength. Prepared now, ready for it, he turned to face the mirror. Rick's face floated there, grinning, an exact replication of Rick in the photograph, a pitiful reproduction.

Raven spoke, his mind-voice low, beseeching, yet imperative.

Rick, listen to me . . . listen to me. You are dead. You are not of this plane. You must move on.

Kat needs me . . .

Kat needs help. I will give it to her. There is nothing you can do. Your presence is helping to keep her here. This odor thing, the after-shave, you must stop it. It confuses and torments her.

She likes living here . . . likes the feeling that I'm close.

Your sister is clinging to the past to save her sanity. But it's wrong. The past, like this house, like you, is dead. She has to let go, build a new life for herself, away from here. If she stays, it will destroy her. Rick—quit this place. Leave her alone. Leave me alone.

The face re-formed into an expression of such poignant anguish that tears welled in Raven's eyes and the pain of pity stretched his throat. Slowly, the apparition faded, unendurably hurt, unimaginably lost. Gone.

Raven turned away with a gasp, moved quickly to the

latticed casement window, and flung it wide. A buffeting blast of wind, his precious *balval,* filled his face with the sweet dank smell of rain, the tang of ocean. He sucked it in and down, swelling, swelling with it until his lungs could endure no more, then tightly braced his body in sheets of muscle and let go his anguish in a gushing, silent roar.

Done, he crossed the room to switch off the wall lights, then returned and sat on the cushioned window seat, breathing slowly, deeply, rhythmically, eyes closed, tongue firm against the roof of his mouth, summoning chi, consciously feeding the balm and power of the universe to every atom of his extraordinary body.

Chapter Six

Kat woke early, just before dawn, and lay there staring at the ceiling of the room she had occupied for the past ten years, a room whose biannual changes of decor had reflected her maturation from child to woman yet still maintained traces of the original pastel-pink softness that was essentially her; never fluffiness but always female.

As she lay there, yesterday—the whole thing—was now totally unbelievable. And the man, John Raven, his powers, constituted not the least unbelievable part of the dream. Did he really exist? Had the ghastly events of yesterday been anything but a vivid nightmare? Was he actually asleep in the adjoining bedroom?

Since Rick's death and the breakup of the family she'd been having trouble with reality. Up to that point in her life she'd never questioned it. Things, even bad-ish things, happened and she'd been able to accept them. Nowadays she found herself asking herself more and more often: Can this be for real? Did that really happen? Is this *really* happening? Maybe it was age. Maybe the older a person got, with more experience piled up, the less capable the human mind became of accepting the crap and threw up uncertainty as a defense barrier.

She strained to listen for any sounds, an indication of human habitation, but apart from the distant predawn twittering of birds in the canyon the house was silent.

Restless, her strung-out nervous system beginning to gear up for the day, she slipped out of bed, drew on a green silk robe, and crossed the room to open fully the already partly opened pink-flowered drapes (she detested total darkness, needed the relative lightness of even the blackest night sky).

She looked out, across the canyon and the state park to the distant smudge of ocean, then down . . . and her heart tumbled. He was there, standing by the terrace wall, gazing off to his right, toward the San Gabriel Mountains, toward the sunrise, the first golden hints of the new sun's rays reaching him, emphasizing the rich dark sheen of his hair, the tan of his face and naked arms, the whiteness of his short-sleeved shirt.

Again, his profile touched her female heart. That nose, so slightly aquiline, was a killer. Hell, so was everything else about him. Standing there, so still, he looked sculpted. His magic and his mystery reached up to her, and suddenly she wanted to be with him, within his presence, to talk to him, to find out all about him. With a glad quickening of the heart she hadn't felt in a very long time, she hurried for the bathroom, stripping off the robe, hoping he would not move until she had showered, dressed, and joined him.

Memories.

The good kind.

The sun rising over the San Gabriel Mountains behind the old frame house, as it was rising right now, spilling a golden shower of light over the meadows and down into the packed-earth yard where Grandpa George and Dad would be saddling their first mounts of the day. The horses snuffling, whinnying belly-deep, greeting the crystal morning; the jingle of harness; the comforting slap of hand on solid neck; the murmur of Romany and Comanche magic, secret communications between man and horse.

Grandma Rupa and his mother, Lila, in the kitchen, the metallic clatter of pots, the scrape of plates, good smells of coffee, frying bacon, and fresh-baked biscuits. Wolf, their German shepherd, all eyes and ears, slavering in anticipation.

Pintsize, his own Shetland, golden as the sun, angel-eyed and butterball round. John riding before he was three.

The stables: cool shade, rough wood polished smooth by the abrasion of oily flank; the wonderous pervading odor of horse.

The barn: shafts of white sunlight, mote-drifted, spearing through knothole and sprung weathered board. The intoxicating aroma of newly turned hay.

Five years of paradise. All that a boy could dream of.

He was born not thirty miles from where he now stood, up there to the northeast of the city on the edge of the Angeles National Forest, on land his father and grandfather leased for the raising, training, and provision of horses. For the movies.

Back in the late fifties and up until 1963 when it all fell apart, if you were making a movie in the Los Angeles area and needed horses, you went to see George "Nanosh" Candey and his son-in-law, Will Raven, because the service they provided was the best. Or—if you were making a movie anywhere on the continent—Arizona, New Mexico, wherever—and you already had horses but wanted a first-rate wrangler to handle a tricky remuda, you still went to see Will Raven because Will, of Comanche blood, being a descendant of Quanah Parker, knew more about the structure, physiology, rearing, training, riding, and handling of horses than just about anyone in the United States—with the possible exception of George Candey, a Romany of the Lowara tribe.

* * *

Memories.

The other kind.

Dad gone. Away on location—New Mexico, Arizona, Colorado, Nevada. Endless waits for his return.

Mom, pregnant, kicked by a bee-stung horse. Ambulance, hospital, murmured talk of "no more babies." The end, he somehow sensed of the good times, the beginning of the bad.

His fifth birthday. That awful day. A small celebration, a chocolate cake with five candles; Dad home for the occasion, hammering out "You Are My Sunshine" on the rinky-dink piano that came with the rented house; John dancing with his Mom; Grandma Rupa and Grandpa Nanosh gently jigging and singing along. Then . . . Grandma crumpling, dead before she hit the floor.

The bad times had begun.

And something else. Something weird, bewildering, frightening. Standing there, in that instant of shocked silence, he saw his grandma rise from the floor, except she was still lying down there on it. This was a second grandma, not quite as substantial, but the same in every detail. She looked at him and smiled, an expression of peerless peace, of acknowledgment of his recognition, and then she disappeared.

No one else had seen her.

Days later, at the funeral in Gorman, as her coffin was being lowered into the ground, he saw her again, alongside Gramps, who was standing, stunned by Romany grief, facing John across the grave.

Gramps sensed something, came out of his trancelike state and looked piercingly at John, then turned his head to his immediate right, following his grandson's wide-eyed gaze. When his eyes returned to John they were alive with a radiance of joyous understanding.

A new relationship with his grandfather began that day, involving something secret and intimate that was not to be shared by anyone else.

Later, Gramps choosing his time, alone with John in the evening-dark stable, said gently in a tone that conveyed pleasure, pride, awe, "You saw her."

Then Nanosh enfolded him in a gentle-giant's embrace and spoke of Romany things, of "second sight," and "perhaps of other gifts."

From that moment he became Nanosh's heir, heir to a thousand Gypsy secrets and incalculable Gypsy wisdom.

Astride Pintsize, overshadowed by his Gramps on a seventeen-hand quarter horse, he would accompany Nanosh up through the meadows, dismount, settle on a log, his elbows on his knees in imitation of his elder, and listen with awe and fascination to stories of the Rom: their travels, adventures, philosophy, beliefs, and of their kinship with all natural things.

And his grandfather spoke of other, darker things, of the dangers of the outside world, of the need—now that John was about to start school—for vigilance, alertness, and of the necessity of learning to defend himself.

"You have inherited a sad world," Nanosh told him, pointing off, by way of illustration, to the south, to where the purple-gray miasma of monoxide poison hung above the city, a Satanic shroud shutting out the sun. Seen distantly, the manifestation of madness. "People have lost touch with nature. They've placed themselves above it, no longer feel part of it. They are destroying the earth. They're all insane." He smiled, tempering the seriousness of his tone, patted his grandson's knee. "Pretty heavy stuff for a five-year-old, I know, but this is now your world and I want to protect you from its madness, best I can. New and unsettling things will be coming at you every day, maybe dangerous things, like boulders down a mountainside. You'll soon be starting school. You'll meet up with meanness, violence, drugs. Drugs make people do crazy things. The Rom owe their existence to eternal vigilance. You must learn the habit of alertness until it becomes as instinctive as breathing. You must learn to protect yourself. I will teach you.''

Memories.

The very worst kind.

Christmas 1963. His sixth birthday come and gone, his father appearing magically on that November night, home from location in northern California, then gone, promising to be home for a long happy Christmas vacation for them all.

The last day of the school semester, excitement leaping inside him like popping corn. Two whole weeks with his dad, picture finished, no more quick hello-goodbyes.

But something went wrong. Instead of his mom, Gramps was there to meet him at the school gate, Gramps's face and aura telling him *trouble* long before he reached the gate.

There'd been an accident. Something had happened to his dad in northern California, in the Cascade Mountains, but nobody was saying what. His mom had flown up there, would be home in a few days. When she returned she was near insane with grief.

Confusing times. John's world now became unreal, the old order gone forever. Strange things happened every day. People arrived at the ranch in cars, some with cameras, but were chased off by his furious grandfather.

Then, the ultimate blow. His dad, they told him, was dead.

Quickly now, as though he were the operator of his own life Moviola, he reviewed poignant moments of his life since he last laid eyes on these sunstruck San Gabriel

Mountains: the nightmare flight from L.A. to escape the voracious newshounds, just Grandpa, Mom, their German shepherd, Wolf, and himself, all that remained of the family; the ranch in Arizona where Grandpa Nanosh took a job as horse-handler to support them; his mom's sudden and secretive departure from the ranch, the ensuing bereft and lonely years when she never returned, first with Nanosh in Arizona, later with the Gypsy psychic Jack Shanglo in England, then two years traveling with the Rom *kumpania* across Europe.

At age fourteen he was reunited with Nanosh, by now manager of the Arizona spread, the ranch owned by wealthy industrialist William Meeker. Raven smiled inwardly as he recalled the incident just one week after his return to Arizona that radically changed the course of his life. Bill Meeker's only son, Rob, lost in the mountains, Rob's lame and riderless mount found in the yard. Fifty men searched Buck Mountain for three days to no avail, Bill Meeker desolate with grief. Then, as though guided there, Raven had wandered into the stable where Rob's saddle was kept. When he had reached out to touch the well-soaped leather he had *seen* Rob lying in a gulley with sudden, shocking insight, the mountain behind him identifiable not as Buck Mountain, where Rob had said he was heading, but Baker Butte, twenty miles to the south.

Rob was lucky. His father had believed in psychic ability, had listened to young John Raven, and had acted on his psychometric sensitivity. Three hours later Rob was home, emaciated by hunger and exposure, leg broken, but alive. And in William Meeker Raven had found a powerful friend and generous patron for life.

Raven recalled how, that same night, Meeker came to visit Nanosh and himself at the small house provided for the ranch manager, telling them of his interest in psychic phenomena and expressing his earnest desire to help John develop his obvious talent. And, reluctant as Nanosh was to be separated again from his grandson, he readily agreed that Bill Meeker's offer of a first-class education was a gift John could not afford to refuse.

The frames of movie reeled swiftly through the gate of memory as Raven reviewed the development of his psi abilities throughout his years at school and the university. His gift was a mystery to him; its parameters unknown. Often it had been a frightening, unwanted thing that brought confusion and bewilderment. With the onset of puberty his power had grown. Nanosh had explained that it was being nourished by chemical changes in the body. And with keen Romany insight, fearing the ridicule of nonbelievers, Nanosh had warned him to keep his talent secret.

As always, his grandfather had been right. On the few occasions Raven had inadvertently demonstrated his ability at school, he had paid the price. John Raven was "different," "weird," to be avoided. It was not until after graduation from the university, after he had begun to work as a researcher at the Alcott Institute and was steeped in the field of extrasensory perception, that he was able to reveal, to any degree, his own talent. And even then he held back.

Raven's thoughts now progressed to recent times, to one week earlier when he received the news of his grandfather's illness.

He had dreamed Nanosh was dying several hours before the phone call from Bill Meeker came. What Raven had not anticipated was the shocking revelation concerning his father—and his mother—told to him by Nanosh in his final living moments, information that had brought Raven, on extended leave from the Institute, back to California, where it had all begun twenty-four years ago.

As he stood now, eyes closed, the rising sun over the

San Gabriel Mountains warming his face, in the world yet not quite of it, he tried to read the future, to reach into the days ahead and so prepare and arm himself against the danger he could sense as a pervasive but nonspecific threat. But he could see nothing. One of the mysteries of ESP appeared to be just that. Like doctors who cannot diagnose their own illnesses, psychics with precognition were notoriously unable to predict their own futures. Probably just as well. Raven had never wanted to "see" his own future. Though right now, so certain of pending danger, he would have given much for an inkling of its timing, nature, and direction.

"Good morning."

Her voice startled him from his trancelike concentration.

Opening his eyes, he studied her as she walked toward him from the kitchen door, read her aura as she advanced through the shadow of the terrace, arms folded against its chill, smiling as she drew close, moving from shade into sunlight.

She was wearing jeans and a white T-shirt, a white cardigan about her shoulders. Her blond hair was styled in a half-ponytail, its wisps glinting golden in the sun. Considering her recent ordeal she looked fine, though dark smudges beneath her eyes and a resonance of nervousness belied her brave effort of concealment.

Raven said, "Good morning. You're up very early. Couldn't you sleep?"

An ambiguous shrug momentarily revealed the treasure house of trauma, of uncertainty and insecurity lurking behind her smile.

"I did okay. How about you? You were up earlier than me."

Raven grinned. "I'm a dawn man—when the topography warrants it.'' He gestured to the vista. ''This is spectacular.''

''I was watching you—from my bedroom window. You looked so at home with all this, as though you belonged.''

He smiled, acknowledging again her intuitiveness. ''I once did belong. I was born in those mountains, lived here until I was seven. This is the first time I've been back.''

''You sound . . . sad about it.''

''Not sad to be back. Just sad about the things that made it necessary to leave.''

She nodded, understanding. ''Another unraveled life.''

He said more cheerfully, ''Well, we're not going to dwell on unraveled lives today or on any other kind of unhappiness. You and I are going to make breakfast and a big pot of coffee, and we're going to sit out here in the sun and talk and enjoy the view and to hell with the mad, bad world out there, okay?''

Her smile sparkled. ''Okay.''

''Well, look at them up there, don't they look cozy,'' Max murmured to himself, almost nauseous with excitement.

He was high in a pine tree down in the canyon, five hundred yards from the house, a pair of Zeiss Jenoptem 7×50 binoculars he'd boosted from a parked car in Will Rogers State Park glued to his sweating face and trained on little Miss Katherine Anne Tyson as she stood up and took the coffee jug from that weird son-of-a-bitch bastard who'd killed Luke.

So, she'd made it back—and Hero had come with her.

Why?

For protection? Thinking that Bad Max would come looking to finish what he'd started in El Centro and take revenge for Luke's death?

Nah, you didn't rely on one-guy protection against a rapist killer armed with a cutthroat razor. You called in the cops. And there were no cops anywhere to be seen, either on the road in front of the house or around back up there on the terrace. He'd checked that out, driving past the house several times that morning before heading through the park and then into the canyon on foot—a bird-watcher out with his binoculars should anyone notice.

No, the cops figured he was in Mexico. Hero had brought her home for one reason: he fancied some of that sweet cunt Luke had been fucking when Hero had arrived on the scene and spoiled the party. And spoiled Luke.

Shaking with excitement, with rejuvenated fury trained on Raven's face (all he could see above the low stone wall from that angle) in jerky long-shot, Max drifted into the fantasy visualization of what he would do to that face—and to all of Hero, and to all of Kate Tyson—later that day. Oh, yes, it was all there and very possible. Though the canyon side beneath the house was steep, it was climbable—along there, up there, over the terrace wall. No problem.

He pictured the scene, saw it all in thrilling detail. It was a hot day. They'd have lunch on the terrace, drink a few beers, get a little sleepy, maybe a little horny—boy, that would be something, catch them in the sack. Zip, zip, zip—there goes Hero, cut his cock off, make him eat it. He'd have to slug the bitch to keep her quiet, but he'd make sure she was wide awake when he started on her.

He prayed he'd have a nice long time with her, like the chick in Daytona, coupla days, maybe, up there in that big house. Jesus, the things he could do to her in two, three days. Drive her insane with terror—telling her if she did this and that he'd forgive her for killing Luke and let her go. Then, seeing that look in her eyes when she finally realized all the dirty stuff she'd been doing wasn't going to save her, that she was going to *die*.

Vengeance is mine, sayeth Max Koenig.

He'd wait till they left the terrace and went into the house, then make his move.

Later, sitting there in cushioned patio chairs at an umbrella table, the sun high behind them and hot for November, the steep, rugged canyon sweeping down and away from them like a tumbled, overgrown amphitheater, their conversation gradually veered from the lightness Raven had insisted upon to more serious matters.

Kat knew what he'd been doing, knew she was being gently bullied and manipulated for therapeutic reasons, and loved him for it. He was, she had decided, a very lovable man.

Now sufficiently stable to consciously consider such things, she began to analyze both her feelings toward him and the qualities in him that evoked those feelings. He was, of course, physically attractive, and that was great; and he had saved her life and was now here protecting her, and that was wonderful, too. But there was so much more to him than beauty, bravery, and kindness, more than strength and understanding and mysterious ability. John Raven was more than the sum of his parts. He was "different" from any man she had ever met.

But how much of himself, she wondered, would he reveal? On the drive up from El Centro he had promised to tell her about his "exotic" upbringing, and yet she felt his innate self-containment, mystery, secretiveness would never permit him to tell all—at least not until he got to know her much better. And she couldn't see how that could be possible. Today, probably, he would be returning to San Diego, then to Kansas City. She would be staying in California . . .

The thought of separation from him triggered a sudden and surprising spasm of near-panic in her. She marveled at the force of the feeling. What was going on here? Was it from fear of being alone again? A reaction to the rape? Or something else?

She couldn't be sure. All she knew was that she didn't want Raven to leave. She *needed* to be near him.

"I want to know more about you," she found herself blurting, astounding herself.

He regarded her oddly, with an amused smile lifting the corners of his mouth.

Those eyes, she thought—so goddamned knowing. Despite his denial of yesterday, she was certain he could read her every thought.

Holding the smile, he released her from the tyranny of his gaze and returned it to the view. "What would you like to know?" he asked, his voice a deep hypnotic vibration.

"Everything."

He laughed softly. "That could take a while."

That's the idea, she said to herself, smiling. Stay a while and tell me.

"Who are your parents? What do they do? Are they still alive?" she asked.

The smile disappeared. His jaw tightened. A muscle ticked at the side of his face.

Kat could have bitten her tongue. "I'm sorry, I . . ."

He was quick to ease her discomfort. "No, no, it's all right." He was silent for a moment, gathering the words. "Kat, if you'd asked me that a week ago I could have given you a straightforward answer—based on what I've believed about my parents since I was six."

"Since you left California."

He nodded, acknowledging that she had remembered. "But a week ago my grandfather died. I was with him at the end. And he told me things about my parents I never knew and could never have suspected." He shook his head. "I'm still having trouble accepting it."

"John, I don't want to pry."

"No, it's all right. I'd like to tell you. I feel I want to share it with somebody, and I'd rather it be you than any-

97

one else. You've had family problems—have got them still—and I know you'll understand.''

He looked at her, his expression earnest, kindly. ''But, Kat, understand this, too. I won't be telling you these things merely to share a burden. I'm doing it to try and help you. You told me yesterday you wanted to write but didn't know what or how. I think you know ''how'' very well. It's just a matter of finding the ''what.'' I believe you're struggling against a psychological block—your father's success. You fear failure, fear comparison to him, and can't bring yourself to start. You can't even settle on a subject. But you seem very interested in the American Indian and in psychic matters, so I'm going to give you a true story involving both of those things—plus background material on one of the most fascinating people on earth, the Romany Gypsies, plus—''

He paused again, frowning, as though disbelieving what he was about to add.

''—plus murder . . . and ruthless ambition . . . and the evil destruction of human lives.'' His mouth twisted in a tight, humorless smile. ''In short, all the ingredients for a potential best-seller.''

Kat stared at him. ''My God—all this happened to you?''

He nodded. ''I didn't know most of it till a week ago. My grandfather had kept it to himself all those years under a promise of secrecy. He—'' Raven broke off, roused himself, reached for the coffee jug. ''Well, look, now that we've started, why not do the thing properly? What do you use for note-taking—a pad, a tape recorder?''

Kat shrugged. ''Both. Right now I'd prefer to record you, transcribe it later. Shall I go get the recorder?''

''Sure.'' He proffered the jug. ''And bring a refill, hmm? This is likely to be a long session.''

Chapter Seven

Kat returned with the coffee and a Sony cassette recorder, angled the table microphone toward Raven, and did a test run.

"Good," she said. "It's all yours."

"I've been thinking where to begin," he said slowly. "Maybe with my grandfather, how he got to the States and met up with my father. I could talk to you for a month, nonstop, just about the Rom. They're an incredible, fascinating people, but secretive. Very few books have been written about them. Maybe this can be your edge—authentic inside information from a rare source."

"Is that what you are, John—Romany Gypsy?"

"Half. The other half is Comanche Indian."

She laughed, delighted. "My God, how romantic! But I could never use you as a hero. No editor would accept that overabundance of glamour as realistic."

He grinned. "They would if they knew anything about the Rom and Indians. The races have a lot in common. To borrow your description of the Pueblo Indians, the Rom and the Comanche are of the earth. They belong. They have a miraculous affinity with animals, with all of nature. It was horses that brought my grandfather and father together."

"I love it already," Kat said, refilling the cups. "Go ahead—talk. I promise not to interrupt, I'll save the questions for later. I'll just lie here with my eyes closed and picture what you're telling me.''

''Okay.'' He smiled at her enthusiasm, her excitement, pleased to see the gradual change in her from the mood of yesterday. A new Kat Tyson was visible inside the despairing chrysalis of the old. If he could ignite the fire of her literary interest, get her writing, he felt sure the transformation would be permanent and profound. She had great potential for happiness.

''My grandfather's Romany name was Nanosh,'' he began, experiencing the pangs of sadness as he brought Nanosh alive again with memory and with words. ''But like all Gypsies who step into the *Gaje* world''—he pronounced it ''Jorje''—''he was required to have a Christian and a surname, so he called himself George Candey. *Gaje*, by the way, is the term Gypsies use for all non-Gypsy people. It means 'peasant,' and will give you a hint as to how Gypsies feel about the *Gaje*.'' He smiled. ''Me—I'm lucky. I'm only half peasant.''

Eyes closed, Kat grinned and nodded.

In a more serious tone, Raven went on. ''In nineteen-forty Nanosh had good reason to regard one particular strain of Gaje as peasant, to say the least. They were the Germans. In nineteen-forty Nanosh was traveling through northern France with his *kumpania*—that's a group of family units living, in those days, in horse-drawn wagons, called *vurdon*. Suddenly the German blitzkrieg was upon them. I want you to try and imagine the horror and terror of the scene: the roads choked with refugees fleeing south, mostly on foot, staggering along with what few possessions they could carry, and the German fighter planes swooping down, machine-gunning the crowds.

''Blind panic broke out, and that panic turned to savagery against the Rom, the Gypsies, who not only had wheeled transport but were obviously coping with the terror with greater coolness and composure."

Raven smiled. "Forgive my grandfather's partisanship, but I know from personal experience that it's true. I traveled with the Rom for two years and can testify to their courage and dignity in threatening situations. Every day of their lives is a struggle for survival."

Kat opened her eyes and met Raven's gaze, acknowledging that his comment was directed at her, that he was telling her she, too, would have to be courageous if she were to live life to the fullest. With a faint smile that she had received and understood, she again closed her eyes.

"To avoid destruction, the *kumpania* dispersed. In my grandfather's wagon were Nanosh, his wife, Rupa, and three of their four children. Their fourth child, Lila, who was then three years old, was traveling in another wagon. There was no time to transfer Lila to her family's wagon, and this undoubtedly saved her life. Good thing, too—otherwise I wouldn't be here to tell the story. Seventeen years later, Lila became my mother."

Kat smiled slyly. "I think it was a good thing, too."

"Using his great hunting skill and knowledge of the country," Raven continued, "Nanosh escaped along rural trails in wooded country, circling all the time with a plan to meet up with his *kumpania* at the river Marne. But when he reached the river he discovered the German army already in occupation, his *kumpania* gone. So Nanosh headed for the woods and joined a *kumpania* of the Kalderash tribe—Nanosh was of the Lowara tribe—planning, at the first opportunity, to escape across the Marne and find Lila. But it never happened. It was nearly five years before they saw my mother again."

Raven paused and took a sip of coffee.

"At first the Germans treated the Rom well enough, provided they kept out of sight and trouble. The danger lay, rather, with the French authorities who were handing interned Rom over to the Gestapo for deportation to extermination camps in the east. The whole world knows about the Holocaust and the terrible plight of the European Jews under Hitler, but few people know that half a million Gypsies were exterminated in camps like Sobibor, Chelmo, and Dachau. Like the Jews they became *Rassenverfolgte*, enemies of the Reich, and were legislated out of existence. They were massacred by Croatian nationalists, by Ukrainians in the forest of Wolyn, and by innumerable other enemies. For, literally, centuries, attempts have been made to wipe them off the face of the earth, and yet, like Nanosh and Rupa, they have managed to survive.

"How?" he asked rhetorically. "By their elusiveness, by their mobility, and the smallness of their widely scattered groups. Gypsies are like quicksilver, difficult to grasp. They are here—and gone, their *kumpanias* constantly merging and dividing. And they are supreme psychologists. No race understands human nature better than the Rom. But above all, they are *hunters*—fierce, proud, cunning, instinctual—and, when their family's or friends' survival is threatened—utterly ruthless."

Kat's heart stirred. Into her mind flashed the picture of Raven standing there in the clearing, legs and body braced, face contorted by the most awful anger—his destruction of Luke Shand utterly ruthless.

Several things were happening here, she realized. In telling her about the Rom, John Raven was, ostensibly, providing her with unique and fascinating material and with the encouragement to write, but beneath this he was telling her about himself, about his culture, philosophy, training, beliefs. But for her, his story had taken on a new and disturbing dimension. He was telling her that he was an instinctual hunter—and when *his* family's or friends' survival was threatened, utterly ruthless himself.

As though reading her thoughts, sensing her apprehension and wishing to allay it, Raven said with a smile, "Don't misunderstand, the Rom are not, generally speaking, a violent people. They prefer other forms of defense. They can radiate a frightening animal magnetism. Many of them possess a gaze so fierce no *Gajo* can meet their eyes. They use the power of their personalities to deflect possible danger. They use their voices. Living in the open air, all Gypsies develop loud, carrying voices that can be used devastatingly at close range. And they are nature's actors, will switch moods to gain advantage—one moment meek, the next menacing, extremely volatile. . . ."

Kat's thoughts again sped back to the bus and to Raven's own mystifying change of behavior at the onset of the hijacking: his pretense of meekness—cowardice, even—while faced with the shotgun, followed by his act of extreme bravery that saved her life.

". . . and all these defenses, and more, Nanosh had to employ in the years to come to save his family and *kumpania*.

"At first they lay low in thickly wooded country, scavenging what food they could from the woods, the countryside, the nearby towns. Then, quickly, the situation worsened. German requisitions started. Food was rationed and there were severe shortages. One day a German patrol arrived at the campsite and took away all of the Rom's good horses. A strict blackout was enforced; campfires were forbidden after dark. German soldiers would open fire at any burning light they saw.

"When winter came and natural sources of food became nonexistent, Nanosh was forced to register his family for their ration cards. He used several sets of identification papers he'd accumulated on his travels—such material identification is meaningless to the Rom. They use aliases to confuse the Gaje whose laws and legal impositions they resent. The name George Candey, with which Nanosh eventually entered the United States, is one of the fictitious names he used during the German occupation.''

Raven paused for thought, sifting through his storehouse of memories before deciding in which direction to continue.

"During this period an interesting dichotomy afflicted the Rom. On the one hand they were naturally opposed to helping the *Gaje,* yet they didn't hesitate to hide and protect a wounded British airman who'd been shot down in their area. This tells you a great deal about their sympathy for and their affinity with the persecuted and the hunted. But for Nanosh it had devastating consequences.

"The action drew the attention of the local resistance movements, and several more Allied airmen were brought to the Gypsy camp for temporary safekeeping. Gradually, Rom participation in resistance against the Germans increased, particularly in the supplying of illicit ration cards and false identification papers. Naturally, it was only a matter of time before the Germans learned of the Rom involvement.

"One day Nanosh was returning on horseback to the camp from a local town where he'd been liaising with a resistance group when he heard the sound of machine-gun fire. He spurred his old horse into a gallop and came upon a terrible sight. A German patrol, four *Geheime Feldpolizei,* were raking the wagons with their machine guns. Murdered Gypsy men, women, and children were strewn around the campsite. A Polish airman they'd been hiding was sprawled facedown in the campfire. Rupa, still alive, demented, screaming curses, was kneeling beside three

104

young bodies that Nanosh recognized immediately as his own children. He went berserk.

"My grandfather was a huge man of great physical strength. He drove his horse into the Germans, knocked them down, jumped off his horse, and grabbed one of the weapons. He killed them all, but took two bullets in return, in his thigh and side. His children, two boys and a girl, were dead. Rupa had also been shot, above the hip. Only six other Gypsies, an old man and five women, remained alive. There was no time for burial, little time for anything but escape. The Rom placed their dead in two of the wagons and set fire to them, then escaped in the German patrol vehicle."

Kat was staring at him, shaking her head, appalled. "My God, how terrible."

Raven nodded. "I've seen the site of the massacre. I was taken there when I lived with the Rom in Europe. They've erected a stone in remembrance. But even standing there, in that solemn little clearing in the French woods, it was impossible to fully appreciate the grief Nanosh and Rupa must have suffered over their murdered children. The Rom idolize their children. And all Rom grieve extravagantly, give themselves to sorrow totally. A Gypsy funeral is a harrowing experience. My grandfather's funeral last week was no exception."

He shook away the image. "For Nanosh and Rupa the nightmare continued. A massive manhunt was set up to capture the infamous Rom who had dared kill four Germans. Reprisals were taken against other Gypsies unfamiliar with Nanosh or known to him. In fear of this retribution, and possible betrayal, Nanosh decided to avoid contact with all Rom, which imposed a great additional burden on Rupa and himself. A Gypsy denied Rom fellowship is a man robbed of his soul.

"Both of them badly wounded, Rupa soon dangerously

ill with pneumonia, reliant on *Gaje* strangers for their lives, they moved constantly from one hiding place to another— a rat-infested cellar, a forest cave—unremittingly hunted. That they lived to see the end of the war was a miracle— and a tribute to their enormous spiritual strength and courage, and to Nanosh's great skill as a hunter and instinctual survivor. And yet, typically, he gave credit for it all to God.''

Kat, watching the play of emotions evoked by vivid recall pass across his face as he gazed out over the canyon, said, "He was very religious."

Raven shook his head. "Not in the accepted sense. God to him was not an old man with a white beard, but nature, all things natural, the cosmic forces that affect our lives. Nanosh was very wise. He sought no revenge against the Germans for the death of his children. He used to tell me that revenge, like sustained anger, plays no part in a wise Lowara's philosophy. But don't misunderstand. Nanosh fought with resistance groups for the next two years and killed many Germans. He did it with an awareness of a need to destroy the evil—the *beng*—of Nazism, in order to protect the Rom way of life for future generations of his people. To him it was a very important distinction."

Kat said, "I can understand it. What an incredible man. I would love to have met him."

Raven smiled. "You would have loved him had you met him. He was incredible . . . so vibrant, so totally alive. Strong yet gentle. And you wouldn't believe his affinity with animals. I've seen him . . . but that's getting ahead of my story. Let me just finish with the war."

He drank his coffee, put down his cup.

"In August nineteen forty-four, when the Allies liberated Paris, Nanosh regarded his and Rupa's contribution paid in full, and he set about the difficult job of locating Lila and rejoining the world of the Rom. Telephone communication was in a bad state in Europe at that time, and it took almost a year—five years since their separation in northern France—before they were reunited with their only surviving child. And it happened in the unlikeliest place: a little semidetached house in the suburbs of Manchester, England.

"The story of Lila's experience in, and escape from, Europe was scarcely less horrifying than that of her parents. All through it she'd been under the protection of a truly remarkable Gypsy whose assumed name was Jack Shanglo, a man of great psychic sensitivity, who now owned the house in Manchester.

"Jack told Nanosh and Rupa an appalling story of murder, rape, and brutality against the Rom in Europe, of wild flight in the dark of night, hiding in forest and bog in freezing temperatures, near starvation, and of their eventual escape across the English Channel in a leaky sailboat. Jack's family, too, had been decimated on the way. His wife and two sons had been shot to death by Germans in Normandy."

Kat groaned and shook her head. "My God, and I think I've got problems."

"Miraculously, Jack's mother, though in poor health, had survived the ordeal. And it was with regard for her that Jack had decided to abandon the freedom but hardship of the road and settle in a permanent home. Well, Jack's decision gave Nanosh cause for thought. Rupa's health was also poor. Although the war was now over, conditions in Britain and Europe were harsh. Rupa needed a warm climate and an easier life. It was time to find new lands, time to travel *perdal l paya,* as the Rom say—beyond the waters. And so, in June nineteen-forty-seven, Nanosh, Rupa, and ten-year-old Lila—by then having become George Candey and family—arrived here in the United States."

Raven paused to collect his thoughts. For the briefest moment while his mind was unfocused—

Something—

The slightest presentiment of unease—

No more than the vaguest sensation of presence, an awareness of being watched.

He felt a compulsion to move. With a smile at Kat, he stretched and eased his shoulders, saying lightly, "We'll break for a minute. I'm not used to talking so much."

"Of course." She switched off the recorder.

Raven got up, moved to the wall, stretching and deeply breathing, his gaze surreptitiously scanning the canyon, searching between its rocks and trees. Max nagged at him like an aching tooth. Could he have been wrong about Max? Could the psycho freak be south of the border, terrorizing Mexican girls with his Mark of Zorro technique?

He closed his eyes, put his conscious mind on hold, willed his subconscious to provide an answer. The voice was there instantly, the thought-form, a silent mental whisper, insistent and undeniable—

Max is in L.A. Here. Close.

Kat's voice, concerned, intruded. "John—you sure you want to go on?"

He turned, smiling. "Of course. Why shouldn't I?"

She shrugged, expressing uncertainty. "You looked— strange just then, kind of worried. Is talking about your grandfather upsetting you?"

His smile was placatory. "No, it wasn't that. It was nothing. I tend to go off into these brown studies now and then, you mustn't mind it."

She held his gaze, frowning, unsatisfied, and asked, "What were you listening to? You looked as though you heard something."

Now he laughed. "Boy, you are perceptive. Yes, I was listening, to the canyon, to the cosmos, but if we get into that we'll never finish the story." He sat down and drained his cup. "Now, where were we?"

Kat switched on the recorder. "George Candey and family had arrived in the States—June nineteen forty-seven."

"Right. Well, Nanosh had to earn a living and horses were his thing. He knew them as well as any living man and loved them better than most. As a very young boy he had learned all the Rom secrets and tricks concerning the *grast*—the horse: how to diminish a good horse's qualities by running him slightly out of step and by holding its head a little too low for comfort; how to transform a tired old nag into a prancing thoroughbred by secretly placing a piece of ginger under its tail."

Kat laughed, enthralled.

"And these tricks served their purpose when trading with the unscrupulous *Gaje*. But Nanosh's interest was focused on the animals themselves. He admired and respected them. Many people believe the horse is stupid and lacks the ability to reason. But it isn't so. The animal requires respect and understanding—and Nanosh understood them as well as he understood men, which was very well indeed."

And so do you, thought Kat.

"Some people thought his control over them was supernatural. I've heard men murmuring that Nanosh possessed the power of the Devil. And I understood how they could think that. His rapport with them was unbelievable. You had to see it to believe it, and even then you'd have trouble with it. Many times I've seen him handle an incorrigible renegade, a thorough badass, its eyes wild, ears laid back, muscles all aquiver, desperate to stomp any human that came close to the ground. Nanosh would just stand there, looking at the animal, keeping his respectful distance, and the ranch hands would watch with disbelief the gradual change in the horse's behavior. It would grow still, whicker softly. The wild whiteness would disappear from its eye. Its ears would spring erect as though tuning in to Nanosh. And that's exactly what it would be doing. For Nanosh was what they used to call a Horse Whisperer.''

Kat released a laugh of amusement and fascination. ''A *Horse Whisperer*? I've never heard that term.''

Raven, unexpectedly, reached into his shirt and withdrew the ankh that hung about his neck on its gold chain.

''Remember this—from the bus?''

Kat nodded, preferring not to remember.

''A little side story for you,'' Raven went on. ''In eighteen seventy-three, a Victorian writer named William Smith visited the Lee Gap horse fair in Yorkshire, England, and came away convinced he'd seen a magician at work. He wrote about a 'gypsyman' who had the ability to control horses from a distance without a word of command, and Smith believed the power lay in a charm that possessed—his words—'some preternatural efficacy over the beasts.'

''Well, the 'gypsyman' was Nanosh's grandfather Dodi, my great-great-grandfather. And this ankh was the 'charm' Smith referred to.''

Kat gasped with delight and rolled her eyes. ''God, I love it. How incredibly romantic. Does it really possess magical properties?''

Raven laughed and shook his head. ''Sorry to disappoint you. No, the power lay in Dodi himself. He, too, was a Horse Whisperer. They weren't uncommon in Britain in those days. They even formed a 'Freemasonry' with secret signs and passwords. Most of them used herbs and substances in their art. Sweet-smelling plants such as bryony, cinnamon, and rosemary were used as 'drawing' charms. Conversely, a piece of raw and rotting meat or

110

animal grease concealed in a pouch would repel the animal.

"But, according to Nanosh, neither his grandfather nor his father, who also inherited the gift, ever needed such devices. And neither did Nanosh. They all relied on the power of their personalities. Their 'charms' were respect, patience, understanding, and a hypnotic quality of voice."

For Kat, these words provided another piece of the jigsaw to add to the puzzle that was John Raven. Gradually, the picture was beginning to form.

"The ankh has been handed down to me as a symbol, a reminder of my illustrious and talented forebears, and, I guess, of the essential and eternal difference between the Romany people and the *Gaje*," Raven said solemnly.

Kat regarded him quizzically. "Do you feel different from us, John?"

Raven sighed, contemplatively. "Yes. Because I am different. Not physically or physiologically, of course—at least, I don't think so. But certainly culturally, mentally. I've been raised to believe as possible and natural things most people scoff at."

"You mean—the paranormal."

Raven smiled. "There you are, you see. You call it the 'paranormal.' I think of it as 'normal.' "

Kat laughed. "Yeah, you got me. But how can you think of psychic gifts as normal when so few people seem to have them?"

"Kat, you'd be amazed how many people find they do have them—once they give themselves *permission* to have them and learn how to develop them. But first you've got to *believe*—in both the reality of the so-called gift and in yourself. Acceptance is the first and most important step."

Kat shook her head. "I don't know. I don't feel I've got any talent at all in that direction."

He laughed. "Great. That absolutely ensures you never

will have. You've just fed your subconscious a truckload of self-doubt.''

She sighed despairingly. "Oh, boy, I can see I'm going to have trouble with you. Would you mind getting away from me and back to Nanosh? He's far more interesting.''

"Okay, we'll deal with you later. So—horses. About the time Nanosh arrived in the States, Western movies were enjoying their heyday. Thousands of horses were needed, together with expert handlers and riders, and Nanosh had no trouble finding work.

"One day, in the mid-fifties, Nanosh was breaking mustangs on the Mogollon Plateau in Arizona, with Rupa and Lila—who was now eighteen and a brilliant horsewoman—camped nearby in a trailer, when a movie director arrived on the spread looking for locations and an expert wrangler. With him was another horse-handler, a tall, muscular, handsome Indian of noble bearing and striking presence—Nanosh's description, not mine.''

Kat smiled, knowing what was coming.

"The director introduced the Indian to Nanosh, and in that first instant, as Nanosh told it, there was forged between them a bond as strong and enduring as the love of life itself. It was as though Nanosh were looking into the eyes of one of his own sons, reincarnated. The Indian, it transpired, was Comanche and a direct descendant of the great chief Quanah Parker—who, incidentally, married a white woman, so I do have some *Gaje* blood in my veins.''

Kat sighed and rolled her eyes. '' 'Exotic' was definitely an understatement.''

"The Indian's name,'' Raven went on, "was Will Raven.''

Kat nodded. "Of course. And he and the lovely Lila took one look at each other . . .''

". . . and fell madly in love,'' Raven completed. "You're absolutely right. They were married within the year. By now, Rupa's health was deteriorating, and for some time Nanosh had been considering a permanent home. So when Will Raven suggested a partnership, that they rent some land near Los Angeles where they could train and supply horses to the movie industry, Nanosh jumped at the chance. And that's what they did.'' Raven pointed to the distant San Gabriel Mountains. ''Right over there. There was an old clapboard house on the land. I was born in it a year later. And for seven years I led the happiest life you could ever imagine.''

Kat nodded. ''If it was anything like my first year in this house, it must have been heaven. But, obviously, as with my family, something terrible happened.''

She saw Raven's expression, in profile, change from the gentleness of wistful remembrance to the grim severity of deep, abiding hurt, and once again alarm stirred within her as she recalled his propensity for awesome violence. In these moments she sensed that no matter how much he told her, there were aspects of John Raven she would never know; not she nor any other human being. The man was an enigma and would always remain so.

''During my seventh year,'' he went on, his voice now quieter, more gratingly vibrant, and more threatening to her ear, ''my father was away from me a lot, on location—Arizona, New Mexico, all over. I missed him terribly. Rupa was dead by now, and with Dad gone so much the house wasn't the same. I sensed, as you did here, that the good times were over, that bad times were coming. But I had no idea how bad.

''At Christmastime of that year, something strange and awful happened. Dad was due home from northern California, but he didn't arrive. And suddenly our house was in an uproar. People with cameras arrived in cars, wanting to take pictures of the family, the house, everything, and there was my grandfather, driving them off with an ax handle. It was a madhouse. Then Nanosh took me aside and told me my father was dead, killed on location upstate.''

Kat murmured an empathetic groan.

''From them on I lived in a world of unreality. Yesterday you said you had trouble believing what was happening. During that period it was the same for me. I couldn't understand what was going on—the mysterious whispered conferences between Nanosh and my mother, the persistence of the people I learned later were the press. Then my mother went away for a few days and came back emotionally devastated. The next day we were on our way to Arizona, to the ranch of a man named William Meeker, where Nanosh was working when he met my father.

''This was bad enough but worse was to come. One night, shortly after we'd arrived in Arizona, I heard a heated argument between Nanosh and my mother, heard a door slam and a car drive away. The following day Nanosh told me my mother had returned to northern California on business concerning my father. The days passed, then weeks. My mother never came back.''

''My God, how awful.''

Raven drew a sigh. ''I never knew what happened to her. She simply disappeared. Nanosh was inconsolable. Except for me, he had now lost his entire family. As much as he hated the idea of being separated from me, he knew he couldn't look after me by himself, so he sent me to England, to stay with Jack Shanglo in Manchester.

''At first I loathed it. I really thought I'd die of heartbreak and culture shock. Can you imagine what life in a Manchester semidetached house was like after the San Gabriel Mountains and the Mogollon Plateau?''

Kat shook her head. ''I know how I'd dread to go back to Lennox after living up here, so I guess if I multiplied that by a factor of one hundred it might be close.''

Raven smiled grimly. "By at least a hundred. One thing saved my sanity—Jack Shanglo. In his way he was as remarkable a man as Nanosh. Jack was a very gifted psychic, talented in all the so-called phenomena: telepathy, clairvoyance, precognition, psychometry, and psychokinesis, the most rare gift of all."

And that is how you developed yours, thought Kat.

She said, "I'm not sure what they are. I know telepathy is communication between minds, and precognition is seeing the future, but I'm not clear on the others."

"Clairvoyance is knowledge of things happening in another place right now. Psychometry is the gathering of information by touching an object. And psychokinesis is the movement of an object without touching it."

Kat frowned. "And all these things are really humanly possible?"

"Oh, yes. In varying degrees, of course, and with practice. Jack Shanglo was unbelievable. He could take a ring, a scarf, whatever, and reel off details of the owner's past, present, and future that were astonishingly accurate."

"I find it all fascinating," said Kat. "I could get very interested in psychic phenomena. I'd like to write about it. Would you help me get started?"

"Of course. Jack Shanglo is, alas, now dead, but"—he gave a wry smile—"maybe I'll send you over to live with the Lowara in Europe for a while. You'd learn more about the mysteries of life and human nature in one month with them than you'd learn in a lifetime here in L.A."

"And that's what you did."

He nodded. "Jack knew I was pining—for my family and for ranch life. So he sent me to Europe, to travel with the Lowara. I was with them for two years, and, oh, the things I learned. My formal schooling may have suffered, but they taught me things no student in L.A. ever learned—mainly, how to survive."

She smiled. "*That* is a story I want to hear."

"You will, in time."

"So, what happened then? Did you come back to live with Nanosh?"

Raven nodded. "When I was fourteen. I'll skip over some years. After that just say I picked up on my schooling, took a degree, began work at the Alcott Institute in Kansas City. The important part I want to get to is a week or so back, when I got word that Nanosh was very ill. I want to stress this part, Kat, because . . . it might affect your future and I want you to be prepared."

She frowned at him, puzzled. "Affect *my* future? Do you see me involved in—well, in your affairs in some way?"

He was hesitant in answering. "Yes. It's—not a precise picture, but it's there, a feeling. And it could be dangerous, so I want to prepare you."

She was staring at him, nonplussed and a little frightened. How could she be involved in Raven's future when he would probably be leaving that day?

She said, "Go on."

"I was shocked by Nanosh's condition. Lying there, he was so emaciated I hardly recognized him. I swear he had willed himself to live until I arrived. When I entered his room, his eyes lit up and for a moment I saw a vestige of the vibrant energy that had always radiated from this giant of a man. I wept as I hugged him, knowing he, the last of my family, had so little time to live. I couldn't believe I would never see him again after that day."

Picturing the scene, thinking of her father and his illness, Kat felt the sting of tears and let them come.

Raven saw, said quickly, "Kat, I'm sorry, I didn't mean to upset you."

"No, no, go on. Please, it's all right."

"His condition was the first shock. Then came the second. Nanosh ordered the nurse from the room, and in a whispery voice said he had something very important to tell me. He said that for twenty-four years he had upheld a promise to remain silent, but felt that a recent event had released him from the promise, and he wanted me to know. Kat, what he told me just blew my mind. He told me my father is still alive.''

Her mouth dropped open. ''Oh, John . . .''

Raven sighed. ''Twenty-four years ago, on location in the Cascade Mountains, my father didn't 'die.' He was accused of murder, tried, and sent to San Quentin for life. That was why all the press descended on our house. He served twenty-three years. In deference to me, to the disastrous effect he imagined the notoriety of his crime would have on me, my father made Nanosh and my mother promise to tell me he was dead. The recent 'event' that allowed Nanosh, in his mind, to tell me was the release of my father from prison. Will Raven is now free and living''—he spread his hands interrogatively—''where? That's what I was doing on the San Diego bus. I came here to try and find him.''

Kat's mouth was still open, her mind swimming with surprise and so many questions she didn't know where to begin. ''I don't know what to say! It's incredible. Who—who was your father supposed to have murdered?''

Raven smiled coldly. ''Thank you for the 'supposed.' You're right, he didn't murder anybody. He was incapable of killing any*thing*, let alone anybody. He was framed.''

Kat continued to stare. ''By whom? Do you know?''

''Yes. This is where it gets really fantastic. He was framed by Frank Vollner.''

Kat blinked. Her mouth tweaked in an incredulous grin. ''*The* Frank Vollner? The movie producer?''

Raven nodded, held her gaze, enforcing his assertion. She gasped.

"The person who was murdered was Frank Vollner's first wife—Barbara. Nanosh told me as much of the story as he was physically able. After he died, I returned to Kansas City to arrange a leave of absence and look up any newspaper accounts there might be. I couldn't find much in the files, but the case was exotic enough to warrant some space. I was horrified by what I read—by the details of the murder and to see my father's pictures in the papers. I understood why he wanted me to believe him dead. It was a brutal, gruesome crime."

Kat's expression was still frozen in shock and incredulity. "What happened?"

"According to the press? Back then, Frank Vollner was a struggling young producer making low-budget movies, mainly Westerns. He'd recently married Barbara, aged twenty-two, an heiress to the McKenzie Oregon and California timber fortune. She was also an actress and was starring in the picture Vollner was shooting in the Cascades. My father was working on it as a wrangler for the remuda. According to the trial evidence, my father fell insanely in love with Barbara, and when rejected by her, got drunk one night, lured her into his trailer, and cut her throat. Vollner found my father unconscious on the floor, his bloodstained hunting knife in his hand, Barbara dead on the bed."

Kat shut her eyes. "Dear God, what a terrible shock all this must have been for you. You know, when we first met on the bus, you looked so . . . desolate. Now I know why. First, this news of your father, then Nanosh's death."

"There's more," Raven said distractedly. "You remember me telling you about the heated argument I overheard between Nanosh and my mother at the Meeker ranch? Nanosh explained that to me. My mother was near insane with grief, as grief-crazy as only a Gypsy woman can be. She knew my father was innocent, knew a defenseless In-

118

dian had been framed by an influential *Gaje*, and that Will would get the chair or life imprisonment. She also knew Frank Vollner had to be behind the murder of his own wife. Before we left L.A. she'd met Vollner in the Cascades and *knew* he'd done it. The reason she left the Meeker ranch that night was to confront Vollner and try to find some evidence for my father's defense. As I said, she never returned. Nanosh was sure Vollner was responsible for her disappearance, and possibly her death."

Kat said, "I'm speechless. Frank *Vollner*. I mean, I *know* there isn't a successful Hollywood producer who isn't also a ruthless bastard, it's a synchronization of terms . . . but *murder*? I've met Vollner several times, at charity things. He and that simpering wife of his, Sissy, are neck deep in good works in Tinsel Town—and I wouldn't trust the guy as far as I could throw a Rams' tackle. But murder. What was his motive—his wife's money?"

"That's one of the things I intend to find out."

Kat's eyes widened. "You're going after Vollner?"

Raven frowned. "I don't know. I've got three objectives. One: I'm going to find my father. Two: I'm going to clear his name. Three: I'm going to find out what happened to my mother. If, in order to achieve those things, it's necessary to go after Vollner, then I will."

Kat looked at him, into those dark Gypsy eyes that were capable of expressing such extremes of emotion, such gentleness, and, as now, such depths of anger and determination. And a wave of apprehension rippled through her.

"How will you begin?" she asked.

"Nanosh gave me a name. Joe Santee. He's a Comanche Indian, lives in the desert near Live Oak Springs, near San Diego. Santee knows my father, shared a cell with him in San Quentin. Nanosh believed if anyone knows where my father is, Santee will."

Kat groaned. "And you were heading there when all

this happened. And now you're wasting your time here with me when you must be desperate to speak to Santee."

Raven broke the severity of his gaze with a smile, reached across the table to take her hand. "I am not wasting my time, get that out of your head. Everything will happen when it's supposed to happen, believe me."

The recorder clicked off.

Kat said, "The tape's finished."

"And so am I," said Raven.

Chapter Eight

The front gate buzzer sounded at eleven on the rear terrace. Kat went to answer it, released the gate, and a moment later an unmarked blue Plymouth swirled into the turnaround. Raven was standing with Kat at the front door when the men—two policemen in plainclothes and one in uniform—entered the house.

Introductions were made. The one heading the trio was Detective Lieutenant Anthony Marco. The others: Detective Whales and Officer Brawley.

Marco looked young to be a homicide lieutenant, a factor that, without a doubt, confirmed Raven's immediate impression that Marco was exceedingly bright. Raven liked him on sight and sensed the feeling was mutual.

Marco, wearing a gray lightweight suit which seemed, miraculously, to have resisted the heat, stood four inches shorter than Raven, his hair as dark as Raven's and styled similarly straight back from his forehead but cut shorter. He had a handsome, well-proportioned face with dark, lazy lidded eyes that looked at little but saw everything. His aura was that of quiet dignity. Shaking his hand, Raven read openmindedness, and knew he'd have no trouble with this man when they got into the psychic thing, which he knew they would.

Marco needed to speak to Raven alone, so he suggested

they go into the kitchen while Detective Whales and Officer Brawley accompanied Kat into the library.

"I want to save Miss Tyson, as far as it's possible, any further reminder of what happened yesterday," Marco said, crossing the kitchen to look out of the window at the canyon. "I'd say she's suffered enough."

His voice was softly modulated, the delivery that of an educated man whose thoughts outdistanced his words.

"You're right." Raven moved up beside him. "On her behalf I thank you."

"Wonderful view. I've only been in Los Angeles a month, so all this is still new. Do you think Californians appreciate how lucky they are?"

"Of course not. Where are you from?"

Marco glanced at him, his smile a mock challenge. "You tell me, you're the psychic."

Raven returned the smile with his eyes. "Who said so?"

"Lieutenant Plaidy. He told me what you said about Max being in San Diego, not Mexico."

Raven nodded. "You're from New York."

"Right. Anything else?"

"Your wife—she's from L.A. She wanted to come home."

Marco grinned. "You're very good. I wish I had it, it would sure help in this job."

"It's easier with people who understand—and believe."

Marco nodded. "I believe. My wife has it. On good days she makes my neck hairs stand on end."

"That's the problem," acknowledged Raven. "Good days, bad days. It's rarely consistent."

Marco changed tack. "Regarding yesterday, there'll be no need for you or Miss Tyson to attend an inquest in El Centro."

"That's good news."

"Two things interest me. One is this 'Mark of Zorro'

M.O., the other was your certainty that Max was in California, not Mexico. Do you have any updated feelings about that?''

''Yes. I feel he's here—in Los Angeles.''

Marco studied the view for a moment before saying, ''So do I. Last night two people—a black prostitute with her pimp—were murdered in Hollywood. Both were killed with a razor. The girl's face was slashed with a Z. It can't be coincidence.''

Raven's pulse erupted. ''Jesus. Then he *is* here.''

Marco turned toward him. ''We've got to put a face and a surname to this maniac, Raven. The Hollywood victims were discovered only this morning, so we haven't had time to cover the area yet, try and get a positive I.D. We're running Luke Shand, Max's partner, through the computer in the hope they've both got records and are linked together down the line. And I've put out an all-states flyer on this Mark of Zorro M.O. What I'd like you to do is come down to the station and help us build a composite of Max.''

Raven felt the insidious brush of unease. ''Of course. But what about Miss Tyson?''

''What about her?''

''I don't want her left here alone.''

Marco regarded him searchingly. ''You think Max is here for her?''

''Why else would he risk coming here? He could have been in Mexico twenty minutes after the rape.''

''Okay, this shouldn't take long. I'll leave Officer Brawley with her. Let's go.''

Max was sitting behind the base of the pine tree, hidden from the terrace. Every now and then he'd take a quick look to see if they were still there. He might have to wait a couple of hours and it was too uncomfortable to stay up in the tree. In fact, even from ground level, he could just see the tops of their heads, and a short while back Hero had stood up and given the canyon a good once-over, as though he was looking for something. Max couldn't bring himself to believe Hero was looking for him, that Hero suspected he'd come looking for Kate. To Max, no cops meant no suspicion that he was within five hundred miles of Cleves Cottage. No, Hero was merely taking in the view, and everything was cool.

So, he let five, ten minutes go by, thinking about Luke, still struggling with the impossible reality that his friend was dead, thinking about Kate and what he was going to do to her, working up a throbbing blue-vein boner visualizing her stretched out naked on the bed, ankles and wrists tied to the bedposts, and what he'd be doing to her, then ducked his head around the tree and saw—

Nothing.

Nothing?

He shot to his feet, heart pumping, the binoculars trained on the terrace, cursing himself for daydreaming. How long had it been since he'd last looked? Ten, fifteen minutes? Asshole. They could've been gone fifteen minutes, be in fucking Malibu by now.

So, calm down, go take a look. Maybe it was better if they *had* left the house, give him a chance to scout it, find a neat hiding place, a bedroom closet, maybe! He chuckled, finding the picture hilarious. There she'd be, locking her bedroom door, shutting the bad world out for the night, taking off her clothes, walking around the bedroom ass-naked, maybe eyeballing her cute body in the closet mirror, saying to herself, ''Hey, not bad, Kate, old girl, nice slim hips and good, good tits,'' and then slowly, slowly the closet door would swing open and there he'd be, grinning like a loony, saying from the shadows, ''Surprise, surprise!''

Man, would she die.

Yessir, she certainly would die.

He loved it. Please God, let it be just like that, and I'll never ask another favor the rest of my life, okay?

He stood up and started across the canyon.

Lieutenant Marco gestured to a chair. "Would you like coffee? I can't recommend it—except as rocket fuel."

Raven smiled. "No, thanks."

He felt uncomfortable in Marco's office, in the police station. Through the glass partition he studied the huge room, occupied by shirt-sleeved men he presumed were detectives, who were sitting at metal desks and walking around, some talking to people who might be witnesses or suspects and some typing reports. On the walls of the room were all kinds of notices and photographs and composites of people wanted for various offenses. Murder, it seemed, was a front-runner for L.A.'s most popular crime.

Raven felt ill at ease with the ambience of the room. Like a radio picking up a squall of nerve-grating static he was assailed by an onslaught of negative vibrations. Nothing specific, but a general feeling of sordidness, paucity of human spirit. But what did he expect? In this room had sat countless murderers, rapists, armed robbers, drug pushers, people so devoid of compassion and dignity they didn't deserve the appellation "human being." Nor that of "animal." Certainly not that. So, what were they?

"You feeling all right?" asked Marco, seated behind his desk.

Raven turned to face him. "Why do you ask?"

"The room getting to you? My wife won't come in here, it makes her feel sick."

"She sounds a highly sensitive lady. I'd like to meet her sometime."

"You ever do any police work?"

Raven shook his head.

Marco toyed with a pencil, pushing it through his fingers. "Not too many police officers welcome psychic assistance. If the psychic fails, it makes the cop look like a fool for believing. If the psychic succeeds, it makes the police look inept. I'm not one of those cops. We have so many unsolved crimes in this division, I welcome all the help I can get. You see those mug shots and composites on the wall out there? Every one represents an unsolved crime—a murderer or whatever still on the loose, a conscienceless, lawless, black-hearted son of a bitch who right at this moment might be doing again what he's already wanted for. If I can prevent it happening, I'll take all the help I can get from any source—including psychic sensitivity. Mind if I ask what your particular talent is?"

Raven experienced the familiar rush of aversion to the question, the intuitive urge to deflect it. In the past it had been asked by far more skeptics than believers, by ridiculers poised to mock. In addition he had a lifetime of Rom caution to contend with. But this man Marco was different, his query genuine, his interest sincere. The silent voice of instinct told Raven something was happening between himself and Marco, that he should do this thing.

Holding out his hand, he said, "May I have your pencil?"

Marco gave it to him, watched as Raven held it, stroked it, ran it between his fingers as Marco had been doing.

Raven's gaze became fixed upon the surface of the desk. The light of conscious awareness faded from his eyes, replaced by the unblinking glaze of trance, of meditation.

After several silent moments, Raven spoke, his voice a dark, husky rumble. "I feel pain . . . right leg. I see mountains. Snow. You are skiing . . . falling." Raven closed his eyes. "Bad fall. Your leg is broken. Bone sticking through the skin." Raven's breathing rate increased.

His face began to distort. Sweat broke out on his forehead. Now his hands were trembling, his breathing became labored. "Danger. I see a dark passageway . . . old tenement building. There is a shadow . . . a man." He gasped, jerked, clutched at his right shoulder. "You've been shot . . . here . . . small-caliber bullet."

Marco turned white as a sheet and whispered, "Jesus."

Raven drew a deep breath, opened his eyes, blinked, returned the pencil to Marco, saying nothing.

The lieutenant gave an astounded laugh. "Psychometry. Boy, I could use you around here. Listen, why aren't you making a fortune in Hollywood? With your looks and talent . . ." Marco dismissed his own question with a wave of his hand. "I'll demonstrate my own telepathic talent by answering for you." He grinned mischievously. "Actually, there's nothing telepathic about it. It'll be the same answer my wife gave me. She wouldn't touch the West Coast psychic circus with a tent pole, wouldn't want to be identified with the regiment of con artists who pass for psychics in this town. Also, she believes if she uses her gift to make money, she'll lose it—right?"

"I've never considered it, Lieutenant. I know about the L.A. psychic scene, but it's never interested me. I have a well-paid and interesting research job at the Alcott Institute in Kansas City and—"

A rap on the open door interrupted him. A young, burly, red-haired detective in shirt sleeves, carrying a sheet of computer printout, entered.

Marco said, "Bill, say hello to John Raven. This is Detective Frazer."

Raven shook the big man's hand. "Nice to m . . ."

Frazer waited, frowning, puzzled by Raven's staring expression. He laughed uncertainly. "What's the matter, I got pizza on my chin?"

"Don't buy it."

"Huh?" Frazer shot a glance at Marco, found his lieutenant looking at Raven and grinning with secret knowledge.

"Listen to the man," Marco advised the detective.

"Don't buy what?" Frazer grimaced at Raven.

"The car."

Frazer gaped. "How did you . . . oh, hey, you heard me on the phone, right? I was just talking to the guy."

Raven shook his head. "No."

"Then how . . . ?"

"Are you thinking of buying a car, Bill?" asked Marco, holding out his hand for the computer sheets. "What you got there?"

"Well, yeah, I met this guy . . ."

"He's not what he seems," said Raven. "Get the car checked thoroughly."

"It's been checked," protested Frazer. "It's in A-one condition."

"No, it isn't," Raven insisted. "Check it again. And check out the guy as well."

Frazer stood, nonplussed.

Marco suddenly got excited. "Listen to this," Marco said to Raven. "We're getting cross-country reaction to the flyer. We asked for razor kills with a *Z* mutilation and so far we've got ten!"

Raven grimaced. *"Ten."*

"In date-of-discovery order they go El Paso, Abilene, Shreveport, Mobile, Tampa, Daytona Beach, Pittsburgh, Detroit, Chicago, Kansas City."

Raven closed his eyes. "Any same-day kills?"

Marco scanned the printout. "No."

"It has to be Max and Luke. They were traveling counterclockwise around the country. El Paso was the first, hmm?"

"The first to be discovered."

"What I'd do," Raven suggested, "is get autopsy reports from these places, find out how soon after death the bodies were discovered. That'll give you an accurate order of killing. My guess is those psychos made no attempt to hide their victims, so the order of killing ought to match the order of discovery. That being so, they started in El Paso. Why El Paso? Neither of the men had Texas accents. Either the El Centro police or the FBI should have traced Luke Shand's background by now—they've certainly got his picture and fingerprints. I'd advise them to start looking for a connection between Luke and Max in El Paso. There has to be a reason why both of them were there at the same time. Did they meet casually in a bar, start talking over a drink, and decide it'd be fun to go around the country mutilating people with a razor? If I had something of Shand's—an item of clothing—maybe I could pick something up about him."

Marco nodded. "I'll get Plaidy to send a few things up. Meanwhile, I think the El Paso angle's a good idea." To Frazer he said, "Get on it, Bill. Contact the El Paso PD, see if they've got anything on Luke Shand. Then call Plaidy."

"Will do." Frazer gave Raven a bemused parting look. "You're sure about the car, huh? It's a beauty—a four-point-two Jag."

"You buy it, you'll regret it."

Frazer glanced at the lieutenant, heaved a disconsolate shrug, muttered his thanks, and left.

"Trouble is," said Raven, "he'll never know for sure."

Marco shook his head in wonderment. "John, how d'you do it?"

Raven answered pensively, "I can't explain it. It just—comes. It's a mental image, but not quite. Or a head voice, but something more. Who can define the form and substance of a thought? Can you explain the process when you get a hunch?''

"No. Is this the kind of stuff you research at the Institute?''

"We test for every form of psi talent.''

"No wonder you find it interesting. I could really get into it. Maybe I'll give up police work and . . .''

"No, you won't.''

Marco laughed. "No, I won't. But maybe I could do something about combining the two.'' He glanced toward the outer room. "Here comes Joe for the composite. I'll leave you two alone.'' He stood up. "Listen, thanks for the help on the El Paso thing. I've got a feeling you could be on to something.''

Raven grinned. "There you are, you see—you're psychic too. Everyone is.''

"Sure. And there are a lot of fiddle players in the world, but not too many Paganinis.''

The canyon was easy, good finger- and toeholds all the way up, bushes and rocks and trees for cover. Max wondered how many of these houses got hit from the canyon. Maybe not many because of the difficulty of quick getaway. All the homes would be alarmed, with invisible rays connected silently to the local cop shop. Trip one of those mothers and the next thing there'd be ten black-and-whites waiting at the front gate as you came out, a helicopter hovering up there if you took the canyon route. Sneaky bastards, the rich.

How could a guy make an honest killing with all this high-tech security shit around?

Well, *he* could make an honest killing, even two, he thought, chuckling at the joke. Yessir. Because he was doing it the bold way, in broad daylight with the folks at home. People didn't switch on alarms when they were at home, and they didn't expect guys coming over the canyon wall while the sun was shining. He couldn't wait to see their faces when he popped up out of nowhere and hit Hero with the Blade of Zorro.

He paused to catch his breath and looked up. Nearly there. The terrace wall, built of gray artificial stone, grew out of the natural rock, six feet above his head to the capping stone, though on the other side the wall would be only three feet high—waist-high on Hero—so there'd be no noise-making long drop to contend with.

He looked along the wall for some cover once he got his head above the capping stone, and found a flowering shrub growing out over the wall that would do nicely.

His heart accelerated as he dug a Nike into a crevice and hauled himself up another two feet, then found a niche and went up again, reaching way up and getting his fingers over the capping stone directly beneath the shrub.

Slowly now, doing it right, fighting the urge to rush up and over and get into it, he raised himself up until his eyes were level with the top of the wall. Peering around the shrub, his first sight of the house, its closeness, its sumptuousness, sent a wave of excitement through him. Jesus, there had to be good pickings here . . . money, jewelry, antiques, checkbooks, plastic. And a car out front. Yeah, everything. After he'd finished Kate and Hero, he'd take his time, go through the house, load a pile of stuff into the car and head down to Mexico. This was his lucky day, he knew it. Maybe Luke's spirit had guided him here, had told him to go after the bitch instead of heading straight for Mexico. If it was you, Luke, thanks, he thought. Because this is *the* perfect scam.

Up to this moment he'd given no conscious thought to the possibility that there might be other people in the house. Now, seeing the close reality of it, its size, he was struck by doubt that it belonged to Katherine Anne Tyson.

She was too fucking young to own such a place. So, whose was it? Her old man's?

A fresh flood of adrenaline surged through him as he conjured up a vision of maybe four, five, six people in the house. Maybe servants, too! Hey, what did we *have* here? Images of the possibilities tumbled feverishly through his mind. That multiple-murder case that shocked the world a few years back happened right here in L.A., in Hollywood . . . the actress Sharon Tate and her buddies . . . that mad asshole Charlie Manson butchered a bunch of them . . .

Now, wouldn't that be somethin'—another shocker for the world. Four, five, six people die in a Manson-type slaughter in beautiful downtown Brentwood Park. Except it wouldn't be Charlie this time. It would be Max Koenig. How's *that* for a monument, Luke? The whole fucking world would know about it!

There—it was decided. No matter how many people were in the house, they were all going to die.

His heart took a tumble. There was movement inside the house. Somebody had come into the kitchen. Jesus, it was Kate! Look at her, not thirty feet away, so beautiful in her titty T-shirt, standing right there at the window filling the coffee jug.

Where was Hero?

He'd be back there on the cool side of the house, slumped on a sofa, watching TV.

But, hey—if Kate was making the coffee, there couldn't be any servants, right? When you were this rich, you didn't make coffee yourself, huh? So maybe there weren't any servants. Maybe there wasn't any family. Maybe it was just Kate and Hero. And maybe you'd better get over the wall and find out, asshole, or you'll still be hanging here thinking come Christmas.

The door into the kitchen was at the side of the house,

to his right. Keeping an eye on all that plate glass at the back of the house, he waited until Kate left the kitchen, then quickly slipped over the wall and ran across the terrace to the door. He turned the knob, eased it open, stepped inside and stood listening, his senses raw, every nerve in his body zinging, his heart trying to break out of his chest.

Silence. Not a fucking sound.

His eyes ranged around the room. Except in the movies, he'd never seen such a kitchen. It looked unused, unreal. In the far wall he could just see a partly opened door, leading into a hallway. On Nike tiptoes, he crossed the kitchen and stood behind the door, his ear angled to the opening.

A voice.

Kate's voice. Distant. Indistinct. From a room across the hall.

Another voice. A man's deep rumble, no more than a murmur. Hero.

Max slid the razor from his pocket. He opened the blade, kissed its surface, grinning inanely, breathless with excitement now, blood pounding in his heart and head, guts churning. How would he play it? Tear across the hall into the room, hit Hero where he stood, sat, whatever, stun them both with his speed, with shock? Or wait for one or both of them to come into the kitchen?

His gaze went to the coffee percolator, plugged in, red light on, by the sink. Kate would come for it. He didn't want that. He'd have to lay her out, maybe make a noise, warn Hero. He wanted Hero first, get him out of the way, then take his fuckin' sweet time with Kate.

The first way was the best. Go in there now, fast, shock the shit outta them. Right!

But it didn't work out that way.

Suddenly Kate's voice was getting louder. She was coming into the hall from that far room. No talking now, just footsteps.

Max eased behind the door, slipped the razor back into his pocket, took a stance, ready to grab her with one hand, belt her senseless with the other.

He waited.

What the *fuck*? No more footsteps. A door in the hallway closed.

Nonplussed, he peered around the kitchen door. No Kate. The hall was empty. He saw other doors. Where in hell had she gone?

The john?

One of those doors was a toilet.

Perfect!

The Lord—and Luke—was on his side.

Get in *now* and fix Hero.

Geared for an instant kill, adrenaline and insane hatred flooding his system, Max burst into the library, prepared to move in any direction, knowing Hero would be paralyzed by shock, incapable of any action during the time it took to reach him.

But it was Max who suffered paralysis.

Four strides into the room he came to a mortified halt. Sitting there on the sofa was not Luke's killer, Hero, but—

Holy shit!

A uniformed cop!

They stared at one another.

Officer Brawley, ten years on the force, made a swift appraisal of the guy—six-four, blond hair, built like a bull—took in his demeanor, analyzed his expression, computed his intention, now saw the open razor, realized with blood-freezing awareness that the impossible was happening, and reached reflexively for his gun.

The movement jerked Max from his stupor. In two strides and a leap he cleared the end of the sofa, landed on it, crashed into the cop who was halfway to his feet, and fell sprawled on top of him on the floor.

Max saw only a face, a throat. He had to die. His right hand came down. But something got in the way. Blood spurted from the cop's left wrist, splashed down into the cop's face as he fought left-handed to defend himself from the terrifying blade, his right hand trapped at his side, still grasping the gun butt.

Brawley groaned, pleaded, "Christ, no . . ."

Max struck again . . . and again, slashing uniform, dueling with the limb until muscle and tendon severed and the arm flopped down onto the carpet like a dead fish.

There.

Good-bye, friendly neighborhood pig.

Behind him, over the sounds of his own raucous breathing and the rattling, bubbling, throat-cut noise the cop was making, Max heard an outcry of horror that could only mean Kate had returned.

He sprang to his feet.

She was in the doorway, paralyzed, stone-stunned with shock and horror.

He grinned. "Hi, Kate. I've come for you. Where's the asshole who killed Luke? Where's . . ."

With a piercing cry she turned and ran into the hall, mindless with panic, primal instinct turning her toward the stairs, urging her to climb, to get high into the trees, away from the predator. She raced up them, driven by terror, senseless to everything but the next step and the next step, so many of them, so many of them she'd never make it but suddenly she was on the landing and running along it, reaching her door, smashing through it into the safety of her room, marveling that she'd made it, that he hadn't caught her, almost convulsing with shock and disbelief.

Looking up from the hall, Max made a note of the room

Kate had run into but had other things on his mind. She'd keep.

Hero.

He had to find that bastard and put him away. Where could he be? What was the cop doing there?

Standing there, instinct told him Hero wasn't in the house. Christ, there'd been enough noise. Somehow the cop had replaced him. In the short time between seeing Hero on the terrace and now, there'd been a switch. Why? It couldn't have been a trap. They'd been expecting him; there'd be a dozen cops here and he'd be dead.

So—what?

Figure it out. Like Luke would do.

The cop came to the house. How? A step into the library and a glance through the front windows showed him there was no patrol car there.

Cops don't walk in L.A., he knew that from TV.

So, a squad car had dropped the cop here . . . and taken Hero away?

Why?

To question him?

What about?

About yesterday. About El Centro.

Why should the L.A. cops be in on that?

Just keeping tabs, maybe, on Kate . . . and on Hero, Luke's killer.

Or—

His mind working now—

Or they'd found that black gix and her pimp in Hollywood, razor-cut, and were putting a few things together.

He looked at the bloody razor in his hand. Maybe using it, the Mark of Zorro thing, wasn't smart anymore. It'd been fine as long as Luke and he didn't leave witnesses, no one to link it to them. But in El Centro they'd left witnesses. Hero and Kate. And maybe right now Hero was . . .

A white light blinked on a telephone at the end of the sofa. He stared at it. Then—

Shit!

He ran and made a grab for the receiver, hearing Kate's sobs as she punched out the number.

Grinning, thanking his luck he'd stayed in the room instead of being up there kicking her door down right now, he said, "LAPD, Captain Koenig here, what can I do for you, sweetass?"

He got a big kick out of her scream before he tore the phone out of the wall.

So—okay.

Hero was out to lunch and there was nobody else in the house.

Except Katherine Anne.

Again he regarded the razor.

"Just one more time, Luke, then we'll put old Zorro into retirement."

Leaving the library, he started up the stairs.

"The eyes still aren't right," Raven said. "They were narrower, colder. I don't know, maybe the shape is right but the killer quality is missing. Can you do a killer quality?"

Joe, the composite compiler, selecting another transparency, said, "One of these days someone will invent a method of photographing a witness's memory, then we'll be getting somewhere."

Raven was about to tell him this had already been done in experiments in Thought Photography at the Institute when Lieutenant Marco entered the office, beaming, brandishing more computer printouts.

"Give that man a cigar. You were right on the money,

John. I've been speaking to Plaidy. The FBI ran Luke Shand and came up with a dishonorable discharge following a spell in the army brig in El Paso for knifing a sergeant. On your suggestion I pushed the Luke/Max linkup in El Paso and, whaddya know, one Max *Koenig* escaped from the brig two days after Shand was released—and on the same day as the first razor killing.''

Marco seated himself, opened the printouts. ''Joe, we can scrap this, the army is telexing a mug shot of Koenig from their records any time now.''

Joe shrugged at Raven, gathered up his equipment, and left.

Marco, studying the printouts, grimaced and shook his head. ''Two more victims have come through that fit into the killing timetable: a woman in Denver, a couple of days before they hijacked the bus, and a second victim in El Paso, date of death unknown. The body of the Reverend Wesley Parker was found decomposed in the Finlay Mountains, but razor slashes in the clothing link this one to Shand and Koenig, too.'' Marco stared pensively at the printout. ''Interesting pattern. The first two victims were men, all the rest women. Why?''

''Who was the first?''

Marco shuffled the sheets. ''A guy named Dowson, owned a gents' outfitters, Macho Modes, in El Paso.''

''Clothing. Max escaped from the brig, he'd be wearing prison garb. He'd need civvies fast.''

Marco nodded. ''Right. Of course. And the Reverend?''

''How did the killers get from El Paso into the Finlay Mountains? Even money it was in the Reverend's car.''

Marco grinned. ''John, how about we do a swap? You stay here and level L.A.'s crime mountain, I'll go study psychic phenomena at your institute.'' Slowly Marco lost his grin. "Maybe I'm not kidding—not about the first part. You planning to stay long in L.A.?"

Raven shook his head. "No. I've got things to do near San Diego. I plan going down there . . ."

Kat.

"I plan going . . . down there . . . tomorrow . . ."

Kat!

A voice. Her voice. Calling his name. There in his head. Marco was staring at him.

Sweat broke out on Raven's face. Icy fingers touched his neck. He shivered.

Marco asked worriedly, "John, are you all right?"

"Call the house," Raven grated. "The Tyson house."

Marco reacted instantly, asking as he located Kat's number in his notebook, "What is it, John? You picking something up?"

Raven's eyes were shut tight. His face was contorted, breathing labored. "She's—in trauma. She's terrified. Something bad is happening there."

Marco stabbed out the number, listened, slammed the receiver down, and jumped to his feet. "Line's disconnected. Come on."

Raven stood. "No! Get your nearest patrol car there fast as they can. Tell them to use their siren. Tell them to break down the Tyson gate, ram through it, anything, get in there fast."

Marco winced. "John, private property . . ."

"Just do it! I'll pay for any damage. Goddamn it, Lieutenant, *do* it!"

"JOHHHNNNN!"

Max heard the desperate cry, its volume, though not its searing poignancy, stifled by the stout oak bedroom door. Hey, how Luke would've dug hearing this one externalizing. How very right that one of the best should be the last—and should be the bitch who had cause Luke to die.

Trouble with so many of the others was you couldn't allow them to externalize too loud, either because it was outdoors and you didn't know who might be passing by, or because of the neighbors. The black chick in Daytona had been an exception, but he reckoned Kate was going to run a close second. Yeah, Katherine Anne was going to be a prizewinner, a blue-ribbon screamer, tearing her throat raw in this big old empty house before he cut it.

Grinning, fizzing inside with excitement, he scratched on the door with the razor. "Johnnie's not here, Kate . . . only big bad Max. Open up, sweetheart, I've got something real nice for you!"

Another scream. Pure, vibrant terror. Great. She was paying for her crime. But was going to pay a whole lot more. Everything.

"Open the door, Kate." Soothing, playful. "Come on, sweets, you *know* you're gonna die, why not get it over with quickly?"

He tried the doorknob, knowing it would be locked, put his shoulder to the oak paneling, and gave it a shove. Tough mother. He stepped back and drove his foot into the top right panel. It was like kicking steel plate. The place was built like a frigging castle.

"Open up, Kate! Hey, don't even think about jumping out of the window, huh? It's a long drop. You'd break your legs, an' I don't want damaged goods, you hear me?"

Something solid bumped against the door. Christ, she was piling furniture against it. He had to do something. He looked along the landing, saw the fire extinguisher, a gold one to match the decor, on the wall at the far end. He ran for it, released it from its bracket, came back and rammed it against the door panel.

Better.

Three, four more blows. Better still. The panel split. Another couple of good ones and half the panel tilted inward but came to rest against something, a chest, pressing against the door. He slid his hand into the gap, pushed against the piece with his fingertips, but couldn't get enough leverage.

Shit.

"Hey, come on, let me in, bitch! You're makin' this worse for yourself. You don't open this door, I'm *really* gonna hurt you!"

He went back to the battering ram, attacking the door with maniacal anger.

Every shattering, splintering blow resonated through Kat's head with such intensity she thought her brain would explode. Clamping her hands over her ears had no effect. She stood in the center of the room, watching the two three-drawer chests, which she'd piled one on top of the other, shift precariously with every blow. Soon the top one would fall. His face would be there. His razor. She would stand helplessly and watch him batter out the remaining panel, climb into the room, taunting her all the while, telling her what he was going to do. And then . . .

She couldn't let it happen.

But what else could she do?

He was right about the window. If she jumped, she probably would break her legs—and have to lie there helpless while he killed her.

She could attack him as he climbed through the door. With what? A hairbrush, for Crissake? If she had a knife . . . if she had a gun . . .

If . . . if . . . if . . .

None of these were rational thoughts. They were fleeting fragments, subliminal flashes through a mind paralyzed with terror, desperate survival urges from an increasingly despairing subconscious. But to no avail. She knew she was doomed. Knew she was going to die. Knew all she could do was stand there and watch it happen.

And yet . . .

When the top chest finally teetered, tipped, crashed to the floor, when he was revealed in the broken doorway, his face a mask of murderous jubilation, she snapped from her trance, gathered herself, and screamed out *his* name in a storm of belief and pleading and defiance.

"JOHHHNNNN!"

And again as tears streamed down her face contorted with the torment of terror.

"JOHHHNNNN . . . *HELP ME*!"

And with a wracking sob sank, kneeling, to the floor.

Leaning in through the broken door, elbows resting on the lower chest, leering, enjoying it now, Max knew he had it all, could take his time and play with it. He ogled her beautiful breasts and her slender thighs in the skintight jeans and said in a quiet, croaky voice, "Kate, honey, that weird boyfriend of yours ain't here to help you this time. *Max* is here to help you. Look, I'm coming in right now. See—I'm putting one leg inside the door. Now the other one. Hey, Kate, would you believe this—I'm right here in your bedroom! Bet in your wildest dreams you never thought one day I'd be standing right here in your bedroom, huh? Nice room, Kate. Nice house. Rich folks, huh? Your daddy's rich an' your momma's good lookin' . . ."

Kate screamed as he grabbed her hair and wrenched her head upright, exposing her throat.

"Look at me, bitch, when I'm talkin' to you!"

She stared up into the face of insanity, the razor there, inches from her eyes.

"You killed Luke!" he screamed at her, stunning her with sound. "You and the prick! The best friend I ever

142

had. You think I'm gonna let you get away with that? Huh? *Huh*? You think I'm not gonna make you *pay*?''

Releasing her hair, he grabbed the neck of her T-shirt, pulled it away from her body, and with a terrifying downward stroke slashed the cloth to her navel.

The shocking nearness of the blade sent Kat into hysterics.

Max slapped her hard. "Shut the fuck up!" He hauled her to her feet. "Get naked and on the bed. DO IT! NOW!"

His push threw her across the room. She hit the bed and sank to her knees, gasping for air, dizzy with terror, close to unconsciousness. She clung there, expecting the follow-up: a punch, a kick, more verbal abuse. Then gradually, mystified, she became aware that his attention had been distracted. With disbelief, she slid a glance in his direction, found him rooted, facing the door, braced in an alarmed, listening attitude.

Something had frightened him.

Now she also heard it . . . the distant wail of a police siren!

Hope flooded through her. The prospect of survival galvanized her. She sprang up and rushed for the bathroom door, knowing the door was flimsy, knowing the lock would never hold against a determined assault, but knowing, praying, this animal was fast running out of time.

Over the slamming of the door she heard his roar of fury, then a silence that seemed to convey, to her, his indecision. Through it came the siren, steadily louder, closer to the house, but how could they have gotten through the locked gates?

She knelt, too weak to stand, stared unseeing at the door, sobbing softly, shaking uncontrollably, listening, not comprehending, incredulous.

A timeless time passed. In the silence she drifted mentally. What had happened to her? Had she fainted here in her bathroom? What year was it? Were Mom and Dad and Rick downstairs? Surely it had all been a dream?

Then, glancing down, she touched the raw edge of her severed shirt and knew the truth.

His silence tortured her nerves like fingernails sliding down slate. She pressed her ear to the door, heard movement, the rustle of . . . bed sheets? A window opening?

Silence.

The sound of distant shouting . . . male voices . . . down in the hall. Her heart gushed with relief. But still she remained there, fearing a trick, that Max would be outside the door, waiting to grab her, use her as a hostage.

Now a gruff male voice from the direction of her bedroom door. "Al! Open window here . . . sheet tied to the rad! Get around back! Where the fuck's that backup? We need a chopper in the canyon!"

And then—

Climbing-through-the-door sounds. Closet doors wrenched open. Footsteps outside the bathroom door. The knob turning, the door tried.

"This is the police! Who's in there? Open the door. Come on out, hands behind your head."

Kat cried out, "It's me! Katherine Tyson!"

"Okay, open the door. Come out on yuh hands and knees."

She almost burst into hysterical laughter. She couldn't have stood if she'd wanted to.

She unlocked the door, pulled it open. Shock slammed at her. There was nobody there. For a nightmare moment she knew it had been a trick. He'd lured her out. She'd fallen for . . .

Suddenly he was there in front of her—a uniformed cop, frozen in firing stance, geared to shoot.

He snapped, "You alone?"

She managed a nod.

"Come on out."

She crumpled to the floor and he went in over her, slamming the door back, ripping away the shower curtain, only then allowing himself to become aware of her condition.

"Jesus Christ . . . are you all right?"

He helped her to stand, drew her to the bed, then moved quickly to the window, looked out, called down. "Al—any sign?"

Kat stared and rocked, hugged the T-shirt to her breasts, listened to the thunder of her heartbeat, hearing also now the crescendo of brutal, wonderful sound as car after car sirened up to the house and men moved quickly about and shouted to one another.

"You got a key for this door, Miss Tyson?"

She fumbled, then produced it from her pocket. The cop moved the chest and opened the door, then went out.

Moments later someone entered the room, breathless.

"Kat."

At the sound of his voice she looked up.

Raven held out his arms and she came up into them, letting go the tears in an explosive, racking sob.

Chapter Nine

Within twenty-four hours Kat was back on the freeway, heading for San Diego, floating in a waking dream of déjà vu, same rented car, the ocean now on her right, Raven beside her, a Max Koenig nightmare again behind her. So fragile was her hold on reality that every now and then she felt compelled to reach out and touch something solid—the seat upholstery, the door handle—to reassure herself that she was who she was and where she was and with whom, and not about to waken from all this safe security and gaze up into the face of the psychopath who was raping her and about to end her life. Inwardly she prayed *pleaseGodpleaseGodpleaseGod, let this be real.* And quite calmly she wondered whether she was losing her mind.

If it had not been for this man on her left—provided *he* was real—she was convinced she would, by now, either be dead or lying monstrously sedated in a Totally Mad ward of a Psychiatric Hospital for Eternal Incurables, never to be heard of or from again. For the second time in forty-eight hours John Raven had saved her life, and for the second time he had used his psychic powers to rescue her from the brink of a breakdown, and the odds against that happening, against the very human *possibility* of it happening, were so high that even his hypnotic ministrations left room for doubt that she was not right now in that Totally Mad ward or lying under Max the Maniac.

PleaseGodpleaseGodpleaseGod, let this—and him—be real.

In the kitchen of the house Lieutenant Marco, that nice man, had questioned her gently about all that had happened, and at one point had asked, in a tone that was somehow different, more personal, somehow more intrigued than officially inquiring, "Miss Tyson, this may seem an odd question, but can you remember, at any time during your ordeal, appealing to John for help, consciously reaching out to him?"

She had answered, "Yes. When Max Koenig was breaking down the door. I'm sure I called John's name. He'd helped me before. I guess he was the only person I could think of."

Marco said in a way that made her shiver, "He heard you."

"Heard me?"

"He picked up on your terror, knew you were in desperate trouble. He insisted we smash the gates open. He saved your life."

Awed, she had whispered, "For the second time."

The lieutenant smiled. "I guess he's doubly responsible for you now. You know what the Chinese say about a life saved."

She shook her head. "I won't see him after today. He has important business in San Diego."

Saying it, the prospect of separation again afflicted her with a feeling of emptiness.

But it was, so gratefully, short-lived.

A while later, Raven came into the kitchen, cutting short Lieutenant Marco, who was telling her he'd leave a policewoman and a male officer with her until Max Koenig was caught. "Lieutenant, under any circumstances I don't think Miss Tyson should stay here."

"I'm inclined to agree," Marco said. "But what's the alternative? Miss Tyson, is there anywhere else you can—"

And Raven had said, "I have to go down to Live Oak Springs. Miss Tyson knows about it. If she'd care to, she can come with me."

If she'd care to!

The offer transformed her state of mind. Raven's presence did this to her. She wondered and marveled at the effect he had upon her. It was as though with a word, a look, a gesture he could erase bad pictures from her memory and supplant good ones. Pondering his power over her, she was aware of an increasing inclination to think of him, with his dark good looks and hypnotic eyes, as a benign Rasputin, and felt empathy with Tsarina Alexandra, who fell under the sway of the infamous Siberian mystic.

Not that there was anything sinister about John Raven. She knew he would never use his powers to take advantage of her—or anyone else. And yet the very presence of that power was sufficient to set up in her a tingle of—what? Apprehension? As a child she'd been taken to the zoo, had stood close to the tiger cage and watched a big cat lope lazily back and forth along the wire fence. Though it had offered no overt sign of aggression, the tiger had radiated such innate power and potential threat that Kat had stepped back involuntarily and hidden behind her mother's skirt. Her reaction to Raven was not dissimilar: attraction mixed with apprehension.

Kissinger said power was the ultimate aphrodisiac.

He might well be right.

Raven said softly, "Penny for 'em."

Fearing he had read her thoughts, she felt the start of an embarrassing blush and battled to restrain it. "I . . . was thinking about you."

148

"Oh?" He gave her a whimsical smile.

"Lieutenant Marco told me what happened in his office—that you . . . heard me call out to you."

"I sensed something," he conceded.

"It must have been more than something. You insisted he smash the gates open. You must have been very sure."

A frown clouded his brow. "It wasn't just that moment. I'd had a bad feeling about Max since we arrived at the house. I didn't like that canyon."

She nodded. "I remember—early morning, I saw you looking down into it. Then, later, when we were talking, you broke off and went to stand by the wall. I thought you were listening, but you were looking."

He smiled. "Listening, looking, sensing, it's all the same."

She laughed. "To you."

He shrugged. "It's all vibration. Electromagnetism and vibration. The kids in the sixties had it right with their 'good vibes' and 'bad vibes,' though most of them didn't know physiologically what was happening. We are electromagnetic creatures. *You* are a power plant of fizzing, sparking electrical connections. You have a force field. You respond to the earth's electromagnetic field. And the sun's. You are also a tuning fork that resonates to the vibrations of the universe. You respond to the gravitational pull of the moon. You are sixty percent water. If the moon can lift the oceans away from the skin of the earth, imagine what it does to your blood and the water in your body.

"You are also a living, breathing radio receiver. Every moment of your life you are being bombarded with signals—electromagnetic waves and vibrations. You are being hit by so much stuff right now that if your conscious mind didn't filter it out you'd go stark staring mad. Fortunately, nature is conservative. What it doesn't need, it shuts down. We come back to what I said about people being numbed out. We no longer need keen senses to see and smell and hear our sources of food or our enemies, so nature has taken the edge off. Compared to dogs, cats, birds we are practically senseless. And the same applies to ESP abilities like telepathy and psychometry. It's *there*, Kat, in you, in all human beings. But in most it's dormant. All it needs is rekindling.''

"But *how*?" she asked with a laugh. "I mean, I'd *love* to have your gifts . . ."

"By practice. And most of all by *belief* that you already possess the gifts. I'll give you a for-instance. A while back I took a vacation in Africa, a photographic safari in Kenya. Now, some of my senses might be better developed than most people's, but my eyes I never use, right? Who needs eyes at the Alcott Institute?

"There I was, out in the bush in a VW wagon with five people and the courier, an English guy, who kept saying, 'Look, folks, over there—a rhino, a buffalo, a lion, a warthog,' whatever. And we couldn't *see* anything. It was all just a mess of bushes and undergrowth and stuff. The courier laughed and told us, 'Give it time. In three or four days you'll have your "game eyes" and you'll be spotting things before I do.' And he was right. For the first time in our lives we had to really *use* our eyes, to look instead of merely seeing, and by the fourth day I could tell a lion from a bush at half a mile. And it's the same with all our senses. What you've got to do is wake them up again.''

Kat said, "Well, that's easy enough to understand when it applies to one of the normal senses, like eyesight, but telepathy and psychometry and precognition are not *normal*—oh, God, you've got that look on your face again—but you know what I mean. They're regarded as *para*normal.''

"Yes, they are, but wrongly so, by people who don't believe they exist in every human being. Belief is everything. I wish you could witness some of the things that happen at the Institute—especially with kids. Before they become numbed, polluted by adult disbelief and disapproval, most children are psychically sensitive. Their senses are fresh; they have no inhibitions about using and demonstrating them. I've worked with kids who can *feel* colors, can differentiate them with their fingertips, who can *see* while blindfolded, who are incredibly telepathic. They have to be. Life to them is a new and bewildering experience. A child too young to communicate by language does so by telepathy. The young function at a far more intense sensory level. And they haven't yet learned to doubt their capabilities.''

Kat was nodding acquiescently. "It doesn't take long, hmm?''

"No. And it's happening more and more quickly. Noise is the killer. Noise is vibration. TV, radio, cassette players, discos . . . they assault the mind, numb the senses. How can people hear themselves with all that crap and racket battering at them all the time? Why d'you think the great mystics choose to live on silent mountaintops?''

Kat nodded. "Of all the so-called psychic phenomena I think I can most easily accept telepathy. I mean, I can *just* see myself, with practice, being able to do it. But the other stuff—psychometry and precognition and psychokinesis— how do you develop that? Where do you start?''

Raven took a moment to study road signs. They were approaching San Diego and he needed to pick up Interstate 8 to Live Oak Springs.

When he had joined the traffic on I-8 he said, "You start with your subconscious mind.''

"Oh?''

He glanced at her with a smile, making it light. "Kat, I'm not going to kid you there's an easy way into this. I don't pretend to know all there is to know about psi phenomena. We're dealing with the human mind, and to date man's knowledge of its miraculous abilities is infinitesimal. Psychology and psychiatry are infant sciences. Most of the orthodox scientific community refuse to investigate psi phenomena, and some scientists even deny its existence.''

She grimaced at him. ''How can they, when people like you can provide so much evidence?''

''They refuse to accept it as 'evidence.' They call it coincidence or ignore it all together.'' He grinned. ''Scientists, as you might by now have gathered, are a funny lot. They're a closed community who protect their reputations fiercely. They're terrified of ridicule, refuse to accept any discovery that isn't replicable—that can't be repeated under so-called controlled conditions. And when you're dealing with the human mind, with something as nebulous as human psychic sensitivity, replicability is difficult, often impossible, to sustain. So, with obvious exceptions like Duke University, investigation is limited to organizations like the Alcott Institute, which is privately funded.

''So, okay, let's take the Alcott Institute. What do we do there and what has been discovered? We test people. We use Zener cards and dice to test for telepathic and precognitive ability. We have a sleep laboratory that explores astral projection. We conduct distant-viewing experiments for telepathy, and run endless tests for metalbending and other psychokinetic talents. We hypnotize people and put them in Faraday cages to exclude electromagnetic influence and wire them up to EEG and EKG machines and countless other bits of hi-tech bullshit. In short, we do our very best to stifle them in as artificial and unnatural an environment as we can and expect them to demonstrate abilities that are intrinsically delicate, sensitive, and spontaneous.''

Kat stared at him, then exploded an incredulous laugh. "Oh, wow. Would it be an understatement to say you sound vaguely disillusioned in your work?"

Raven grinned. "Not with my work. The powers that be just don't understand how the phenomenon works."

Kat nodded her understanding. "But how can they ignore tangible evidence—like metal-bending, for instance?"

Raven laughed wryly. "How can people ignore the cries of an old lady being mugged in the street? They simply do. People believe what they want to believe. If a scientist believes metal-bending is the result of trickery, sleight-of-hand, then that's what it is."

"And what do you think it is, John?"

He shook his head. "I honestly don't know. It could be electromagnetic influence at the atomic or subatomic level, but I'm not sure. Nobody is. All I know is, it happens. When you accept psi phenomena as fact, when you believe all human beings possess the abilities and give yourself *permission* to possess them, then things begin to happen. It all comes down to belief."

"You said I'd have to start with my subconscious mind. . . ."

Raven nodded. "Same thing. You plant the belief in your subconscious, then wait for things to happen."

Kat shook her head, her smile apologetic but dubious. "It surely can't be that simple."

Raven sighed histrionically. "O ye of little faith. Kat, I could talk for ten days straight about the incredible *power* of the subconscious mind, about its control over every cell in the body, about its infallible memory, about things I learned about it from Nanosh and Jack Shanglo and the Rom in Europe involving spells and magic, but we haven't got time. And I believe all we still *do* know about the subconscious is only the tiniest tip of a vast iceberg. But believe this: it is a miraculous facility, a veritable nuclear power plant, waiting to serve us. And all we have to do in order to achieve miracles is learn to harness the power of the subconscious.''

Kat laughed. ''I know, I know—mind over matter. I do believe in that.''

Raven shrugged. ''So—believe in psychic phenomena. Tell yourself over and over: I am psychic. I can communicate telepathically with John Raven's mind, with all minds. Practice. And *believe*. And right now I believe we've reached our destination.''

Up ahead she saw a sign for Live Oak Springs.

Kat sensed a change come over Raven. Gone suddenly the gentle instructor, the hypnotist who, for the duration of the journey, had been working on her mind, distracting it from the horror of yesterday. Raven's thoughts now belonged totally to him. Sitting there, he looked almost as though he had turned to stone, grave with concentration. Kat disliked the eerie sensation of being completely shut out, and found no comfort in her awareness of what the forthcoming meeting with the Indian, Joe Santee, meant to Raven.

Once again, at that moment, she found herself afraid of this complex, different, mystical man.

Chapter Ten

"There."

It was one of the few words Raven had uttered in the past twenty minutes, since they had quit the interstate and driven tortuously along back roads and rural tracks, between stands of pine and bleached desert. Raven followed a map locked in his memory, the details of which appeared to materialize one by one as the relevant geographical feature appeared, confirming the accuracy of his recall.

And now they had arrived, the "there" referring to a sandblasted mailbox at the road's edge, bearing the almost indiscernible name: Santee.

The house, fifty yards back off the graded road, was an adobe flat-roofed dwelling of exceedingly basic construction. To Kat's eye, its features—two small windows and a door—set in the skin-toned mud of the front wall, resembled the physiognomy of an inscrutable Indian, an interpretation, she acknowledged, deriving from her awareness of its occupier's nationality.

The shack, backed distantly by the Cleveland National Forest and surrounded by reaches of flat, inhospitable, almost featureless scrub desert, existed in isolation.

Raven drove into the scrabbly front yard, stopped the car a short distance from the dwelling, and cut the engine. He looked about him, studied the old Chevy pickup parked in the shade of a lean-to attached to the right side of the building. He took his time, getting the feel of the place.

"I'll be okay here," Kat said, rolling down her window, sensing his struggle between his indecision to have her accompany him and his reluctance to leave her alone.

"I don't know this guy," he said, explaining it but knowing she understood.

"That's all right. Go talk to him. Good luck."

He thanked her with a smile, got out of the car.

He was halfway to the door when a dog appeared from the shade of the lean-to. It was big and brutish, a yellow battle-scarred roughneck. It came on slowly toward Raven, its gait stiff, ruff bristling, head lowered, fangs exposed in a truly diabolical snarl, muscles bunched for the charge.

Kat's heart went wild.

Her stark stare flashed between the dog and Raven.

Raven stopped, stood absolutely still.

With stifled breath, Kat watched the confrontation. The dog would surely attack. She felt compelled to do something, open the driver's door, blow the horn, something, yet was frozen by fear and indecision.

Raven appeared inhumanly calm, just standing there, facing the dog, his body poised yet somehow confident, relaxed. In profile, he appeared to be smiling, his expression changing subtly, as the human face does in conversation. Yet she could hear no words.

Her glance went to the dog. Amazingly, a subtle change was taking place in *its* expression. The snarl was less decisive. The animal appeared confused. Its gaze slipped sideways, as though the car suddenly appeared more interesting, and returned to Raven with unmistakably less murderous intention.

Then suddenly, incredibly, it capitulated.

Head lowered, tail wagging boisterously, it advanced on Raven as though greeting a vaguely remembered acquaintance, not too certain but willing to take a chance, sniffing his clothes, his skin, licking his hand, finally giving him the okay and trotting beside him to the door.

Reaching it, he knocked, then turned toward her, grinning, his shrug telling her jokingly: See, that's how easy it is.

Laughing with relief, she gave him a mock-dismissive wave, then saw the door behind him open. The figure was lost in shadow. There was a brief exchange, then Raven stepped inside. The door was closed, the dog left outside.

Kat slid lower in the seat, feeling the heat, turned her face to the open window and stared out at the barren desert, experiencing, in Raven's absence, the encroachment, again, of unreality.

What was she doing here . . . in the front yard of an adobe shack a stone's throw from the Mexican border? Had she yet been home? Was Max real? Was any of it?

Her thoughts drifted, lulled by the warmth and the silence. She thought about Raven, about writing, reviewed the things he'd told her about Nanosh, Jack Shanglo, the Gypsies, about his father and Frank Vollner, and wondered whether she could weave this fascinating weft and warp into an acceptable literary whole. Certainly she could write it from the heart. Nothing she had ever encountered enthralled her as much. Maybe she would go to Europe, research the Rom Raven had traveled with. Maybe . . .

She screamed.

The dog was there, in her face, its huge head filling the open window, drooling and dripping, its great yellow fangs naked and flashing as it filled the car with a horrendous barking cacophony.

Kat hurled herself sideways across the driver's seat, stunned, then terrified, finally this-is-just-too-fucking-much furious, and yelled, "You . . . AAASSS . . . HOLE!" and lashed out at the door with her foot.

A man's voice bellowed from the house. The dog gave her a parting shot and dropped out of sight. The driver's door was wrenched open and she almost fell out.

Raven said imploringly, "Kat, I'm sorry. I was sure he'd accepted us."

"He's accepted *you*!" she pouted, shaking with anger. "How in hell can you *practice* telepathy with a thing that's trying to tear your throat out?"

Raven grinned, finding her fury irresistibly comical. "Maybe he doesn't go for your perfume."

"He sure went for my throat."

"Come on. Santee said to come in the house." He helped her out.

Kat jumped as the dog appeared from around the front of the car.

"Easy," Raven murmured, placing himself between the dog and her. "Stay here."

Though desperate to get back in the car, into the house, anywhere, she stood her ground and watched as Raven approached the dog, stroked it, whispered to it.

After a moment he reached behind him for her hand. "Kat, come here."

"Perhaps you shouldn't use my name. Maybe that's what's doing it."

Raven chuckled. "Red's had a change of heart. He wants to be your friend, don't you, old fellow?"

The dog barked, but his tail was wagging.

"Was that a 'yes'?" Kat asked.

"Unqualified."

She approached hesitantly. Raven took her hand and brought it to the dog's nose. The ferocious killer gazed up at her with dopey brown eyes and slobbered a kissy lick over her hand.

"I don't believe it," she muttered.

Raven stood. "Like I told you, belief is everything.

Come and meet Joe Santee, you'll find him . . . interesting.''

Kat looked at him, hearing uncertainty in his tone, suspicious of the euphemism. ''Interesting?''

He gave a slight shrug, indicating ambivalence. ''I've told him who you are. He's a little odd, but harmless, I think. He's difficult to read.''

Kat smiled to herself. Inscrutable Indian. Maybe she was psychic.

They crossed the yard, Red muzzling Kat's hand as though asking forgiveness.

The interior of the shack was cool but musty, redolent of the desert, a not-unpleasant aroma of warm earth mingled with the fragrance of spices that might have emanated from the kitchen. Kat found herself in a single adobe-walled room with a wooden floor and a ceiling laced with pine poles. To the right was a rudimentary fireplace containing an iron grate and a small pile of split logs. A shotgun hung on nails above a smooth plank mantel. A single iron bed and a rickety pine dresser occupied the left wall. In the center of the room a scrubbed-wood table and four wooden chairs stood on a woven circular Indian rug. The rest of the furniture comprised a pine sideboard on the rear wall and a couple of dilapidated fabric armchairs arranged near the fireplace. There was a bottled-gas camping lantern on the sideboard, and another hanging from a rafter above the table.

In the rear wall, over to the left, was a doorway through which Kat could see, at an angle, part of what was obviously a kitchen of sorts. From it came the hiss of a gas camping stove and the rattle of crockery. She presumed Joe Santee was making coffee. She also presumed, as women must, that there was no indoor plumbing, and sent up a prayer that they wouldn't be there so long she would be forced to use a desert privy.

A second glance around the room told her something about Joe Santee. The place was quite devoid of personal memorabilia. There were no photographs, keepsakes, objets d'art. It was a lonesome house, little more than a cave to shelter a wilderness dweller. Recalling that Raven had told her Santee had been in prison with his father, she saw Santee as the most pitiful of human beings—a penniless, friendless, Indian ex-con, situated so low on the social totem pole as to be, literally, out of sight. Her heart went out to him, as it had to so many in the pueblos. She felt anger at the injustice of it all, at the decimation of a once-proud spirit.

Catching Raven's eye, she saw his empathy, his nod telling her he read her mind and shared her feelings.

Santee came in then, carrying three coffee mugs, pausing for the briefest moment in the doorway to observe Kat, but offering only the slightest expression of greeting before heading for the table with the coffee.

Kat was unnerved by his strangeness in both manner and appearance. She saw a striking man, once handsome, his age unguessable. Six feet tall, he was a physical anomaly, his pallid, care-creased Indian features, dark somber eyes, gray, lank shoulder-length hair, and seemingly spiritless posture at odds with a muscular, almost youthful body clothed in worn blue jeans and a red-check short-sleeved woolen shirt. He was two men in one: a mind upon which time and life had wreaked their havoc; a body they had somehow overlooked.

Kat glanced at Raven. He was studying Santee with intensity, trying to read him, his frown of perplexity indicating a difficulty that mirrored her own.

Santee sat down, cupped his mug of coffee in strong, corded hands, and stared at it. His mental process was impossible to interpret. He might have been gathering his thoughts concerning Raven's visit or simply staring, entranced by the rising steam. His demeanor was, to say the least, odd.

Kat felt a touch of discomfort. She had never been at ease with eccentric behavior. In her father's heyday she had encountered many a Hollywood oddball: drunks, addicts, genuine neurotics and psychotics, and those who wore the cloak of eccentricity for affectation, and she had always been repulsed by them. Madness frightened her, and she was not at all sure Joe Santee was not that way inclined. She didn't presume to judge the man. From the little she knew of him he undoubtedly had enough reason to be unbalanced. But no amount of justification could lessen her apprehension at that moment.

Sensing her unease, Raven slipped her a reassuring wink and, glancing at two chairs that he had thoughtfully arranged side by side facing Santee, indicated they should sit down.

A strange silence enveloped them. To Kat the house was no longer cool but oppressively stuffy. The room was dim, the only light coming in through two small dust-covered windows. She wished the door had been left open. A view of the desert—the *car*—would have been comforting.

The silence dragged on. They resembled three actors on a Western set, waiting for the director to call "action." Kat wondered why Raven didn't say something, start the ball rolling, then thought maybe he'd already asked a question, before Red's attack on her had interrupted them, and was now waiting for a response.

But this was not the case.

Suddenly, without raising his eyes from the table, in a tone which seemed the embodiment of weariness, disillusionment, reluctance, perhaps indecisiveness, and yet in a timbre and accent more educated and polished than Kat had anticipated, Santee said, "Tell me what you want to know."

Raven answered, "Most importantly, of course, I want to know where my father is."

Santee shook his grizzled head. "I can't tell you that."

"Can't or won't?"

"John," Santee said almost pleadingly, "your father is a proud man. What he did, he did for your sake—I mean, of course, pretending to be dead. Can you imagine how hard it was for him to make that decision? You were his only child, his son, and he loved you dearly. He still does."

Raven pounced, revealing his desperation. "So—you're still in touch with him."

Santee didn't answer.

Raven, sighing, said, "Look, I won't pressure you. I know you're bound by a promise, as Nanosh was. Just tell me what you can about him. Is he all right? In good health?"

Santee nodded. "He's fine."

"How well do you know him—really know him?"

"Better than any man. We shared a life together."

"In San Quentin."

"Yes."

"How did my grandfather know to send me here?"

"I went to see Nanosh. Your father had been in touch with him for a year, since his release. When Nanosh fell ill, I visited him on your father's behalf."

Raven drew a sigh, an expression of bewilderment and distraction. "But why didn't my father go himself? And why hasn't he contacted me?"

For the first time Santee's voice and eyes took on life. Looking directly at Raven, he said with a firmness that revealed to Kat the energy that lurked, concealed, beneath the enervated exterior. "Because your father is a convicted

162

murderer. And whether or not he has paid for his crime, and whether or not he was guilty of the crime, in the eyes of society he is still a murderer and he wanted none of the scandal to affect Nanosh's life or your future.''

Raven flashed in response. ''Well, I don't give a damn about my future, I want to see my father. So would you please get that message to him. Tell him I understand why he did what he did and I am grateful for it, and even though his decision has denied me a father for twenty-four years, I accept it. But now it's over. Tell him if he won't come to me, I'll go looking for him—and I'll find him. I don't care how long it takes.''

Santee had returned to his fixed staring at the table. He said gruffly, ''I'll see he gets the message.''

Raven took a moment to calm himself. For a long moment the room returned to its somnolent silence. A fly buzzing against a window, trying to escape, seemed unnaturally loud. Kat empathized with its desire, though she no longer shared its immediate desperation. Her feelings toward Santee had changed from disquiet to fascination, and she was totally absorbed by the exchange between the two men.

Raven cleared his throat. ''Can you . . . tell me what happened? You must know everything there is to know about the murder. Nanosh was too weak to tell me much, and I could find only a mention in the Kansas papers.''

Santee nodded pensively. ''Your father didn't kill the woman.''

''I know that. I barely remember him. I was so young and he was away most of the time. But I know he was a good man, gentle with people and animals, and Nanosh said he could never, purposely, have killed the woman.''

Santee shook his head. ''He was framed. I'll give you the background, help you see it. Will was working horses on a Western movie that was being shot in the Cascade

Mountains, up near the Oregon border. You know that area?''

''No.''

''It's very rugged country—mountain peaks around five to seven thousand feet. I hunted buck up there. Most of it's national forest—Shasta and Klamath—but there's private land, too. The movie was being shot on land owned by the wife of the producer, Frank Vollner. Vollner, as you must know, is a big shot now, but back in those days he was struggling. The way your dad put it, Vollner had only one major asset—his wife. Barbara was young and beautiful and rich. Her folks were big in timber up there, owned the mountain Vollner was using for the movie. She was also working on the picture as the leading actress.

''Seems she had a lot of riding to do, dangerous stuff, and your dad was told by Vollner to keep a special eye on her. They became good friends. Like your dad, Barbara loved horses, and Will spent a lot of time with her, teaching her how to handle them as only a Comanche—and a Gypsy''—he added with a hint of a smile—''can. There was never anything more than friendship between them, but I guess, seeing them ride off together, people started getting the wrong idea. Hell, you know people, they *wanted* to get the wrong idea—a dreary location needs a bit of a scandal to liven it up.

''And conditions were rough. The nearest big town was Redding, fifty miles south, too far to commute daily, so the company was housed in trailers. The weather was bitter cold, it was nearing Christmas, and to make matters worse the picture was running behind schedule. Seems Frank Vollner was pushing the company hard for a quick finish and morale went through the floor. There was a lot of drinking, some fistfights. Several of the crew quit, putting the production in jeopardy. Vollner had to return to L.A. to hire more crew. He was away several days, and when he got back things had really deteriorated. There'd been a heavy snowfall. The leading man was sick. The cameras couldn't turn. Vollner was facing big trouble.''

Raven interjected, ''But his wife had a lot of money.''

''Sure, but it was hers, not Vollner's. Her parents didn't like Vollner, they'd objected to the marriage, and had made him sign a prenuptial agreement that protected her fortune. Barbara told your father all this. I guess she was beginning to see a side of Vollner she didn't like and was having second thoughts about the marriage. She told Will she was glad her parents had insisted on the agreement, and that the only way Vollner could get her money was if she died.''

Raven frowned. ''Surely all this came out at the trial?''

''Oh, sure. Will's lawyer tried to present it as defense, but it was thrown out as irrelevant. It was Will Raven who was on trial, not Vollner. The body was found in Will's trailer.''

Raven compressed his lips, not wanting but needing to know. ''Tell me what happened, Joe.''

Santee drank his coffee, lowered the mug, spoke to it as he cradled it in his hard, callused hands. ''The weather got worse, the leading actor got sicker, and Vollner was faced with a big financial loss. One night he invited Will into his trailer to talk about the remuda, what they were going to do with all the horses if the production was forced to fold. He started pouring out his troubles. He also started pouring out the whiskey. Now, your dad hardly ever drank. He didn't like liquor and knew he couldn't take a lot of it, but Vollner needed a drinking partner and Will could hardly refuse. He swears he only had one drink—not even that. After a couple of swallows he began to feel dizzy, and the next thing he remembers is waking up to find state troopers bending over him, his hunting knife in his hand, and Barbara dead on his bunk.''

"Neat," Raven grated.

"Sure, neat. There were fifty witnesses ready to testify to Barbara's relationship with Will, so her visit to his trailer was in character. And everybody *knows* Indians can't hold their liquor. And after the evidence Vollner gave about Will's visit to *his* trailer that night, no one, especially the jury, doubted that Will killed her."

"What evidence was that?"

"Vollner testified that your father was already fighting drunk when he arrived. He said Will forced his way in, told Vollner he loved Barbara and was leaving with her, then got really mad when Vollner laughed at him. He swore Will pulled out the hunting knife—which he always wore in the mountains—and threatened that if he couldn't have her, nobody would. Vollner said he'd dismissed it as drunken bravado, but began to get worried when Barbara didn't show up later on. He started a search, got the company in on it, and Vollner and an assistant director found her dead in your dad's trailer."

Raven asked, "What did Dad figure happened? Was he drugged?"

"Must have been."

"And the woman? How did she get into Dad's trailer?"

Santee shook his head. "Who knows? Maybe Vollner drugged her—or slugged her."

"Dad is sure it was Vollner who killed her?"

"Who else? Maybe he didn't do it personally, maybe he had it done, but Will's certain it was him."

Raven's face contorted with disgust and puzzlement. "Jesus, to cut her throat . . . and . . . there must have been an autopsy. If she'd been drugged or slugged, surely it would've been detected?"

Santee's eyes rose to meet Raven's, their gaze steady and vehement. "What do you know about Frank Vollner?"

"Practically nothing. Only that he's a top producer/ director and given to good works."

Santee's lips twisted in a cynical smirk. "Oh, yes, good works. He and that blue-blooded wife of his, Sissy, raise millions for charity. Barely a week goes by he isn't on TV and in the papers handing a big check to somebody or other. Mister Squeaky Clean himself. But let me tell you about the real Frank Vollner. All those years your dad was inside he made an intensive study of the guy. It became an obsession with him. And why not? A man's likely to take a keen interest in someone who ruined his and his family's life. Being with him, I got to know a lot about Frank Vollner, too.

"The Vollner everybody knows and loves doesn't exist. This is one *hard* son of a bitch—'scuse me, miss. And I mean hard. Vollner came out to the Coast twenty-five or twenty-six years ago, from New York. The story is that he managed a chain of respectable movie theaters back East, but it isn't true. What he did was run a string of porno flea pits for some very ugly people."

Raven frowned. "How did Dad manage to find that out in San Quentin?"

"John, when you're in the hole for life, you meet some very weird people and make some very peculiar friends. In prison, nothing surprises you and anything can happen. Will Raven was Indian, but he was a popular guy. There was someone in there who knew Vollner, knew his connections, maybe somebody Vollner had hurt, who knows? We never did find out where the help was coming from. But the word went out that your father had been framed, and this stuff about Vollner started coming through."

"When you say 'very ugly people' who're you talking about—the Mafia?"

"The Mob, yes. Vollner was—is—connected. Back in the sixties they sent him out to the Coast to sort out some

167

problems they were having with an independent production company that had borrowed money from them and looked as though it was going bust. Vollner took over the management, saved the Mob's money, found he had a flair for production, and stayed in L.A. to make movies with Mafia backing.''

Raven nodded, seeing it. ''So the picture my dad was on—when it ran into trouble, it meant Vollner was in trouble with the Mafia.''

''Right. Those people are very unforgiving. Vollner was messing up and his future with the Mob was at stake. Who knows? Maybe it was New York that suggested, 'Hey, Frank, we want our money back and we know where you can get it. We'll even help you.' Those guys wouldn't have thought twice about knocking Barbara off to get their money.''

''Wouldn't the production be insured?'' asked Raven.

''Sure. That's how the Mob got its money—the insurance paid out on the lead actress's death. But there was a double bonus in it for Vollner. He not only saved his neck with the Mob, he also inherited Barbara's fortune. He got ten million dollars and the land in the Cascades. From that time on he hasn't looked back. His pictures have made a lot of money for New York. He married Sissy Grant, Pasadena old money—though there was none left when he married her—and became socially acceptable, and he's worked hard ever since on his Mister Clean public image. Now he's as close to sainthood as any Hollywood producer can get. But it's a big fat crock. The guy is a hunter/killer, figuratively and literally. His passion is big-game hunting. He's got a trophy room in his lodge up in the Cascades filled with heads he's collected all over the world. And he's just as deadly in business. Well, when you front for the Mob, I guess you've got to be.''

Pensive, Raven drank some coffee. "You know about my mother, Joe?"

Santee took a moment to answer, and it seemed to Kat, watching him closely, that the Indian was working for inner control. Finally, in a gruff, constricted voice, he said, "I know she came to California from Arizona, trying to help your dad, and didn't return to you and Nanosh. That's all anyone knows—except, of course, the person or people who arranged her disappearance."

"This source in San Quentin didn't know anything about it?"

Santee shook his head. "The first and last Will knew about it was from Nanosh. He didn't want to add to your father's troubles, but he knew Will would be suspicious when your mother didn't visit him, so he told him."

"How did Dad take it?"

Again Santee took his time answering, then did so in a voice ragged with spiritual despair, a reluctance to drag these memories out of the horrible past.

"John, the day you lock a Comanche in an iron cell, separate him from his family, cut him off from the sun, his mountains and horses, is the day his soul begins to die. It's the same for the Romany. You must know this because the blood of both races flows in your veins. But tell that same Indian that his wife, while trying to help him, was murdered by the same people who framed him and put him away, and he comes alive again. Only not as the same man. Perhaps not even as a man. He's no longer the soul who loves all nature and talks to horses. He's a shell, a machine, programmed for revenge. Your father had twenty-three years to think about Frank Vollner . . . about the wonderful life with you and your mother and Nanosh that Vollner ended. Twenty-three years of watching a murderer climb up the ladder of success as the direct result of killing his own wife, your mother, and destroying your father's family. How did your father take it? The same way you would. Very badly."

Raven said quietly, "So he's going after Vollner."

Santee nodded. "In his own time and in his own way."

"Which is why he won't contact me. He's still protecting me. Joe, I want to help him."

"He wouldn't like that."

"Why not?"

"Because it's dangerous, John. Very dangerous. Vollner is protected. He has a constant bodyguard, a couple of murderous thugs. He has a small army up there. He *is* Mafia. You take on Vollner, you take on the Mob."

"No man is invulnerable. Even presidents get killed."

"And then their killers get killed," Santee retorted sharply. "Or put away for life. Either way, for himself, your father doesn't mind—as long as Vollner pays and knows he's paying. But he wouldn't want you involved."

Raven's hand curled into a determined fist. "Joe, I know I can help. Tell me where I can find him. As I told you, Kat's father is Scott Tyson. She was brought up in Hollywood, she has a lot of movie connections. Even if it's only finding out Vollner's movements, where he's going to be . . ."

Santee interrupted, "Your father knows where to find Vollner. Right now he's at his hunting lodge in the Cascades. He's shooting a Vietnam war movie up there on his mountain—"

"Die Young," Kat blurted in confirmation, the first words she'd contributed since entering the house. "I read about it in the trades."

Santee nodded. "Big budget . . . forty million dollars with promotion. He's been at it six months. Interesting thing about this movie . . ."

"What's that?" Raven asked.

"There's a saying: Everything that goes around comes

around. Twenty-four years ago Vollner got himself into a desperate situation shooting a movie in the Cascades. And right now history seems to be repeating itself."

"How so?"

"Vollner isn't infallible. No movie producer is. Otherwise every picture made would be a hit. Vollner's had his share of failures, though overall, as I said, he's made money for the Mob. His trouble right now is he's on a slide. His last two big-budget pictures were box-office disasters. He lost thirty million on *Andromeda* and another twenty million on *Man of Steel*. Now he's chasing the Vietnam war bandwagon with *Die Young*."

Raven frowned. "So what's his problem?"

"He hasn't got one—yet. All I'm saying is he's desperate. He's throwing everything he's got into this one. He's built a fourteen-block Vietnam city up there that he's going to reduce to rubble in a spectacular finish. It's going to be the bloodiest war film ever—and one of the most expensive. And if anything should go wrong . . ."

"Like what?" asked Raven.

Santee shrugged, a gesture of carelessly concealed evasion. "Who knows? On a major production like that a thousand things can go wrong. Maybe the lead actor could take sick, as happened on your dad's movie. That would be an incredible coincidence, wouldn't it? And a disaster for Frank Vollner. You know, I don't think New York would forgive him if he lost them money a third time."

Raven said, "But if he's been shooting for six months, surely most of the movie's already in the can?"

"Yes," said Santee. "But not the big, spectacular finish. That's the expensive bit, vital to the movie. There's another two or three weeks to go before the city is destroyed . . . and as I said, anything can happen."

Raven met the dark, unreadable eyes and realized that Santee had given him all he was going to get. "Joe, I want to thank you for your time." He got to his feet. "We'll go now."

Santee took them to the door and opened it. "Sorry I can't tell you more, but I'll let your father know the things you've told me."

"Thanks." Raven shook the Indian's hard, strong hand, felt the power of the man and other confusing things.

Red was there to walk them to the car, best of friends.

Raven started the engine, waved to Santee standing in the doorway, and drove away.

About a mile down the road, out of sight of the house, Raven pulled the car off into the desert and cut the ignition.

Hearing him murmur "Son of a bitch," Kat asked, "What?"

He seemed to be smiling to himself.

He asked, "What did you think of Mister Santee?"

She shrugged. "I'm not sure. He's a paradox. I couldn't get into his mind at all. I liked him, felt sorry for him. I think he's very lonely. And yet I sensed a tremendous inner strength there that confused me. He speaks well. He's obviously educated, yet chooses to live like this in a desert shack." She shrugged again. "Eccentric, I guess. Maybe prison did it to him. To answer your question: I just don't know. What do you think?"

He was shaking his head as though sharing her confusion. "I think two things. First, I think he just told me where to find my father."

She shot a glance at him. "But he refused . . ."

"That's what he said, yes, but he gave me clues, either accidentally or intentionally. He said Dad would go after Vollner in his own time and in his own way, then implied that he'd do it through some kind of sabotage of the movie, which will have to be done some time in the next two or three weeks. Okay, in order to know how the production

172

schedule is going, you'd either have to get the information from the company offices, which I presume are in L.A., or pick it up on the actual location."

"Right," Kat said. "And the office wouldn't give out much information because they're very secretive about such things. And considering where your father's been for the past twenty-odd years, it seems unlikely he has a spy on the inside."

"Agreed. Which leaves the actual location." That half-smile came again. "Hey, how about this for a supposition: Vollner is shooting a big war movie, requiring, presumably, many extras . . . and my father is biding his time, keeping an eye on its progress, while actually *working* on the movie, obviously under an assumed name. How does that grab you?"

"It's the ultimate irony. I love it."

"So do I. I don't see how else Dad could get close enough to know what's going on. Still, it is only supposition. I'd have to view the situation myself, see how closed or open the location is, how available the information. Dad could be working on a local ranch, or in a bar, anything. I'll have to go up there and take a look."

"I want to go with you."

Raven looked into her eyes, saw her need of his presence, of him. He couldn't abandon her, yet felt, in that instant, a resurgence of the presentiment of future-shared danger he had sensed that first night in Cleves Cottage.

He asked gently, "Kat, is there no one you can stay with?"

She answered adamantly, "No. I don't want to be with anybody else. I want to be with you."

"Look, I know how you feel. You're putting on a brave face, but what happened with Max at the house really put you through the shredder. I understand you wanting me around. But Santee said Frank Vollner is dangerous, and

173

I don't know what kind of situation I'm going to walk into up there. If my father's into something and I have to help him, I don't want you exposed to . . .''

"John, I don't *care* what's up there. It can't be any worse than what I've just been through. I won't stay at Cleves by myself, and there's nobody I . . .'' Tears glistened in her eyes. She looked down at her hands. "*Please*—take me with you.''

"Okay, okay,'' Raven capitulated with a smile.

She looked up, a smile breaking through. "Thank you. Besides, it could turn out to be fantastic material . . . and you do want me to write a best-seller, don't you?''

Raven eyed her narrowly. "You're a blackmailing little hussy.'' He reached out to touch her face, an affectionate caress. "Beautiful—but quite shameless.''

Pleasure surged through her. His touch was a magical thing that warmed her, calmed her, yet excited her. She loved the smell and feel of him, his skin against hers. Almost involuntarily her hand rose to capture his, to hold it there against her cheek.

He smiled at her, giving the moment its due, then withdrew his hand, saying with quiet insistence, "Okay, but we do this properly.''

She thought: Any way—as long as we do it together.

Raven turned to face the desert, his brow creasing with concentrated thought. "We'll be going into rugged country,'' he murmured, almost to himself. "It'll be getting cold up there. We'll need appropriate clothing. The Oregon border is—what?—nine hundred miles from here, say three days' drive. This car's no good for the mountains. We'll return it to El Centro, pick up a camper with four-wheel drive. When we can, we'll stay in motels, use the camper when we must. When we get to L.A. I'll check with Lieutenant Marco in case he needs us for the cop's inquest. You can find out all you can about the *Die Young* production, anything that might help us. Can you think of anything else?''

"No."

He started the engine.

"John . . ."

He looked at her.

"You said you thought two things about Joe Santee. What was the second one?"

Uncertainty crossed his expression and he spoke slowly. "I'm not sure. I believed what he told me about my father and about Vollner, but there was something wrong. When I shook his hand I picked up some strange feelings. The guy was nervous, Kat. I think he was lying."

"About what?"

He put the car in gear and drove back onto the road, the presentiment of danger hugging his shoulder like a familiar, treacherous arm.

"I don't know. And I don't like not knowing."

Chapter Eleven

During a speech paying tribute to Frank and Sissy Vollner for their charity fund-raising accomplishments, somebody once said that Frank was the screen's archetypal tough-guy-with-the-heart-of-gold. This prompted Frank to smile with secret amusement because only that morning he had ordered the disappearance of a Cuban gardener who had inadvertently observed him playing exotic games in his bedroom in the Cascade lodge with a blond starlet.

The speaker had gone on to say, with tongue sycophantically in cheek, that if Frank Vollner ever got tired of movie production he could always step in front of the camera and make an equally impressive fortune playing the type of role for which Lee Marvin was the uncrowned king. This pleased Frank enormously; at last he was receiving public recognition for a performance he had been perfecting since he saw Marvin disfigure Gloria Grahame by throwing a Kona flask of boiling coffee in her face in *The Big Heat* in 1953.

For more than half his life Vollner had idolized Marvin, had attempted to emulate the actor's unique screen presence, his animalistic potential for precipitate violence, his gangly, effortless communication of extreme threat. Trouble was, it was difficult to appear loose-limbed and rawboned like Marvin when you more closely resembled Rod

Steiger. Nevertheless, Vollner combined everything he had into a hybrid performance embodying certain characteristics of both of these fine screen personas, with his own background quite as sordid and violent as any endured by either actor in any of their films.

Born illegitimately into an ambience of extreme social deprivation on New York's Lower East Side (his father was a head-breaker for anyone with the price; his mother a whore who had serviced her tricks within the infant Frank's hearing and sight), and nurtured on every conceivable racket and vice extant during the fruitful forties, he was, by 1953, intrinsically well prepared to adopt a Marvin-type persona. Slickly attiring himself with a languid, laid-back pose, accompanied by the mandatory hooded, dark-eyed look, he discovered, to his everlasting joy, that he could really scare the shit out of people merely by looking at them.

Such talent soon attracted the attention of people who were interested in such matters, and Vollner began his lifetime association with organized crime as a debt collector in the Family's loans division. From there he graduated into prostitution as a collector and protector, and thence into the administration of the production and exhibition of pornographic movies. These experiences rapidly inculcated in him a disrespect for women that verged on loathing, and brought the discovery that their abuse gave him an incomparable pleasure.

Women were born to be used.

In 1961, now a fully fledged enforcer, he was sent to the Coast to collect on a loan made to a small but promising film company engaged in the production of a low-budget spin-off of *Spencer's Mountain,* Warner Brothers' biggest commercial hit of that year. Vollner found chaos in the production department, took over the reins, enjoyed scaring the crap out of everybody, and brought the film in under budget.

Suddenly he was a movie producer and loved it.

What he liked most was the power.

In New York he was nothing, a mere tick on the hound of organized crime. On the Coast, with Mafia backing, he was a demagogue; Christ, a god! He had any trouble, like with a union, he put in a call to New York. Bingo, the trouble disappeared.

He had the power. He had good spending money. He had weather you wouldn't believe. He had women to play with.

Jesus, the women.

Within a year he possessed stature, a bearing impossible to attain in New York. It attracted women like crazy.

What he needed now was serious money and recognition by the Establishment. Barbara McKenzie miraculously entered his life to fulfill both those needs in abundance.

A year later Barbara was dead, he was ten million dollars and a heap of land richer, and through the publicity and sympathy engendered by the notorious murder case, Frank Vollner was known and recognized by the people in California who mattered.

Who says there's no God?

His first two years on the Coast were, if nothing else, instructive, and in them he learned the most crucial lesson of his life: the need for adaptability. So he learned the rules and put them into practice. He became a better actor than most members of the Guild.

Supported by a phony curriculum vitae concocted in New York, he went a-courting respectability in the angular, old-maidish form of Sissy Grant, a well-connected but near-impoverished Pasadena blue-blood sociologist, and won her heart by being the first man in her thirty-year-old life who wanted to fuck her.

And there he had it.

Everything.

The rest became a matter of amply recorded history.

The Land Rover entered the valley on an unpaved road that ran twenty miles in a northerly direction from State Highway 89 to U.S. Highway 97 through some of the most awe-inspiring, rugged, and treacherous topography in northern California.

The Cascade Range.

Fifteen miles to the west, the jagged peak of Mount Shasta soared fourteen thousand feet to scrape the heavens. Up ahead, separating the Klamath and Shasta national forests, the eight-thousand-foot Ash Creek Butte dominated the skyline. And all around and on every hand— minor mountains, buttes, hills, escarpments, valleys, rock formations, and trees and trees and trees.

Frank Vollner loved it all, loved its danger, its violence, its raw solitude. Here in the wilderness there was virtually no law. Sure, there were rangers and state police, but so few to cover so vast and rugged an area, and the few there were could be counted upon to be cooperative. Cops all over the world looked after their local own, and here in the Cascades Frank Vollner was king. He had brought wealth to the area. He'd shot a dozen movies up here, had used the Cascades as Ford had used Monument Valley, though not solely because the landscape was so dramatic. There was another major consideration: he owned the land, which gave him control, which gave him power. Here, while Sissy dwelt in Bel Air mansion comfort, he could play Napoleon, Adolf Hitler, Attila the Hun, or the Devil himself. He could snap his fingers and get things done, make people rich or make them disappear. Here he could do any fucking thing he liked and get away with it. Love it? You bet your ass.

Vollner sat up front with his driver. "Stop here," he ordered.

In addition, there were three other men in the vehicle: two bodyguards and the director of *Die Young*. All were dressed for the terrain in quilted hunting coats, waterproof pants, and heavy boots.

Filling the seat behind Vollner, his massive head scraping the roof of the cab, was a six-six, two-hundred-eighty-pound Korean subhuman bodyguard named Ken Dok, a martial arts master for whom human life—his own or any other, with the obvious exception of his employer's—held no consequence. He broke paving slabs and vertebrae with equal equanimity.

The other bodyguard was Ed Bussey, a raw-boned country boy, six-four, two-forty, who also liked to hurt people.

The director was Allan Schenk, a feisty, precociously confident thirty-year-old Californian anxious to convince the world that anything Spielberg and Lucas could do, he could do better, faster, cheaper. It seemed as though he was about to do it, because after six months of prepro-duction and principal photography, *Die Young* was mi-raculously on schedule and within budget. Had it not been, Schenk would not have been riding in the Land Rover.

Vollner was staring through the windshield at an incred-ible sight. They were in the middle of a city street, a main thoroughfare that stretched away in a straight line for seven long blocks, terminating in an impressive square before the towering façade of an ancient Buddhist temple. It was an impossible city center for northern California—or any-where else in the world. For although its apartment blocks flew the Vietnamese flag and its fashionable shops bore names in Vietnamese symbols, it was a fabulous fantasy, a marvelous make-believe, constructed of wood and plaster and fiberglass, and in three weeks' time it would cease completely to exist.

It had cost seven million dollars. Its controlled destruction, the climax of both the movie and the principal photography schedule, would take two weeks to shoot and would require the expertise of a small army of highly qualified technicians—and a great deal of luck.

In one week all other photography would be completed in other parts of the Cascades, and close to two thousand people—film crew, actors, extras, technicians—would pour into the valley for the Quang Hoi city sequences.

Vollner nodded with satisfaction, told his driver, "Drive on—slowly."

Right now, as the Land Rover crept along the eerily deserted thoroughfare and approached the end of the avenue, there was not a living soul to be seen.

The vehicle came to a halt in the center of the city square. The four men got out, Vollner, at five-ten, dwarfed by his bodyguards yet looking powerful and solid in his hunting garb, his bulk concealing muscle developed and maintained by his worldwide hunting activities.

For a long moment he stood looking around at his creation, his dark, penetrating eyes under hooded lids set like jet stones in a strong, round, heavily jowled face, sweeping the façades of the plaster buildings, searching for imperfection, discord, something not yet done that ought to have been done but finding, to Allan Schenk's relief, nothing amiss. An irate Frank Vollner was not enjoyable company.

Vollner nodded his approval. "Looks great."

"You have a fine art department, Frank," said Schenk, a wiry, collegiate man with a mop of black, curly hair, a matching beard, and wire-rimmed glasses. "Damn good team all through. *Die Young* will be a landmark, make a pile of money."

"It'd fucking better," muttered Vollner. He walked off toward the temple, stopped before its impressive steps, and gazed upward at its face. "This is where the marines are beheaded, huh, where I'm standing? They come down these steps . . ."

"Right," said Schenk, leaping to it, showing the man he had it all in his head. "The platoon is hidden in those side streets, on both sides of the avenue. The square is filled with gooks, forming a big semicircle. The first six prisoners are brought out of the temple, made to stand on the steps, watching. Then one by one they're brought down for execution . . ."

Vollner's head snapped around. "Where's the platform? There's supposed to be a platform."

"No, Frank, the platform gets built . . ."

Vollner waved his hand dismissively. "Oh, yeah, yeah, the prisoners hear it being built, wonder what the fuck's going on, sure." Vollner quickly reeled the key points of the story through his mind.

A company of U.S. Marines gets hammered by the North Vietnamese Army. Twenty are taken prisoner and transported to a fictitious N.V. city, Quang Hoi. The survivors, returning to base, demand action to rescue their buddies. Top brass, explaining that delicate negotiations are taking place between North and South Vietnamese officials, will do nothing. Through a spy in Quang Hoi the survivors learn that their buddies are to be publicly executed on a given day. The surviving platoon again demands action and is again refused. On being told they are to return to the States on extended furlough, the platoon decides to act on its own initiative. They hijack the helicopter gunships taking them to Saigon and head for Quang

Hoi. They arrive in time to witness the first of the executions. Incensed, they become an avenging death squad and, while rescuing the remainder of the prisoners, are instrumental in reducing Quang Hoi to a Hiroshima-style pile of rubble. The final thirty minutes of the movie were to be devoted to the biggest, bloodiest, and most expensive battle sequence in cinematic history.

Looking at it all, thinking of the coming weeks, about the precision of timing, the expertise that would be required to bring the battle sequence off successfully, Vollner was assailed by the sickening surge of apprehension that had haunted him since the *Andromeda* disaster. That mother had severely shaken a confidence built up over the past twenty-six years. Thirty million bucks down the hole. Those pricks in New York—what did they know about making movies, about the marketplace, about the time to get in and the time to stay out? They were trendchasers. "Frank, look at the money Lucas is making with his *Star Wars* trilogy. We gotta get into space." So they got into space—a year too late. Then it was "Frank, look at the bucks Stallone is coining with the *Rocky*s. We gotta get into boxing." So they got into boxing with *Man of Steel,* again a year too fucking late. Another twenty mil down the toilet. And none of it his fault. They were good movies. But that didn't matter. His name was on the door as president of Vollner Productions, and if the axe fell his head would be on the block. Now it was "Frank, Vietnam movies are making a bundle." So they were into Vietnam. Twenty million bucks into it, with another twenty for promo. *Die Young* had to succeed. If it didn't . . .

"When are the explosives being shipped in?" he asked Schenk.

It was a logistical question he would normally and more correctly have asked of a member of his production staff, not his principal director, but it came out almost subconsciously, as a facet of his unflagging concern for the success of the picture, and in any case he knew Schenk would have the answer.

"Tomorrow."

"I want top security on it from the moment it enters this valley," growled Vollner. "I don't need some hophead technician flicking a live butt into a hundred tons of dynamite."

Schenk grinned. "Leastwise not without the cameras rolling."

Vollner turned his eyes on him and Schenk lost his grin.

Vollner took a last look around the city square, then up beyond the buildings to the mountains that rose steeply to the north and south, the beginning of their inclination from the valley floor perhaps a quarter-mile distant on both sides of the valley. Though the afternoon light was fading, the rugged peaks stood out in sharp relief against a clear, darkening sky. He prayed the good weather would hold. The production had been scheduled to beat the winter rain and, eventually, snow. Freak weather could put him in real trouble.

He headed for the Land Rover, opened the passenger door, and said to his driver, "Take me back to the lodge, then drive Mister Schenk to the unit."

He was about to climb into the front seat when Ed Bussey, behind him, said with a grin, "Hey, Boss," and pointed off.

In the center of the thoroughfare, a long way down the valley, a rabbit, raised on its hindquarters, sat looking in their direction.

Vollner returned Bussey's challenging grin. "How much?"

"Ten bucks."

Vollner stretched out his hand toward the driver, who unhooked a rifle from its rack and passed it to him.

"How far d'you reckon?" Vollner asked Bussey, working a cartridge into the spout.

"One-fifty."

"Two hundred," said Vollner, adjusting the sights.

He took a standing stance, raised the rifle to his shoulder, eased it into his quilted coat, took aim. "Wind fifteen from the left," he muttered, telling Schenk how he did it; the others knew. "And good-bye . . . Bugs."

The valley reverberated with the crashing explosion.

The rabbit flew backward as though jerked by a string.

"Jesus," murmured Schenk.

They got in the vehicle. The driver started up and drove down the thoroughfare to the rabbit. Bussey got out, held up the body by its hind legs. The torso was intact. Only the head was missing.

"Je-*sus*!" laughed Schenk.

Vollner turned his head to him, frowning with contrived puzzlement. "What?"

"You took the fucking head off!"

Vollner's expression embraced the others, asking if they could explain Schenk's surprise. "Yeah, well? What else? You hit a rabbit anywhere but in the head with a seven-six-two, you kill the meat."

Schenk's look at Ken Dok said: Is he kidding?

The Korean's impassive stare was answer enough.

"You wanna keep it?" Bussey asked at the open door.

Vollner nodded. "Sure, the dogs'll eat it."

Bussey threw the warm body into the back of the vehicle and climbed in.

Vollner put his hand out to him.

"What?" said Bussey.

"C'mon, you cheap fuck—ten bucks."

As they drove west out of the valley Vollner felt better

than he had in weeks. He thought back over all the hunting he'd done, enjoying again the old elation.

Goddamn, there was just no thrill to compare to a kill.

Maybe when the movie was done he'd go back to Africa and get him an elephant. Shooting rabbits or shooting movies, he was still up there with the best. So screw 'em all.

Chapter Twelve

They were driving north toward Monterey on Route 1, the Pacific Coast Highway, in a four-berth Ford camper hired in San Diego. Kat, feeling the time was as right as it ever would be, believing she now knew John Raven well enough to bring it up, yet still with a certain hesitant diffidence, said, "John, may I ask you something?"

The expression in his eyes as he glanced at her told her he knew what was coming, that he'd been waiting for it, and that it was all right to pursue the matter. "Shoot."

She gave that exasperated eye-rolling smile by now familiar to him. "I think I don't need to. You already know."

He said, "Luke Shand. You want to know what happened . . . what I did."

It was their fourth day together. Following their visit to Joe Santee they had rented the camper and returned to Los Angeles where Kat, using the phone, had worked her own brand of magic to find out as much as possible about the progress of *Die Young* and general information about Frank Vollner's operations in the Cascades, including the location of his hunting lodge. For two nights they had stayed in a Santa Monica motel, in adjoining rooms, compelled— as far as Kat was concerned, though she sensed this also applied to Raven—by a curious, almost mystical restraint to observe sexual decorum. Her relationship with him puzzled her. In every sense he was the most attractive man she'd ever met. His touch, while never overtly sexual, triggered thrills throughout her body. The very thought of his flesh in contact with hers made her shiver. And yet the authoritative voice of instinct told her that sex with him would be wrong. She hadn't the slightest doubt it would be marvelous, that he would be a passionate, sensitive, magical lover, but felt that while gaining this new experience she—they—would lose something much more important and valuable.

Throughout the two nights at the motel, knowing he was close, separated from her by only the thinnest of walls, she had thought about him, had tried to visualize him lying beside her, holding her, his strong arms around her, his lean, tanned body warm against hers. But the mental picture was illicit and would not hold true. That inner voice whispered, No. And would be obeyed. Let it go, it said. Perhaps in time . . .

Perhaps in time.

A vague, frustrating concession, but one that would have to do.

"It's with me all the time," she said. "I can't shake it. In fact, it seems to grow. I think if I don't find out it will haunt me all my life."

"What do you remember?"

She shook her head, her gaze turning distant and misty as she returned to that time. "I don't know. I'm not sure anymore what I heard and saw. You were standing there . . . looking incredibly angry. And then . . . something hit me. Yet not quite. It didn't hurt. It . . ." Again she shook her head. "The next thing I remember was you holding me and Luke Shand . . . in the cactus."

Raven took a while to answer.

The big tires of the trucklike vehicle thrummed on the pavement, cocooning them in a field of hypnotic vibration. They were in Big Sur country, the San Lucia Mountains close on their right, the endless coppery ocean pounding into the rugged cliffs on their left. Raven had been loath to take this route. Big Sur was where Rick had died, and a reminder of her brother's death was the last thing Kat needed. There had been a choice of more inland routes—Interstate 5 or 101—on which they would have made better time, but Kat had insisted on the coastal road, saying she needed the ocean.

The sun was dying, losing its yellow and orange rays, flooding the world with blood-stirring crimson, burnishing the waters with ethereal sheen. It was an unreal moment of the day and so appropriate for what he had to say.

"The short and honest answer is that I know what I wanted to happen, I know I caused it to happen, but I don't know how. I've always had to be satisfied with the premise 'thinking makes it so.' The mechanics are a mystery.

"I'm a biophysicist. I deal in biological structures and processes in terms of physics. But modern physics is in a state of flux. For two hundred years physics has adopted Newton's theory that everything is measurable, and that with enough information, plus maybe a little calculation and a pinch of inference, everything is knowable. Then along came a man named Heisenberg who showed it was impossible to determine exactly the position and momentum of any body at a single instant of time. This necessitated changes in some of the most basic equations of physics, which led to the development of quantum mechanics, which in turn has begun to bring about a major philosophical revolution." Raven grinned at her. "Are you with me so far?"

Kat laughed. "I got the bit about you being a biophysicist. You kinda lost me after that."

"Well, put simply, the eggheads aren't certain about anything anymore. The more they know, the less they know. Take a solid, real-life, everyday object like this camper. It's made of metal—right? And everyone knows metal is hard." He struck the dash ledge with his knuckles. "It's hard and it's *there*, because our senses tell us so. But take a piece of this metal and put it under an electron microscope. Reduce your observation of it to the atomic and subatomic level and what do you find? You find nothing. You find atoms and electrons and neutrons flying around in *space*. So how can it appear solid? It appears solid because we choose to *see* it as solid. We effect its state by the way we will it to be. In other words, it's solid because thinking makes it so.

"Okay, let us apply this to the world of the so-called paranormal. During my years with Jack Shanglo and the Rom in Europe I witnessed some incredible happenings. I told you Jack was a very gifted man. One day, while we were camped in southern France, a Gypsy boy tripped and fell into the red-hot ashes of the camp fire, burned his leg badly. There was a patch of seared flesh the size of your hand between his ankle and knee. The kid was screaming with agony. Jack laid the boy down on the grass, placed his hand over the burn, talked to the boy quietly, hypnotically, for perhaps thirty minutes. And when he removed his hands there was no sign of the burn. The lad got up and ran off to play, quite healed."

Kat shivered.

Raven continued, "What Jack did was *will* the flesh to heal—or perhaps more accurately willed the boy to heal his own flesh. Who knows which? The point is, Jack's mind had the power to influence another person's mind and flesh. But how? What is the force at work? Electromagnetism? It could be, but I don't think so. I think the force is simply Mind.''

Kat's eyes were glued to his as he spoke.

''The truth is, Kat, nobody in the whole wide world has the faintest notion of how the mind works, let alone how it can affect matter. Theories, of course, abound. Some are very plausible, they sound right. But in the final analysis we're left with Lyall Watson's brilliant metaphor that investigating the working of the human mind is like attacking a grand piano with a sledgehammer to get at the concerto inside.''

A raucous horn, close behind, shattered the peaceful ambience and their rapport. High-beam headlights flooded Raven's side mirror. Instinctively he veered to the right, conscious of the irritation wide-bodied campers evoked in car drivers. But even now, with his right wheels on the shoulder, the horn persisted. *Blaa-dee-dee-blaa-blaa* . . . *blaaa-BLAAA.* Were they trying to tell him something . . . that he had a flat? He turned his head to glance out of the rear window, saw, behind the glare of headlights, that it was not a car. It was bigger, a pickup truck. He got a fleeting impression of three faces before returning his eyes to the road.

He lowered his window, waved them on, heard their engine roar in acceleration. They gave him the horn again, now a continuous blast that sounded angry, threatening. Raven waved again. Kat, frowning at him, equally puzzled and increasingly alarmed, turned in her seat. ''What's the matter with him? Why doesn't he pass?''

''I think he hates campers.''

Raven now sensed that trouble was close behind.

Gradually he eased his foot off the gas, dropped his speed two, three, five miles an hour, continued to wave the truck on.

The truck's fender struck the camper's, not hard, but with patent aggression.

Kat's face blanched. She grabbed nervously for the dash. "Jesus."

"Take it easy," Raven murmured tightly. "They'll get tired of the game in a minute." He slowed his speed another notch.

Another fender collision, harder this time. Then the truck was revving, overtaking, horn blaring deafeningly.

From the corner of his eye Raven saw the face in the open passenger window: sunburned, unshaven, coarse, a colored bandanna around the head, dark lank hair, scuffed leather jacket.

"Hey, asshole, you want all the fuckin' road! Got yuh dick in her mouth or somethin'?"

Beside Raven, Kat was shaking.

He reached for her hand, squeezed it supportively. "Wipe him from your mind. He isn't there, Kat. There's no one there."

"Hey, pussyfucker, I'm talkin' to you!"

Releasing her hand, Raven took the wheel, wound up his window.

The pickup surged ahead. It was blue and old and rusted. Through its rear cab window, in the rays of the setting sun, Raven could see there were three of them, the driver's head an explosion of blond, sun-bleached curls, the middle passenger a black. Their shoulders filled the cab.

The truck swerved suddenly into the camper's lane, forcing Raven to swerve and brake hard. Now the driver began playing games, slowing down, speeding up, braking sporadically. The driver's arm appeared out of the window. An empty beer can flew backward, smashing into the camper's windshield.

Kat cried out. "You stupid bastards! Oh, God, what I'd

give to be a cop right now." She shook with fury. "What I'd give for your power."

The trio appeared to have had enough fun. Simultaneously, Blondie and Bandanna's arms appeared, their middle fingers offering an obscene farewell salute, and then the truck accelerated in a cloud of noxious smoke and quickly disappeared from view.

Kat sagged, trembling, gave a fluttery sigh. "God, this country. What's happening to the people? Is there *nowhere* one can go without running into violence and aggression?"

Raven smiled wanly. "Sun City?"

"Well, hell, yeah, I think I'd prefer to live with those old folks, if they'd let me in! I mean, there you have it—they've had to build themselves that retreat to get away from all this violence."

"It's not just the States, Kat. It's a worldwide epidemic. Per capita there's just as much crime and violence in England, Spain, France."

"How can you be so calm about it?" she flared. "Didn't those three punks make you want to kill?"

"Conditioning," he said. "The Rom have to face this kind of thing all the time, have done for centuries. They've learned that in order to survive you have to avoid confrontation, whenever possible. They've learned to quickly assess a situation and act accordingly."

As you did on the bus, she reflected.

He went on, "Nanosh and Jack Shanglo taught me that the finest form of defense is a quick pair of heels. There's nothing cowardly about it; it is wisdom of the highest order. These days kids are taught badly. They see make-believe fights on TV and in films and think it's the real thing. The real thing, as you well know, is terrible."

She nodded, said softly, contritely, "Yes I do. I'm sorry. I know you did the right thing. They've gone and nobody was hurt. And if you had provoked them . . .'' She heaved a sigh, smiled at him wanly. "What were we talking about before we were crudely interrupted?"

He smiled back at her. "Mind over matter."

"Yes. What a wonderful power to have. I'd give anything to be able to dematerialize punks like that. Is that—in any way—what you did to Luke Shand?"

He became pensive again, did not answer her directly. "There are children in Japan who can turn tennis balls inside out, unbroken, merely by willing it to happen."

She stared at him. "Good God. That's impossible."

"Yes, it is. But they can do it. There's a boy in England who creates sculptures with wire without touching it, merely by willing it to happen. Like Jack Shanglo and his healing, these kids alter the state of matter by choosing to observe a different aspect of it or to observe it from a different aspect. However, in nearly all cases, it proves to be an unstable and short-lived gift. Kids grow out of it, probably through conditioning, by peer pressure to conform. Older children don't like to be different. And even among people whose gift persists into adulthood, it is capricious. The great Uri Geller has his off days. What I'm saying is that psychokinesis requires a particular and precise state of consciousness that is difficult to attain. It appears to be a state that occurs when the firing rate of brain neurons reaches a certain critical level. Do you get what I mean?"

Kat nodded. "I think so. It's like the radio-tuning analogy you made. If you don't precisely hit the station, you don't get the program."

"That's right. Except we have less control over tuning our brain neurons than our radios. I've done a lot of research into poltergeist activity. I've been in homes where furniture moves and crockery flies around and smashes into walls, and always the phenomenon has been connected to a disturbed or frustrated teenager, someone entering puberty. Often they don't know they're causing the disturbances. You see what I'm getting at? Their brain-, mind-, will-activity, whatever, was tuned for psychokinesis, and they didn't even know it.''

The sun, a livid crimson disc, slid into the ocean and darkness was suddenly upon them. Raven turned on the headlights.

"Okay—back to Luke Shand. When I was young I discovered I had the gifts these other children have, maybe more. I went to live with Jack Shanglo and the Rom who believe in such things and encouraged their development. But under controlled conditions. Jack instilled in me the absolute necessity of using the gifts either for good or for survival.

"Jack had traveled the world, had even spent some time with those magicians of the martial arts world, the ninja, who reputedly died out in Japan a hundred years ago, but the incredible art is still secretly practiced today. Jack's forte was the martial arts; he never lost a fight. And yet, always, his sternest advice was: If you can—run.

"Among the techniques he taught me was the weapon of the voice. As I told you, all traveling Gypsies develop loud carrying voices, living as they do in the open. The shout can be a devastating weapon. For centuries men have used war cries to demoralize and defeat enemies before a spear was thrown or an arrow shot. The vibration of the sound plays hell with the nervous system. It can, literally, paralyze.''

Kat stared at him, her eyes wide with sudden enlightenment yet disbelief. "*That's* what you did to Luke Shand . . . you shouted at him?''

"That—and something else. What those bastards did on the bus triggered something in me, started a psychokinetic firing rate in my brain. Later, what they were doing to you completed the process. And when Shand went for his shotgun, I let fly at him with everything I had—voice, will, everything.''

"And I caught the edge of whatever you used on Shand," said Kat, nonplussed. "Your anger knocked me out."

"Yes."

Up ahead, the neon sign of a roadside restaurant glowed in the dark.

Raven said, ''Fancy some dinner? I'm starved.''

"So am I."

He slowed the vehicle, turned left off the highway onto a service road, ran into a parking area that surrounded the restaurant, and drew up near the entrance and cut the engine.

Raven started to get out, but Kat's voice stopped him.

"John . . ."

"Yes, Kat?"

"Do me a favor."

"Sure."

"Don't ever get mad at me."

Chapter Thirteen

Killing the rabbit had made him horny. But it had done much more than that. It had opened his eyes to what had been happening to him over the past two, three years, to the changes taking place in his life, to what he was in danger of becoming.

The revelation had hit him suddenly after he'd returned to the lodge. Standing alone before the huge plate-glass window of his trophy den, facing east, taking in the spectacular elevated view of his own valley (*one* of his valleys), the surrounding mountain peaks daubed with blood by the setting sun, he himself aglow with the satisfaction of having made an incredible shot, he was seized by an awareness of self that was both shocking and exhilarating. In cinematic terms, it was as though he'd been viewing himself in a zoom-lens close-up, moving in and in, focusing on ever-decreasing minutiae, on paltry demeaning detail, and had suddenly zoomed out to take in the whole, to see himself as he had been before the failure of *Andromeda* and *Man of Steel,* and as he himself still *was.*

The awareness had both thrilled and angered him.

He was still Frank Vollner, the guy who had been making things happen for a quarter of a century.

He, Frank Vollner, had made better than two hundred and fifty mil for *them* over the years, before those assholes in New York got to thinking they knew the movie business, what the public wanted, better than he did. How many times had he tried to tell them that trend-chasing was the surest route to disaster, that it took a couple of years to make a major movie, from commission of a screenplay to distribution, and in that time public taste could change six ways from up? How many times had he told them moviemaking, at best, was a crapshoot, that *nobody* knew the secret of success, that the most successful producers employed gut feeling for a good story and right casting, then sat on the cost to make sure they didn't end up with a runaway *Cleopatra* or *Heaven's Gate*?

Jesus, the things he'd done for New York. Taking a leaf out of Lucas's book, he'd pulled production out of expensive L.A. and set it up with a special effects division in Redding, just fifty miles south of the lodge. Redding was cheap and had everything, including an airport. He used Hollywood studio space when it was necessary, but he'd carefully selected stories that could be shot in these fabulous, dramatic mountains and had saved New York millions.

He'd warned them against getting into space with *Andromeda*. He'd warned them against getting into boxing with *Man of Steel*. All the schmucks had seen was Lucas, Stallone, and mega-mega-bucks. And they'd made him feel like shit.

He braced himself, flexing his powerful frame, seeing his features demonically reflected in the plate glass.

Well, he wasn't shit. He was still the same guy who had come out here twenty-six years ago to collect from a pissant production company, had got a foot on the Hollywood ladder, and kicked ass all the way to the top. And he wasn't about to let New York take all that away from him. Whatever it took, *Die Young* would succeed. It would remind New York and Hollywood that Frank Vollner was still a force to be reckoned with. And, by Christ, he was.

He felt strong and unbeatable. The rabbit had done it for him. It was an omen.

He needed a woman.

Production was shut down two days for Thanksgiving. No way was he spending the holiday in Bel Air with Sissy. She'd be up to her scrawny tits in tennis and good works. He needed action.

Oh, yes.

His blood coursed as his imagination took off. It'd been too long since he really cut loose. Time was when the lodge had seen plenty of action, wild parties, crazy games. Up here in the mountains he had been God. It was time to play God again.

In Redding he owned a motel. He used The Crest View to accommodate cast and crew when he was shooting, though it was open to the public, too. For *Die Young* he needed a lot of Asian faces and had brought extras in from San Francisco. Among them was a stunning Eurasian chick, a kid with hopes of being an actress, that he'd spotted in a second-unit crowd sequence and thought wasted. He'd pulled her out, put her on standby at the motel for something more meaty. She'd smiled her appreciation, the kind of smile well known to all powerful producers, telling him there was just nothing she wouldn't do for a crack at stardom.

The fuck was her name? Lin something . . . English name. Samson. Sinden. Siddon. Lin Siddon.

"Lin Siddon," he said aloud, turning from the window, heading for the phone, "this is your lucky day." He punched out a number, the motel in Redding. "Cresswell? Frank Vollner . . . fine, how're you? Listen, you've got a girl staying there, name of Siddon . . . Lin Siddon . . . oh, you do . . . yeah, she is, very beautiful . . . yeah . . . Cresswell, will you cut the shit and get her on the phone?"

Ten minutes later Ken Dok and Ed Bussey were airborne in Vollner's private helicopter, heading for the motel.

The place was more of a diner than a full-blown restaurant, a square modern building with an exposed cooking counter occupying the rear wall. Between the hot plates and the big front picture windows were two rows of tables and red plastic banquettes. Kat and Raven occupied a window table, their camper parked directly outside.

Kat said, "I'll have the same," and the waitress departed.

They'd ordered steak, medium rare, with baked potatoes and a side salad.

They'd bought cold-weather clothing at a sporting goods store in Los Angeles. Kat was wearing a russet turtleneck ski shirt and dark green lightweight ski pants. In the camper was a matching hip-length jacket and more shirts and accessories. Raven had equipped himself with similar gear, in black that he invariably favored, but as yet he was still wearing the soft black leather jacket he had worn on the bus.

Raven smiled at her across the table. "How ya doin'?"

She gave a small, uncertain laugh. "I'm not sure. So much has happened . . . is happening. For about ten minutes back there, our first morning at Cleves, talking on the terrace, I felt I was regaining a grip on reality, and then . . . off we go again. I guess you must have felt like this most of your life, since your father's . . . well, supposed death—being shunted off to Arizona, then England, then Europe. And I suppose working with the paranormal is hardly conducive to a sense of reality."

Raven demurred with a shrug. "After a time the unreal becomes the real. I guess my Romany blood and my time with them have conditioned me to accept whatever comes along as 'it.' Accept it, deal with it, as best you can. The Rom are great realists.''

Kat laughed, this time more openly. "I'll bet they have a thousand wonderful sayings.''

"They do—one to fit every conceivable human condition and situation.''

"Can you give me one in Romani? You do speak Romani?''

Raven nodded, thought for a moment. '' *'Feri ando payi sitsholpe te nayuas.'* ''

Kat frowned. '' *'Feri ando payi . . .'* ''

'' *'. . . sitsholpe te nayuas.'* ''

"What does it mean?''

'' 'It is in the water that one learns to swim.' ''

Kat nodded pensively. "It's true. You can learn only by doing. But it takes courage.''

"Courage is lifeblood to the Rom. Life is meaningless without it. They say: 'Too often the courage about dying is cowardice about living.' ''

Kat nodded again, saying quietly, "That's true, too. After Rick's death and the breakup of the family, I . . . thought about suicide. I really wanted to die.''

"But you didn't. You have more courage than you give yourself credit for. What you've been through in the past few days . . . I don't think many people would've handled it so well.''

Her eyes came up to meet his, moist with emotion. "I couldn't have done it without you, I honest-to-God couldn't. Jack Shanglo taught you well. He'd be very proud of the way you've handled things. Nanosh, too.''

He gave a self-effacing grin. "Jack would've kicked my butt for allowing Mad Max to get away.'' The reminder of Max erased the smile from his face. Almost to himself he said, "When we get to our next motel I'll call LAPD, see if they've caught him yet.''

Their meal arrived. They didn't speak again until the waitress had set it out and left.

Kat asked then, "D'you have any idea what you're going to do when we get to the Cascades?"

He cut into his steak, ate some, murmuring approval. "*We* are not going into the Cascades. If it's necessary, I shall go into the Cascades."

Her face clouded with apprehension, with disappointment. "What about me? You're not leaving me alone."

"Alone, no. There'll be other people with you."

"John . . ."

"Tomorrow we'll get to Redding, try to book into Vollner's motel, the what is it . . . ?"

"The Crest View."

"Yes. We book in and mingle—or we stay elsewhere, in the camper, if necessary—and mingle with the people working on *Die Young,* ask around about my father. There can't be too many middle-aged Indians working on the movie, if indeed he is working. This might be a bad time to get there. Vollner's L.A. office said production was shutting down for Thanksgiving, but the question is will the cast and crew leave Redding? It's only for two days. If they do go home for the holiday, we'll have to hang around until they come back."

"And if we can't pick up any trace of your father?"

Raven ate in silence for a moment, his eyes downcast. "Then I'll go and see Vollner at the lodge."

The quiet deliberateness of his tone chilled her. "And do what?"

His eyes, dark-depthed and somehow too placid, met hers. "Talk to the man. Talk to him about my father and my mother. See what he has to say."

A presentiment swept through her, gnawing at her insides, killing her appetite. "John, you can't go there alone. Remember what Joe Santee said about him. Behind the façade he's a hood. He has thugs for bodyguards. The lodge is so isolated . . .''

"Kat, what's the alternative? I've got to start somewhere. I *know* my father will be up there—somewhere. If, as Santee said, he's going to deal with Vollner in his own way and time, it has to be any time now. My father will know how critical the success of *Die Young* is to Vollner. He'll know about the expensive Quang Hoi set and the plans for its destruction. *If* he plans to sabotage it, he's got to do it in the next couple of weeks, before the end of principal photography. Mind you, I'm saying 'if.' I could be way off target. Maybe Dad plans on blowing up Vollner's production facility in Redding . . . or shooting Vollner at the lodge. I just don't know. But he'll be close to Vollner at some time. And if I can't trace him in Redding, *I* have to get close to Vollner."

Kat threw down her fork. "I hate it."

"The steak? Mine's terrific."

Her eyes lashed at him. "John, don't joke. You walk in there alone, reveal yourself as the son of the man Vollner put away for life and of the woman he probably killed, what d'you think he's going to do? You'll present a terrible threat to him. You think he's going to pat you on the head and say, 'Sorry about your folks, John, but it seemed like a good idea at the time'? He's going to make you disappear, as he did your mother."

"The thought might certainly cross his mind," he conceded dryly.

"John, he can *do* it. He's got the way, the means, and he'll have the inclination. His mountain will swallow you up and nobody will bother looking."

Raven smiled gently at her, with appreciation for her heartfelt concern. "What else can I do, Kat? I have a problem. I can neither escape from it, nor appease it. If I turn my back on it, it will assuredly bite me in the ass.

How can I forget that my father is alive? Therefore I have to fight it, find my dad how and where I can.''

"You could wait until he gets in touch with Joe Santee . . . until he comes to you.''

"Kat, my father's been out of prison a whole year. He's ashamed to face me. He won't come to me. I have to find him.''

"You'll be walking into terrible danger, I feel it.''

"Well, let's not jump the gun. Maybe we'll find Dad in Redding and we can all go home.''

Her gaze was challenging. "Without hurting Vollner?''

He considered it for a moment. "As far as I'm concerned—yes. The Rom have a saying . . .''

She gave a wry smile. "I thought they might have.''

". . . about the wisdom of leaving bitterness and hatred to those not strong enough to love.''

Her frown reflected doubt. "And you could love Frank Vollner—after what he's done to you and your family?''

"No. But I could leave him to his fate. He'll pay in the end. Evil, like goodness, has its own rewards.''

"And what about your father? If you find him, will you be able to convince him to leave Vollner to his fate?''

Raven shook his head. "I don't know. Perhaps not.''

"And if you can't . . . if he's determined to destroy Vollner?''

Raven laid down his fork, pushed the plate away. "Then I shall do everything I can to help him.''

Chapter Fourteen

Vollner heard the helicopter returning. The fine madness of sexual excitement coursed through him, subjugating all conscience, anesthetizing every vestige of morality. The girl was his, to do with as he wished.

Ken Dok had called him from the motel: she needed time to dress, to prepare for the occasion, give her thirty minutes. Vollner had used the time to make his own preparations. There was now a roaring log fire in the den fireplace, drinks and food available, all but essential staff banished to their quarters. Vollner had shaved, showered, and was attired in a long Chinese kimono of red and gold brocade, an exquisitely embroidered dragon rampant across his back, emphasizing the breadth of his shoulders. Beneath the robe, he was naked.

His choice of apparel was in no way a gesture to the visit by the Eurasian girl. It was his "Emperor Look." Down the years he had learned the importance of clothes, the effectiveness of appropriate dress, as both a psychological ploy to gain advantage and as a personal boost to mood-inducement. Dressed thus, he *felt* like an emperor, an omnipotent potentate possessing the power of life or death, to whom all owed absolute obedience, to whom nothing could be denied.

Here, at the lodge, Frank Vollner had absolute control over his environment. The den, this spacious, stone-walled room with its exquisite Oriental carpets and comfortable, deep-cushioned furniture, was his throne room. Here, ranged around the walls, were the mounted heads of his hunting trophies, a further reminder of his domination. There, in his glass-fronted gun cabinets, were displayed the oiled and gleaming symbols of his power.

Vollner, gazing around the room, perceiving its perfection, grunted with satisfaction and moved toward the fireplace to add the final touch to the tableau he desired.

The door opened.

The girl entered.

In the presence of the huge and sinister Korean, she looked tiny, fragile, pale. And exceedingly beautiful. Beauty and the Beast, mused Vollner, finding it all perfect.

He maintained his pose at the fireplace, knowing the effect his position and stance created, the firelight burnishing the gold of his robe, surrounding him with radiant light. His art director could not have set it better.

He watched with pleasure the impact he, and the room, had upon her. Her dark eyes were huge against the pallor of her face, transmitting a variety of impressions and emotions: awe, wonder, nervousness, but above all excitement that *she* had been invited here, and that for her, advantages might follow.

Vollner roused himself from contrived reverie, as though he had been lost in film-producer dreams and was only now aware she was there.

"Ah, there you are." His face wreathed in a welcoming smile, he moved to greet her, enfolding her tiny hand in his huge paw, enjoying the touch of her young firm flesh, the fragrance of her perfume. He looked down into a face of flawless beauty, framed by a profusion of gleaming black hair, her brows jet black, nose small and delicate, her mouth sensuously full and ripe and perfectly fashioned.

"Lin, isn't it? I'm Frank Vollner."

Her delicate smile said: Of course, who else?

"Ken, take the young lady's coat."

She removed her quilted coat, revealing a simple dress of red jersey silk which clung like skin to her slender Oriental figure, its hemline fashionably short, complementing her shapely legs which tapered to slim ankles and tiny feet in red leather shoes.

"Lovely," breathed Vollner, holding her hands at arm's length, his smile avuncular, his eyes and mind stripping away her clothes to picture her naked, her pale silky body and thick black bush. "Quite lovely. You must be cold, come over by the fire. That'll be all, Ken."

The Korean retired, closing the door.

"Sit here," Vollner said, indicating a sumptuous sofa facing the fire. "You like champagne?"

He popped the cork, ignoring her response, poured two glasses. He sat beside her, angling his body toward her so that she would do the same. The dress delighted him. Already short, it now rode higher, revealing smooth young thighs in black shiny panty hose. She was going to be perfect.

He raised his glass. "To success."

She smiled, white teeth gleaming. "I'll certainly drink to that." She was nervous, her hand trembled as she drank.

That pleased him, too.

"Now," he said. "Tell me all about yourself."

Chapter Fifteen

Raven and Kat left the restaurant and walked toward the camper. Though the night sky was black, light from the restaurant windows illuminated the vehicles parked close and threw long shadows across the area.

As Raven headed for the driver's door, Kat went around the front of the camper and was momentarily out of his sight.

He unlocked the door, opened it, and heard Kat scream.

Awareness, the instantaneous knowledge of insight, struck him like a blow. Every instinctual receptor contained in his mind and body reacted. He was transformed.

He yelled, "KAT, GET BACK HERE!" his voice echoing and reverberating around the area as he backed away from the vehicle to encompass the whole scene.

As her retreating figure appeared around the front, the black made his entrance around the rear of the camper, to Raven's right. He was huge, his cutaway leather vest exposing weight lifter's arms.

The others, Bandanna and Blondie, sauntered after Kat, coming around the front, moving in on Raven's left, the classic pincer movement.

Raven retreated slowly, telling her calmly but firmly, "Kat, get inside the restaurant."

She was staring at the slowly advancing thugs, paralyzed.

Raven moved, ran between parked vehicles, out into the open area, drawing them away from her.

The trio looked surprised that he hadn't run into the restaurant. And happy. They weren't interested in the girl. They wanted him.

Forming a semicircle, they followed out into the arena, coming on with punk smiles and the punk swagger that says everything's going their way and they're gonna have fun.

Bandanna started it, grinning a lot of teeth as he showed Raven the brass knuckles on his right hand, indicating they all had them. "Hey, asshole, you busted our truck. We're gonna bust you."

Blondie giggled. "You ain't goin' anywheres, fella, so you may's well stand still an' take it. Look at your camper tires."

Raven did not look. His attention was on them, fixed and immovable. He didn't hear them. Jack Shanglo's voice filled his ears, his mind.

Remember always: A fight is won in the mind before the first blow is struck. Empty it of all other matters. Try always for the unexpected. There can only be one outcome— survival. Do what you must.

They were confident, coming at him slowly, jiving, talking away their life force, thinking that three-to-one odds gave them latitude for bullshit, the black circling around behind him, turning on the swagger, prelude to a rush.

Raven let him come.

Suddenly the black was in motion.

Raven spun, braced himself and bellowed, took the fight to the black, saw the guy's surprise, the shock induced by the shout, the slight falter as he arrived with metaled fist drawn back, legs spread for the blow.

Raven dropped into a crouch, drove his right fist with jackhammer force into the man's testicles, smashing them, hearing the muted squelch a split second before the black's explosive scream of terrible agony.

The unexpectedness, the violence of Raven's attack, stunned the others momentarily. They stared at the black, writhing and vomiting on the tarmac. Before Blondie could gather his senses, Raven was on him, blocking a reflexive right hook with his left arm and driving the point of his right elbow with enormous power into Blondie's ribs.

Raven heard the crack of bone and knew the job was done. Leaving Blondie swaying, eyes bulging with awareness of chronic injury, Raven swung toward Bandanna.

The man retreated, eyes wild, staring with disbelief back and forth between Blondie and the black, seeing them destroyed, hearing the sounds of their pain.

"Hey, man . . ." Plaintive now. Afraid now. Wondering what the fuck they'd come up against. "We was only havin' fun. We wouldn't a hurt yuh. You had no call to . . ." Trying it, lulling Raven off guard, now suddenly attacking, "Well, FUCK YOU!" rushing in, swinging a roundhouse right, knowing he'd got this bastard right on the point, then knowing he hadn't got shit because the guy wasn't there anymore, spinning with the momentum of the blow, turning completely around and finding this weird fucking guy *behind* him!

He wasn't certain he saw Raven's hand move. He felt a blow on the right side of his neck, and suddenly his right side was paralyzed, neck to toes. He stared at Raven, into black, inhuman eyes that gleamed like polished ebony in the distant restaurant light, and knew he was going to die. His senses swam. For the first time in his violent life he was truly terrified. He couldn't move!

"What did you do to the camper tires?" Raven asked, his voice so reasonable, deep and quiet and soothing.

Bandanna swallowed, worked his mouth, found a strangled croak. "N . . . nuthin'."

"Good."

Raven turned away.

Bandanna's cry followed him, stricken with panic. "HEY! What about me . . . I can't move!"

Raven called over his shoulder. "It'll wear off. Call an ambulance, your buddies need surgery."

Kat was standing by the camper, her posture frozen, her gaze riveted on the three distant men, transferring it to Raven only as he drew close.

"You okay?" he asked, catching her gently by the shoulders, looking into her eyes, reading her mind.

She nodded.

"Did anyone in the restaurant see anything . . . call the police?"

She shook her head. "I didn't go inside . . . I couldn't." Tears glistened in her eyes.

"Hey," he smiled, "everything's fine. Come on, let's get out of here."

As Raven started the engine, she asked quietly, "Are they badly hurt?"

"They'll live."

He backed the camper out, turned it around the lot, catching the three figures in his headlights. Bandanna was recovering from his paralysis, stamping his foot and swinging his arm, yelling something at the two lying on the ground. As the camper approached, he retreated, his face stiff with fear, thinking it was going to run over them.

Raven swept past, turned onto the service road, and joined the highway.

Kat remained steeped in silence until they passed Monterey.

"It's the only way, isn't it," she murmured disconsolately. "A situation like that . . . there has to be violence."

"Yes."

"But will they learn from it, learn to leave other people alone."

It was a rhetorical question, but he answered all the same.

"No. That's the futility and sadness of it all."

Chapter Sixteen

Lin Siddon was beginning to get an uncomfortable feeling about Frank Vollner, picking up vibes she didn't like.

At first, when she arrived, he had been paternalistic, kind, listening to her life story, refilling her champagne glass in a natural, attentive way, not giving the impression he was trying to get her drunk or anything. And such a possibility had never crossed her mind.

Sure, his getup was a little weird, the kimono and all, but he was an important movie producer and one expected such eccentricity from his ilk. She'd read about this kind of thing and seen it in TV miniseries. But *because* he was an important movie producer, a man constantly in the public eye and known for his charity work, she knew her visit was regarded by him as strictly business, and that he would behave toward her in a certain way, with regard for their respective positions, and with respect for her vulnerability.

Now she wasn't so sure.

His manner was changing. The way he was looking at her was different. Maybe the champagne was getting to him, making him horny. The prospect alarmed her. For the first time she began to realize how truly vulnerable she was, not only as a nobody bit actress in the presence of a movie mogul, but isolated up here in the mountains and totally reliant on him to return her to the motel.

Thinking about it now, the way the invitation had come about was pretty weird. At the time she'd received the phone call—Vollner telling her he had a possible featured part for her that would advance her career, that he'd be shooting right after Thanksgiving and needed to speak to her, to see if she'd be right for it—at that time she'd been so excited she hadn't stopped to think about the oddness of being flown up here alone.

Okay, crazy things did happen in the movie business. Wonderful things, too. Frank Vollner had seen her on the set, had pulled her out of the crowd, and put her on paid standby at the motel. And now here he was, auditioning her for a featured part.

But now she was beginning to ask herself what he wanted in return.

Was that it?

Would the great and mighty Frank Vollner prove to be no different from the hundred-odd slimeballs, from directors to clapper boys, who had promised her professional advancement in return for sex?

She couldn't believe it.

If he played around, he could have practically the entire female population of Hollywood to choose from: actors' wives pushing their husbands' careers; actresses pushing their own; hookers galore. Glamorous and willing women who would gladly give their all. Why bother with a skinny Eurasian girl who'd given him no encouragement at all . . .

Or had she?

On the set he'd smiled at her, she'd smiled back. That was *it*.

No, she had to be wrong about him.

But her female intuition told her she was not.

His next question wiped all doubt from her mind.

"What d'you feel about screen nudity?"

He was looking at her over the rim of his glass, his dark eyes hooded, insolently direct. She'd encountered eyes like these before, in the bars, Neanderthals who'd saunter up and murmur outrageously, ''Wanna fuck?''

Right now Frank Vollner was asking the same thing.

Her heart thudded. Her hand flew involuntarily to the hem of her short dress. She gave a small nervous laugh, put her glass down on the low marble table, using the action to change position, to remove her thighs from exposure to his gaze.

''I . . . think there's too much of it,'' she said defensively yet truthfully. ''It has become contrived. Like the bad language. Too much of anything negates the effect.''

''Smart girl. Brains as well as beauty.'' His tone was teasing, condescending. ''I've been trying to convince certain morons in New York of that for years. But you would agree that nudity is sometimes called for?''

She nodded. ''If it enhances the story.''

Vollner laughed. ''You should be writing screenplays— or producing movies. Maybe I'll make you my assistant, how'd you like that?''

She smiled at the rhetorical question.

He was silent for a moment, watching her. She felt increasingly uncomfortable under his gaze, was picking up a vibration of desire and intention she didn't like at all.

''You ever done any?'' he asked, his voice a ragged reverberation in his barrel of a chest.

''Any what, Mister Vollner?''

''Nude scenes.''

''No, I haven't.''

''Would you?''

Her heartbeat really took off. ''Well, I . . . I guess every actress has to be prepared to . . . to . . .''

''That's right, she has to. As you said, there's so much

of it these days, every actress, given she has an attractive body, has to go with it.''

She fidgeted nervously with her hem, wishing she'd worn pants. His eyes spent more time down there than on her face.

''I think I'm too small.''

''Is that what you think?'' The leer in his voice chilled her. ''Lemme tell you something. Tastes change. When total nudity wasn't allowed, we filled the screen with fantasy voluptuousness, the kind you see in Mike Hammer, Mat Helm, Derek Flint movies—big tits and fat asses—but always covered up. Now that we can take it all off, the camera prefers less flesh. You get a girl riding a guy, a close-up of big, pendulous tits is ugly. What looks best now is your size: small firm tits; neat slender bodies that can thrash around on a bed and walk bare-assed into the bathroom. Believe me, you'd be perfect. Leastwise, I think so.''

It was coming.

Her voice quavered as she asked, ''Is that what you're offering . . . that kind of part?''

He parried the question. ''Lemme ask you somethin'—how much did you earn last year?''

''As an actress?''

''What else?''

''Well, I told you, I do other jobs. I was a waitress . . .''

''Sure. Yeah, as an actress.''

''About a thousand dollars.''

''And how much have you earned this year, so far?''

She gave a dispirited shrug. ''About fifteen hundred.''

He nodded knowingly. ''If you're right for this part I have in mind, I'll give you ten thousand dollars—only three or four days' work.''

She stared at him, her senses whirling as though she'd been hit on the head. Ten thousand dollars! Her heart was now pounding from a quite different emotion. She could live for a *year* on ten thousand, quit the menial fill-in jobs, take acting lessons. That awful pressure would be off—asking for time off to attend casting calls, never knowing if she'd have a job to go back to. She could send some money home. She could . . . God, she could *live*!

Vollner saw it all and felt the power, the thrill of total control over another human life. Ten thousand bucks and she was his, bought and paid for. Oh, she'd squawk when she heard the details, but she'd go along with it, subjugate her principles. Behind the façade they were all whores, ready to sell the hairy little thing they sat on. The only thing that varied was the price.

Her lush mouth was open but no words were coming out. He could play with her now, say anything he liked and she'd take it. She'd been reborn.

"Cat gotcha tongue?"

She laughed incredulously. "I don't know what to say!"

"It'd mean a lot to you, hmm—ten thousand?"

"Everything."

"The part isn't easy."

"I'll work hard on it." Eager now, seeing the brass ring within her grasp. "I can take direction."

He nodded at her, smiling, as though pleased with her response, enjoying the moment, as he would enjoy every moment from now on, studying her reactions, her give-away body language, watching the displays of emotion reflected in her face, the entire gamut, first, as now, the joy, then the uncertainty, followed by dawning awareness, finally the disbelief and trauma. And always the confusion of greed. She would reach and pass hitherto unknown limits of behavior, give herself reasons, tell herself lies. Well, I've gone this far, what's a little more? It's my career. There are a whole new set of standards these days. Nudity means nothing. Maybe I'm out of touch. And,

Jesus, there's the money. I have to do it. I can always pretend it didn't happen. Oh, God . . . the money . . . the money . . .

One of his best-loved games was discovering the price for which any given man or woman would sell their soul. His mother's price had been ten bucks. This one came a little more expensive.

Vollner moved to get up, saying, "Come with me, I want to show you something."

He crossed the den to a far door, she almost skipping along behind him, so excited, already rich, no longer suspicious of his motives, now one of the team. She followed him into a spacious, deserted office, its center dominated by a pool table on which rested a scale model of mountainous terrain, incorporating a film set she didn't recognize. The office also contained desks and filing cabinets and drawing boards, but its striking feature was the hundreds of drawings that almost completely covered the cork-lined walls.

Vollner moved slowly along them, explaining as he perused the drawings searchingly, "Every sequence in the movie is drawn before it's shot. It's called a storyboard. Walk around the room, you can see the whole movie. Your scenes are over here somewhere. You know what *Die Young* is about?"

"Well, only vaguely, I haven't seen a script."

"A company of U.S. Marines gets hit by the N.V.A.— the North Vietnamese Army. Some die, some are taken prisoner, the others get back to base. For reasons that don't matter here, the American brass won't take action to get the boys back, so, unofficially, the survivors of the mission do it themselves. They find out their buddies are being kept in a Buddhist temple in a city called Quang Hoi— that's a model of the city over there on the pool table— and are going to be publicly executed on a certain day.

How they find out is where your character comes in. Her name is An Loq, but the marines call her Little Annie.''

Lin laughed. "Little Annie. I like that.''

"She's a gentle girl, detests the violence of war. When she learns about the public executions, she makes for the border to get a message to U.S. headquarters. But on her way back she gets caught. She's taken to the N.V.A. barracks, is questioned, tortured, and raped. Here—here's the rape sequence.''

Lin approached the board, studied the drawings one by one.

At her side and a step behind her, Vollner studied her, smiled to himself as she registered horror at what was happening to Little Annie.

"Wow,'' she murmured, frowning. "She really gets it.''

"Yeah, well, it's the only sex in the movie, we've got to make the most of it. And we'll shoot for overseas markets, they allow more sex than we do at home.''

"She's naked an awful lot.'' Uncertainty creeping into her tone. "Full frontal? You really need that?''

"We'll shoot on a closed set, of course, minimum crew. Think you can handle it? It's a small but a very important role. It'll get you noticed.''

"I can see that. Yes, I'm sure I could . . . it's just that,'' she glanced at him with a self-conscious smile, "you know, I've never worked nude before . . . all those actors and technicians around.''

Now it was his turn for uncertainty. "Yeah, well, I realize that can be a problem—for *some* actresses. Most of them, hell, they'd give their eyeteeth to be seen bare-assed. But some, a few, they'd jeopardize their careers rather than do it.''

She spun around to him, eyes wide with dismay. "Oh, no! I'm not saying I won't. Please, don't get me wrong . . .''

He sighed pensively, a man with big responsibilities.

"Lin . . . I've got to be sure. You see my problem. I give you this peach of a part and you fuck it up . . . you get so embarrassed you can't act being raped. I mean, it takes some acting even when the actress is comfortable with nudity . . . naked guys crawling all over her. If you blow it, kid, I'd be in deep shit."

"Mister Vollner, I won't! I'll do anything you want, I promise."

Another sigh, thinking about it, then a glance toward a second doorway, like this brilliant idea had suddenly come to him. "Look, tell you what . . ." He moved to the door, opened it, reached inside, and worked a light switch. "Come in here." He went in, holding the door for her.

As she walked past him she saw it was a bedroom, felt the shock of it, like a fist in the stomach. Her mind reeled, heart rocked. She turned to him. "Mister Vollner . . ."

The door closed.

There he was, hands on her shoulders, smiling his trust-me, avuncular smile. "Take it easy, take it easy. Listen, you need that ten thousand, right?"

She nodded distractedly. "Of course . . ."

"Well, I'm gonna make sure you get it. You have a problem, I'm going to solve it. You need help, I'm going to give it to you. Okay, stand right there."

Leaving her at the foot of the double bed, he went to sit in a fabric armchair ten feet away, showing her he wasn't about to jump her bones. He assumed a relaxed pose, legs crossed, smiled at her.

"Siddown, on the bed, I want to tell you something."

Nervously she lowered herself to its edge.

"Okay," he said, gesturing, "take a look at this room. Looks like a bedroom—right? Double bed, dressers, chairs, lamps, nice thick carpet, all in tones of green. You know why? Green is relaxing. Lin, this ain't a bedroom, it's a rehearsal room. Nobody *sleeps* here. Hey, you think

220

I don't know the problem actors have with nudity? You think it's easy for *anybody* to hit a set cold, eighty-thirty in the morning, strip off and pretend to fuck? And maybe they never even *met* before? Jesus!''

That got a smile out of her.

He went on, ''I learned the secret a long time ago. The people involved in the scene, you bring them together before the shoot, so they know each other. But more than that. You get them used to seeing one another in their undies, and finally naked. And you bring in the director and the technicians, so they all get to know one another real well, so there won't be any embarrassment during the shoot. Well, that's what this room is for. This is where the get-togethers happen. You'd be amazed at the big names that've lain on that bed, bare-assed, telling jokes an' talking football.''

Lin turned to look at the patterned comforter as though expecting to see the entwined bodies.

Vollner said, ''You know how people get used to doing things, Lin? By doing them. You start out slow and easy and build up. Stand up, kid.''

Cocooned still in uncertainty, she stood.

''Okay, take off your dress.''

Hesitantly, she reached for the rear zipper. She was not happy; he could read it in her face. There was the confusion he'd been expecting. She was thinking over what he'd been saying, and she knew it made sense. She was thinking about the part, what it could do for her future. And she was thinking about the money. What was wrong was the setup, how this had come about. She hadn't had time to prepare her mind. She was alone with a man. Maybe if there was another woman in the room . . .

Time for him to apply a little pressure.

He gave a light laugh, just showing his impatience.

"Hey, kid, come *on,* I haven't got all night! You want this part or don't you?"

"Yes, of course . . ." Hurrying now, fumbling the zipper, drawing it down, nervous, shrugging the little red dress from her shoulders, lowering it to her feet, stepping out of it, but holding it in front of her as a subconscious last-ditch defense against his eyes.

"Lin, get rid of it, honey, I can't *see* you. I've got to know what I'm casting for this part, don't you see that? I get you in front of the camera and find you've got three tits or an ugly birthmark, I'm screwed. Now, come on, I know you're a nice kid, and shy, but you're also an actress about to earn *ten thousand dollars* for a nude role and the producer has to see what he's buying."

She tossed the dress onto the bed.

He nodded, gestured. "Now the panty hose."

She kicked off her shoes, hooked thumbs into the waistband, drew down the pantyhose, sat on the bed, and removed them.

Vollner felt the rush of excitement. All that remained was a pale pink itsy-bitsy bra and bikini panties.

"Fine, now the bra."

Her head lowered, she slipped the hooks, peeled away the cups.

He stared. Her breasts were exquisite, on the small side but plump and firm and perfectly rounded, with large dark areolae and nubby, puckered, so-suckable nipples he craved to bite.

"Beautiful," he grated, his voice constricted. "Hey, we're nearly there. Now the panties."

She was hesitant, trembling, then with a sudden surge of determination, almost defiance, stood and yanked them down, stood with her back to him, breathtakingly naked.

Vollner feasted, his heartbeat chaotic. See how easy it was? You could buy anybody, make them do things they hated, subject them to all kinds of indignity, they'd take it. The only thing that varied was the price.

He grunted to clear his throat. "Turn around, kid."

She pivoted slowly, eyes downcast, pretending the body he was ogling wasn't hers.

Vollner was amazed, in this day and age and for an actress, at the measure of her modesty. Hell, most kids, especially L.A. kids, and especially would-be actresses, were as unselfconscious about nudity and screwing as they were about chewing gum. This one was excitingly different, an anachronism. Maybe it was the Eurasian thing, the way they were brought up. Whatever, it was to the good. She had a quality of innocence that would come over on the screen, make the rape scene so much more effective. There was no percentage in raping a kid who enjoyed being gang-banged.

He had never ceased to marvel at how different women looked when they were completely naked, when that last vestige of clothing was removed. Even the flimsiest of fabric made a difference. It was the exposure of the pubes that did it, the three-dimensional reality of the hair. Look at hers . . . a thick black bush spreading upward to her firm flat belly, running down in abundance between her slender, satin thighs, sending out an irresistible invitation: Come, spread me wide and get a taste of Heaven . . .

Christ, he wanted this.

Beneath the robe he was rampant, rock hard. His heart thundered in his chest. His mouth was dry; his lips trembled. He had to cough to control his voice.

"Climb up on the bed. I want to see you lying down."

Her attitude now suddenly changed. She no longer resisted. He had expected the transformation. It was an established psychological tactic: remove a person's clothing, you remove their defenses.

He got up from the chair. Opening a dresser drawer, he

took out a viewfinder, a monocular device used in cinematography for gauging the parameters of a frame. Putting it to his eye, he approached the bed, walked slowly around it, focusing on the girl, telling her in a husky murmur, "Jesus, you're beautiful. You have a perfect body. The camera loves you, you know that? You've got something a lot of our top actresses would die for—a photogenic body, any angle.

"Turn on your side . . . bring your knees up, let the camera see your beautiful ass. Great. Now turn the other way . . . face me. Terrific. Now on your back. Open your legs . . . wider, honey, bend your knees. Really spread 'em. Think of the scene. C'mon, let's see some acting now. You've been captured by the N.V.A., those animals. They've tortured you, beaten you, given you electric shocks, used pliers on your nipples, whatever. Now they're gonna rape you. There are three guys here, all naked. You see what's gonna happen and you react. No, bigger than that . . . much bigger. Christ, kid, you're gonna be fucked . . . gang-banged! Lin, I'm not getting it . . . there's no terror there. I know it's difficult, working cold like this, but use your imagination . . . *see* it. No, that's not it, all I'm getting is facial expression, there's no heart, no terror. It's got to come from inside. Shit, no, this is all surface stuff. Really *feel* the first guy come at you, climbing between your legs, a huge hard-on . . . okay, you need help, I gotta see the fear . . ."

Vollner threw the viewfinder aside, released the tie of his robe, shucked the kimono from his shoulders. There he was, stiff to his navel.

The girl gasped with genuine horror, with perplexity, seeing him climbing onto the bed, not knowing which role he was playing, what he was doing or about to do.

She cried, "Mister Vollner!" and tried to close her legs. He grabbed her ankles, forced them apart. "I'm *not*

Mister Vollner. I'm a fucking slope. Christ, play the scene! React! Give me the terror!''

She screamed. She wasn't acting. It was genuine terror. She tried to scramble up the bed, away from him, but he held her legs, spread them wide, and then he was on her, smothering her with his sweating flesh, grabbing her tiny wrists and hauling them above her head, pinning them there easily with one hand, his right hand now down between her legs.

She yelled, outraged, as his thick finger pushed into her vagina. ''STOP THIS! LET ME GO!''

His voice, ragged and breathless, rasped in her ear. ''That's it! This is the reaction I want! Jesus, this is wonderful . . . wonderful.'' He withdrew his finger, hooked an arm under her left leg, lifted her up, took hold of his throbbing erection and fed it into her.

She writhed, bellowed. ''GET OUT OF ME, YOU FILTHY *BASTARD*!''

He roared with laughter, started working inside her, long, deep, rapacious thrusts, driven by the insane excitement of total male domination over a helpless female. ''Oh, *Christ,* you feel good.'' On and on, roaring his pleasure, gasping into her averted face. ''This . . . is how it will be . . . the scene . . . imagine this . . . when the camera's turning . . . think of me . . . inside you . . . fucking you . . . *raping* you . . . give me this . . . give me this . . . and you'll win a fucking OSCAR! Jesus, I'm coming . . . Christ, I'M COMING IN YOU!''

He exploded in her, filling her, drained himself and collapsed, fighting for breath, feeling no resistance, hearing no sound. She was stunned, shocked, as it should be. This was the reality, the truth of rape.

''This is what I want,'' he gasped, catching his breath now, calming. ''Exactly this. Remember it.''

225

Another moment and he slid out of her, got off the bed, put on his robe.

She curled away from him, beginning to come out of the shock, to tremble and sob.

Vollner studied her, her reaction, making mental notes. "Come *on*," he said roughly. "I've helped you! You'll be terrific. You could never have done it without that."

A despairing sob racked her.

"Hey, d'you want the part . . . the ten thousand bucks? It's yours."

She made no response.

He laughed brutally. "C'mon, who're you kidding? You were no virgin, you've been fucked before. It's natural. It's what women do—and usually for a lot less than ten thousand bucks. You still want the part or not?"

Yeah, a response this time, a vague nod. She was coming out of it, beginning to reason with herself, telling herself he was right, it *was* what women did, thinking about the role, her future, the *mon*ey. Smiling to himself, Vollner went to the bedside phone, punched a number, listened to it ring, said, "Now," and put the receiver down.

Returning to the foot of the bed, he retrieved the view-finder, said to her gruffly, "Lissen to me, kid, I'm gonna give you good advice. You want a career in movies, you'll have to toughen up. You've got a great face an' body and a nice style, but you won't get far in Tinseltown with that Virgin Mary act. The odds are stacked against you because you're Eurasian. The parts are limited. Christ, *all* parts are limited, there're twenty thousand *WASP* kids outta work any one time. So you'll have ta work twice as hard, offer them something extra. You could be one helluva sexy woman if you put your mind to it. Young, defenseless flesh always turns guys on. You could be the Third World Brooke Shields, know what I'm sayin'? But you gotta be prepared to fuck."

He went to the armchair, moved it closer to the bed, sat in it, framed her off in the viewfinder.

"You photograph real good, any angle. The camera loves your body. Your body's gotta love it back. You gotta cut loose, let go, lose your inhibitions, *use* your *cooz,* f'Crissake. It's why God gave it to you. Hey, who's kiddin' who? Ever since Eve opened her legs to that dumb schmuck Adam women have been using that hairy little thing to get what they want—right? Cunt rules the world—okay?"

The door from the office opened. Ken Dok entered, followed by Ed Bussey. Both of them were wearing the green uniform of the North Vietnamese Army.

The girl, hearing the door, conscious of her nakedness, reacted with panic, grabbed for the comforter. At the sight of the giant Korean in the uniform, not immediately recognizing him, seeing another uniform behind, she froze, gaped with shock, then jerked a look at Vollner, found him peering at her through the viewfinder.

"Yeah, great! That's the reaction! But lose the comforter. You've been tortured, remember . . . you're lying on a filthy, lice-ridden bed at army headquarters . . ."

She screamed, "NO!" and in a frenzy made to get off the bed.

Vollner jerked his head at Bussey, who moved quickly and caught her, threw her back against the pillows.

Ken Dok pulled off his boots, dropped his pants, took his monstrous erection to her.

She kicked, screamed, went berserk, while Vollner moved in closer, telling her, "Yeah . . . right . . . great . . . terrific . . . Jesus *Christ,* I wish this was a take."

Chapter Seventeen

The Crest View Motel was a four-story structure designed to resemble a Tyrolean guesthouse. Located ten miles east of Redding, it was sited spectacularly on elevated ground that overlooked the Little Cow River and commanded breathtaking views in every direction, the "Crest" in its name referring not to one mountain peak, but to several: Schell Mountain to the northwest; North Fork Mountain, due north; Crater Park, to the southwest; Table Mountain, due south. And many more all over five thousand feet.

The motel, painted apple green with white trim to blend with the landscape, had an overhanging pantile roof, a flower box beneath every window, and perfectly kept gardens. Its facilities included conference rooms, banquet rooms, two restaurants, a coffee shop, several bars, and a sports complex. Sleeping capacity was close to one thousand.

From the time Frank Vollner moved his production facilities from Los Angeles to Redding and bought the Crest View for cast and crew accommodation when needed, the motel had become increasingly popular among the public movie buffs of Oregon and California. When Vollner was in production and shooting in the Cascade area, the Crest View was the place to stay. Here, over a reasonably priced weekend, one could mingle with actors and technicians in the bars, occasionally catch sight of famous faces in the restaurants, feel part of the film community.

During production, the Crest View was invariably full.

At seven o'clock on the evening following their run-in with Blondie, Bandanna, and the black, Raven turned the camper into the parking area surrounding the Crest View and saw immediately they were probably in trouble. The front lot was filled to capacity.

"Business is good," he murmured. "We may have to sleep in the camper. Let's hope, at least, they're all cast and crew."

He skirted the building, discovered a larger but almost equally occupied lot at the rear, eventually finding a space in the farthest corner.

They entered the motel through a rear door, worked their way through busy pine-clad corridors, passed the restaurants and the coffee shop, emerged into a foyer thronged with people, many of them Orientals. Raven cut through them to the reception desk and inquired about rooms.

The sensuous-looking creature with voluminous blond hair and pendulous breasts, wearing regulation cream silk blouse and apple-green skirt, both garments a size too small, fluttered her false lashes at him and breathed, "Gee, I doubt it."

Her languorous blue eyes shifted to Kat, did their female work, and returned to Raven transmitting the perplexed question: Two *singles*? Who's she, your sister?

Her glistening lips said, "I mean, we don't *do* singles. All the rooms have twin beds, y'know?"

Raven smiled his understanding. "Well, how about two twins, then."

"That's what I'm doubting."

Her name badge, clinging precariously to the upper slope of her left breast, identified her as "Gloria."

Raven nodded, as though he expected as much. Gloria. "Did you know it means Beautiful One? How very appropriate. Gloria, do you think you could possibly check for us, see what you've got?"

She flashed a glance of triumph in Kat's direction, gave Raven thirty-two perfectly white teeth. "Sure." And she moved up the counter to the computer, everything ticking like Swiss clockwork beneath the tight green skirt.

Behind his shoulder, Raven heard Kat's contrived groan. She mimicked sourly, " 'Gloria . . . did you know it means Beautiful One? How very appropriate.' "

He grinned, kept his eye on Gloria. "We need help. Who better than Beautiful One? This kid notices everything in pants that passes this desk—even middle-aged Comanche Indians. If he's here, she'll know."

She sighed histrionically. "Raven, is that, honest-to-God, your story?"

He laughed, modified it to a grin for Gloria, who was flashing at him down the line, punching computer keys.

Kat said, "I'll sleep in the camper. I'd hate to cramp your . . . investigation."

He threw a quick glance at her. "Would you do that? Okay, I'll tell her. One room it is."

He winced as her fingers drove into his kidney.

Gloria returned. Raven guessed by now her teeth must be feeling the cold. "Don't know if this'll help. Someone just canceled. I can let you have one room." Her gaze, concentrated on Raven but fleetingly, insolently, embracing Kat, said: Who're you trying to kid?

Behind him, Kat murmured hostilely, "Just had a great idea—*you* sleep in the camper."

"We'll take it," said Raven.

Kat's heart stirred.

* * *

230

Something was going on in the corridor of the top floor when they arrived there with their overnight bags. A group of young Orientals—four girls and a guy—were involved in a heated discussion outside a room. The focus of attention seemed to be a beautiful Eurasian girl, distraught and crying, encircled by the others, who appeared to be exhorting her to take action about a problem.

As Kat and Raven closed in on them, they heard the young man say, "Lin, you've got to *tell* somebody! He can't get away with this. Christ, it's unbelievable!"

Lin was sobbing bitterly. "Tell who? He owns everybody up here. Nobody would believe me."

One of the girls spat angrily, "So you're just going to take this? You're going to run back home, quit acting, let him ruin your career? Lin, Vollner isn't God. You've got to report this to somebody."

Raven and Kat exchanged a glance.

Now the Chinese male spotted their approach and shushed the group.

Key in hand, Raven was checking the room numbers, already knowing that 446 was the one the group was standing outside. The room Lin had just vacated.

He smiled at them as they eased away from the door. "Hi."

They murmured a subdued response.

Raven unlocked the door, let Kat through, then turned to the group, who were silent, half watching them, waiting for them to enter the room. He looked at them in turn, gently impressing his presence upon them, getting their attention, then settled his gaze on the distraught girl and began reading her trauma.

Lin was sobbing softly, her eyes downcast, absorbed by her dilemma, but in the ensuing silence she gradually became aware that something was happening and glanced up to find Raven's gaze, piercingly direct, hypnotic, yet somehow sympathetic, fixed upon her.

Her heart took a tumble. A warning flashed into her mind: Vollner's man. He'd heard her talking! She tried to avert her eyes, but found his gaze irresistible. Twice . . . three times she was drawn back to meet it. Something weird was happening to her, to the group. They were standing like statues, staring at this striking man. She felt helpless, powerless to move, strangely calm, and yet her heart was thudding like a drum.

He spoke . . . his voice deep, kind, gentle, soothing, its rich timbre flowing through her like warm oil. "Lin, isn't it?"

She frowned, nodded, wondering how he knew.

"My name is Raven. John Raven." He took a step closer, reached out, and gently touched her cheek.

The young man, short but muscular, shifted uneasily, moved reflexively into preparation for the karate square-off stance.

Maintaining his eye connection with Lin, Raven offered him an open palm, a smile of appeasement, murmuring, "Take it easy, I'm not going to hurt her."

The kid demanded suspiciously, "Who are you, mister? What're you doing?"

Raven said, addressing Lin, "I heard Vollner's name mentioned. You've had trouble with him . . . bad trouble."

One of the girls muttered, "You can say that again."

Raven continued, "I'm no friend of Vollner's. Far from it." His gaze now embraced them all. "I'd like to talk to you—to all of you. I need some help. Maybe in return I can help you. Would you come into our room?"

They exchanged glances.

Lin said softly, "I was just leaving. I've got a taxi waiting to take me to the bus station."

"There'll be another bus. I think we ought to talk."

More glances, shrugs, then mutual acquiescence.

"Okay," said the young man.

Kat's expression reflected more intrigue than surprise as the group trouped into the room. Though she hadn't heard his words, she knew Raven had been fishing.

They sat on the beds. Introductions were made. The kids were Billy, Nancy, Belle, and Mo. They struck an immediate affinity with Kat, drawing comfort from her gender, her manner, her "ordinariness." Raven's aura disturbed them.

Raven began with, to Kat, "Lin's had trouble with Frank Vollner. At the lodge. It's so bad she wants to give up acting. I feel we ought to hear about it, if she'll tell us."

Lin, immersed in her disconsolation, took a moment to react, then looked up slowly, puzzled and suspicious. "How did you know that? That it happened at his lodge?"

Kat glanced at Raven, sensed his approval of explanation, said to the girl, "Lin, John is psychic. He . . . reads people, knows things."

The group stared at her, at Raven.

Billy murmured approvingly, "Wow."

Mo nodded, readily accepting it. "My mom's psychic. Whenever I go home, even when I don't phone, she's always waiting for me at the bus station. I guess we're telepathic or something."

It was enough to put them all at ease.

Nancy said, frowning, interested, "I never knew that—about your mom."

Mo shrugged. "She doesn't tell people about it. She's frightened they'll think she's weird."

Raven smiled, his raised-brow expression telling Kat: See, everybody's got it.

To the group he said, "I'd better explain about myself. Professionally, I'm a scientist. Right now I'm looking for a man, a relative I haven't seen in a very long time. This man used to work for Frank Vollner, and Vollner did something very bad to him." He looked directly at Lin, his expression conveying sympathy, understanding, and belief in the cause of her anguish. "I believe my relative is here now, and I've got to find him. Maybe you've seen him, talked to him. He might well be working on *Die Young* under an assumed name."

Billy asked, "What does he look like?"

Raven shook his head. "I don't know. I have no photographs of him. But he's a Comanche Indian, fifty-five years old."

The group exchanged looks, shook their heads.

Billy said, "There're an awful lot of people on this movie, a lot of different races, including some Indians, but I don't remember seeing one that age."

Raven nodded. "What are you guys—actors?"

Nancy answered, "Yeah, well, crowd, really. We've got no lines to say. But we've been told we're getting small featured pieces in the Quang Hoi scenes—you know, maybe a special piece of action when the marines start destroying the town."

"So—you haven't actually worked on the movie yet?" Raven asked hopefully.

Belle laughed. "Sure we have. We've all been part of the crowd in two or three sequences. To Vollner we're just Chinese faces. Only our parents can tell us apart." Her expression changed from derision to anger. "Not Lin, though. She hasn't worked yet. Vollner had her picked for a special part . . ." She stopped, reluctant to reveal the source of her friend's distress.

Raven waited.

Lin shook her head, whispered to Belle, "Tell them."

Trembling, Belle looked at Raven, then at Kat, and

blurted, "The bastard raped her. Three of them did it . . . Vollner and his two goons."

Kat stared at her, uttering a sound of empathy and horror.

Belle went on distractedly, "Only it wasn't done like that—you know, just rape. The pig made it sound as though he was doing her a favor." She drew a sigh, trying to make it sound plausible as she told them Lin's whole sordid story of the night before.

Kat gasped. "I don't believe I'm hearing this."

Belle rounded on her. "Lin wouldn't lie! Look at her! Shit, she *wanted* this part. Vollner offered her ten thousand dollars . . ."

Kat protested, "No, please, Belle, I didn't say I don't believe you! Belle, I know what rape *is*!"

Belle frowned at her, awareness dawning. "You, too? I'm sorry. I . . . well, look at her. That's the way you felt—right?"

Kat nodded.

Belle gave a helpless shrug, continued in a quieter tone, "We don't know what to do. Lin only got back here a short time ago, she's been trapped up there at the lodge, waiting for them to bring her back in the helicopter. Now she wants to go home, to San Francisco, forget acting."

Raven said with quiet assurance, "That's understandable. But she won't give it up. She has a bright future."

Lin raised her eyes to him, frowning with uncertainty. "You see that?"

"Yes. You're very beautiful, Lin. You photograph extremely well."

Her lips compressed bitterly. "That's what he told me. But he also told me I'd have to go to bed with a lot of . . ." She shook her head. "I could never do that. I'd rather be a waitress."

Raven said, "This ten thousand dollars . . . was Vollner serious about it? Does he really want you for the part?"

She shrugged. "I guess so."

"How did you leave him? I mean, what was his attitude toward you when you left the lodge?"

"I couldn't believe it. He was behaving as though nothing wrong had happened, as though he really believed he had helped me get the part by . . . doing what he did. I think he's insane."

Raven nodded. "Absolute power is a form of insanity, and that's what he has over you. As you said in the corridor, he owns everybody up here. You could never make a charge of rape stick. He'd produce a dozen witnesses who'd swear it never happened. He'd say you offered him sex for the part, he turned you down, and this is your revenge, something like that. Whichever way it went, you'd lose. Maybe even your life. If you started a case against him, you might well disappear forever."

The group reacted. Billy said, "Are you kidding?"

"No, I'm not. Vollner is a very dangerous man. He has two faces: the fund-raising do-gooder, and the one Lin saw. You threaten his do-gooder public image, I guarantee you'd meet with an accident."

Nancy rolled her eyes. "My God, who're we working for?"

"You're working," Raven said, "for the Mafia."

He gave that a moment to sink in, then went on, "Okay, let's agree that, with regard to the rape, no legal action is possible. My advice is that none of you says a word about it outside this room. Vollner will have spies everywhere. He owns this motel. You talk about it, he'll get to hear, and the very least that could happen is you'll be kicked off the production. At the moment he thinks he has bought Lin's silence with the ten-thousand-dollar part. Well, he has."

Lin looked at him, shook her head adamantly. "No, I

could never play that part now . . . see him sitting there
on the set, watching . . ."

Raven said, "You won't have to. But you could use that
ten thousand, couldn't you?"

"Of course."

"And you deserve it for what you've been through.
Think of yourself as having already played the rape scene.
Now you collect."

She frowned at him. "I don't understand."

"You have an agent?"

"Yes. In Los Angeles."

"Can you reach him? I mean, it's nighttime and a holiday . . ."

She was nodding. "His office is also his apartment, you
know. If he's not there, he has an answering machine."

Raven indicated the phone. "Call him, I'll pay. Lin,
listen to me . . . you're an actress. I want you to act right
now. When you speak to him, or his machine, you're excited, over the moon about this fabulous part and the ten
thousand dollars Vollner has offered you. Tell him Vollner
sent for you and you went to the lodge for an audition,
and you got the part. But tell him you want it confirmed.
Ask him to call Vollner immediately, not to wait until after
the holiday, and get it tied up. Right?"

She looked bewildered. "But how . . . ?"

Raven said, with a glance requesting confirmation to
Kat, "Movie people agree deals with a verbal handshake,
don't they? Their word is their bond—like bookies and
stockbrokers?"

"Yes," said Kat. "Most deals are done over the
phone."

Raven looked back to Lin. "Right, the moment your
agent gets confirmation from Vollner, the ten thousand is
yours."

"But he won't pay if I don't do the part," she protested.

"In certain circumstances, yes, he will. Or, rather, his insurance company will."

"In what circumstances?"

"If the movie isn't finished. If Vollner doesn't get around to shooting the rape scenes."

Lin took her bewildered look to Kat, back to Raven. "But why shouldn't he?"

"Trust me. Call your agent."

They listened in silence, the Chinese kids exchanging puzzled, intrigued glances as Lin gathered herself, took a moment to rehearse the words in her mind, contacted the L.A. number, and delivered her euphoric news to her agent in person.

She sagged as she came off the phone. "He's thrilled. And why not—he's about to earn a thousand bucks for making a phone call."

"Good," said Raven. "Now I want you to do something for me. I want you to tell me everything you know about Frank Vollner, about his personal staff, and about the layout of the hunting lodge. *Everything*."

Chapter Eighteen

The lodge described to Raven by Lin Siddon bore little resemblance to the original structure built by Angus McKenzie in the late forties.

Emigrating from Scotland after World War Two, Gus had parlayed his experience in a modest Highland lumberyard into a substantial fortune in the redwood forests of the Pacific Northwest, and thence into a multitude of evergreen and deciduous timber and lumber interests, gradually spreading inland from the coast as far as Redding, buying up land by the square mile rather than by the acre.

A nature lover, he had two abiding passions: trees and birds. The site on which he built his lodge had an abundance of both. Being a simple, somewhat dour Highland Scot, he constructed the lodge simply and somewhat austerely, using gray mountain granite to remind him of his homeland. Isolation had also been important. A single graded road, five miles in length, led in from Highway 89. Except by air, or by Jeep twisting through surrounding valleys, there was no way to reach the lodge. Here, until a "widow-maker"—a dead branch falling from a tall sequoia—had crippled him, Gus provided a rustic haven for his toil-worn business associates. Good food and better whiskey had been the order of the day. Hunting was strictly forbidden.

Suddenly mindful, as a cripple, of his own mortality, he took immediate steps to transfer ownership of his estate to members of his family. To his daughter, Barbara, in addition to the sum of ten million dollars, he gave twenty-five thousand acres of land in the Cascades, which included a mountain and the lodge.

Within a year Barbara was dead, and her money, mountain, and lodge belonged to her husband, Frank Vollner.

Gus McKenzie died a year later, a desolate man.

Vollner, seeing its potential as a true hunting lodge and a place in which to royally entertain his nature-starved New York associates, lost no time in transforming it into a luxury retreat, adding self-contained suites, a screening room, an indoor shooting range, separate staff quarters, and a helipad. He extravagantly stretched and expanded the structure until it more aptly required the description "complex."

One original feature, though, had not been changed: its supreme isolation. Vollner guarded his privacy determinedly. The surrounding forest was seeded with electronic warning devices. All approaches to the lodge were protected by closed-circuit surveillance. A guard was posted on the road leading in from 89. Powerful lights lit the terrace and surrounding gardens at night. A wire enclosure housed six Doberman guard dogs, trained to kill on command.

Vollner felt totally secure at the lodge, another reason—added to the obvious ones of comfort, convenience, and separation from Sissy—for spending so much time there, rather than in Bel Air.

During his years in L.A. he had cut throats—figuratively and literally—to get where he was and he had made many enemies. But at the lodge he gave them little thought.

Until the phone call.

It came in the late evening, a couple of hours after a

call from the L.A. agent, and Vollner was pissed at being disturbed.

Alone in the production office off the den, he was immersed in logistical problems concerning the Quang Hoi sequence and had left instructions: important calls only. Okay, the agent's call was important because he didn't know how the Eurasian kid would react to what happened, and was somewhat relieved to hear the guy say how thrilled Lin was to be doing the part and how soon could Vollner's office get a contract to him. Not that Vollner gave a shit how the kid reacted; any potentially troublesome move she made would be blocked. But it was cleaner this way. And as a bonus she'd be very effective in the role. He was pleased with the outcome, even forgave the agent for calling him direct and after business hours.

But there was another call.

What now?

"Yeah, what is it?"

Lenny was on the board. "Boss, I got a guy here I think you oughtta talk to."

"The fuck time is it?"

"Nearly eleven."

"Lenny, this'd better be *real* important."

"I think it is, boss. He says his name's Raven."

Several things happened to Vollner, none of them pleasant. Surprise hit him like a lightning left jab. He broke into a cold sweat as events that had occurred a quarter of a century earlier projected across his mind. Then came disbelief. Finally, bolstered by a reminder of his own strength and invulnerability as opposed to the position of his caller, he relaxed in a burst of sardonic laughter.

"Raven! Jesus Christ, the guy's got a nerve."

He knew Will Raven was out, but knew also the Indian was beaten and penniless, no threat whatever. So, what did the guy want—a handout? Was he trying some kind of shakedown? He couldn't be that fucking stupid. Well, maybe he, Vollner, could work something to his advantage here. Sissy was big in ex-con rehab. It'd go down well with the press if Frank Vollner was seen to be so charitable that he even gave a lift to the ex-con who murdered his first wife. How's that for brotherly love? Jesus, the trades would lap it up, take back some of the shit they'd hit him with over *Andromeda* and *Man of Steel*. Yeah, why not . . .

"Put him on," he snapped at Lenny.

"Mister Vollner?"

Vollner frowned. This wasn't Will Raven. The voice was too young, too refined. Who the fuck was tryin' to pull what here?

"Yeah, who is this?"

"My name is John Raven."

Another left jab. Vollner's mind raced. John Raven . . . John Raven . . . there was a kid. Raven's attorney had made a big thing of it in court. And later that crazy Gypsy wife had screamed at him about depriving her son of his father. But he couldn't recall a first name.

"What can I do for you, Mister Raven?"

"I believe you know my father . . . Will Raven?" The tone was cool, polite.

What was this guy—a fucking comedian?

"You bein' cute, Raven?"

"Not intentionally. Mister Vollner, I'd like to meet you, talk to you about him."

"What about him?"

"I'm trying to find him. As you may know, he was released from San Quentin a year ago. I've only just learned of his release. I thought perhaps you might know where he is."

"No, I don't." He wanted to add, "I don't normally keep in social contact with Indian scumbags who murder my wife," but there was something in this guy's voice that made him hold back. Vollner had always been in awe of education; of itself it demanded a certain respect. Besides, if he was going to pull this ex-con rehab scam, he might need this guy.

Raven said, "I still think we ought to talk."

"Why?"

"Because I have certain information which leads me to believe that you—or your film production—might be in jeopardy."

Vollner jerked forward in his chair. "You what? Say that again?"

"I think we ought to talk."

"Talk now. Whaddya mean—jeopardy? Is Will planning something?"

"Not over the phone, Mister Vollner."

"Where're you calling from?"

"The Crest View Motel."

"*My* motel? In Redding? I'll send the chopper, it'll be there in twenty minutes."

"No, tomorrow morning. I'm very tired, I'm going to bed. Shall we say eleven o'clock?"

"Yeah, right, eleven."

Vollner slammed down the phone button, stabbed out an internal number. "Ken, you an' Ed get the hell over to the Crest View, pick up a guy name of John Raven—*now*. He won't like it, but just bring him."

Raven put down the receiver, got off the bed, and crossed to his traveling case.

"Well?" Kat asked, impatient and concerned.

They were alone now. The group had returned to their rooms, taking Lin Siddon with them.

Raven said, "They're coming for me."

His back was toward her. He took off his leather jacket.

He was wearing a red-and-black-check shirt, and she noticed a four-inch strip of black Velcro running down from the collar between his shoulder blades. He removed something from the case, reached behind him, and affixed it to the Velcro. When he removed his hands she could see what it was, but asked all the same.

"John, what's that?"

"It's a knife."

She got up and went to him, her face creased with growing apprehension. "I don't understand. You said eleven o'clock tomorrow."

"I know Vollner. He won't wait till tomorrow. He flipped when I told him *Die Young* might be in jeopardy. He'll send his goons tonight."

She stared at him. "And you're just going to sit here and wait for them?"

"No, I'm going to sit in the foyer and wait for them."

She erupted. "Are you crazy? After what Lin told you . . . about Vollner and his thugs . . . about the lodge? You're going to let them take you up there tonight?"

He put on his black ski coat. "I have to get close to Vollner. This seems the perfect time."

"The perfect time to disappear! You've just got through warning Lin about what might happen to her if she upset Vollner, and you're about to do the same thing!"

He smiled at her anger. "Kat, I'm not planning to upset him. I'm going to cooperate with him, help him find my father before Will does something drastic."

"So—why the knife?"

"It isn't just a knife." He reached back and withdrew it from its sheath, showing it to her. It had a black seven-inch blade with a jagged spine, and a flat black plastic handle. Embedded in the handle was a compass. "It's a hunting knife. It has the compass and a couple of useful things stored in the handle. I never go into the mountains without a compass."

She wasn't buying it. She turned away, distraught. "It's horrible."

"No more so than a kitchen knife. It depends what you do with it. I don't intend stabbing anybody with it."

"Then what *do* you intend?"

"I intend talking to the man. They'll fly me up there, we'll talk, they'll fly me back."

"Why not just take a compass?"

"I don't have one."

"Why conceal it behind your back?"

"Because I expect they'll frisk me, see if I'm carrying a gun."

"Oh, God, this is awful. John, there has to be another way."

He sighed patiently, sympathizing with her concern. "Kat, my father's up here somewhere, I know it. Joe Santee knows it. The Chinese kids have been knocking around the locations for some time now and they haven't seen anyone fitting Dad's description. We could spend a few more days asking more people, but I've got a feeling we'd be wasting valuable time. Besides, I've spoken to Vollner now and committed myself. So, let it go at that and see what happens. Okay?"

She didn't answer. She had her back to him, head lowered. He went to her, put his hands on her shoulders, turned her around.

"Listen to me . . . I don't want you to use this room until I get back. I don't want you in the motel. Take the bags and wait in the camper, all right?"

Her face, looking up at him, reflected her state of nervousness and worry. "You do expect trouble, don't you?"

"I don't expect it, I'm just preparing for it . . . the Rom's first rule for survival. If—I repeat, *if*—I'm not back by this time tomorrow, drive straight to L.A., contact Lieutenant Marco, tell him everything. Do *not*, on any account, phone Vollner or drive up to the lodge. Will you promise me?''

She lowered her eyes from his, nodded. "I wish you wouldn't go. I've got a bad feeling about this. You do, too.''

"Not at all," he lied. "And who's the psychic around here anyhow?'' He gave her a reassuring hug, kissed her on the forehead. "Come on, I have to get downstairs. Take the bags and get over to the camper.''

She looked up at him with a teary, twisted grimace. "Is that the best you can do—a peck on the forehead?''

He took hold of her face, so gently, and brought his mouth to hers for a tender, gossamer kiss. "That better?''

She didn't answer. She couldn't trust her voice.

Ten minutes later he was seated in the foyer, facing the main doors, when they came in. He followed them with his eyes and other sensory perception as they crossed to the desk, asked for his room number, received the information he had left for them, and turned, surprised, to find him sitting there.

Ken Dok and Ed Bussey came over. He read them, and didn't like the reading. Not one bit.

He smiled amiably. "Hi. What kept you guys?''

Chapter Nineteen

Nanosh had counseled him early on: *You can, with almost invariable accuracy, judge a man by the company he keeps and the help he employs.* On that basis alone, had he known nothing else about Frank Vollner, Raven would have judged him a violent and dangerous man.

They put him up front beside the pilot, a muscular Cybernaut in a flying suit and visored helmet, and sat behind him in the six-seater Bell. Though not a word was spoken during the twenty-minute flight—nor had been since they walked into the foyer—Raven was acutely conscious of their enmity toward him, a radiation of barely suppressed eagerness to render him extreme bodily hurt, as though they had been promised such a treat by their boss when Vollner was finished with him.

That a man like Vollner, a renowned film producer with a reputation for charitable work, could employ such obvious thugs as Ken Dok and Ed Bussey must have surprised a great many people, mused Raven. Then again, maybe he kept them hidden up here in the mountains when he ventured into L.A. wearing his do-gooder face.

As the helicopter descended out of the blackness of the mountains into the blaze of light illuminating the helipad and the adjoining compound, Raven experienced a renewed attack of the apprehension he'd felt at first sight of Dok and Bussey. He was into it now, no turning back. He had no idea how he was going to play it with Vollner; it would depend largely on Vollner. Sooner or later, he had to face the man who had destroyed his father's life and most likely murdered his mother. This seemed as good, or as bad, a time as any. He was only glad Kat was not with him.

Out of the chopper and across the compound yard, Raven noting the dog enclosure, spotting phantom figures skulking in the shadows. It was an armed encampment. Who was Vollner afraid of? New York?

Through an iron-studded, porticoed front door into a marble-floored hall, big oak center table evoking images of medieval banquets, white stucco walls adorned with tapestries depicting hunting scenes, displays of ancient weaponry and firearms, and trophy heads. On the right a robust oak staircase climbed to a gallery landing. A lineup of dour, un-American-looking ancients in ponderous gilt frames climbed up the wall with it. Raven guessed one of Vollner's art directors had decorated the place. He could hear Vollner's instructions: *Gimme English hunting lodge . . . the whole bit.*

Ken Dok indicated he should wait, covered by Ed Bussey, who stood like a statue, arms folded, giving Raven the threatening street stare. Dok disappeared through a door on the right.

Raven gave him an amiable, irritating smile, went to sit in a high-backed tapestried chair, and closed his eyes.

Ken Dok was gone for some time, no doubt telling Vollner about Raven's weird behavior at the motel: *The guy lied. He wasn't in bed, he was waiting for us in the foyer. He knew we were coming.*

That would give Vollner something to think about, make him uneasy. Raven planned on making him a lot more uneasy before he was through.

"Hey—you."

Raven opened his eyes. Bussey jerked his head in Ken Dok's direction, who was standing there in the doorway, filling it, his expression showing puzzlement as to how a guy in Raven's situation could fall asleep.

Raven walked over, offering Dok the same easygoing grin he'd given Bussey. "So—your buddy does talk. The man's got everything . . . charm, poise, breeding . . ."

Dok grabbed Raven's wrists, jerked his arms up over his head, ran his huge, hard-callused hands under Raven's armpits, around his waist, down each leg. The flat throwing knife, nestled between his encompassing shoulder blades, remained undetected.

Dok ushered him through the den to the open door of the production office.

Frank Vollner had sited himself at the far end of the pool table for maximum impact. He leaned forward, hands on its edge, his face dramatically half lit, half shaded by the overhead canopied lights.

Though he knew Raven had entered the room, he continued his contrived preoccupation with the scale model of the Quang Hoi valley set for a long moment, putting Raven down, letting him know he was of no consequence. When he finally looked up at him, he used only his eyes, fixing Raven with the same puzzled manic stare that Steiger had used so effectively as the ruthless studio boss in *The Big Knife*.

Vollner milked the moment, insolently studied Raven from head to toe, his expression unchanging, then briefly switched his gaze to Ken Dok, who stood behind Raven.

"You have something to do?"

Dok departed soundlessly.

Only now did Vollner stand upright, saying to Raven, "Come here," in a tone suggesting he had something to show him.

Raven advanced to the end of the table facing Vollner.

There they stood like a couple of poised gunfighters, squared off for the final confrontation, their faces cast in deep, dramatic shadow. The game, the setting, amused Raven, but it also alarmed him. It told him a lot about Frank Vollner. The man was immature. He was living a role. Perhaps he thought role-playing was mandatory among men who spent their lives creating lurid fiction. But how deep did Vollner's psychosis go? Was he, in fact, mad?

The possibility cleared away much of the difficulty Raven had had in believing the crimes could be attributed to the esteemed producer and fund-raiser. Here, in the mountains, in this isolated hideaway, Raven found it easy to believe everything he'd been told. Here, he sensed Vollner created his own reality. Here he was God.

Now, as Joe Santee's warning about the man came home to Raven full force, he was more relieved than ever that he had left Kat at the motel. The lodge, as Lin Siddon had discovered, was no place for a woman.

A pool cue appeared suddenly in Vollner's hand, plucked from a rack in the shadows behind him. In his white open-neck shirt and black pants, he looked for a moment like an old-time billiards player, but the purpose of the cue was not sport.

He used it as a pointer to indicate the scale model. His voice was gruff, aggressive, as he began. "I own this whole shebang . . . twenty-five thousand acres of wilderness. Here's the lodge. There's only one road leading to it—here—runs in from Eighty-nine, five miles. Here's my mountain, back of the lodge, five thousand feet high. Go north around the mountain, in this valley, here's where I've built a fourteen-block city, Quang Hoi. Cost seven million dollars. The only road into it is here, on the western edge of the property, linking Eighty-nine with Ninety-seven. I've built a service road from it into the Quang Hoi set. The terrain is as rugged as it comes. I've got men guarding the roads, men guarding the Quang Hoi set, and men guarding the lodge. I've got electronic alarms, heat-sensing devices hidden in the woods. I've got six killer dogs.'' He set aside the cue, dropped into his original pose, hands on the table, and stared at Raven through the bright cones of light. "Can you tell me how the fuck a broken-down, middle-aged Indian is going to get past that lot to hurt me or my picture? Hmm? What's this 'information' you've got that leads you to believe I or *Die Young* might be in jeopardy?"

Raven said, "I won't tell you my source. I'll just say this: My father realizes how vital the success of this movie is to your future, and he might see its failure as a means of getting even for what you did to him and his family."

Vollner glared at him, a long I-don't-believe-what-I'm-hearing Steiger stare, then with an explosive, outraged laugh moved from the table to snap on the room lights. "What *I* did to *him* and his family." He rounded on Raven, bristling with fury. "What the fuck d'you think *he* did to me and mine!? He murdered my wife, f'Crissake!"

"No, he did not," Raven said quietly.

"So you say," nodded Vollner, his fists bunched as though he was barely suppressing an urge to smash something. "But the law says otherwise. The law was so certain about it he was put away for twenty-three years. So your opinion, though understandable, ain't worth diddly-shit, sonny. But none of this matters. Will Raven served his time and now he's loose and the only problem is to stop him doing something stupid and getting himself killed or sent back to San Quentin—right?"

"I agree. That's why I'm here."

Vollner paced back and forth, rubbing his face, eyeing the scale model with sidelong glances. "Your father knows pictures . . . picture-making. He's been out for a year. If he's got some kinda sabotage in mind, he's probably kept tabs on the progress of *Die Young* . . .''

"Bank on it," said Raven. "Only don't limit his knowledge to this production."

"What d'you mean?"

"I hear my father dedicated his time in prison to gathering information about you. He made you his life study. And apparently he had a lot of help. Somebody in San Quentin didn't like you, Mister Vollner. Somebody who knows your true New York background, not the phony stuff you've fed the public. Maybe he's not planning to shoot you or sabotage your movie. Maybe he'll just spread the word about your Mafia connections, tarnish your saintly image among your fancy charity friends."

Vollner paled, mouthed wordlessly, stabbed a threatening finger at Raven. "That's a goddamned *lie*! I'm not connected."

Raven shrugged. "Then an exposé can hardly hurt you. Anyway, I don't think my father would take that route. As an Indian ex-con he'd have trouble making people believe his claims. No, I think he'll sabotage your movie, get you in deep shit with the people you say you're not connected to."

Vollner came around the table, closing on Raven, sizing him up, trying to assess what he had here, hearing the words, seeing the style, finding something enigmatic and kinda weird about this guy.

"What d'ya do, Raven, for a living?"

"I'm a scientist."

Vollner circled him, frowning. "Something don't jell. You really Will Raven's son? You pure Comanche?"

"No. I'm half Romany . . . Gypsy."

Vollner's dark eyes flared with sudden insight. "So she really was . . ." He saw his mistake and slammed shut.

Raven peered hard at him, his heartbeat accelerating. "*Who* was really *what*, Mister Vollner? You were going to

252

say she really was a Gypsy, weren't you? My mother. She came to see you, to plead my father's innocence. Did you think she was Comanche like him? Did she come here—to the lodge? Was it from here you made her disappear?''

Vollner's face flushed with fury. ''The fuck you talkin' about? Christ, what else you gonna charge me with? Yeah, she came to see me—and behaved like a friggin' mad-woman, told me she was putting a Gypsy curse on me! But I never touched her. I had her taken to L.A., never saw her again.''

''Why L.A.? We were living in Arizona by then.''

''One of my guys was driving down there anyway. I had her dropped at the bus station, made sure she had enough money to get home.''

''That was charitable of you,'' Raven said derisively.

''Yeah, well, I'm a charitable guy. I felt sorry for her, sympathized with her situation. I even felt sorry for your father, despite what he did. I liked Will, he was a fine wrangler, did good work for me. In a way, it wasn't his fault, he was crazy drunk, didn't know what he was doing. I feel no hatred toward him now. He served his time, the slate's clean. If he needs help to get started again, I'll see what I can do. The important thing is to stop him doing something stupid and landing back in San Quentin.''

Raven smiled, extended his hand. ''For once I agree. Let's work on this together. Thank you for your sympathy and understanding.''

Vollner hesitated, stared at Raven's hand suspiciously, but took it. ''Yeah, well . . .''

It was all there in Vollner's aura: the calumny, the deceit, the lies, the fear, the violence. Raven read the truth of Lin Siddon's accusations. He read his father's innocence, his mother's death. Vollner stood before him psychically naked, stripped of all role-playing pretense: a cheat, a liar, and a murderer. Rotten to the core.

Sensing some incomprehensible but threatening emana-
tion from the handshake, from the staring, penetrating intensity of Raven's gaze, Vollner sought to release his hand from
the powerful grip, breaking away with a shrug and a nervous
laugh. "Yeah, well, we gotta help each other in this rough
old life—right? Charity's the name of the game."

Raven transferred his gaze to the scale model. "I hear
you're planning on destroying this city yourself."

"Three weeks from now, yeah. We got a lot of action
to shoot first." Vollner eyed him narrowly. "You know
the story?"

"Yes, I do. Your avenging marines flatten Quang Hoi . . .
total destruction . . . a sort of latter-day Hiroshima."

"That's right. Except it'll be done with conventional
weapons, not nuclear. Shit, for sure not nuclear. Tell me,
Raven, where d'ya hear about this? That kind of information is protected."

"I can't tell you. Let's just say I know as much about
you as my father does—maybe more."

"Yeah? Like what, for instance?"

"Oh, like the state of your health, for instance. But
before we get into that, tell me about Quang Hoi. To reduce fourteen city blocks, even plaster ones, to rubble,
you'll need a lot of explosives. When are they due to be
delivered on site?"

Vollner glared at him, overtly suspicious. "Why d'you
wanna know?"

Raven heaved a slightly impatient sigh. "Vollner, I'm trying to put myself in my father's position. If I wanted to sabotage your movie, right now is the time I'd do it. You're into
the final phase of principal photography. The battle scenes
and destruction of Quang Hoi is a very expensive and vital
part of the picture. If *I* could blow up your city before you
got around to doing it, you'd be out of business. I doubt New
York would fork out another seven million dollars for a new

set. After your two recent box-office disasters, the Family must be pretty pissed off with you as it is.''

Vollner exploded. ''Jesus Christ, where d'you get all this Mafia shit from?''

''It's not important. Just tell me about the explosives. Listen, I'm trying to *help*. I want to prevent my father doing something stupid as much as you, and the more information I have about the Quang Hoi setup, the more I'll be *able* to help. Are the explosives there yet or not?''

With lingering reluctance to give out the information, yet persuaded by Raven's earnestness and reasoning, Vollner growled testily, ''Yeah, yeah, they're already on site. They were delivered today.''

''And stored where?''

Vollner pointed to six small plastic cubes, sited behind the city buildings, three on either side of the main thoroughfare, each separated from the next by a distance of several hundred feet. ''It's in concrete bunkers, split up in case of an accident.''

''And guarded.''

''I already told you. I got a patrol checking them out around the clock. Nobody gets close until we start shooting. After that, not even Will would be apeshit enough to blow up a valley full of people.''

Raven nodded. ''Good.''

Vollner looked at him. ''So—now what?''

Raven had all the information he needed. He said, ''Mister Vollner, I think we ought to lay some plans. Do you mind if I have a drink?''

Chapter Twenty

As they entered the den, Raven said, "I was admiring your trophy heads. Did you shoot any of these yourself?"

Vollner laughed. "Did I shoot *any*? I shot 'em all!"

Raven frowned, astounded. "All of these? You're kidding."

"Hell, no." Vollner moved to the bar, went behind it. "You do any hunting, Raven?"

"None like this. You must be one heckuva shot."

"Modesty forbids an answer—but, yeah, you're right. In Quang Hoi the other day I killed a rabbit at two hundred yards, took the little bastard's head clean off—standing shot over iron sights, God's my witness."

Raven whistled in admiration.

Nanosh had also told him: *Admire him profusely and let him talk long enough, and any* Gajo *will lose himself.*

Vollner poured two Jack Daniel's over ice, came over to where Raven was inspecting a deer head with a noble spread of antlers.

"Whitetail," said Vollner, handing Raven his drink. "Twelve-pointer, dressed out to two hundred eighty pounds. It scored two-oh-five points by Boone and Crocket standards."

Raven raised his brows in approbation. "Where was that?"

"Illinois."

"You've hunted all over."

"Hell, yes—the States, Europe, Africa, India." Vollner began to move around the room, into it now, proudly reliving his coups, getting to a gigantic moose head that dominated the wall over the fireplace.

"Look at this guy. Seventy-seven-inch spread, scored two-hundred-and-fifty points. Took that mother on the Kenai Peninsula, Alaska."

And if moose could shoot, thought Raven, your fat head would be hanging in his den. "Impressive," he said.

They moved on to the mounted, alive-looking head of a beautiful antelope with graceful backward-and-upward sweeping horns.

"Impala," said Vollner in a tone of wistful remembrance. "Shot this one on the Mara River, Kenya. Stunning creatures. The most acrobatic of all African antelope. You scare them, they take off in incredible leaps, spanning thirty feet. I knocked this one outta the air, midleap. *Hell*uva shot."

"You like to hunt," Raven observed dryly.

Vollner jerked a look at him. "Yeah, I like to hunt. I don't give a shit for these bleeding-heart critics of blood sports. What are they—all vegetarians? They raise hell about hunting, then go off to the market and buy lamb chops or sirloin for dinner. Bunch a fucking hypocrites."

"What is it you like about hunting?"

Vollner veered away from his trophies, headed for the bar, went behind it and poured himself another drink, hitting Raven with a glazed Steiger-stare as he drank. "Do I hear disapproval, Raven?"

Raven slipped onto a rattan stool. "As a biophysicist, I'm interested in people, in their behavior, what makes them tick. I've never met a big-game hunter before. I'd like to hear your philosophy."

Vollner gave a cynical laugh. "My phi-los-o-phy. Yeah,

you can hear my phil-os-o-phy. I believe the compulsion to hunt is as natural and basic a part of man's makeup as his need to fuck. That's the way it's been since the first hairy Neanderthal clubbed an animal to death for meat, or kicked the shit out of a saber-toothed tiger to save his own hide. It's there inside every man, Raven—latent or not. I like to hunt because it gives me the feeling of *power* . . . of *control*. Sitting in a fucking boardroom, listening to some ignorant asshole telling you what to do, you've got no control. Out in the bush, facing a wild animal that's out to scrag your ass or stomp you into a bloody pulp, it's you or it, baby. You've got your gun, you've got your nerve, you've got your ability. *That's* your control. You get it before it gets you.''

Raven nodded, smiling with his eyes. ''Interesting. You know, you sound angry . . . defensive, as though you've used hunting to hit back at a world that has handed you a lot of shit. Was that it—a rough childhood in New York?''

Vollner's pupils, like polished onyx, glared at Raven. He pointed a finger. His voice was ominously low. ''Mister, I'm warning you, lay off this New York thing now. Knock it off!''

Raven sighed, gave a dismissive shrug. ''Vollner, fact is fact. I know your true background. There's not much point in denying it. Okay, you had a rough childhood. So did I. We compensate the best way we can. You took up hunting; I went for education. Tell me something . . . is that why you moved up here from L.A., hid yourself away up here in the mountains, surrounded yourself with armed guards and electronic devices and killer dogs? Does all this give you the control you need over life?''

''Yeah, that's right!'' Vollner erupted. ''Up here I'm the *Man*! Up here I'm the *Law*! Up here I'm the king of the fucking castle, and anyone—'' He stopped abruptly, stared at Raven through narrowed, manic eyes. "Mister, I don't think I like you."

"And anyone who gets in your way gets his—or her—head chopped off. Isn't that what you were going to say? That's exactly what you were going to say."

Vollner murmured, "Who the fuck are you?"

Raven said easily, "You ought to be grateful to my father. If he hadn't so conveniently killed your wife, you wouldn't have got your hands on all this. She was beginning to see you for what you were, wasn't she, Vollner? For what you still are. She was beginning to realize her father had been right about you after all—and why he'd insisted you sign a prenuptial agreement. That was why Barbara was spending a lot of time with my father, not with any romantic interest, but because he was a kind, gentle, dependable guy who shared her love of horses. Another year, maybe, she'd have divorced you and you'd have lost the lot."

"Bull-*shit*!" exploded Vollner, pounding the bar with his fist. "She was a whore! An Indian-fucker! And your father was a violent drunk!"

"My father hardly took a drink in his life."

"How in hell would you know? You were, what, six, seven at the time?"

Raven turned the full impact of his ferocious Rom gaze on the man, gave it a moment to work, followed it with a voice that was low yet incisive and penetrating, vibrant with emotion. "I know because my grandfather told me."

"Your *grand*father." Vollner laughed scoffingly, but there was nervousness there, a need to avoid Raven's eyes.

"Yes, Vollner. Will Raven's father-in-law. A full-blood Romany, and one of the most honorable men who ever walked the earth. Listen to me, Vollner . . . listen to me . . ."

Vollner stared at him, finding himself suddenly unable

to shift his gaze from those dark, glistening, magnetic eyes, feeling his mind lulled, his body immobilized by the deep, resonant caress of the man's voice. He wanted to listen . . . had to listen . . .

The voice continued, seeping deeply into him, soporific as a drug. "My grandfather died two weeks ago. Until that time—for the past twenty-four years—I believed my father was dead. Rather than risk the chance of his imprisonment ruining my life, Will Raven made my grandfather promise to tell me he was dead. Can you grasp the degree of honor required, on the part of both men, to make and keep a promise like that? No, you cannot—because such human values are quite alien to you. You neither possess such qualities yourself nor associate with men who possess them. You don't even know what I'm talking about. But the point of my telling you is this: If my grandfather said Will Raven didn't drink, that is fact. It is indisputable. It is not open to question."

Vollner's lip curled in a clever sneer. "Your grandfather lied about Will being dead, didn't he? He could've lied about his drinking."

Raven slowly shook his head. "Vollner, if you don't know the difference . . . but you do. Anyway, what does all this come down to? Well, obviously to a frame. You were married to a wealthy woman, you needed money, but you couldn't get your hands on hers—until she died. You saw a growing friendship between Barbara and my father, worked out a plan, put it into operation. Barbara dies, my father goes away for life, you collect. Very neat.

"But then along came a minor complication. My mother. Lila Raven was no ordinary woman. She was full-blood Romany, dynamic, volatile. She was also desperately in love with her husband. She *knew* Will to be incapable of murder, knew somebody—you, the beneficiary—had framed him. So she went for you, made

a lot of noise, spit curses at you, threatened you enough
to make you believe she was dangerous. She was your wild
animal, Vollner, out to scrag your ass, stomp you into a
bloody pulp. And it was her or you. You had to get her
before she got you. How did you do it? Did you shoot her,
like one of your trophies? Or—as king of the castle—chop
off her head? How did you kill her, Vollner?''

From a low, rumbling beginning, Vollner's voice
climbed to a furious, bellowing crescendo. ''You're crazy,
you know that . . . your entire fucking family is crazy!
It's your mixed blood . . . Comanche and Gypsy, Jesus
Christ, what a fucking weird combination!'' The telephone on the bar rang suddenly, shockingly, but Vollner
did not reach for it. Instead, he retreated across the den,
backing toward a phone extension set on an antique desk
against the far wall, stabbing his finger at Raven as he
continued his vociferous protestation. ''You're insane,
coming up here and making accusations like that. Hey,
d'you realize who you're talking to? I'm Frank Vollner—
and *nobody* talks to me like that!''

''*I* just did.'' Raven sipped his drink.

Vollner reached the desk, did a quick about-face,
snatched up the phone, listened for no more than a second, snapped, ''When I ring,'' put down the receiver. He
opened a drawer, took something out. When he turned to
face Raven, there was an automatic in his hand. His smile
was a twisted, triumphant scowl. ''Yeah, you just did.
And you're about to realize the mistake you made.''

Raven eyed the gun with no great surprise. ''What d'you
intend doing with that—kill me as you killed my mother?''

Vollner returned to the bar, a madness evident in the
flare of his eyes. ''What's your game, Raven? First, you
tell me you're here to warn me about your father, help
save him from gettin' into more trouble. Now you're beg-

ging for trouble yourself, making serious accusations. What the fuck are you up to?''

Raven met and matched the man's ferocious gaze. ''I just wanted you to know how much I know about you, Vollner, what you're capable of. I'm here as insurance for my father. If he turns up in the Quang Hoi valley, I don't want to hear he's been 'accidentally' shot by one of your goons. You're going to pass the word—no shooting.''

Vollner smiled, moved behind the bar, the gun trained steadily on Raven. ''Is that a fact. And what's to stop me shooting him *and* you, make you both disappear, get you fucking Ravens outta my hair forever?''

''Maybe nothing could *stop* you, but you wouldn't get away with it.''

''Oh, really? Why not? I'm the king of the castle, remember? I can do anything I want.''

''Not this time. If I'm not back at the Crest View within twenty-four hours, word goes down to a cop friend of mine in L.A. He knows I'm up here, what I'm doing. If my father and I don't walk out of these mountains, unharmed, he's going to come looking for us—and you.'' Raven finished his drink, put down the glass. ''Your reign is over, Vollner.'' He inverted the glass, peered at it as though it were a crystal ball. ''Shall I read your future, tell you what I see? The state of your health is . . . short. You won't live to finish *Die Young. You* are going to die.''

Vollner stared at him, held captive for a beat of time by the seriousness and intensity of Raven's prognosis, then, rousing himself, girding his will to overcome the spell of the other man's voice, he began moving away toward the end of the bar, countering with, ''Is that what you see? Okay, now I'll tell you what I see.'' He turned quickly and the automatic roared deafeningly. The drinking glass disintegrated in an explosion of lethal fragments. ''I see a mountain of bullshit! I see a smartass bio-phys-i-cist who knows fuck-all about people. You got too much college and not enough knowledge, Raven. You really think I'd fall for that shit about a cop in L.A.?''

Raven picked glass off his ski coat. ''You'd better.''

''Yeah, and if you're not back at the motel in twenty-four hours, who's gonna get the word to him?''

''You don't really think I'd be stupid enough to tell you that.''

''You don't have to.'' Vollner reached under the countertop, appeared to press something, smiled coldly at Raven. ''You're a good-lookin' guy, you oughta be in movies. You got presence. You got guts. What you *ain't* got is ability to read people. You under-read me badly, Raven. You shoulda said all this over the phone, not walk into the castle. Let me promise you somethin' right now— *any*body fucks with Frank Vollner, he gets whacked. I catch your daddy in the Quang Hoi valley, he gets whacked. D'you think I'd be stupid enough to let him go, so he can take another shot at me? And when he gets whacked, you get it, too. *That's* what I see.''

Vollner deflected his glaring gaze from Raven as the door from the hall opened, his anger dissipating, turning to triumph at what he saw.

Icy fingers of premonition stroked Raven's neck as he turned to see who had entered, already knowing but unable to believe.

Vollner smiled at Raven. ''Now I see something else: a family reunion . . . your momma, poppa, and you. All in the same hole in the ground.'' Vollner waved the gun in the direction of the door. ''Let's go.''

Ken Dok stood there.

With Ed Bussey, grinning.

And Kat.

Chapter Twenty-one

Raven and Kat were handcuffed together, his right wrist to her left, making any sudden movement impossible. While this was happening, they exchanged glances, both in their way apologetic, but Kat's attempt at words was brutally discouraged.

"Are you all right?"

Ed Bussey: "Shut the fuck up!"

They were led from the lodge across a compound lit up like broad daylight to the helicopter, its rotors still turning. The compound was alive with activity. There were armed men everywhere. Six of them, each with a Doberman, were heading from the kennel enclosure toward a canopied army truck parked near the helipad.

Raven and Kat were pushed aboard the Bell, seated directly behind the pilot. Ken Dok and Ed Bussey swung in behind them. Vollner, wearing the khaki parka and carrying a rifle with a light-intensifier sight, emerged from the lodge, headed first for the truck to deliver instructions, then climbed into the helicopter, telling the pilot, "Go!" as he settled beside him.

The rotors accelerated, the chopper lifted. Brilliant spotlights lit up the ground in front and below. The nose dipped and they sped away, turning west to circumnavigate the mountain in a clockwise direction. The pilot, intimate with the terrain, flew at minimum altitude, barely skimming the treetops. The effect, for Kat, was dizzying, a disorienting switchback ride of rushing, swooping hazard.

Raven, sensing her discomfort, her fear, squeezed her hand, his tight smile telling her things weren't as bad as they seemed, though instinct told her they were exactly that.

Raven was mystified as to why, if she had been brought to the lodge by Dok and Bussey under duress—which must have been the case—he had received no telepathic warning of her stress. Had he been too preoccupied with Vollner to notice? Had they told her a convincing tale to lure her into the helicopter? How, in fact, had they known she was *there*?

In a while they reached a road, a livid scar separating dense stands of pine trees, and turned north to follow it. Raven's remembrance of the scale model told him this would be the road marking the western boundary of Vollner's kingdom, the one linking highways 89 and 97. For the time they flew above it, it was quite deserted.

Soon the pilot veered eastward, following the contour of Vollner's mountain, which rose steeply to their right, densely wooded, and picked up another, graded road. Raven identified this as the one Vollner had built to gain access into the Quang Hoi valley.

Suddenly they were over the city, flying low down the main thoroughfare, the concentrated beams of light illuminating its surface intensely and turning the strip into a resemblance of an airport runway. The make-believe buildings—apartment blocks, shops, offices, public buildings—looking totally real in the peripheral light—flashed past on either side, each of the seven blocks separated by a cross street.

As they approached the square and Buddhist temple that formed the buffer end of the avenue, Vollner shouted to the pilot, "Take it up and around . . . back of the buildings! Circle the set!"

The chopper gained altitude, flew directly over the temple, turned to the right, to the south. Raven spotted the three concrete bunkers that housed the explosives, set back maybe a hundred feet behind the buildings and spaced widely apart.

Reaching the entrance to the city, they turned right, recrossed the avenue, turned right again, and covered the rear of the buildings on the north side of the valley, again flying over three concrete bunkers. To their left, its heavily timbered presence pressing close to the bunkers, leaving no more than two hundred yards of flat grassland behind them, rose the mountain that formed the north wall of the valley.

It was not until the helicopter had landed in the city square, close to the steps of the temple, that they saw signs of occupation. Headlights burst suddenly from a cross street and raced toward them, the vehicle becoming identifiable as an open Jeep carrying two uniformed guards as it drew close.

One of the men got out and ran at a crouch to confer with Vollner at his open door.

Vollner yelled, "Everything okay?"

"Yessir! No sign of anyone in the valley. Only a coupla rabbits."

Raven assumed Vollner had been in radio contact with these guards from the moment he'd received Raven's phone call.

Vollner nodded. "Okay, keep patrolling. I've got six men with dogs comin' in by truck, maybe twenty minutes. I'm putting one on each bunker. Meantime, you see *anything* move—*anything*—waste it!"

The guard grinned. "Even the rabbits?"

"Yeah! The sound of gunfire will help change this ass
hole's mind."

"Yes*sir*!"

The guard ran back to the Jeep and it took off across
the square.

Vollner turned to Ken Dok. "Get these two outta here."
He climbed down, stood guard with the rifle while Raven,
Kat, Dok, and Bussey got out.

Vollner came close to Raven, said into his face, "You
better pray your daddy doesn't come looking to blow up
my city. If he does, you two go up with it. That, Mister
Bio-phys-i-cist, you can take to the bank." He turned to
Dok and Bussey. "You know where to put them."

Bussey, carrying a battery lantern, led the way. Dok
shoved Raven in the shoulder to get him moving. They
trouped across the square toward a cross street on the north
side. The eerie feeling as they went down it that they were
walking down a real street in a real city added to Kat's
state of extreme apprehension.

Behind them, the helicopter took to the air, swung over
them almost maliciously, battering them with its blinding
light and down draft, lighting up the cross street. Then it
was gone, circling out over the no-man's-land between
them and the north mountain, heading back down the valley.

They emerged into flattened grassland, the valley floor
here almost denuded of growth by the construction activity
of the past weeks. Bussey headed for the nearest bunker,
a structure of cement blocks larger than Raven had gauged
from the air, perhaps twenty feet square, eight feet high,
with a single steel door facing the city, and no window
that he could see.

Bussey went ahead to open a padlock. He slid open a
dead bolt, pushed the door inward, took hold of Raven's
arm, and shoved him inside, dragging Kat with him. The

door slammed shut. The bolt went home. The lock snapped on.

They were in absolute blackness.

Raven shouted, "Hey, come on, give us some light!"

He heard Bussey laugh. "Fuck in the dark like everybody else."

"At least take the cuffs off!"

"Ain't you into S and M? Gee, fella, you don't know what you're missin'!"

The sound of laughter, muted voices, receding.

Silence.

Kat was shaking.

Raven wrapped his free arm around her, drew her close. "Ssh, ssh, take it easy. Come on, now, listen to me . . . *listen* to me . . . relax . . . it's all right . . . I've got matches . . . give them a minute to get well away."

His voice, close to her ear, deep, soothing, confident. Her senses swam with his voice, with the darkness. She felt the panic drain from her. Her heart still pounded but she was no longer jittery with fear.

She clung to him tightly, drawing from his strength, marveling at his effect upon her. "I'm okay now."

"Good girl. All right, let's see what we're into here. Relax your arm, I have to get the knife out, fiddle around a bit here."

"The knife!" she whispered. "Thank God you brought it."

"Uh-huh." He laughed.

The handle contained a small assortment of emergency aids: fish hooks, needles, a length of flexible sawblade, and a dozen matches wrapped in waterproof paper. Raven extricated a match, struck it, held it aloft. His first priority was a means of prolonging a flame. Immediately behind them rose a wall of boxes and containers, reaching almost to the roof. Most were constructed of metal, some of cardboard, some of wood. He passed the match to Kat. During the brief life of the flame he hurriedly pulled down one of the cardboard boxes and three of the wood. By the time he had arranged them in the space by the door, the match was burning her fingers.

Blackness enfolded them again.

He said, "Kat, sit down here, on this box. We've got to think this through." When they were both seated he went on, "There has to be some kind of ventilation in here, otherwise we'd be dead in an hour and I don't think Vollner intends that. He's going to keep us in here until my father turns up, and that could take all night, if at all. So—there's probably a grille on the rear wall, up behind the boxes. That'll be the weak point of the bunker. To get at it, we have to shift some boxes, stack them in this space. We need light to work by. I've only got a few matches. I'm going to cut strips of cardboard from this carton, twist them together to make spills. But first we have to get rid of these damned handcuffs. I've got a length of flexible sawblade here, it's a wire covered with diamond dust. Given time, it'll cut through anything." He was unfolding the wire as he spoke. "It has a ring on either end. In an ideal situation it would be stretched across a length of bowed wood. We'll have to do it by hand. Okay, I'm going to strike another match, get us set up for the cut."

The match flared. He passed it to Kat, then lifted the spare wooden box on top of the one he'd been sitting on, making a table. He knelt beside it, arranged his manacled wrist along its edge to give clearance between his wrist and Kat's for the saw cut. It was an awkward, unnatural angle. Though Kat would have unobstructed use of her right hand, Raven would have to go in with his left, under his right arm, using a downward pull.

He had time to pass a ringed end to her before the match died.

He said, "Okay, we don't need light for this. Let's get the wire in a solid groove . . . that's it, take up the tension . . . now, pull toward you."

She pulled. He pulled. After a few tentative strokes they got a steady rhythm going. Raven could feel the diamond dust begin to bite.

"Good. Now it's only a matter of time."

"How much have we got?"

"Vollner told that guard the men with the dogs would be here in twenty minutes."

"We have an awful lot to do in twenty minutes."

"This won't take long, it's only mild steel. Just keep at it—and tell me what happened at the motel."

She drew a fluttery sigh. "Oh, God . . . I was so stupid. I was in the camper. Those two creatures knocked on the door, said they had a message from you. Like a fool I opened the door. They grabbed me, put something over my face, almost carried me to the helicopter. I felt terribly dizzy. I think they used chloroform. I should never have opened the door."

"Kat, you weren't to know. Well, at least *I* now know why I didn't pick up on your trauma—you were sedated."

"But how did they know where I was?"

"I've been trying to figure it out. I was waiting for them in the foyer. I'd left a message at the desk that I *was* waiting for them, so they wouldn't ask questions about room numbers and whether anyone was with me. I don't know—maybe Vollner sent them back to pick my things up, they asked for the room number and found out you were booked in with me."

"But how would they know I was in the camper?"

"The registration form. I had to put down our vehicle registration number."

"Oh, God, of course! They checked the room, found it empty, went looking for our vehicle."

"I was dumb. I should've put down a phony number."

She said, "Come on, don't blame yourself. When we signed in we didn't know it would come to this. If we hadn't run into the Chinese kids, it would've turned out differently."

"Maybe. But I did something wrong, otherwise we wouldn't be here. I underestimated my adversary."

Kat said, "I disagree. No secondhand information can prepare you for a firsthand confrontation. How could you possibly fully estimate Vollner when you'd never met him?"

Raven smiled in the darkness, touched by her loyalty. "Thank you."

She panted, "How're we doing here?"

"Keep at it. It's biting fine."

"And what happened to you—at the lodge?"

"Vollner has a production office off the den. When I got there he was studying a scale model of his property, I guess figuring the best way to deploy his men. Whatever, it gave me a chance to get my bearings in relation to the lodge. I know which direction we have to take to get out of here."

"Well, that's something," she said hopefully. "So . . . what did he say to you?"

"At first he came on with his social benefactor image—agreed with me that saving my father from himself was the important thing. But then I shook his hand and read the truth. So I led him on, encouraged him to talk. We went into the den. I got him bragging about his trophy heads, and the real Frank Vollner emerged. The man loves to kill. It gives him control. He sees this mountain as his kingdom, believes up here he has the divine right of kings, power over all life. I got him mad, talking about his New York background, his connection with the Mob. I wanted the truth about my mother, wanted to be absolutely certain

I knew what I was dealing with. Then he took a phone call. It must have been the goons reporting that they had you outside. Vollner changed then, dropped all pretense of saving my father. If he finds him, he'll kill him. Us, too. I don't mean to frighten you more than you already are, but it's vital you know the truth. We are now fighting for our lives . . . and we may have to take some drastic action to save them. And I mean *drastic*.''

As though on cue, the bracelet links parted.

Kat let out a gasp of relief.

Raven felt around in the darkness, swiftly began cutting strips from the cardboard container.

He struck a match.

Kat cried out when she saw the blood—on the wooden box, on Raven's wrist.

He shook his head. "It's nothing, the blade caught me a couple of times. Come on, twist these strips together, two or three to a spill." He lit a single strip from the match, used the strip to light her bundle, got a decent torch going. "Good, you keep the light going, I'll shift the boxes."

He tore into the job, pulled down the top containers nearest the rear wall and stacked them against the door, piling them high, grunting and sweating as he lifted heavy metal containers above his head.

"My God, there's enough stuff in here to start a war."

"What is it?" Kat asked, unable to decipher the cryptic military descriptions stenciled on the boxes.

"Everything . . . explosives, smoke grenades, blank ammunition."

She gasped. "And we've got a naked flame in here!"

He grinned, his face gleaming with sweat in the flickering light. "Just don't light any blue touchpaper, otherwise we'll surely retire—and in several directions."

He attacked the boxes, pulling them down, carrying

them across, lifting them high, working frantically, conscious of the value of every second.

Kat watched him with a feeling of helplessness, wanting to do more than crouch there, lighting twists of cardboard, yet knowing he could never work this fast in the dark.

As one spill died, she lit another, watched it catch, flare, begin to burn brightly. She was drawn by the flame. As she stared into its blue and orange depths, her mind became hazy. Her thoughts began to drift with the swirling smoke. It was all so unreal. This place, this prison, was a surrealist nightmare . . . Raven working, his shadow leaping, the two of them *being* here. Madness. How could it be *happening*? What applied here was a completely different level of consciousness, unknowable to the nonparticipant. An interesting facet of life, but a huge problem for a writer. Words alone could never bridge the chasm separating the real from the related . . . especially when the real itself seemed so unreal. Where was she going with this train of thought? Where had she begun? Her brain buzzed, her mind whirled, her eyes were losing focus. She looked up in slow motion and with tremendous effort into Raven's demonic face, dirt-streaked and gleaming with sweat, grave with concern. . . .

He coughed. "Kat . . . are you all right?"

"I feel . . . faint."

"We're losing air. Give me the torch."

As he moved away from her, she realized he had made a narrow passage halfway along the rear wall. He now squeezed into it, edged along it, stepping sideways, his chest scraping the cement blocks. As the meager light diminished, darkness and the poisonous air overwhelmed her. A claustrophobic panic welled inside her like a wild thing. She curled against the rear wall, hugging her knees, her face pressed against the cold cement. She was going to die. They were both going to die in this awful place.

That was the unbelievable reality. They had poisoned their own air . . . and they were going to die . . .

His muffled voice reached her.

What was he saying?

He turned his head in her direction. "Kat! I've found it. It's a metal grille . . . head high . . . two rows along. Kat, get on your feet! I've got to shift more boxes and I need your help."

His torch went out.

"We'll have to work in the dark." He gave a grunt, lifting a box. "Come into the passage. I'll get them down, you drag them out. Pile them anywhere, we won't need to move many."

A metal container crashed to the floor.

Kat squeezed into the passage, hating its confinement, shuffled along, sensing the air getting minimally fresher. Her foot struck the box. She stretched down, finding it difficult to bend, located a handle, took a grip, and began an inching-backward shuffle, grunting with every tug, cursing the weight of the box, the narrowness of the passage, wanting to cry, wanting to give up, knowing for John Raven's sake she would do neither.

"Aaagh!"

"What?" His voice, crackling with concern.

"I broke a goddamn nail!"

His laughter boomed. "Kat Tyson, you are beautiful. I promise you this—if I ever get into a mess like this again and need a partner, I'll ask for you."

"That's . . . the best . . . news . . . ohhh, *shit*!"

"What now?"

"There goes another one."

Awful, there, working in the dark, enshrouded by absolute blackness, the air suffocating, their dilemma exacerbated by the need for speed, by the uncertainty of what might be awaiting them if they did manage to break out.

But worse for him, buried in the boxes, entombed in a tight-fitting sarcophagus with barely enough room to move. Another grunt, another crash. Lifting them over his head and dropping them behind, the nylon of his ski coat scratching the cement wall like footsteps in dried grass. Two boxes . . . three . . . four . . . five . . .

She gasped, groaned, cried, "John . . . how're we doing? *What* are we doing?"

"I'm . . . making a ledge. I have to get on top, with support for my back . . . to get at the grille with my feet. I can feel it. It's not that strong."

. . . six . . . seven . . . eight . . .

"That might do it. I'm going to strike a match."

"You want cardboard? I think I buried it."

"No, I'll only need a quick look."

The match flared.

Kat winced at its blinding brightness.

He had built a step-up, created a deep seat in which he could recline, his feet level with the grille. He was sitting up there now, head scraping the concrete roof, leaning forward inspecting the grille, panting, smearing dirt across his face as he wiped sweat from his eyes, telling her, "We're in luck, kiddo. These bunkers weren't built to last." He raised his left foot, placed his boot against the grille, and pressed, testing its strength.

He gave a satisfied nod. "It'll go."

She frowned. "But we'll never get through a hole that size."

"Trust me. And stand well back." He blew out the match.

She retreated along the passage, heard him shifting on the boxes, settling, taking up a position. For a moment there was silence. She heard a long-drawn intake of breath, repeated, sensed the intense concentration attending it. Though blind, she could see him there, coiled, hands grip-

275

ping the leading edges of the boxes, one booted foot poised like a drawn-back battering ram. There was another moment of silence.

Then it came.

The blast of sound shocked and deafened her. It was as though she had been struck on the head by a solid object. She dropped into a crouch, ears ringing, believing she could smell dust . . . coughing now . . . because it was dust . . . propelled down the passage by a draft of unbelievably cool—unbelievably *fresh*—air.

Raven was moving. His hands felt for her in the darkness, took hold of her arm, and drew her to her feet. "Are you okay?"

She swayed against him. "I'm deaf . . . dizzy."

"It'll clear in a moment. Okay, I've made a hole. We have to climb up on the boxes, squeeze out through the blocks. There'll be a six-foot drop outside. I'll go first, show you how, and I'll help you from the outside. We can't risk a light, we'll have to do it by feel. You ready?"

"Absolutely."

He edged back along the passage. She followed, hungrily sucking in the fresh air. She could now see the hole as a patch of less concentrated darkness, and marveled that his kicks had removed not only the grille but a couple of adjoining concrete blocks. The darkness in the passage was no longer absolute. Faintly she could see Raven as he mounted the stepped boxes, swung into the seat, stretched his legs out across the passage, and began to inch forward into the hole.

The difficult part came when his buttocks passed the supportive leading edge of the seat and he hung suspended on the passage. He lay back, used his elbows to push himself forward, gained additional propulsion as his legs progressed through the nine-inch wall and he was able to bend his knees and heel the outside wall.

Now he was halfway through.

With his head and shoulders supporting his weight on the boxes, he reached forward, took a grip on the concrete blocks, and pulled himself into the hole. The last phase was the most difficult of all. Ideally he should have been facing the floor, not the ceiling, so he could slide out of the hole using the natural bend of his body. But such a beginning was impossible and there was no room to turn. Now, until his shoulders and head were clear of the hole, his spine was under assault from the outside edge of the blocks and the downward drag of his torso. Kat realized now why he had insisted on going first: he would be there to give her the support he now desperately needed.

She winced as he struggled to make the last few inches, arms raised above his head, using his heels now to pull himself through. For a moment, in the most meager light penetrating through the gaps around his body, she could see the top of his head and his extended arms. And then, with a final grunt of effort, he was gone.

A long and awful silence followed.

Panic gripped her. Terrible possibilities flooded her overcreative imagination: he'd snapped his spine . . . fallen forward and cracked his skull . . .

Another interminable fifteen seconds dragged by.

Raven—where are *you?*

Terrified now, she climbed up onto one of the stepped boxes and peered through the hole. Suddenly his face was there, filling the hole. She stifled a scream, gasped, "Where've you *been*?"

"Taking a look around. Come on, out you come."

She stared at him. "What are you standing on?"

"The blocks I kicked out."

She gave a ridiculous laugh. "Of course."

"Kat, will you come *out* of there?"

"God, yes."

The first stage went easily enough. She got her legs through the hole to a point where she was able to bend her knees. But her torso and arms were shorter and much, much weaker than his, and when she reached the position where she had to relinquish her hold on the boxes and grab for the blocks, she didn't make it. She grabbed and missed, raking her nails down the concrete, and with a cry fell backward, her head and upper torso hanging down in the passage, Raven clamping her legs from the outside.

His voice, an imperative hiss, came through the hole. "Don't panic!" Now his hand and arm appeared, snaking in across her thighs, waving at her above her head. "Grab hold, Kat, I'll pull you up."

She clung to his arm, felt herself being raised effortlessly into a horizontal position, then catapulted through the hole and was suddenly out of that hellish place and clinging to him, panting, weak with relief, gasping, laughing. "Thank you . . . thank you."

He grunted a laugh, hugged her tightly. "Yuh done good. Real good."

They took a moment to settle, get their bearings, check the area, though there was little to see. The strip of land behind the bunker was all darkness, the loom of the northern mountain all but invisible against a starless, moonless, overcast sky.

Raven pointed. "We head west, stay behind the bunkers until we clear the town, take a direct route out of the valley until we hit the road that'll take us south to Eighty-nine. How d'you feel about a twenty-mile hike?"

"These boots were just made for walkin'. I don't care if it's two hundred, so long as we get out of this god-damned place."

"Stay behind me, and be prepared to go to ground if I stop suddenly. And no more talking—sound travels at night."

They started off. Their journey was short-lived. As they cleared the end of the bunker, the blinding beam of a powerful flashlight paralyzed them.

From the blackness behind the light came a dog's rattling, deep-chested growl.

The guard's voice said, "Now let's see you get back in the same way you came out."

Chapter Twenty-two

Jack Shanglo had cautioned him: *Never attack until you know your enemy's strength. He might be secretly armed or have concealed reinforcements.*

Blinded by the flashlight, Raven couldn't be certain if the guard was carrying a gun, though he assumed the worst. At best there was the dog to contend with. What he had to do in order to better assess the situation was get the light out of his face, even briefly. And that entailed separating himself from Kat, dividing the guard's attention.

While Kat stood frozen, Raven went into an act, held out his hands imploringly and backed up quickly toward the hole in the wall, pleading convincingly, "Hey, man, take it easy . . . we'll get back in, just keep that dog away from me. I hate dogs, all right?"

He was backing away so quickly he appeared to trip over his feet and fall down.

The flashlight beam followed him, then immediately switched back to Kat to check she hadn't moved, then came back again, Raven still lying there, groaning, "Jesus, I think I've busted my ankle."

The guard was getting confused, suspicious. "What you tryin' to pull?"

"Nothing! I've sprained my ankle!"

"Get on your feet." The beam swung onto Kat. "You—move. Get over there to the hole."

Raven could see the gun now, a shoulder-slung submachine weapon, maybe an Uzi. And he could see the dog, a Doberman of course, well trained, hanging slightly behind and to one side of the guard. The man himself was no giant: six feet, one-eighty. But with an Uzi size didn't matter.

Raven, still on the ground, called to her dispiritedly, "Kat, I'm sorry. We've had it. You'll have to give me a hand here."

She started toward him. "Is it the ankle you sprained in El Centro?" she asked, telling him she knew he was working something.

"Yeah, the same one, goddamn it."

The guard followed her closely, nervous. "Cut the crap, you two. Get him on his feet."

Raven made a big thing of getting up, then staggered a few steps, dropped to his knees, educating the guard to sudden moves. "Christ, I think it's broken!"

The guard yelled, "Cut the shit! You're not up in two seconds, I set the dog on yuh!"

"No! Look . . . I'm getting up! Kat, get back in the *bunker*." His tone telling her to move *now*.

She moved quickly away from Raven. "I need some light here."

Instinctively the guard swung the beam toward her, then back to check on Raven, almost one hundred eighty degrees, then back to Kat, not liking their separation but sure of the dog, knowing it would take Raven if he tried anything stupid.

Raven was also sure of the dog: sure he could not reach its mind. Given time, all animals could be reached, no matter what their temperament. But this Doberman would need far more time than was available. It was a programmed killing machine. He would regret its death, as he regretted the untimely death of all things, but the law of survival was immutable.

He would wait until Kat had gone through the hole.

He would take the guard first. With the knife. Fend off the dog with the guard's body. Then expose himself to the dog's attack and kill it.

That was the plan.

But it didn't work out that way.

Raven saw the spot of light, red, about the size of a quarter, creeping along the bunker wall while the guard's flashlight was on Kat. At first he was puzzled by it. Then, with quickening pulse, realized what it was.

A laser sight.

Someone out there in the darkness was lining up on . . . whom?

It didn't make sense that the hunted could be either Kat or himself. The hunter would have come in to give help to the guard.

So—

His excitement built—

They had an ally.

His *father*?

Was Will Raven out there in the mountain dark?

Raven waited breathlessly, expecting the spot of light to move, to settle on the guard, expecting the shot.

Nothing happened.

What was he waiting for?

Kat was struggling to climb up into the hole, the guard behind her, right-angled to her, keeping half an eye on Raven.

Raven closed his eyes, reached out with his mind to the hunter, put himself up there to see what he was seeing.

Yes.

The guard was presenting a side-on view, a narrow target, with Kat immediately behind him.

Raven had to move the guard, turn him.

He begged, "Hey, man, give her some help there. Can't you see she can't get in by herself?"

The guard came at him. "On your feet, scum, you help her."

"Okay, give me a hand up here."

"Jesus, you must think I'm fucking dumb." He kicked Raven in the thigh. "Get the hell up!"

Raven crawled away, protesting, dragging his fake game leg, turning the guard until his back was toward the mountain.

There was no shot. Instead: a curious whiffling sound, like a cane shaken rapidly through air. And a thud.

The guard bucked as though struck between the shoulder blades. In the flashlight's beam Raven saw the bloody glint of metal protruding from the man's chest. An arrowhead.

The guard fell facedown. The dog was a beat late, confused. It focused on the guard, turned toward the mountain. Raven snatched up the flashlight, leapt to his feet, poured the blinding light into the animal's eyes. It howled and came on, hurled itself at Raven in seething fury, blinded. Raven swung away. The dog hurtled past, smashed into the bunker wall, recovered, and came on again.

This time Raven took its force, ramming the flashlight into its gaping jaws, his knife deep into its throat.

Kat missed it all.

Halfway into the hole, she yelled as Raven came up behind her, took hold of her by the waist to pull her out. "Let go of me, you bastard!"

"There's gratitude."

She whirled to face him. "John . . . ?"

He shone the flashlight on the guard, the dog. "We've got help."

She gaped uncomprehendingly, trying to fit it together. "What happened?"

"There's somebody out there with a crossbow equipped with a laser sight, probably a light-intensifier, too."

Kat grimaced at the reaching darkness. "Who could it be—your father?"

"Can't think of anyone else out there playing with a bow and arrow," he quipped.

She gasped, expelling confusion, emotional exhaustion. "My God, I don't believe any of this. What do we do now—head over there and try to find him?"

"No. If he wanted that, he'd be with us right now. I think he has things to do in the valley, then he'll follow us out. We'll stick to our original plan. Only this time we'll have a gun, a flashlight, and someone to watch our backs. Are you okay?"

"I'll do. But how about you, your poor broken ankle? God, what a performance. You should get an agent."

He chuckled. Taking her arm, he led her away from the presence of the dead bodies, his mind focusing on their escape route as they cleared the bunker and entered the area separating it from the buildings of the city. Recalling Vollner's conversation with the Jeep guard, it was obvious that guards with dogs were already in place at the two bunkers down the line, so that direction of exit was closed to them. They would have to detour.

At the corner of the first cross street they encountered, Raven halted and set his thoughts to alternatives. They could go back, work their way around the Buddhist temple, and head east into unknown territory, getting away from the activity in the Quang Hoi set, but also away from their most direct route out of the valley and toward a known road.

He didn't like it, the unknown territory. Traversing rugged terrain, even a comparatively flat valley, in such darkness was extremely hazardous. There was no guarantee the valley would remain as flat and wide as it was at this point. It might narrow, even cease altogether, box them in. There could well be rockfalls to negotiate, fast, icy streams. To use the flashlight extensively would be suicidal; it would be seen for miles.

He dismissed that direction.

They could head north, again away from the set, work their way into the lower slopes of the mountain on their right, then circle west, around the set, to reach the road. But, again, it was unknown terrain. By himself, he would have taken this route. For him, a night mountain held no terrors. But Kat was pure city. She had neither the experience nor the temperament. Every rustle in the undergrowth would be a source of trauma, and she'd had enough of those to last a lifetime.

So—

Only one route remained.

Raven, indicating the cross street, whispered, "Let's take a look at Main Street, Quang Hoi," and led the way, hugging a building wall.

Reaching the end of it, indicating by touch that she should stay put a few paces behind him, he went ahead to peer around the front of the building.

To his left, across the square toward the temple, there was utter blackness, neither sight nor sound of any activity. But to his right . . . way down the valley at what must have been the beginning of the set: lights. A lot of them. Vehicle lights. And pinpricks of flashlights, milling around, grouped as though in preparatory assembly.

Then, as Raven watched, the helicopter made a sudden

appearance, as though it had swept around the obstacle of Vollner's mountain and entered the valley. It came on to circle the group, its powerful searchlights spotting them in cones of brilliance like performers in a son et lumière production.

An amplified, distorted voice addressed them, resonating between the mountains. Raven guessed it was Vollner, issuing instructions. He had no need to hear the words. They had to be: *Spread out, search the valley, shoot to kill.*

Now the group divided, half to search each side of the city. Raven counted their flashlight beams . . . six to each side . . . and made a calculation: twelve men in the group, plus five guards on the bunkers, two in the Jeep, the truck driver, helicopter pilot, Ken Dok, Ed Bussey, and Vollner . . . at least twenty-four men and five dogs were in the valley, searching for his father.

It was time to get out of there.

But how?

In which direction?

The helicopter now began to traverse the valley, zigging first to the south side, sweeping over the buildings to light up the terrain behind them, then zagging across to cover the north. The vehicles—the truck and the Jeep—were heading slowly up Main Street, keeping pace with the searchers, their high-beam headlights lighting up the thoroughfare.

In which direction?

There seemed only one available choice: a retreat to the temple and into the unknown territory behind it.

Raven turned to confer with Kat, but in the next instant was stunned by the explosion that came from the direction of the temple. A burgeoning glow relieved the intense darkness of the cross street and showed him Kat's face, stark with shock. He whirled, moved quickly back to the corner, peered cautiously around it, aware that they no longer had the cover of the night.

As his eyes took in the scene, another explosion devastated the façade of the temple. In moments the entire structure was a huge burning pyre, sheets of flame leaping a hundred feet into the night sky, showers of orange sparks spiraling upward in the vortex of the intense heat, drifts of burning material floating down onto surrounding buildings and into the city square.

Kat was behind him, gripping his arm.

Raven gasped. "He's doing it. He's blowing up the bloody set! We've got to get out of here. . . ."

And then the helicopter was on them, over them, hitting them with its down draft, heading for the fire, cutting off their northerly retreat. The vehicles would arrive next, bringing the guards. In seconds every man and dog in the valley would be passing their hiding place.

In seconds they would probably be dead.

If they stayed.

But where . . .

Raven glanced past Kat, back along the cross street. In the wall to their left were several windows. If they got inside the phony shop, they might be able to work their way through an entire block of buildings, moving away from the temple and a concentration of guards, negotiate a cross street, get into the next block, and so on down the valley.

They would have three things in their favor: darkness— once the guards and vehicles had passed them; the fact that Vollner, preoccupied with the fire, believed Kat and he were still locked in the bunker; and cover for most of the way.

That had to be the way.

He grabbed Kat's arm and pulled her across to the win-

dow. He tested it: real glass. No wonder the set had cost
Vollner seven million. It was a sash frame, four feet by
three. But fake, unopenable. The glass in the lower half
had to go. He moved Kat aside, drove the Uzi butt into
the pane. The sound of shattering glass seemed deafening.
Quickly he knocked the remaining shards from the frame,
picked Kat up and fed her through, climbed in after her.
Immediately the interior of the shop blazed with light as
the truck and the Jeep approached, racing for the temple.
Raven brought Kat down into a crouch, below the level of
the shop's front window.

As the vehicle swept past, the light within the shop
diminished to the fire glow. Raven glanced around the
interior. It was, as he'd expected, no more than shell,
wood-strutted vertically all through to support the roof,
with a chipboard wall—presumably the stud wall between
this fake shop and the next—about thirty feet away. An
open doorway in the wall, giving access to the next section, heartened him, though its position—at the front of
the building—did not. He would have preferred their progress to have been along the solid rear wall, as far as possible from the big shop windows facing Main Street.

Raven tapped Kat on the arm, pointed at the door, and
they scuffled across the packed-earth floor at a crouch.
Pausing at the door, he looked back through the windows.
The timbered structure made a feast of fuel, and the fire's
fury was undiminished. Against the fifty-foot wall of brilliant orange flame he could see the silhouettes of the vehicles and of the guards they had disgorged, standing by
helplessly as the centerpiece of Vollner's set was reduced
to ashes.

As Raven watched Vollner circle the fire in the helicopter, he bored into his mind. The man must be demented
with fury, with fear, as he thought of the retribution of
New York, of Will Raven, reflected on what he had done

to Will and Lila Raven, and imagined what he *would* do to their son in revenge.

Raven also thought about his father, certain that it was he who had shot the guard, and asked himself: Had it been pure accident that Will had been so fortuitously in that spot at that time? Or had he seen their arrival by helicopter and their incarceration in the bunker, followed them, and been about to release them when he; John, had effected their own escape? Did Will know his *son* was in the valley? Or were he and Kat merely two unknown people Will had been able to help before blowing up the temple?

The speculation brought further questions: How had Will set off the explosions from his position out there behind the bunker? He wouldn't have had time to reach the temple before the explosion. Therefore, it must have been detonated from distance by—what?—an electronic device. Did his father know how to handle such things? A naïve question. San Quentin would have provided any knowledge Will wished to acquire. That Will Raven of twenty-four years ago was dead and buried.

Okay—another thing to figure out before he and Kat headed out. If Will had set a charge in the temple and triggered it from, say, the tree line at the base of the north mountain, and if his aim was to destroy the entire set, it followed that he had planted charges throughout the set—including the section in which Kat and he were now hiding!

Will had probably, through his light-intensifier, seen them enter the shop. Perhaps he had even set off the temple explosion first in order to draw Vollner and the guards to this end of the valley, giving him and Kat a chance to escape. But now that they were out of Will's sight, he wouldn't know where they were at any one time. He might, therefore, make wrong assumptions—and blow them up! So they'd better get the hell out of there fast.

He turned to Kat and was able to say only, "We've . . ." before the building across the square, adjoining the temple, went up with a deafening roar, followed almost instantly by another explosion on their side of Main Street, which Raven couldn't see but knew was also close to the temple, the swift sequence of detonations proving his theory that Will was setting off the explosions by remote control. His father, sitting up there in the mountain dark, was blowing Frank Vollner's dreams and hopes and future into oblivion, tasting the sweetness of revenge. Raven figured maybe there would be five more explosions before the block they were in went up, and whirling again on Kat he yelled at her, "GO!"

He followed her through the door at a crouch, urging her on, weaving between the vertical struts, conscious that there might well be guards up ahead of them, that Vollner, realizing by now that Will was triggering the explosions by remote control, was issuing commands for a block-by-block search for the explosive charges and/or Will Raven.

It's what I would do, thought Raven—try to save at least some of the set down the line.

Just then the truck and the Jeep raced by, carrying guards, heading for the west end of Main Street.

Great.

Now he and Kat were caught between guards approaching from their front and explosions coming up behind.

What to do.

Think.

Difficult, just then, because another detonation, a monstrous explosion, on the south side, behind the buildings, went up, shaking the valley floor, lighting it like day with a billowing mushroom of flame that soared and curled and licked two hundred feet.

Kat screamed, went to ground, too late, hands clasped to her head.

Raven gasped, "Jesus . . . he's hit a bunker."

Think!

They had to get out of the buildings, away from the bunkers, into the north mountain. Vollner's men were stretched thin. They couldn't cover the entire width of the valley now. They would be concentrating on their search of the blocks, of the bunkers.

He caught hold of Kat's arm, pulled her to her feet. He moved fast, passing through shop after shop, heedless now of exposure to the street. If they were seen, if anyone or anything tried to stop them, he'd use the gun. The situation had changed drastically since the first explosion. Now, seeing the devastation his father was causing, Raven knew that Vollner and his men would shoot them on sight.

There it was—the solid wall indicating the end of their block.

Beyond it would be a cross street.

What would be waiting for them out there?

Raven moved to the front window, checked the street. To his left, an entire southside block was violently aflame. Its northside counterpart would be burning likewise. There were no guards, no helicopter. Vollner had removed all his forces from an already lost situation.

To his right, far down the set, Raven could see the vehicles, headlights first but also their dim shapes in the fire's glow. He could see no guards; they would be inside the blocks, searching. He would wait until the next explosion, use the cover of its noise to break the shop window, get Kat out and around into the cross street, then race for the darkness of the north mountain.

He went to her, put his arm around her, pressed her body to his, comforting her. She looked distracted, shocked, and almost out of it. He had to motivate her for this final effort.

"Listen to me . . . you're okay, you're fine. We have to get out of here, up into the mountain . . ."

The building shook.

Raven released her, ran to the window, smashed at it with the Uzi's butt. He kicked and knocked away the jagged shards, took Kat by the arm and helped her through, followed her out and around the corner into the cross street, as brightly lit, goddamn it, as sunrise, their shadows long, cast by the fire behind them.

His left arm around her waist, the Uzi in his right hand, Raven all but carried her along.

Then suddenly a guard with a dog and an Uzi appeared around the rear end of the building. Momentarily shocked by the unexpected sight of them, he recovered quickly, snapping a command to the dog as he fumbled to release the safety on the gun.

Raven threw himself sideways, to his right, away from Kat, drawing the guard from her, slamming too hard into the shop wall but getting his gun up and squeezing off a burst that didn't completely miss, and he saw the guard fly backwards, firing as he went, stitching a line of splintery holes along the shop wall a foot above Raven's head.

The dog was on Kat, its jaws clamped on her padded arm as she tried to hold it off. She was down, yelling, screaming for help, kicking at the animal as it abandoned her arm and tried to get in closer for her throat.

Raven couldn't shoot it without shooting her. He ran at it, took it on the run, drove his boot into its throat with a kick of such force it lifted the heavy animal up in a backward somersault and dropped it, twitching, its neck broken, ten feet away.

Raven jerked Kat to her feet, dragged her on, bullying her with movement, not permitting her to dwell on the horror, knowing that if he let her stop she would drop and never get up again.

Reaching the rear corner of the street, he released her momentarily, bent to pick up the guard's Uzi, then moved into the lead to peer around the corner of the building. To his right he could see the distant bunker they had been imprisoned in, and the surrounding area, lit by the flames of that burning block. There was no one there.

To his left . . . a long, narrow swath of impenetrable shadow stretching from the buildings out past the bunkers, a dangerous, visible no-man's-land between the bunkers and the mountain.

Away from the cover of the cross street, he and Kat would be clear targets out there in the open.

There was no alternative. They had to go.

He turned back to her, finding her slumped against the wall, head tilted back against it, eyes closed.

"Kat, listen to me . . . we have to run—*hard*—for the mountain. If you hear gunfire, ignore it, keep running. If anything should happen to me, if I fall down, *don't stop,* keep running . . ."

She groaned, "No . . ."

"Yes!" He thrust the guard's Uzi into her hands. "If anybody gets in your way, point this at them and pull the trigger. I guarantee they'll go away. Are you ready?"

Again he moved to the corner, looked hard down the corridor of shadow, took a firm grip on her wrist, and they flew, knees pumping, feet drumming, breath sawing . . . out past the line of the bunkers and into the twilight zone of fire glow. No shouts. No shots. They were doing fine. A hundred yards to go and they'd be moving into darker terrain, into ever-deepening shadow as they closed on the mountain.

Then block two, north side, went up in a storm of fire.

The flare of light hit them. It was as though a movie technician had switched on a dozen brutes to light up their section of valley. Raven pulled Kat to a halt, turned, appalled by their sudden exposure, grating "Bad *timing*!" between his teeth, then saw, off to the right near the second bunker, flashes of light in the deep shadow and simultaneously heard above their heads the rush and crack of bullets. The stutter of gunfire reached them a beat later.

He jerked Kat into motion, stretched out into a long, powerful stride, pulled her with him, her own stride lengthening until she felt she was wearing seven-league boots, her feet barely touching the ground.

Metallic bugs fizzed and snapped above their heads and all around them. Raven knew the range was too great for submachine-gun accuracy, but knew also a chance hit could kill. From the volume of the fire it seemed only one guard was shooting; and from the diminishing sound Raven guessed he was not following them. But the shooting would attract other guards. The helicopter would be alerted by radio. And in seconds Vollner would be upon them.

Fifty yards to go . . . the mountain looming above them, no longer a black featureless mass but a steep incline of visible trees and granite outcrop, a haven of a thousand good hiding places, protection from the light.

Kat was almost out on her feet, her limbs floppy with exhaustion, body slack with defeat. She pleaded with him, "I can't . . . I can't . . ."

He erupted with unexpected laughter. "You *can't*! Girl, you're carrying *me*! Look—we're nearly there! Come on, another fifty steps . . . count! . . . one . . . two . . . three . . ."

"My legs . . ."

"Beautiful legs. Did I . . . never tell you . . . what terrific legs . . . you've got? Meant to . . . *count*, damn it! . . . ten . . . eleven . . . twelve . . . listen to me . . . this is Rambo country . . . rugged, dense trees, ravines and caves . . . a million holes to hide. Good God, he held off the National Guard in country like this."

It got to her. She laughed, then groaned pitifully. "I'm not . . . built like . . . Stallone."

"No, but you're almost as pretty . . . that's what counts."

Then they were there, scrambling up a shale slide and into the first of the trees, into their blessed shadow, Raven helping her up onto a rock ledge, over it, and down onto a lower shelf with a deep overhang, gasping, "Rest here a minute," Kat dropping like a folded tent, faceup to the night sky, panting and gulping and groaning, her breath streaming white in the mountain cold.

Raven knelt, hands on thighs taking the weight of his upper body, and sucked in ozone, relishing the rush and reach of cold, clean air into the bottom of his lungs. He had been taught the technique of restorative breathing, the deep, slow inhalation that revitalized the body with the power of chi. With his eyes closed, he did not merely breathe, but focused his mind on the element of air, to the Rom *balval*, the essence of life, directing it to every atom of his being, feeling it heal, knowing and believing in its miraculous restorative powers.

Kat's hand on his made him start.

Her face was a pale blur against the rock. "We made it," she whispered, her voice choked, breaking. "Thank you—again. How many more times . . . will you save my life?"

He smiled, squeezed the hand he held.

Suddenly he froze, listening.

She came up on one elbow. "What?"

Then she heard the approaching chop of the helicopter.

Chapter Twenty-three

It beat, first, along the edge of the mountain slope, searching with its powerful lights for signs of their entry into the trees. Then suddenly it swung high and in, clattering directly over where Raven and Kat lay hidden by the overhang, but not, thankfully, hovering, sure of their position. It peeled away to the west, circling slowly counterclockwise, disappeared from their view and hearing for a full minute or two, then came in again from the east, this time higher up the mountain, flying a circuit perhaps half a mile in diameter.

Kat was trembling, following the flickering progress of its lights through the foliage of the trees with fear-filled eyes.

Raven said, "They can't see us. They know we're here somewhere, can't have got far, but they can't see us."

"What are we going to do? We can't stay here." Even though she knew she couldn't be heard she was whispering.

"You're right. We'll move when they move. Right now, Vollner's got a whole bunch of more pressing problems than finding us. I don't think he'll spare any men to chase us. He'll be desperate to find the remaining explosives, stop the destruction. Give him a few minutes, I think he'll go away."

The whistling clatter of the rotors increased, came in

again directly over their position, and then their senses were battered by an onslaught of noise: engine scream and down draft storm and submachine-gun fire, bullets ripping through foliage and whining off rock.

Raven threw himself on her, fearing ricochet as the fusillade of bullets strafed the area, thudding and cracking around them, seeking them out. There was a brief pause, perhaps as Vollner fed in a fresh magazine, and then it came again—a continuous cacophony of noise at a hideous level.

Then, just as shockingly as it had begun, it ceased.

The helicopter peeled away, ran back down into the valley, heading for the set.

Raven eased himself up, stroked her face, murmured reassuringly, "It's okay, he's gone. And I don't think he'll be back."

They heard the reverberating crump of another explosion.

He said, "Lie still, I'm going to take a look around, see what's happening."

He left her, climbed around the overhang, descended cautiously over rock outcrops and through the tangled trees until he gained a clear view of the valley. What he saw awed him. It was obvious that the noise of the helicopter had drowned out more than one explosion. The set was an inferno, the fire spreading rapidly from block to block. Even if there were no more explosions, nothing could now prevent its total destruction.

Raven reached out to his father, wondering where exactly he was, whether he was perched, as was Raven, in an elevated position, observing the holocaust as he timed and triggered the detonations. Or had he by now escaped, leaving the spreading flames to set off the remaining hidden charges.

Raven received no response. There was no voice, no

sensation, no vibration. He would have been surprised had it been otherwise. His mind was numb with shocking, violent input. It was akin to listening for a whisper at a rock concert. It would be pointless and dangerous to search for or wait for his father. He had an obligation to Kat to get her out. That had to be his only concern.

He returned to her, stage-whispering, "It's me!" as he approached her hiding place. He found her curled fetally, shivering from shock and cold. He gathered her in his arms, rubbed her back and shoulders, said comfortingly, "They're not going to bother us anymore. Half the city's gone. It's like the inside of a volcano down there. All we have to do is get out without breaking a leg. Are you ready?"

She nodded distractedly.

He helped her up, looked about him, choosing a route. The mountain was no longer utterly dark. Up through the pine trees the clouded sky was aglow with a pink-orange bloom that reflected down, provided the faintest twilight at ground level. It was a hallucinative and dangerous ambience, one that would have to be traversed slowly and cautiously.

He started off, Kat close behind, testing rocks for stability before adding his weight, taking small steps so that she could follow them exactly.

The terrain varied extremely. One moment the going would be soft and steeply inclined, the scant soil slippery with moss or pine needles into which he would need to drive his boots at an angle, creating steps; the next, the stone would break through, either as a solid outcrop or a partly buried boulder, treacherously insecure. They would encounter an impassable barrier of trees or undergrowth, a tangled deadfall, a dense growth of ferns or saplings and have to detour. No ten-yard stretches were alike.

Raven paused frequently to check on Kat. Movement,

coupled with the prospect of escape, had been therapeutic. He grinned at her and received one in return. Her spirit was restored.

They had traveled maybe three hundred yards when he received a sharp prod in the back. He turned to find her wide-eyed with alarm. Frantically, she pointed back along their trail. He peered into the ethereal gloom, whispered, "What is it?"

"I heard something."

He motioned her into a crouch, his Uzi pointed down the trail. A breeze from the east was blowing up. He cocked his head and listened, reached out for any sign of human or animal presence. There would be wildlife on the mountain: deer, rabbits, rodents, birds, undoubtedly disturbed by the fire. He peered hard into the darkness, saw no movement, smelled nothing, heard only the riffle of the wind.

And yet he knew there was something out there.

Neither confirming nor denying Kat's suspicion, he made a sign that they should continue. Had he been alone, he would have broken trail, doubled back, lain in wait, sacrificed ten minutes of progress for peace of mind. But Kat was not trained for forest stealth, and whoever or whatever was following them would hear the detour and simply wait them out.

Within fifty yards the tree line abruptly ended. Before them stretched an outcrop of gently sloping, naked rock, twenty feet across, ending in a crevice. From the trees Raven could not see its depth, but guessed from the close sound of rippling water that it was quite shallow. Beyond the cleft, perhaps ten feet, he could barely see the rock's continuance, and beyond it, again, a continuation of the trees.

He welcomed this feature. Once they were across and into the far trees, they could lie low and wait for whatever was following them to emerge onto the rock, settle it either way.

Making a sign for Kat to stay put, he flattened down prone and snaked out across the rock. Reaching its edge, he discovered, as he had expected, a narrow, shallow defile, six feet deep, ten feet across, its shallow tinkling stream rippling over tumbled rocks and boulders.

He lay still, peering and listening into the tree gloom on the far side, seeing and hearing nothing but the stirring of the breeze.

Waving at Kat to join him, he slipped over the edge to find a good foothold within the wet, slippery rocks. He helped her down and across, took her into the trees, then went to ground, the Uzi trained on the defile.

A minute passed . . . two. Their breathing calmed, but not their nerves.

"You did hear it?" Kat whispered, wanting, not wanting his confirmation.

"I . . . felt it. It was probably an animal."

She shivered. "God, I hate this mountain . . . this forest. Give me good old boring concrete anytime."

He smiled. "We'll soon have you back in nice old safe L.A."

Another minute dragged by. Raven shook his head. "If anything was following us, it's given up. Come on, let's . . ."

He stiffened, whirled around.

Kat's heart leapt. "What is it?"

He was staring into the black grotto of trees behind them.

A twig snapped.

Raven shot to his feet, grabbed Kat's arm, and hauled her up, hissing, "Into the stream—move!"

As they hit the open, a shocking explosion of gunfire came from behind them, the bullets singing off the rock to Kat's right.

A man's voice commanded, "Stay right there! Don't move a fucking muscle! Throw those Uzis into the water . . . downstream!" Another burst of gunfire reinforced the command.

Kat screamed and sent her weapon clattering into the gulley. Raven's followed it.

Ken Dok and Ed Bussey emerged out of the gloom, came up behind them with flashlights, Dok holding them at gunpoint while Bussey did a quick, one-hand frisk, finding Raven's flashlight which followed the Uzis into the stream.

Bussey's flashlight played on the defile. "Get across there. Try anything, Raven, the girl dies first."

They handled it with extreme caution: both of them covering Raven and Kat while they crossed, then Ken Dok standing guard until Bussey joined them, then Bussey taking over as his partner made the crossing.

Now here they were, Raven and Kat standing upstream, facing the thugs, Raven computing distance and strategy and their chances, preparing himself for attack, yet knowing without a shred of doubt that if he made an unsuccessful move they would shoot Kat first, knowing also that unless he tried *something* they would both die very soon.

Behind the flashlights' glare he saw Bussey take something from his pocket and hold it to his mouth. "Bussey to helicopter . . . you there, boss?"

The radio squawked. Vollner's voice came through, metallic and distorted. "Yeah, what is it?"

"We got 'em! Where you said. We're on the rock now."

"Jesus Christ, stay right there! Three minutes!"

Bussey stowed the walkie-talkie away in his pocket, played his flashlight on Raven's face, then on Kat's, chuckling, "Like to hear what's gonna happen to you? You're goin' for a ride in the chopper. Not far, though. You ever hear what some marines did to Cong prisoners

in 'Nam, Raven? They took them up coupla thousand feet
and threw them out the chopper. That's what Mister Vollner's gonna do to you—right into the fire down there.
He's *really* pissed off with your daddy, Raven. Oh, we'll
catch him, too. Then the same thing'll happen to him.
That crazy asshole is gonna be real sorry he ever messed
with Frank Vollner. . . .''

There was a curious squelchy thud.

Bussey hurtled sideways, colliding with Ken Dok, Bussey's gun and flashlight clattering to the rock. Dok's beam
jerked from Raven's face, swept across Bussey as Dok
staggered backward under Bussey's weight. For an instant
Bussey's face was gruesomely lit. A crossbow bolt pierced
his skull, the feathered flight all but contained within the
brain, the bloody hunting head protruding several inches
from his left temple.

Raven had a mere split-second advantage. Already Dok
was recovering, thrusting Bussey's body from him, but
using both hands—one holding the flashlight, the other the
Uzi. Raven went for the gun, took three strides and kicked
the weapon out of Dok's grasp, sent it spinning into the
defile.

Ken Dok, now free of Bussey, swung with the heavy
flashlight. Raven blocked with his left arm, took an ago-
nizing blow that shattered the flashlight, drove his right
fist into Dok's ribs.

It was like hitting steel plate.

The giant Korean retreated—laughing!—relishing the
contest. With his back to the defile, keeping Raven between him and the forest, he went into the karate square-
off stance, legs spread, huge fists balled. Raven adopted
the same stance, but had no intention of making this a fair
fight. Vollner had said three minutes. One had already
passed. He had to finish this juggernaut off in sixty seconds.

Raven asked over his shoulder, "Kat—you all right?"

She answered tremulously. "Yes."

"We've got no time to mess around here. Pick up the Uzi and the flashlight . . . and when I give the word, shoot this bastard."

Ken Dok flung himself into an attack.

Raven parried a pile-driver left fist to the face with his right hand, went in low with a left to the Korean's ribs, swung in behind, blocking Dok's leading foot with his own left foot, smashed three lightning punches into Dok's kidneys, the impetus of the blows toppling the foot-trapped giant.

Dok went facedown on the rock. Raven was instantly above him, his foot raised for a heel strike into the back of the neck. His heel drove down. Dok sensed it coming and rolled, caught Raven's ankle with a sweeping right arm, bringing him down.

Dok grabbed for him but Raven drove his fist into the Korean's face, smashing the nose. In an instant both were on their feet, Dok moving very fast for so huge a man, circling to place Raven between him and the forest, between him and the crossbow.

Kat ran in to pick up the flashlight and the Uzi, dreading the prospect of having to shoot a human being, no matter who, but knowing she would if Raven gave the word.

One further minute had passed. Raven could waste no more time. He backed toward Kat, reaching for the gun.

Dok came at him very fast, drove a right into Raven's chest, tried for a second blow but found it blocked by Raven's left hand. Raven exploded, hit the Korean with a flurry of strikes—right elbow into the throat, left elbow to the gut, a fist to the face . . . chop, kick, punch . . .

. . . nothing worked. The monster *was* made of steel. Raven threw yet another punch to the Korean's face. Dok took it dismissively, grabbed Raven's fist, held it with contemptuous ease in an inhumanly strong left-hand grip, drew Raven to him, grinned into his face as he raised his right chopping hand for the coup . . .

The gift—that resonance with all things, the sensation of certainty that if he wished to destroy the world he merely had to will it to be so—*was there.*

He gathered himself, attuned his mind to that of the Korean, and let it go.

Dok flew backward as though flung from a catapult. Clutching his head and with a spiraling scream he went over the edge of the defile and disappeared from their view.

Raven took the flashlight from Kat's hand, played it down into the stream. Dok lay facedown in the water, one arm twisted grotesquely behind his head.

Trembling, Kat moved up beside him. He slipped his arm around her, drew her to him, turning her away from the sight of the body.

"You . . . used that . . ." She didn't know what to call it.

"I had to. He would have killed me."

"I would have shot him . . . to save you . . ."

Her words were drowned by the rushing roar of the helicopter. It was a sudden and shocking arrival, a battering downpour of noise and wind and light, the rotors thrashing the trees on both sides of the gulley. It hovered there, fifty feet above them, while its occupant took in the scene. Raven could sense Vollner's initial confusion, then his identification of the two bodies and his realization of what had happened. He had lost control of the situation. His men were dead. He could see the Uzi in Raven's hand, must know Raven would use it, would never be captured.

Vollner would shoot to kill.

The lights.

Raven was blinded and exposed.

He raised the Uzi, squeezed the trigger. The monstrous

little gun jumped in his hands. Perspex shattered. One light went out. The helicopter, seeming to roar with pain and fury, lifted and wheeled violently, battered away over the trees to the east, Raven continuing to shoot until the submachine gun suddenly ceased, its magazine empty.

He yelled at Kat. "Get in the trees—deep into them. They'll be back."

She shouted at him, frantically. "What're you going to do?"

"There are three Uzis in the stream. We need them."

"I'll help you find them!"

"No, Kat! Don't argue! Vollner's going to come back shooting. Get in there—find my father. Now *go*!"

As she started off across the rock, Raven dropped down into the defile. In the meager light of the fire glow, the water was black, opaque. He began to move downstream at a crouch, dredging the rocky bottom with his hands, the water elbow deep and icy cold.

He hated the many uncertainties he harbored about the Uzis. He knew next to nothing about the Israeli guns beyond the fact that they were potent close-range weapons with a murderous rate of fire. He did not know whether they would function after immersion in water. He did not know their magazine capacity, though guessed it was in the region of twenty rounds. He did not know how many rounds had already been fired from the respective guns. Added to this uncertainty, he knew nothing about helicopters, their construction, their vulnerability. He was going into battle with uncertain knowledge of his *own* strength, as well as the enemy's.

His fingers touched a shape and texture that wasn't stone. Thank God, he'd found one. He lifted the weapon out of the water, shook the excess from it, aimed at the water, and gently applied pressure to the trigger. The weapon bucked in his hand. Well done, Israel, but he'd wasted three or four bullets proving their workmanship.

His first objective was to put out the helicopter's remaining spotlight. In its light, even down in the gulley, he was vulnerable. The sides of the defile were vertical, offered no protection. Vollner would most certainly come in shooting. He might even have returned to the set for guards, for additional firepower. If he didn't get the light on the first attack, he would die very suddenly.

His hand touched the second Uzi. . . . .

But the helicopter was on him, coming in below the tree line and soaring at the last moment. It swept across the plateau, Vollner shooting blindly at the moment from the open passenger door, fire-storming the arena.

Raven flung himself against the gulley wall, rough-aimed the Uzi, and opened fire. His bullets thwacked against the underbelly of the helicopter, hit the skids, circled the spotlight, missed the goddamned lens.

The Uzi quit.

Raven threw it from him, went into the stream, probed for the weapon he had touched, found it.

But now the helicopter was gone, swinging west this time, up over the trees, out of sight.

Raven plunged down the stream, searching frantically for the fourth Uzi, the one he had kicked from Ken Dok's hand. How many rounds did it still hold? Who had fired those bursts from the trees—Dok or Bussey? Questions . . . questions . . .

He reached Dok's body, felt all around it, found nothing, moved farther downstream . . .

Then the helicopter was back, sweeping in from the west, coming in upstream of him with Vollner right there in the open door, machine-gunning the stream.

And Raven thought—

Screw the light, get Vollner.

He raised the Uzi, took careful aim on that thick, squat body filling the doorway, and—

Squeezed the trigger.

Nothing happened—

Because the magazine was empty or because the water had penetrated the powder or whatever—

But NOTHING HAPPENED and now—

Vollner saw him and yelled something to the pilot, pointing, then took aim at Raven and couldn't miss, but for some reason—maybe because Raven wasn't firing, knowing he couldn't—didn't shoot, but kept his weapon trained on Raven as the helicopter slowly circled the plateau and circled Raven, holding him in the defile.

It was play time.

Vollner's amplified voice boomed around that rocky place. "Hey, Raven, why don't you shoot? No bullets? You've got ten seconds to join your momma . . . she's buried in those trees behind you. Where's your girlfriend? No matter, I'll find her. And your crazy father. Oh, he'll die, believe me. A family reunion, like I promised. Five seconds, Raven . . . four . . . three . . ."

Vollner shuddered.

As though he had changed his mind about shooting, he slowly lowered the weapon he was holding in his right hand, bent forward out of the doorway in an attitude of obeisance, then gun and man pitched out and somersaulted down into the stream, the submachine gun narrowly missing Raven, Vollner landing faceup six feet from him, damming the stream.

In the moments before the helicopter soared away, withdrawing its light and plunging the defile into darkness, Raven saw the cause of Vollner's death and the source of his own salvation—the feather flights of a crossbow bolt, all but hidden in Vollner's throat.

Snatching up the submachine gun, he fired a burst at

the retreating helicopter's tail, knowing he missed, knowing it didn't matter. It wouldn't be back.

He yelled, "KAT!" scrambled out of the gulley, met her as she ran from the trees.

She clung to him, gasping, "God, I thought you were dead. Two more seconds . . . what *happened*?"

Raven looked off into the trees. "Did you see anyone?"

She shook her head.

"He shot Vollner with the crossbow." He stood for a moment, undecided, then cupped a hand to his mouth and shouted, "WILL RAVEN!" Then, wondering still if Will knew it was his son's life he had saved, shouted, "DAD . . . THIS IS YOUR SON, JOHN! PLEASE—SHOW YOURSELF!"

The only responding sound was the wind through the trees.

Now, beseechingly, "DAD—CONTACT ME . . . *PLEASE*!"

The plea in his voice touched Kat. She said, "John, he will, in his own time, I'm sure. He wants us to get out of here, out of danger. He's protecting us."

Raven came back to her, nodded. "Yes." He brought his mind to bear on the trek still facing them. "How're you feeling?"

She said wearily, "Better—now Vollner's dead. I don't think the guards will come for us—do you?"

"No, I don't. With Vollner gone, there'll be confusion down there. But they'll come for these bodies, then maybe head back to the lodge, contact New York." He shrugged and abandoned further speculation. "Let's get away from here. We'll stay on the mountain for a while, drop down into the valley for easier going when we can." He looked at his watch. "It'll be dawn in two hours. I want to be on that road before first light."

* * *

The mountain continued hard, dangerous going. Traversing its face, they encountered frequent crevices and gulleys, some narrow enough to stride or jump across, others needing to be climbed down into and up out of, but all hazardous in the near-dark.

At first they had had the benefit of the fire glow, sustained by the fire as it spread westward through the set, the direction of their course. But gradually, as they left the fire behind, the glow diminished and their progress slowed.

Faced suddenly by a wide, deep, difficult defile, a great gash in the mountain's side filled with jagged rocks and tumbled boulders, Raven decided to head down toward the valley. The terrain was steep and slippery. Cutting steps with his boots, he forced a way through banks of ferns, encountered a wide stand of almost impenetrable sapling, came out of it onto a steep table of treacherous, moss-covered rock. Kat slipped and fell frequently, often slithered down to meet him, probably hurt badly but never complaining.

Finally, exhausted, bruised, cut, soaked with sweat and dew, they broke out of the tree line onto level grass and dropped, gasping for breath.

To their left, way up the valley, the fire still burned, the set no longer discernible as the buildings of a city but as twin, parallel holocausts of flame. The air they so hungrily inhaled was redolent with smoke, clouded with the white ash that drifted on the breeze.

Staring at it, Raven shook his head and murmured, "Unbelievable."

Kat nodded, replied in a weak, croaking voice, "It is. Just that. The whole thing. I can't believe it's real."

Raven said, "Disbelief is a form of shock, designed to save one's sanity. The next stage would be amnesia."

She said distantly, "That would be nice. I wish I could forget every rotten thing that's happened in the past two years." Tears welled in her eyes. "I wish . . . I wish . . . I wish . . ."

It was time to move.

Raven got up, helped her to her feet, held her close, telling her with seriousness yet with lightness of tone, "A very wise man, Nanosh by name, once said to me in our blackest moment, 'John, life may seem at times to resemble one gigantic cow pat, but it's all we've got. And it's to be lived—with hope, with courage, and with gratitude.' Kat, old girl, you are an extraordinary woman . . . courageous beyond words. I'm filled with admiration for you. I hold you. I read your aura. And I tell you this: You will put the past behind you, start afresh, and live a glorious, joyous future. Raven has spoken."

She sobbed, "Oh, John . . ." and kissed him, and held him. "God-*damn,* you are beautiful."

He tensed, shifted his gaze to the valley, moved her away from him, listening. "Helicopter."

"Oh, no."

"Get in the trees."

From the darkness they watched the parade approach, heading away from the fire, the Jeep, the truck, and above them the half-blind helicopter.

In moments they were past and gone.

Kat groaned with intense relief.

Raven said, "Now we're in the clear. Let's go."

Dawn was smudging the sky behind them when they broke through a line of trees and came unexpectedly upon the graded road.

Kat all but cried out with joy.

Raven, shushing her, drew her back into cover and down into a crouch, whispering, "We're not out of danger yet. If they're laying for us, this is where they'll do it." He indicated the direction to their left. "That's the shortest route, down to Eighty-nine, but it takes us along the perimeter of Vollner's land. I think we ought to go right, up to Ninety-seven. It's twice as far, but it might be safer."

Kat nodded. "Whatever."

"Remember this—we trust *nobody*. We can't beg a lift. We hear a vehicle, we dive into the trees." He drew a sigh, grinned at her. "Last leg, kid. Play this right and we're on our way home. You okay?"

She returned his grin wearily. "I'm bloody marvelous. I've got blisters, cuts, bruises, palpitations, but I feel . . ."

A male voice behind them said, "Well, fancy findin' you two here."

Shocked, they spun around, and were shocked again.

Standing there, in checkered hunting coat, cradling a shotgun, was Joe Santee.

He smiled twistedly. "You don't seem overjoyed to see me."

Raven, aghast, came slowly to his feet. "You . . . working for Vollner?"

Santee stared, bemused, amused. "For that scumbag? Hell, no, I came up to maybe help your daddy."

Raven deflated with relief.

Kat fell backward, groaning with an outpouring of the same emotion.

Pointing his thumb, indicating the fire, Santee said, "Seems like Will didn't need much help. I could smell the fire in McCloud. You seen him, John?"

Raven shook his head. "It's a long story. Joe, we have to get out of here."

"Damn right. This place is going to be swarming with fire fighters and police any minute. I've got a pickup hidden up there in the trees. I'd like to wait for Will, but maybe we shouldn't."

Raven said, "No, I think for Kat's sake we should get

going. From what we've seen, I'm sure Dad can more than take care of himself.''

Kat got shakily to her feet. ''Mister Santee—did any girl ever tell you you're the prettiest sight she ever did see?''

The Indian grinned. ''No, miss, can't recall one ever did.''

She went to him and kissed his cheek. ''Well, this one's telling you, right now.''

Santee caught her as she collapsed against him.

Raven moved in, swept her up into his arms, and carried her through the trees to the truck.

Chapter Twenty-four

They took their time, three days, returning to Los Angeles. Joe Santee proved himself a staunch friend, a streetwise counselor.

That first day, as they drove the long, circuitous route back to the Crest View Motel, having listened intently to Raven's concise account of all that had happened since their arrival in Redding, Santee said, first, "Jesus Christ," then, gathering his thoughts, said, "Okay, well, let's think about this carefully, the implications, and decide what to do. First off, we have to collect the camper and your bags from the motel. We drive back there now, you wait in the truck out of sight, I'll drive the camper away, you two follow me in the pickup until we're well clear of Redding."

Kat, recovered from her fainting spell but exhausted, nestling against Raven, seated between the two men, asked, "What're you afraid of, Joe?"

He glanced at her, his smile reassuring. "Not afraid, Kat, just cautious. When the Mob are involved you never know how things will go. They'll arrange this situation to suit themselves. Don't be surprised if you read a totally different story from what happened. Business is their only business. If they can capitalize on Vollner's death, maybe collect insurance for the producer's accidental death in an accidental fire, that's how it'll come out. A lot of people owe Vollner—therefore owe the Mob—a lot of favors around here. They'll find witnesses to testify to anything. Be assured, New York will minimize their loss, maybe even turn a profit. Who knows? Maybe Will did them a favor getting rid of Vollner.''

Raven said, ''Does that mean Dad could be in the clear on this?''

Santee frowned, took his time answering, did so in a tight, less-assured voice. ''That's one of the unknowables. Depends on several things: how New York comes out of it financially; how much they're told about Will's participation in the fire by Vollner's men; and whether they blame the whole thing on Vollner's stupidity and bad management. See, what I'm thinking, you said, as far as you know, only those thugs Ken Dok and Ed Bussey were privy to everything that happened from the time the Eurasian girl—what'shername?—Lin Siddon, went up to the lodge. Well, they're dead. And Vollner's dead. So, who's going to be able to tell New York exactly what happened?''

Raven looked at him. ''The helicopter pilot?''

Santee nodded. ''Yeah, well, maybe. So, the Mob will have your father's name.''

''And ours,'' said Kat.

There was a ruminative silence in the cab for a while, broken finally by Santee. ''You two are implicated only by your connection to Will. You didn't kill anybody, didn't cause the fire.''

Raven said, ''I killed Ken Dok . . . shot one of the guards.''

Santee threw a glance at him that conveyed something akin to anger. ''In self-defense! Don't go blaming yourself for that.'' Immediately he recovered control of himself, returned his gaze to the road, said more quietly, ''Anyway, the Mob won't be concerned about those two expendable punks.''

In the silence that followed, Raven reflected on the vociferousness of Santee's reaction. There was something not quite right about it. Santee was mad at him. Why? Because he'd ignored Santee's warning about getting involved with Vollner? Because Santee was deeply concerned about the welfare of Will Raven's son?

He liked Santee, instinctively trusted him, but was disturbed by the man. He couldn't read him at all. Maybe prison had added a veneer of impenetrable armor to his natural Indian inscrutability. Whatever, it was like trying to read the mind of a totem carving.

Again, Santee broke the silence. "Tell me—when you booked into the Crest View, what address did you give?"

Raven, applauding Santee's direction of thought, said, "My Kansas City address."

"And does anyone in K.C. know where you are?"

"Not specifically. I've taken indeterminate leave of absence from work. Even I didn't know where I was going to be staying."

Santee nodded. "Good."

Raven frowned. "Maybe not so good. When I registered, I put down the camper license number. We rented it in San Diego. Down there, Kat filled out the rental agreement, gave her Los Angeles address. If the Mob wants to find us . . ."

"Shoot," said Santee, then gave a shrug. "Well, hell, if they're bent on finding you, they'll do it anyway."

Kat raised her cheek from Raven's shoulder, arched her brows in a comic-serious expression of fatalism laced with concern.

He said, "Kat, I'm sorry. I should never have got you into this mess."

She gave a dry laugh. "Do I have to remind you that if it wasn't for you I'd have died in El Centro?"

Santee shot an incredulous look at her. "You serious? What happened in El Centro?"

In the next hour Kat told him the story.

It went as they planned. Santee driving the camper, Raven and Kat following in the pickup, they headed out of Redding down Interstate 5, covered the one hundred and sixty miles to Sacramento without stopping, propelled by a desperate psychological need to escape the wilderness of the mountains, the autonomous threat of Frank Vollner's kingdom. The safety of Sacramento might be delusional, but the city's size and bustle was comforting. By mid-afternoon they were booked into an anonymous motel, sleeping like the dead.

The story broke on TV late that evening.

Santee had joined Raven and Kat, bringing pizzas and coffee from a local restaurant. He told them he'd listened to the pickup's radio but had gleaned nothing. Then they turned on the TV for the evening newscast and there it was.

The report was pretty much as Santee had predicted: Renowned film producer Frank Vollner had been killed in an explosion that had totally destroyed the multimillion-dollar set vital to the climactic action of his latest, forty-million-dollar production, *Die Young*. Four other men had also died in the fire.

The report was protracted, involving eyewitness accounts from two surviving guards (whose performance, obviously orchestrated by New York, was that of bemused, benign security watchmen), and interviews with Allan Schenk, the director, and a company man from New York. The consensus report: Frank Vollner's death would be an irreplaceable loss to the industry; how ironic he should die on the verge of completion of his greatest cinematic triumph; and, yes, *Die Young* would be completed as a tribute to the superman whose achievements in film were outshone only by his tireless and exemplary work in the sphere of charity fund-raising.

"America's first saint," said Kat, snapping off the TV.

"You hit it right on the nose, Joe," Raven complimented Santee.

The Indian nodded. "The movie probably will make money. New York will milk this publicity, and Vollner will go out in a blaze of glory. Well, I guess that's okay—so long as he has gone out."

To Raven's eye, Santee seemed suddenly weary, depleted, as though afflicted by the aftermath of emotional involvement in Will Raven's cause. John was touched. He felt he wanted to know more about Joe Santee and his friendship with Will. It seemed a rare and precious fraternity.

"D'you think my father wanted Vollner dead?" he asked.

Santee shook his head, the weariness evident in the weight of the gesture. "No. Leastwise, not at his hand. He wanted to ruin Vollner, then leave him to New York. But things appear to have gone very wrong. Your father's not a killer. As I told you at Live Oak Springs, he has avoided you because of his reputation as a killer. And now you *know* him to be one."

"In our defense!" Raven retorted. "Joe, what you said to me about the deaths I caused also goes for my father. He must never blame himself for saving our lives. I don't in any way blame him. Whether he knew it was his son up there or not doesn't matter. He saw two people in trouble and did what he had to do. We thank him for it, love him for it. Please . . . get that message to him."

"Amen to that," said Kat.

Raven went on, "What d'you think he'll do now? Will you be able to contact him?"

Santee said, "He'll lie low, watch the outcome. He'll be very concerned about your involvement. Rest assured, he'll be keeping an eye on you."

Raven frowned. "How? If he gets that close I'll see him."

"Through me. I'll be doing the watching. Oh, I don't mean I'll be living in your ear, but I'll keep in touch. And you know where to find me."

Raven nodded. "I'd like that, Joe." After a moment he said, "Another thing. As I told you, just before Vollner died, he told me through the megaphone that my mother was buried in the trees by the stream. When things cool down I want to go up there, secretly, find her remains, bury her beside Nanosh in Arizona. I don't want her resting on Frank Vollner's land forever."

Santee nodded gravely, his mouth compressed too tightly for response.

Raven said, "I want this to end, Joe . . . put behind us. I love my dad and I want to be with him. Please—tell him."

The second day, Raven now driving the camper, Santee his truck, they made two hundred and seventy miles to Bakersfield, stayed again in an off-highway motel, approaching Los Angeles with caution, reading the news reports for signs.

By now the media was full of it, TV, radio, and newspapers offering glowing obits, in-depth profiles, interviews with film pundits, with charity heads, with famous movie names, with anyone who was anyone and had rubbed shoulders with Frank Vollner, and many who weren't and hadn't.

And throughout it all there was not one intimation of murder or foul play, not a single mention of Will Raven or John Raven or Katherine Tyson or of gunfire or of crossbow bolts or of anything that might smudge the perfect picture New York was painting of death by misadventure.

"Were we really *there*?" asked Kat, casting aside the L.A. *Times*. "It doesn't sound like the same scene!"

She sighed, shook her head. "I guess I'll always have trouble believing people can really do such terrible things, even when I see them happening."

Santee nodded. "In prison, terrible things happen most days, Kat. After a while you give up trying to figure mankind and just accept and expect the worst. It sounds sad and cynical, and sometimes you're wrong, but in the game called survival, which is what all of us are playing, suspicion is forgiven."

Raven, staring at a scene on TV of the smoldering, devastated Quang Hoi set, said, "What we need to know is— have *we* been forgiven. And how do we find out?"

Chapter Twenty-five

It was early evening on the third day when they arrived at Cleves Cottage, laden with groceries from a market on Sunset. Since their hurried departure for Live Oak Springs a week earlier, the house had been locked and unoccupied, the domestic staff on paid leave. In the past week Kat had given no thought to her home; God knew she'd had more than enough to otherwise occupy her mind. Now, drawing up to the gates, vivid memory of that nightmarish last day with Max came rushing back, and as she searched for the electronic gate control in her bag, she was afflicted by an ambivalence toward the house which manifested itself in a nervous fumbling.

Raven, sensing her mood, said, "Kat, don't be afraid, I'll stay with you for a while. We have to talk about your future. Joe and I will check the house over, we'll have a meal, you'll feel better once you're settled."

With a compliant nod and a grateful smile, Kat took out the control, leveled it at the gates, pressed the button.

Nothing happened.

She groaned. "Goddamn, now the batteries *are* dead."

Grinning, Raven opened the camper door. "The cops rammed the gates, remember? We'll get them fixed tomorrow."

He climbed down, pushed the gates open by hand and

secured them, then drove in, followed by Santee in the pickup.

Santee had spoken to Raven at the market, out of Kat's hearing. "If the Mob wants you and have worked it out fast enough, they could be waiting at the house. When we get there, you two stay in the camper, ready for a quick getaway. I'll go in first with the shotgun. You hear shooting, get out of there fast, go down to Live Oak Springs. I'll join you when I can."

Raven protested, "You mean *if* you can. Joe, this is not your fight. You've done more than enough already. I'll go in with the gun, you look after Kat."

The Indian's smile told him he was wasting his breath. "Hell, I'm not doing this for you, it's for your dad. You want to argue with that? Get the house keys from Kat and fill me in on the alarm system."

Now, as they entered the turnaround, Raven kept going until the camper was positioned for a fast escape, the engine running.

Santee drew up opposite the front door, his pickup shielding the camper from it. He climbed down, shotgun at the ready, began a check around the house, peered into the downstairs windows, checked the garages for alien vehicles, disappeared around back, reappeared to give Raven a sign that all was clear here, then opened the door and went inside.

Kat said, in a voice taut with tension, "What you said about my future . . . I don't think I can live here anymore."

"I agree." He glanced at her but quickly returned his attention to the house, ready to fly out of there in an instant.

She sighed. "I suppose—being up there in your father's presence has made me think a lot about mine. And I feel ashamed . . . ashamed that I allowed that mercenary bitch to keep me away from him. I'm going back, John. I'm going to stay with him until he either recovers or dies. I have a right. And if Lady Bloody Elizabeth tries to stop me, I'll . . . I'll . . ." Her voice faded.

Raven looked at her again, saw and felt her utter exhaustion, her confusion, the devastating effect her recent past had had on her. He reached for her hand. "I think you ought to go. Get away from all of this, give it time to settle. I'll keep in touch, let you know what, if anything, happens. But cover your tracks. Don't tell anyone where you're going. Don't fly direct from L.A. to London. Take some domestic flights under a false name, leave from Dallas, maybe, or Miami."

Her eyes widened at him with alarm. "You think the Mafia would go to those lengths to find me?"

Raven shook his head. "I wasn't thinking of them. I was thinking of the police. But if things get really rough, I'll talk to Lieutenant Marco, convince him you were only an innocent spectator, that you should be left alone."

"And you," she asked worriedly, "what about you?"

He returned his eyes to the house. "I'll stay in California. I'm going to find my father, Kat. Maybe I'll do some work for Marco. He's a believer in psi, would like to experiment with it in police work. I need a change from the Institute. I'll use L.A. as a base, look for my dad, see what the world of crime has to offer. You know, this past week, crime has taken on a new meaning for me. I guess anything does when it hits you and the ones you love personally. If I can, I'd like to help Marco reduce his caseload, put some bad people behind bars. I'd like that very much."

"You could stay here, if you wanted—look after the house for me. You'd be doing me a great favor. I'd hate to think of it abandoned, maybe vandalized."

He nodded, smiling. "We'll see."

A light went on in the library. Santee was there, waving them in.

With a sigh of relief, Raven cut the engine. "All clear.

Come on, let's broil those steaks, open that wine, and get absolutely legless.''

Kat beamed the first real smile he'd seen from her in days.

Joe Santee set down his knife and fork, leaned back, patted his hard, flat stomach, and groaned, ''Young miss, you're ever looking for a job as cook, I know a fine residence down in Live Oak Springs that'd hire you on the spot.''

Kat laughed. ''Thanks, Joe. I'll bear it in mind.''

They had eaten in the kitchen, thick sirloin steaks, salad, and a bottle of superb California cabernet that slipped down like liquid silk.

Raven had drunk little, just one glass, and noticed that Santee had been equally abstemious. Although, for Kat's sake, they had fostered a relieved, relaxed atmosphere, teasing her a little, Joe making her laugh with desert stories, each man was aware of the unremitting alertness of the other, listening for the sound of an approaching car, whatever. In this matter their rapport was perfect. In a more personal direction, it was not.

Raven had hoped that here, in this more intimate, domestic setting, having spent three days together, he would be able to break through Santee's formidable mind-barrier, catch him unaware, and read a little of what was happening back there behind the façade he voluntarily presented. But he could not. It was akin to attempting to investigate the many rooms of a great mansion, and finding each door in turn politely but firmly closed in his face. Raven considered, half amusedly, that he'd like to test the Comanche's brain-wave energy at the Institute, but suspected Joe might blow the circuits of the EEG machine.

Santee, making a point of looking at the kitchen clock, which indicated nearly ten o'clock, said with regret, ''Well, folks, if you'll spare me the dishes, I guess I'll be on my way.''

Kat looked at him aghast. "Joe, you're not going. I thought you'd stay the night."

"Like to, Kat, but Red's down there by himself and gets peevish if I'm away too long."

"Oh, your dog! I'm afraid I forgot about him—but please don't tell him."

Santee grinned. "Red can look after himself. He's got water and biscuits and he'll hunt a bit, but, like I say, if I'm away too long he sulks and gives me general hell for a few days."

Minutes later, taking his leave, Santee paused for a moment on the porch to look out across the turnaround and the lawn to the descending density of trees and bushes that hid the house from the road. "You got a gun?" he murmured to Raven.

"No."

Santee proffered the shotgun. "Take this. You can bring it down when you visit." He dug into the pocket of his mountain coat for a handful of extra shells.

"Thanks for everything, Joe." Raven offered his hand.

Santee did an unexpected thing. Ignoring the hand, he caught Raven's shoulders in a brief, affectionate embrace, whispering into his ear, "Make sure she gets out tomorrow. This place makes me nervous."

"Me, too."

"What are you two whispering about?" asked Kat.

"Men's stuff," said Santee, and made to shake her hand.

"Don't I get a hug?" she complained.

Santee smiled. "You sure do."

They waved him off, watched his pickup exit past the camper and disappear down the serpentine drive.

"Quite a man." Kat sighed. "I'm going to miss him. Funny, isn't it, when we first met him I thought him a real oddball. Now . . ." She shrugged and smiled. "Well, he's still a little odd, but I really like him."

"Me, too. But he's a hard man to read. In fact, impossible."

They went into the house, back to the kitchen.

As Kat prepared coffee, she asked in a worried tone, "What did Joe whisper to you?"

Raven removed dishes to the sink. "He only suggested what I've already suggested—that you get away tomorrow. He feels you're very vulnerable here."

"That's why he gave you the gun."

"It's only a precaution. I don't intend shooting anybody—unless it's absolutely necessary. God knows, there's already been more than enough killing."

They drank their coffee in the library, seated on the sofa before the open fire, the heavy drapes drawn across the windows against the disturbing darkness of the night.

Kat sat hunched forward, sipping meditatively, absorbing the comfort of the fire, enjoying the lassitude now, weary through and through but knowing her own bed awaited her and that she could sleep around the clock.

"Strange," she said, her voice an enervated monotone. "Here we are again. Did we ever leave? Did those terrible things really happen? Were Frank Vollner and the others real?" She shook her head slowly, staring at the golden flames. "So recently passed, but already it is taking on the substance of a dream. T. S. Eliot was right, humankind can't bear very much reality. He wrote: 'Time present and time past / Are both perhaps in time future / And time future contained in time past.'

"It's all very bewildering. More frequently these days it seems I know nothing about anything, never have, never will. Could it be that what we've just gone through hasn't yet happened . . . that we have yet to suffer it in the future? I'm rambling. I'm boneless with exhaustion and I'm talking nonsense."

Raven smiled. "No, you're not. The whole of science

is now bewildered about time. Einstein did that. Nothing is as it seems. All is illusion. Except, perhaps, that you are quite done in and ought to get to bed."

She nodded exaggeratedly in agreement. "That I *am* sure about." She put her cup down on the table. "What about you?"

"I'll stay here awhile. Don't worry about me, I'll sleep."

He got up with her, saw her to the foot of the stairs.

There she put her arms around him and hugged him with a great intensity of feeling. "I can't begin to thank you, so I won't begin to try."

"Words are quite unnecessary." He raised her chin, kissed her tenderly on the mouth.

She said, "I love you, John Raven . . . really, deeply love you."

He smiled into her eyes. "And I you."

With his eyes he followed her up the stairs, felt his heart stir with fondness as she plodded, comically exhausted, to the top. She called down, "They fixed my door."

"So I see."

"I wonder who . . ."

"Probably Lieutenant Marco."

"What a nice man."

She turned and flapped her fingers in farewell salute, entered her room, and closed the door.

Raven returned to the fire, to sit in silence and to think, to turn his mind to the reality of their situation, and not least to analyze the feeling of unease he had experienced since entering the house.

Something about it was wrong.

Chapter Twenty-six

He had no intention of sleeping, his sense of foreboding was too acute. Around midnight, he had switched off the library lights, opened the drapes, and sat there in the dying firelight, shutting down his sensory input, regulating his conscious state to a condition of alpha alertness, the better to locate his source of unease.

Nothing came.

Still on edge, he made a complete tour of the house, covering ground that Joe Santee had already checked, downstairs and upstairs, pausing outside Kat's room for a long moment, satisfying himself that she was asleep, then continuing his search outside the house, moving like a shadow in shadow.

The exterior of the house yielded nothing but night noise of the city: the distant thrum of traffic, barking dogs, the faint whine of jets over LAX.

The threat was not outside the house. It came from within.

Returning to the library, Raven laid the shotgun down beside him on the sofa, closed his eyes.

Think.

If the Mafia were pursuing them, how would they come? Really, it was unreasonable, even ridiculous, to presume hit men would arrive in the dead of night, creep up from the road, pick a doorlock, and take their revenge with

silenced weapons. They could so much more easily do it
in daylight, disguised as deliverymen, repairmen, take the
bodies with them, end of story.

This was the problem, of course, the one voiced by Kat:
reality. How, in reality, did the Mob exact revenge on their
enemies? For surely they did it. They shot people and
garotted people and car-bombed people. So why *not* creep
up through the trees in the dead of night and—

Another thought—

Was his perception faulty?

Never before had a sense of unease as acute as this
proved unjustified. Long ago he had learned to trust his
inner voice implicitly. Nanosh had advised him: *Compared to the animals, most men are as sensitive to danger
as a scarecrow in a field. Animals sense the approach of
fire, flood, earthquake, predator—and act upon the warning. Men die of stupidity. You have been blessed with such
sensitivity. Trust it. Act upon it always.*

Fine.

While living with the Rom, it had been easy advice to
follow. At the Institute he was aware that his intuitive feelings had fallen somewhat into abeyance. There he tested
other people's gifts, had had less call to exercise his own.
And what nature no longer requires, she withdraws.

Suddenly, in the past week or so, he'd had reason to not
only bestir his somnolent talent, but to exercise it more
energetically than ever before. Had he overdone it? Had
the psychic pendulum swung too far the other way?

Was he sensing danger that did not exist?

Swayed by uncertainty, tempted by fatigue, he did the
unforgivable and fell asleep.

It was not a gradual withdrawing from unconsciousness
but an instant, shattering awakening. His eyes flashed
open. Dimly, in the near-darkness, he saw the fireplace,

its ashes dead. Reaching for alien presence, his other senses flared. Behind him danger loomed as awesomely as a charging animal. His hand streaked to his right, grabbing for the shotgun. It was not there. He turned his head, saw with peripheral vision the bulk of human shape silhouetted against the window light, huge and close.

A voice, larded with chuckling triumph, grated, "Lookin' for this, man?"

There was no upswing, no wasted effort that might have given Raven a chance for movement; just a vicious, full-blooded, pile-driving jab with the butt that caught him flush on the left temple and sent him keeling to the floor.

A roaring blackness, speckled with darting, kaleidoscopic lights, engulfed him. He was leaving the world. And yet, as he slid away down the long black slope to oblivion, one lingering spark of conscious thought remained. It brought no comfort. Rather, it sent him on his way in dread.

He knew the man.

Kat dreamed of death. She was on the rock—not there exactly, but in some distorted surreal representation that embodied Vollner's mountain and the terrace beneath her room. She was looking down upon Ed Bussey's body, its head grotesquely skewered by an Indian arrow, brain tissue seeping from the ghastly holes. Quite dead, of course. Then how . . . could his eyes be opening . . . be staring up at her . . . be smiling with insane intent? Now he moved, rose to his feet, grinning, the arrow an obscenity through his skull . . . he came at her, hands extended, fingers clawing for her, she backed away, screaming, tearing her throat with screams, but quite alone, John where was John where was his father where was her own father the terror came on toward her . . .

She retreated, but now the rock was steep and slippery

her feet could get no hold and she was sliding sliding down the rock faster and faster to meet the nightmare at the bottom . . .

. . . on her back defenseless and he was beside her leering over her blood and brain matter seeping from his shattered head his hands upon her kneading her breasts trailing across her naked flesh to finger her vagina . . .

Kat.

He knew her name

Wake up, Kat.

It was a dream.

Kat Kat Kat.

She was slipping from it thank God she was coming out of it into reality into safety . . .

Her eyes were open but somehow the nightmare was still there. Her room—she was in her room, dim, the drapes just parted, but he was *there,* sitting beside her, his hand on her pubic mound.

JOHN!

Christ, no . . . he couldn't . . . wouldn't . . .

Her mind exploded with terror and she screamed for real.

He laughed, clamped his free hand over her mouth, said in the gruff, dirty voice she recognized but didn't believe, "Hey, Katherine Anne, is that any way to greet an old friend?"

Max.

Impossible.

But *here.*

With a frenzied sideswipe she knocked away his hand and bellowed, "JOHN!"

He chuckled. "Save your breath, sweets, it'll do no good. Hero's out of it. Hey, you've kept me waitin' a long time, you bitch, stuck up in that fucking loft. Yeah, I've bin up there all this time, crept out at night for groceries.

Even bought me a brand-new razor! Know what I've been thinkin' about, waitin' for you to come home?'' His thumb worked deeper into the crevice of her vagina. "I've been thinkin' about shavin' your sweet li'l pussy. . . .''

Kat convulsed, twisted and kicked with such violence she wrenched his hand out of her pajama pants, hurled herself sideways off the bed and reached the door before he caught her, grabbed her hair in a savage backward jerk.

He panted in her ear. "Okay, we'll skip the shave.''

Something cold and metallic pressed against her cheek.

"Did you really think you'd gotten rid of me? *Huh?* Those cops, dumb shits. Followed the sheet and the razor like a pack a crazed hounds, thought for sure I was in the canyon. Never searched the attic 'cause there was no pole to pull down the trap.'' He rattled a laugh. "There was no pole 'cause I took it up there with me. I heard 'em figuring I couldn't be dumb enough to get cornered in the roof. Open the door, sweetheart, let's go play games with Hero.''

He told her, "Hit the lights.''

Kat, her hair still captured in his punishing grip, the razor there against her cheek, reached for the switch, her terror swelling as the wall lights revealed Raven lying beside the fireplace, hands tied behind his back with curtain cord, his twisted posture and the slackness of his body indicative of death.

"Nah, he's not dead,'' Max said, reading her reaction. "Just a good crack on the noggin. Hey, you think I'd kill the guy so easy—an' without you being here to watch? But first—*he's* gonna watch. Me an' you. In memory of Luke. Take off your jimjams, Kat, lie down on the couch.'' He threw her onto the sofa. "Do it! Try to run, I cut Hero's throat!''

331

Oh, God, for it to end like this. To come through it all and have it end like this.

Devastated by shock and terror, still, it seemed, not totally awake, she sat staring at the floor, her trembling fingers working spastically at the buttons of her pajama jacket. Unbidden and ridiculously, T. S. Eliot drifted through her mind: 'This is the way the world ends.' Her world was ending. Hers and John's. Together.

Max was hauling Raven into an upright position, his back against the fireplace surround, positioning him to face the sofa, to view the spectacle to come.

He slapped Raven's face hard. "Come on, man, wakey, wakey, the show's about to start."

Raven groaned. His eyelids fluttered, his eyes rolled up into his head, finally settled on Kat, blinking for focus. Finally making it all the way, seeing her, seeing Max, putting it together, he tensed violently, discovered his bonds, fell sideways into the fireplace.

Max yanked him upright. "This is how it's goin' down." He cracked Raven's head back against the stone surround, stared maniacally into his face, an insane fury barely contained. "I got your attention! It's a party for Luke. You remember Luke, don't you, Raven? My best buddy, the guy *you* killed. What we do, we all take our clothes off. I fuck Kat, you watch. Then you fuck her, and I watch. You don't make it, I cut your pecker off, she eats it. Then she dies, we both watch. Then you die, I watch. Then I take your beautiful camper, fill it up with goodies outta the house, and go to Mexico, live happily ever after. Any questions?"

Raven was staring into the eyes of madness. There were no redeeming human qualities of compassion, reticence, or morality there at all. They were the eyes of a stalking cat: fully focused, conscienceless, evil.

In the exercise of his psychokinetic gift, Raven had never

been sure of the mechanics involved. Since its discovery while living with the Rom, he had used it seldom. Subsequently, he had absorbed enough knowledge to conclude that the effect was achieved by a combination of dynamic life field, intensely focused will, and an innate ability to attune his brain wave and vibration rate to that of his aggressor. He literally hit them with body, mind, voice, and soul.

But in this present situation the mechanics were awry. His coordination was imperfect. His head reeled from the blow to the temple. His energy field was depleted. And bound and seated thus, it was impossible to generate vocal kinetic power through muscular tension.

But, Jesus, he would try.

Max whirled on Kat, the stridence of his voice making her cry out in terror. "YOU—GET NAKED!"

Destroyed, she slipped the jacket from her shoulders, sat hunched forward, arms protecting her breasts, tears flooding her cheeks.

Now, in a maelstrom of lunatic activity, Max tore off his clothes, pranced naked and erect before her, berated her, "Get those pants off or get cut!" He slashed the open razor before her face, leapt up beside her on the sofa, jumped up and down, waved his arms in the air, cut *Z*'s in the ether. "Zorro is here! Rest easy, Luke, baby, this is for you!"

Now.

Raven gathered himself, brought to fine focus every atom of mind and being, clenched and strained against his bonds until he trembled and shook, lasered his will at the cavorting, murderous animal . . . and let it go in an explosion of sound.

Max Koenig flew backward in a perfect somersault, struck the floor with his heels, staggered backward three steps, and slammed the back of his skull into the wall beneath a window.

Raven yelled, "Kat!"

She was lying where the periphery of his force had flung her, face pressed against the rear cushions of the sofa. She stirred, turned slowly to face him, her vision glazed, stunned.

"Kat—get the razor! Cut these ropes!"

A sleepwalker, she moved so slowly to get up.

A low, crackling, diabolical chuckle paralyzed her. "Stay right where you are, Katherine Anne."

Max rose slowly to his feet like a creature from the dead, the shotgun aimed at Raven. "That's how you killed Luke. Man, I don't want you at his party. Say good-bye to Katherine Anne . . ."

The shattering of glass was as shocking as the shotgun blast it preceded.

Max gave an epileptic jerk, pitched forward, toppled over the sofa, sprawled facedown across the coffee table.

The flights of a crossbow bolt were just visible in his spine.

Epilogue

A week passed before Raven was able to visit Joe Santee in Live Oak Springs, to return the shotgun, to tell Joe of the incredible happenings on the night of his departure from Cleves Cottage, but most of all to reiterate their thanks for his help during their escape from the mountains.

It had been a week in which a great deal happened, and yet nothing happened.

Stunned by the unexpectedness of Max Koenig's death, by the manner of it, by the implication that Will Raven had followed them from the Cascades and was actually out there in the garden, and delayed by his bonds, by the time it had taken to rouse Kat from a condition close to catalepsy and persuade her to retrieve the razor and cut the ropes, Raven had lost several precious minutes in the pursuit of his father.

Standing there on the dark lawn, facing the darker gloom of trees—the direction from which the crossbow bolt had come—he called, pleaded, riven with a frustration that verged on anger, torn by indecision, wanting to plunge into the trees, to follow his father, who must still be close, yet knowing Kat was in desperate need of care.

He returned to the house.

With Kat in bed, sedated, Raven returned to the library to think and make decisions.

Summoning control, all the mental discipline he could muster, he shut out thought of his father, subjugated his own shock, frustration, and curiosity, focused his mind on immediate practical necessity, on the implication of Max Koenig's presence, on the possible effect a report to the police could have on Kat's future, on their joint survival. And then he decided Max would have to disappear.

Steeling himself for the task, he withdrew the bolt from the body, dressed it, loaded it into the camper. Two hours later Max, the mass murderer, the cop killer, the cutter of women, was buried with his razor under a pile of rocks in the San Gabriel Mountains.

While Kat slept, he planned her escape. She needed a few days to recover sufficiently to travel alone, but could not afford those days. The alternative: Raven would accompany her part of the way.

By midmorning, when she awoke, he had booked flights under assumed names from San Diego to Dallas, from Dallas to Washington, D.C. From Washington she would fly alone to England.

Her departure was tearful.

"Why," she asked, clinging to him, "does life seem mostly to consist of meeting people we have no wish to meet, and leaving those we love? Why, goddamn it, can't we *do* what we want to *do*?"

He smiled into her tear-filled eyes. "Believe that it all has a purpose. If nothing else, it saves you from going stark, staring mad."

She choked a laugh. "Oh, John . . . you've saved me from that."

"Go see your dad. Give Lady E. hell. And think about the book you're going to write when you get back."

Fearful doubt formed furrows between her brows. "Will you really be there?"

"I'll be there. I'll look after the house. Call me, but if

I don't answer, don't worry. I'm going down to see Joe, tell him what happened, see if I can persuade him to get my father to contact me."

"Perhaps," she said mistily, "from a distance, I'll be able to put this whole weird period into some semblance of perspective. Right now, you alone are the one real thing in my life. Please don't, for pity's sake, disappear from it."

He had returned direct from Washington to Los Angeles.

After entering the house, he found on the answering machine a request to call Lieutenant Marco, LAPD.

His heart raced. Possibilities tumbled down upon him like deadly boulders . . . Max . . . Vollner . . . his father. What did Marco want?

Well, screw it, he decided finally. His conscience was clear, he'd face whatever they threw at him. At least Kat was out of it.

He called Marco.

Hearing the lieutenant's friendly tone, his spirit soared.

"John, how are you?"

"Fine, Lieutenant, how're you?"

"Not good. I have a problem."

His spirit wavered. "Oh?"

"Actually, I have about six hundred problems—all of them unsolved crimes." He cleared his throat. "John, you remember the talk we had . . . about psychic matters, about applying them to crime?"

"Of course."

"I was telling my wife about you, what you did in the office. She convinced me I ought to recruit you— unofficially, of course. I wondered if you'd be interested, have a beer sometime, talk it over?"

"Yes, I would. I'm going away for a couple of days, I'll call you when I get back."

"Terrific."

"Lieutenant . . . any word on Max Koenig?"

"Not a goddamn thing. It's as though he's disappeared from the face of the earth."

Indeed he has, thought Raven.

Raven turned Kat's bronze Porsche off the desert road onto the track leading to Joe Santee's house. Pulling into the front yard, he sensed the place was deserted and felt a visceral pang of disappointment. A week's separation, he suddenly realized, had aggregated his good feeling of respect and general liking for the older man into something more, into a deep affinity which now made itself felt as a reaction to Joe's absence that bordered on loss.

Raven cut the engine and climbed out, hoping he was wrong, almost willing Red to come charging around the corner in canine greeting.

The desert place sang with silence.

Perhaps Joe had just driven somewhere, to the market, maybe. Perhaps he had a job. Mentally he produced more alternatives to bolster hope, but all the perhapsing he could come up with would not assuage the inner certainty that Joe had left for good.

Why?

And where?

Knowing it would be fruitless, he knocked on the door.

Silence.

Something stirred inside him, a compulsion, as real and insistent as a hand upon his shoulder.

Open the door.

He reached for the latch, tried it, felt the door give. He pushed it wide, stepped inside, calling "Joe?"

The interior was hot and musty, the odor of a room closed for days. Dust motes floated in the slash of sunlight he had admitted through the door.

He looked around. All seemed the same as when he had first seen the room. And yet there was something different. Slowly he surveyed the room, beginning to his left, panning around past the kitchen annex, clockwise toward the fireplace . . .

The fireplace.

His heart leapt.

There it was, the difference, the object he had caught in peripheral vision, mounted above the mantel, suspended on wooden pegs that had previously held the shotgun.

A crossbow.

There was a note on the mantel, written anonymously as a protection from alien eyes, but telling Raven all he needed to know and more than he could ever have hoped for.

Beloved Son, my heart yearned to tell you. Joe died six months ago, so I borrowed his name. Of course, Nanosh knew. There's danger still, and I don't want you hurt. I'm going for your mother, to bury her beside Nanosh. When it's all done, we'll meet again. I am proud to call you Son. *Ashen Devlesa, Romale.*

Tears stung Raven's eyes as memory swept him back through the years to childhood, to an Indian father hugging him good-night, blessing him not in the Comanche tongue but in the language of his Romany mother.

Ashen Devlesa, Romale.

May you remain with God.

"You, too, Dad," he whispered.

Dad.

With a bursting heart he went out to the car.